THE
BEASTS
OF
PARIS

STEF
PENNEY

QUERCUS

First published in Great Britain in 2023 by

QUERCUS

Quercus Editions Ltd
Carmelite House
50 Victoria Embankment
London EC4Y 0DZ

An Hachette UK company

A CIP catalogue record for this book is available
from the British Library

HB ISBN 978 1 52942 155 2
TPB ISBN 978 1 52942 156 9
EBOOK ISBN 978 1 52942 157 6

10 9 8 7 6 5 4 3 2 1

Typeset by CC Book Production
Printed and bound in Great Britain by Clays Ltd, Elcograf S.p.A.

Papers used by Quercus are from well-managed forests and other responsible sources.

In memory of my brilliant dad, Jo Penney

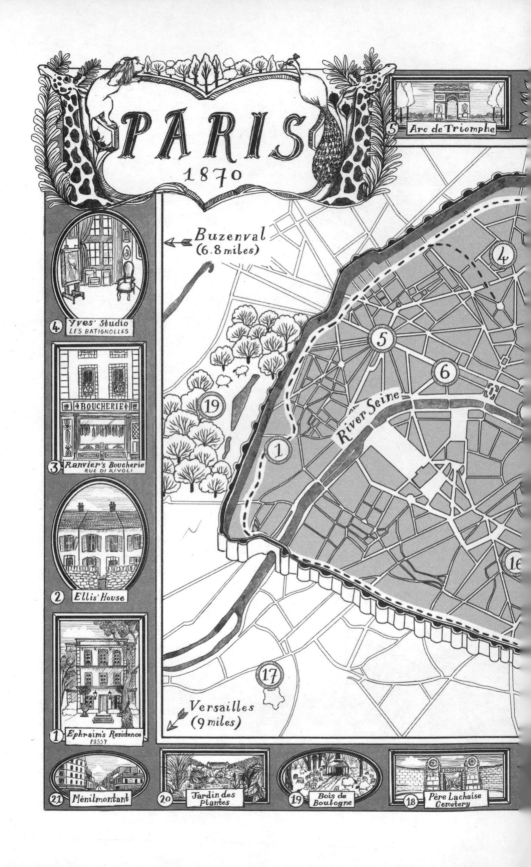

PARIS
1870

← Buzenval
(6.8 miles)

River Seine

5 — Arc de Triomphe

4 — Yves' Studio
LES BATIGNOLLES

3 — Ranvier's Boucherie
RUE DI RIVOLI

2 — Ellis' House

1 — Ephraim's Residence
PASSY

Versailles
(9 miles)

21 — Ménilmontant

20 — Jardin des Plantes

19 — Bois de Boulogne

18 — Père Lachaise Cemetery

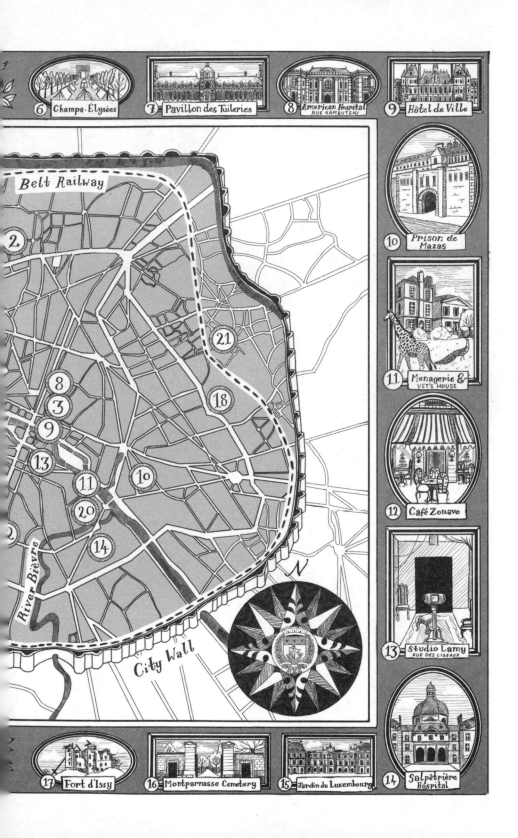

6 Champs-Élysées
7 Pavillon des Tuileries
8 American Hospital RUE RAMBUTEAU
9 Hôtel de Ville
10 Prison de Mazas
11 Menagerie & VET'S HOUSE
12 Café Zouave
13 Studio Lamy RUE DES CISEAUX
14 Salpêtrière Hospital

Belt Railway

River Bièvre

City Wall

N

17 Fort d'Issy
16 Montparnasse Cemetery
15 Jardin du Luxembourg
14 Salpêtrière Hospital

Under all great cities there are dens for lions, cellars sealed with thick bars in which savage, stinking, poisonous beasts are kept.

One day the distracted keeper forgot the keys to the menagerie doors, and the wild animals spread out across the city with savage cries.

Théophile Gautier, 1871

Prologue

May 1871

Blue smoke swathes the avenue in drifting veils, making it hard to see, and there is a peculiar noise outside: a constant spitting and humming, as of angry insects. The blue smoke is gun smoke and comes from the cannon and rifles; it eddies through the warm air and mingles with black smoke from the burning buildings. The fires themselves speak with a low, intermittent roar. The weather has been so dry that everything burns with a demented, ferocious joy.

Trees that survived the winter are innocent casualties. Showers of green confetti flutter to the ground as bullets whip the leaves from the branches. Soon, they are leafless again. And throughout the city a black snow is falling – flakes of charred paper rain gently down on the pavement, stinging eyes, coating throats, clinging to skin.

From behind the curtain, she peers down at the ghostly street, hearing the strange sound without knowing what makes it. She sees dusty figures creeping around, clothes and faces the same nondescript grey. Outside the café, a barrel pierced by a bullet belches wine into the dirt.

A man lies on his back in the road, one hand to his forehead, as if he were trying to remember something. Half an hour ago, she saw him suddenly toss away his rifle and fall over. Another of the ashy figures picked up the weapon and continued firing. She stopped watching. When she looks out of the window a little later, he has disappeared.

The bodies lie here and there, but her attention becomes fixed on a horse lying across the central gutter, jerking its head and limbs in a hopeless effort to get up, its coat matted with ash and blood. She has not shed tears until now. She prays that it will die; begs out loud, even though no one can hear her, that someone will put it out of its misery. The animal goes on struggling, making those awful, convulsive movements, although, as the afternoon wears on, it becomes weaker and at last is still.

1

One year earlier

Great quartz lamps: that's what he always thought. He'd tried to come up with other ways to describe them, but always came back to lamps. More than gold: there was the outer ring of golden brown, which became paler, reticulated with cream and yellow, then dissolving into green and blue, though always more green than blue, and that depending on the light. Even a hint of mauve, at times, before plunging into darkness. To stare into them gave Victor the sensation of falling. Sometimes he saw a landscape of unmapped rivers, or polished marble, or sun-struck water. Or himself, reflected. Lamps, but never illumination. Marguerite would stare back at him, or through him, or past him; impossible to say which. He had known her for years, and he didn't know her at all.

Victor Calmette's days did not contain much time for dreaming, but, after his rounds were finished, he stopped by the *fauverie* and watched, trying with his mind to reach through the bars, cross the gulf between man and beast. His training had hardly equipped him for the needs of animals like these. Despite superficial similarities, zebras were not horses, antelopes were not cattle, and tigers were, most emphatically, not house cats.

The great cat pavilion in the menagerie had some fine speci-mens – like Tancred, the venerable lion, and the panther, Nero, a minor celebrity in his own right, who had briefly belonged to an actress from the Comédie-Française – but Victor's favourite haunt was outside the last cage in the row. Marguerite was the Caspian tigress. She had never known her vague, unimaginable homeland; she had been born in the zoological garden at Berlin, and they, having a surfeit of tigers, sold her to the Jardin des Plantes. Victor and the tigress had arrived at the same time – he, a newly qualified assistant to the chief veterinarian; she, a cub a few months old, malnourished and listless. Given responsibility for the new arrival, Victor fed her by hand, first on goats' milk, then rabbits, offal and horsemeat. At first there was little hope she would survive, and indignant letters passed between the menagerie's director, Monsieur Lapeyre, and his opposite number in Berlin. But, in a few weeks, she grew stronger and wilder, until it was no longer safe to sit with her in the cage. Ten years on, she was a magnificent, full-grown beast. More than once, Victor had suggested that Monsieur Lapeyre write to another zoo, asking for the loan of a male Caspian, but nothing had come of it. They had no cages to spare for such a dangerous animal, said Lapeyre. Victor, who was still, after ten years, the assistant veterinarian, was not best placed to argue.

He liked to think that Marguerite recognized him as different from the other humans who passed in front of her eyes, that she returned his gaze and some inchoate, tender memory stirred in her feline brain. He sometimes fancied that he discerned a softness in her expression, and that she would have been happy had he reached through the bars and stroked the broad slope of her muzzle, or caressed the rough velvet behind her ears. Some of the cats were relatively docile: Tancred, for all his fearsome appearance, was lazily tolerant; Olga, the lynx, could be as playful and affectionate as a kitten; but Marguerite was always aloof and unpredictable. Last year, a keeper had gone into her cage to remove some rubbish. He hadn't startled her, hadn't done anything foolish, but in less than the blink of an eye she lashed out: there were roars, screams, blood. The man was lucky not to lose the arm, or worse.

Victor did not reach through the bars; he might be sentimental, but he wasn't stupid. Nevertheless, he loved Marguerite with a devotion that sometimes puzzled him. For her part, the tigress blinked lazily. Folly to imagine there was any feeling there for him, yet she seemed to focus on him, and a soft, deep growl emanated from her throat. He felt it thrum in his ribs and pelvis, his bones a tuning fork she casually struck. Then, just as casually, she turned her head away, bored (not bored? How would he know?), lifted a massive, cinnamon paw and began to wash.

Mondays were always busy for the veterinarians, as Sunday was the day of free entry to the public, and the hoi polloi of Paris had a tendency to throw things into the cages. The keepers tried to prevent visitors from poking umbrellas through the bars (with or without needles attached) or chucking rotten eggs into enclosures, but there weren't enough of them to prevent mishaps – and, sometimes, tragedies. Robitaille, the head keeper, was a good man, who truly cared for his charges, but some of the keepers were little better than the trash who threw stones at the quagga, or fed the bears meat laced with poison. Just last week, someone had ripped the wings off a Reeve's pheasant – God knows how they had got hold of it, or why. No one had been caught.

Today, due to the rain, there were few visitors, and Victor's eye was drawn to a lone figure. A young woman gazed down into the bear pit. She held herself very upright. Her dark hair was barely hidden under a little straw hat; her attire was careful, but shabby. It was the rigidity of her posture that held his attention. She gripped the railings with both hands, and he had a feeling that she had not moved for some time. He was aware of a sense of foreboding. Not that she would throw poison to the animals, he felt . . . What, then?

Slowly, he drew nearer. In the pit, the bears were lying in a heap. The smell was like a wall one had to walk through. The big male lifted its head and peered, scenting humans. Victor stopped a few yards from the visitor. Her hat glistened with rain. To his own surprise, he spoke.

'They won't do much, at the moment. They won't move until they're fed, around four.'

He wasn't surprised that she didn't turn her head, but neither did she walk away. He willed her to look in his direction.

'People think that bears are friendly animals. They aren't. They can be ferocious, believe it or not.'

The bear rolled his head back on to the ground and sighed, as if ferociousness would be too much effort.

'That's Clovis. He's a bad-tempered old devil. I'm fond of him, though – he's been here longer than I have.'

Victor was unused to speaking with strangers; he was not a forthcoming man at all, really, especially with women, but something about this girl and the singleness of her attention spurred him to keep talking.

'I'm the assistant veterinarian of the menagerie, Victor Calmette. I've been here ten years. Clovis has been here for nineteen. He was born here. The female, next to him – she came from Finland. Her name is Aino.'

'How long do they live?' Her voice was barely more than a whisper; her accent Parisian.

'Oh, bears can live about forty years.'

She gazed at the animals. The floor of the pit was made of stone flags, the walls were brick. A tree trunk, cemented into the centre of the pit, spikes hammered through it at intervals, served as a climbing post.

'A long time to live in a pit.'

'They have everything they need. They have company, plenty of food. No predators. Animals live longer in zoos than they would in the wild.'

He meant this to sound reassuring, but, somehow, it wasn't. He cast around for something to appease her.

'Have you seen the tigress, Marguerite? I looked after her when she first came, as a cub. When I first started. She had come from another zoo and was starving. She wasn't expected to live.'

The girl looked towards him and allowed him a brief glimpse of her face. Victor was put in mind of a Russian icon: a slim, sombre face, with melancholy, reproving eyes.

'You saved her?'

'It was my job. Anyone could have done the same.'

The hands on the rail loosened their grip. He wondered if she lived nearby.

Victor was about to speak again, but she moved away from the railings, nodded in his direction and, in the same action, turned and walked away. He hung on to the railing and rocked back on his heels, surprised by the depth of his disappointment.

Anne Petitjean marched away from the bears, her heart clattering against her ribs. Being addressed by strangers had this effect. This one had been polite, neither aggressive nor insinuating, yet she was almost blind with panic. She never knew what to say, or how to extricate herself without causing offence. Sometimes the panic was so overwhelming, she took refuge in silence, although it was a poor refuge, as it made people angry. She didn't want to be silent. She formed words in her head, sentences that seemed normal, but nothing would come out. Sometimes, it was as though a hard thing like an apple rose up and blocked her throat – not that there *was* a thing, she knew perfectly well, but that was what it felt like. At other times, if she did manage to speak, the things she said sounded odd, or rude.

Anne made herself slow down; she would not be panicked – not here, of all places. The menagerie was her place. She came whenever she could. Here, she revelled in a solitude that was otherwise denied her. Even when the park was busy, people generally left her alone.

Even the sort of man who persisted in bothering young women could be repelled if she turned her eyes on him in a certain way. It cost her, that look; she had to reserve it for the worst offenders. But having that power pleased her.

Her friends begged her to teach them the secret.

'No, it's like this! Look, I'm doing it now,' said Marie-Jo, making her eyes bulge.

'You look like you're constipated,' said Lisa, her sweetheart, snorting with laughter. 'Anne, do it again! How do you do that?'

Anne didn't know what to tell them. It felt as though she simply allowed the fear that lived inside her to look outward. The nightmares showed in her eyes.

The animals in the zoo didn't ask questions. They didn't expect her to talk. She felt calm around them. Anne would have loved a pet – a dog or cat, a rabbit, anything, really – had that been possible, but, as it was not, she made do with this: in her free hours, she would come to the menagerie and stare through bars.

Impossible to shake off the feeling that the man's words had given her. He had disturbed her – first, by talking to her at all, and then, by mentioning Marguerite as though she belonged to him. The tigress had a special place in Anne's affections, and now that small, private territory had been trespassed upon. She was compelled to look at him when he said he had raised her, because she had to see what sort of man had done something so wonderful. What she saw was unremarkable: not very tall, a pelt of dark hair, round brown eyes, and a big moustache that made her feel he was peeping at her from behind a hedge. The eyes seemed kind, but who knew what went on behind a face? He was just anybody, like a thousand other men, but he had stroked the tigress's rich, golden fur. Did he still do so? Did she like him? Was that possible? Marguerite was so superb, an exiled queen. Complicit, surely, in her imprisonment, for she could have killed a man like that with one swat of her paw.

Anne turned down the path to the cat pavilion, hoping, in the increasingly heavy rain, she would have it to herself. But she was not in luck: a couple were loitering by Nero's cage, sheltering under a large umbrella. The man was saying, '. . . surely be too difficult; it's so dark – what about the contrast?'

In one glance, everything about them was printed on her mind; she noted the young man's longish hair, his attempt at growing whiskers, his dark eyes. The woman was a little older, with the sharp features of a falcon. She was saying, 'We have to have him; he's famous.' The man spoke in a foreign accent. The woman was bourgeoise, her voice silvery and sure, and she wore a dress of violet cloth caught up in elaborate flounces. Even to Anne's untutored eye, an expensive dress, a fashionable woman. But stupid. Didn't she know the animals were not for sale? Alongside their appearance and their words, her mind recorded the flat smack of raindrops on umbrella fabric, the warning half-breath, half-growl of the black cat; his rank smell of fear.

Anne walked past, trying to erase the imprint, and sent her fare-wells to Nero, expressing the wish that he soon be left in peace. Nero was sensitive; the actress's scars were hardly his fault. The panther was the midnight prince of the zoo, a pale-eyed shadow. Sometimes, he seemed more absence of light than flesh, melted into invisibility in his shelter; she wondered why he did not just slip out of the cage and vanish.

Further along, Tancred paced, a malign light in his eyes. The lion was rumoured to have killed a man in his native land, but maybe they made that up to make him more interesting. The zoo visitors loved murderers. The hippopotamus was known as Kako the Terrible because he had attacked two of his keepers. This was no rumour: one man had died, the other had been crippled for life. But a hippopotamus is a fat, lumbering thing. It is not a golden monarch; its eyes do not glow like topaz held to a flame. Tancred gazed at Anne through his bars, head lowered. Irma the lioness lay beside him like a lumpy, dun rug. The patch of mange on her flank was worse than last week. She, though his mate, and dear to Anne, was not the queen of the zoo. There could only be one queen, and that was Marguerite.

Anne glanced back at the couple, still arguing, when the violet woman turned and caught her eye. Anne stiffened, her breath stopped, sweat dampened her armpits and her heart hammered. She dreaded meeting someone's eye; it was as though something painful and dangerous shot between them and scalded her very being. She tore her eyes away too late, trembling. She knew the man was looking at her too. Why couldn't they leave her alone?

The tigress was curled into a massive cushion on the concrete, where her coat glowed like fire in a hearth, one paw reaching through the bars in a casual reminder of her power. Marguerite was huge, three metres from nose to tail. Even in repose, she was defiant. As Anne stared, she lifted her head and gazed at her. The lambent eyes were calm, and Anne could allow her eyes to be held, because this gaze didn't hurt.

Anne had known the names of the bears before the man told her. She knew the names of all the animals – at least, of those important enough to have been granted names. The zoo giants had names: the elephants were Castor and Pollux; the rhinoceros, Murielle. They were like headline actors at the theatre. The other animals were members of the chorus. It wasn't just a matter of size. Mostly, if you ate other animals, you were given a name. The antelopes and bison, grass-eaters that lived in peaceable herds, didn't have names. But the zebras and the quagga, the solitary freak that looked like an experiment and made her feel sad, did. The lemmings didn't have names, nor did the various small, brown, desert creatures. As for the birds, through the whole rainbow of gaudy parrots and turacos, down to the smallest finch, they were nameless.

Anne sometimes thought that, where she lived, the women were like small, herbivorous creatures. Men were predators: important and memorable. Women were prey, like lemmings, or like the birds that so many visitors walked past without even stopping – sometimes noisy, occasionally decorative, but not individually of interest. Unless you paid the closest attention, you couldn't even tell them apart.

Most women – certainly most of the women in the hospital where she lived and worked – were like the sparrows of Paris: ubiquitous, inconsequential; their voices a nondescript background blur. She – Anne Petitjean – was unusual, because she had a name that had acquired a certain notoriety. Granted, the name she was known by was not the name she had been given at birth, nor was it one she had chosen for herself. Still, to be known by anything at all – surely that was something?

2

An easy stroll from where Anne lived on the Left Bank would take you to the avenue that was being driven through the districts of Sorbonne and Montagne Saint Genevieve. Here, as throughout the heart of Paris, a merciful operation was taking place. What was narrow and crooked was uprooted, what was stinking and unsanitary was pulled down, and in its place went broad, tree-lined thorough-fares, where you could see trouble coming from a thousand yards. The Boulevard Saint Germain already carved a swathe from the Quai Saint Bernard to the Boulevard de Sébastopol, but, at various points along its length, it followed the plan of existing streets, appropri-ating the grander and nobler buildings, excising the poorest and most dilapidated.

Number 104, Boulevard Saint Germain, had started life on the old street still known to locals as the Rue des Ciseaux. It was a well-proportioned building, its south-facing frontage dappled by the shade of a plane tree. Plate-glass windows bore the words *Studio Lamy, Portraiture Photographique* and displayed a rustic bower, framed photographs and a camera. Someone had done a fine job of arranging the display; passers-by slowed as their eyes were caught by the col-ours of the backdrop and the glimmer of what appeared to be a pool of water surrounded by flowers.

The building had two entrances. The door on the boulevard repre-sented its public face: prosperous and respectable. Its neighbour on one side was a bakery; on the other, a dealer in fine art and majolica. The back door opened on to a crooked alley that ran behind the boulevard: a dark canyon between unseeing walls, where the sun never hit the ground and the gutter never ran dry. This was a much older street that had survived the operation by clinging to its neighbour, burrowed in like a louse. The clientele who used the front entrance to commission a portrait or some *cartes de visite* would never dream of setting foot in that smelly, dark street. There was no street sign, but it was the Impasse de Bièvre, and it marked the ancient course of a river that had, long ago, been diverted. The back door, always in shadow, had no name or number. It gave on to a windowless corridor and a staircase which wound its way up the back of the building.

Both doors led, ultimately, to the attic: a huge room, which spread the length and depth of the building. Five floors above the street, the roof was pierced with skylights, which flooded the room with light. From the rafters hung calico screens, which could be positioned by pulleys to reflect or soften the light. A number of cheval mirrors stood at odd angles, like party guests arrested in mid-conversation; from a hook in the ceiling dangled a stout, leather harness.

A large mirror lay flat on the floor, next to which knelt a young man. The day before, Lawrence Harper had been at the zoo, discussing the challenges of photographing a black animal in a dark cage. Now, he was gluing artificial ferns and flowers around the edge of the mirror to give it the appearance of a pool. He had been adding foliage since before dawn and was cold and stiff. The skylights let in draughts and the stove struggled to drive off the damp.

Footsteps on the stairs. Mademoiselle Ernestine Lamy, his companion from the zoo, swept a glance over the arrangement on the floor.

'Quickly, if you please, Monsieur Harper. The model will be here in quarter of an hour.'

'I'm finished. We need more coal.'

Ernestine tugged on a bell rope and frowned at his ferns.

Lawrence was ready for criticism. 'I thought too many flowers would be distracting. You need some darkness here.'

Ernestine pursed her lips, then nodded.

Lawrence was never quite sure what tone to take with her. She wasn't his employer; strictly speaking, he worked for her parents, but she made him more nervous than either of them. She was a few years older than he and a Parisienne to her fingertips. Not exactly pretty – her face was too sharply defined for that – but she was considered handsome and was sophisticated in ways that were unfamiliar to him.

Lawrence spoke excellent French, but in Paris he felt clumsy, unsure of the nuances of words, too uncertain to assert an opinion or attempt anything as bold as humour. And his accent (he hadn't previously realized he had one) brought people up short. During his first weeks in the city, stallholders had stared at him in incomprehension and children laughed. 'Quack quack! He talks like a duck!' they would shriek, flapping elbows and flattening their vowels. Gifted with a quick ear, he learnt to modify his vowels, but he couldn't eradicate all traces of his otherness.

Ernestine dressed the set. There was a backdrop – one Lawrence had painted recently – depicting a ruin in front of mountains and waterfalls. In front of this, she positioned a plaster column, draping swags of silk ivy over it. She stepped away to judge, twitching the ivy so that it mingled with the ferns. To the naked eye, it looked crude and artificial, but Lawrence knew it would be transformed through the camera lens into an enticing pool in a forest glade. Lawrence left her fussing over the ferns and went to the darkroom, at the other end of the studio.

He turned up the gas, casting a red glow over the counters with their neatly squared dishes, the shelves of bottles, the wooden drying racks. He ran a finger around the glass squares to check the edges were sufficiently filed. He gave them a final polish and covered them with a cloth. He picked up a bottle and held it to the light. Yesterday, he had made the collodion, this syrupy, golden fluid with the power to stop time. The thought still gave him a thrill.

He emerged from the darkroom to see Madame Lamy with a young woman. Madame turned to him with a smile.

'There he is. Fanny, you haven't met our assistant yet. This is Monsieur Harper – we have an American in our midst. Monsieur Harper – this is our model for the day, Fanny.'

Fanny shook his hand and smiled shyly. She was pretty, but unremarkable looking, with a head of beautiful chestnut hair.

'Hello, Mademoiselle—'

'You can call her Fanny. Anyway, she is a madame, now – aren't you, dear? Madame Klein, for all of, what is it? Two months? I trust Monsieur Klein doesn't mind you continuing to model for us?'

The new Madame Klein shook her head and blushed. 'No, not at all.'

'Fanny is one of our best models. Very popular. Ah, here's Monsieur Lamy. Everything ready, Monsieur Harper?'

'Yes.'

'Then I'll leave you. Fanny, dear, I'll see you downstairs afterwards.'

The galleries of the Louvre and the Grand Palais are full of naked women: acres of painted flesh are purchased by the state and stared at by its most respectable citizens. The postcards that emerged from the Lamys' studio were smuggled out the back door, furtively sold by roving salesmen, pored over in private. It was a puzzle to Lawrence why a painting of a nude woman was a different kind of thing from a photograph of a nude woman. Was it because a painting took longer? Was it because it claimed to represent something that happened in myth? A painting could be named *The Rape of Lucretia* or *Susanna and the Elders*, and be held to edify (the Bible, in particular, lent a gloss of respectability to any amount of skin). It could not be due to artistic merit, as there were terrible paintings, and beautiful photographs, and Monsieur Lamy's photographs were beautiful. Lawrence had tentatively brought up the subject with Madame Lamy – he couldn't discuss it with her husband, who was deaf and mute – and she simply laughed. Then, more seriously, she said, 'Of course, what *we* do are academy studies. We don't do *smut.*'

Fanny came out from behind the screen wrapped in a robe, her chestnut hair streaming down her back.

Ernestine held out her hand for the robe, looked the girl's body up and down, and tutted. 'You shouldn't have laced so tightly. You can see corset marks.'

Fanny rubbed at the pink welts on her skin. 'I had to. I can't do up my dress otherwise. I'm sorry, Mam'selle; they won't last.'

Ernestine directed Fanny to lie on a blanket on the floor and gaze into the make-believe pool. Serge Lamy took up his station behind the camera and signed to his daughter, who added a wreath of flowers to the girl's head and twirled a hank of her hair so that it snaked down her spine. Fanny lay with her bottom towards the camera, her face visible in the glass. Ernestine gazed at the effect, then pointed to the girl's hand.

'Wait! The wedding ring . . . Papa, should she take it off?'

Her father shook his head, then raised a screen and angled a cheval mirror to throw more light into Fanny's face. He signalled to Lawrence, who leapt to the darkroom to sensitize a plate and place it in the camera. Serge Lamy raised his hand and the studio went very still as he pulled out the dark slide. After several seconds, he slotted the slide back in, pulled out the plate and took it to the darkroom. Once he had teased out the image to his liking, he passed it to Lawrence to fix in a bath of hyposulphite of soda. Serge went back into the studio while Lawrence washed the plate and put it on the rack to dry. The vapours of ether, alcohol, bromide, pyrogallol, guncotton and silver nitrate, mingled with the fumes from the gas lights, began to give him a headache.

He heard Ernestine directing the next pose: 'Kneel here . . . on one knee, like that, and put your hand on the pillar. Turn a little to the left . . . No, twist more . . . All right, Papa?'

Fanny could find a pose faster than any model Lawrence had seen. She would subtly transform herself, for those few seconds, from a demure young woman lying awkwardly on a cold floor, into an exotic seductress, a forest nymph, a pagan goddess. It was the first time he had seen a model do this – and he couldn't say exactly what it was she did, but she became more graceful, more magnetic, her face intent with inner life; even her skin seemed to draw the light. When the pose was captured, she went back to her everyday self, and, if the scenario were to change, pulled on a robe and slumped in a chair while Ernestine and Lawrence stripped the set and created a new one – a Moorish bedchamber, say, with a divan, arabesques of organza, a suite of paste jewels.

When he first started working at the studio, Lawrence had been astonished that Mademoiselle Lamy took such an active part in the work. But then, the Studio Lamy was an unconventional business. Serge Lamy could not speak or hear. It did not seem to matter: the Lamys communicated with rapid hand movements that were just as complex and subtle as actual words. With the models, his wife or daughter interpreted for him, and things proceeded no slower than in any other studio. Some of their regular models had even learnt some basic signs – and that was down to him. Monsieur Lamy was a man of natural charm; good humoured and thoughtful, his presence cheered and soothed those around him. He had a loyal clientele who appreciated this; they also, perhaps, appreciated his discretion.

Ernestine's presence with the naked girls made the business seem more domestic, almost innocent, as though she and the model were sisters, one adorning the other for her wedding night – except they weren't. Every eye in the room constantly assessed the desirability of Fanny's body. She was uncovered, decorated, adjusted for the pleasure of others who were not in the room, but whose desire was nonetheless palpable. Lawrence found her beautiful, but felt no twinge of desire. He had learnt early that there was nothing less erotic than the creation of erotic photographs. A session meant hours of concentration, each image meticulously prepared for, then executed quickly and without error. While Ernestine ran the studio, ringing for refreshments, checking the stove, dressing and undressing the set and keeping a list of poses, Lawrence ran back and forth to the darkroom to prepare plates, or rush exposed ones into the developing bath. They hardly had time to eat, snatching sandwiches and coffee that Madame Lamy sent up, and at the end of the day they were exhausted.

When the last plate was fixed and set on the rack to dry, the daylight was fading. Lawrence's eyes stung and his head throbbed; his fingers and palms were stained black with chemicals. He coughed and spat to rid his mouth of the taste of metal. He scoured his blackened hands with a stiff-bristled brush until they hurt. He scrubbed them every day, but the stains never entirely faded. He was used to it, was even proud: it was the badge of his profession.

3

Anne was crossing the hospital courtyard when there were shouts from the door to one of the wards.

'Anne! *Coucou*, Anne!' It was Marie-Jo and Lisa. 'We've been looking for you. Where've you been? Jospin wants to see you.'

'What did he say?'

'You're to go to his office,' Marie-Jo said, with a suggestive leer. 'When you have a *moment*. He wants to see you on a very important matter.' She made an obscene gesture. 'The Saint's in his bad books.'

'Oh? Why?' The Saint was Jospin's pet patient, everyone knew.

Marie-Jo leant towards Anne, her eyes alight with joy. 'I heard she hit him in the face with her bloody napkin. Wouldn't I love to do that – if I still could.'

Anne's eyes widened. She wouldn't have thought the Saint had it in her.

She found Dr Jospin in his office, surrounded by tottering stacks of files. Philippe Jospin was the medical director of the Salpêtrière, a doctor world-famous for his pioneering work with the insane. Anne knew this because the other doctors in the hospital said so. He was a vigorous man in early middle age, with a strong resemblance to Napoleon Bonaparte, but today he looked tired, his boulder-like head sunk into his shoulders, as if weighed down by all it contained: lists of patients, reams of pathologies, the hydra-like proliferation of all the women's disease. But his face brightened when Anne came in.

'Anne – wonderful! Come in, come in. Sit, please. Will you take a glass of wine?'

When she hadn't seen Jospin for a while, Anne forgot the power of his voice. It was round and musical, with a warmth that made you want to draw near. Anne nodded and he got up to fill two glasses from the decanter on the shelf.

'Your health, Anne. I see from your records that you haven't had an episode for some months, now.'

'No.'

'Excellent. How are you finding the work?'

'All right.' After a pause, she remembered to add, 'Thank you, monsieur.'

He nodded. 'You don't find it too hard?'

She almost smiled at that. 'No. Not too hard.'

Anne's work as a ward girl consisted of cleaning up after the worst-afflicted and most troublesome patients. In a week, she would mop kilometres of floors, carry tons of linen, strip hundreds of beds. She scrubbed out slop buckets and cleaned up mess – anything the nurses considered beneath them. The smell of shit and vomit was so pervasive she hardly noticed it. Her muscles had grown hard since she began on the wards, and her hands were calloused and raw. There were hundreds of ward girls – most, like her, current or former patients of the Salpêtrière. Anne wasn't sure which she was. Sometimes, it was hard to tell.

'Good.' Jospin tapped steepled fingers together, his elbows on the desk. 'Well, I know that it's been a while since you took part in a Tuesday session.' He cleared his throat. 'But I wondered if you would take part tomorrow?'

'Eleven months.'

'I'm sorry?'

'It's been eleven months since the last one.'

'Yes, it must be.' He smiled. 'You have a better memory for dates than I do. I had to look it up.'

'What about Odile?'

'Odile?' He looked politely enquiring, as if he didn't know the name.

'Odile Sabatier. I thought . . . nothing.'

Odile Sabatier, the Saint, was the current star of the Tuesday lectures. A flaxen-haired eighteen-year-old who specialized in religious ecstasies, she had been referred to, in Anne's hearing, as 'a perfect hysteric'. Perhaps less perfect, now. Jospin blinked and looked down at his desk, as if the memory was too much even for his formidable composure.

'We will do what we used to do – all right?' He smiled, confident in her acquiescence, as well he might be; within these walls, Jospin was God.

Anne looked down. 'What if I can't . . . you know.'

Jospin laughed. 'Let me worry about that, Anne. Have no fear. You always were a most responsive subject.'

He rolled the words over his tongue and Anne felt a twinge of pleasure. Words of praise were so rare; it was nice to be complimented for something, even if it was for her illness.

The Salpêtrière was so vast, it was more like a small town than a hospital. It had been on the site on the Left Bank of the Seine for centuries – first arsenal, then prison: a holding pen for prostitutes and other women awaiting deportation. After that, it became a women's hospital. It had sprawled over the years, benefactors adding buildings in a jumble of styles: here, classical symmetry; there, a Swiss chalet. Now, it boasted an indoor amphitheatre, a church (and a smaller chapel for Protestants), a library, vegetable plots, an orchard and, in its public spaces, many fine paintings. It had stables, bakeries and shops, a café, a dairy, a butcher. There were sewing workshops for the inmates and a photographic atelier for the staff. It contained scores of wards, endless corridors. Some on the upper floors had barred windows, but the elegant symmetry of its courtyards gave a civilized air to the confinement. Some wards had no bars, and some had no windows, like the subterranean dormitories where the ward girls slept. Altogether, the buildings housed thousands of women.

It was a hospital, but not a hospital like most others. Few of the patients were expected to recover, but then, how could they? Some were simple, some were violent or hopelessly deluded. Others had made the mistake of being abandoned by their lovers, or of growing old without family to care for them. Some were the victims of accidents, like Lisa, who had been kicked in the head by a horse; now, she suffered from fits and her words were hard to understand. But by far the greatest number were indigent and desperate: drunkards who couldn't hold down the most menial job; wives on the run from violent husbands; worn-out women of the town, like Marie-Jo. One thing united them: they had nowhere else to go. With its modern facilities – there was even a ballroom – it was far from the worst place an unfortunate woman could end up.

On Tuesday, at half past twelve, Anne waited her turn outside the amphitheatre. Her skin was up in goose bumps; the corridor was chilly and smelt of damp stone. She felt nauseous – as usual, on these occasions – but focused her attention on the grain of the dado rail under her fingers. Various sounds came through the double doors in front of her: deep murmuring, a shriek, yelled commands that she couldn't understand; gales of laughter.

Dr Jospin was on the other side of the double doors, declaiming to a full house. Anne listened to his muffled voice, and the adenoidal breathing of the orderly who waited with her. There would be a number of patients brought on to illustrate Jospin's public lecture. Today, Anne was preceded by a middle-aged woman known as the Colonel, whose special gift was being told, under hypnosis, that she was an officer in the Prussian army, whereupon she would bark commands in a fearsome baritone. Only under hypnosis, she spoke fluent German.

As her demonstration concluded, the lecture hall resounded with laughter. Anne had never seen this performance, but she had heard it, through this door, on many occasions. Now, the laughter died down, and Jospin's voice could be heard again, bringing the Colonel out of her trance, gently asking her questions, to which she responded in her normal voice, which was breathy and monotonous. There was applause, more laughter, coughs.

The door opened and the Colonel came out; the orderly grasped Anne's upper arm and led her into the theatre. She took a deep breath and deliberately unfocused her eyes.

'Now, ladies and gentlemen, we come to our next patient – Honorine,' Jospin said, and a murmur of recognition rippled through the auditorium.

Behind Anne, on the wall facing the audience, hung a painting on a heroic scale. It showed a man standing in the courtyard outside, surrounded by women in various states of derangement. He wore a cloak and Napoleonic bicorne, while the women were either in the process of, or had recently finished tearing their blouses to reveal their breasts. His face bore a look of stern sympathy; with one hand, he gestured towards the prettiest *déshabillée* girl, while the other hand was kissed by a kneeling woman who had managed to keep her clothes on. The painting depicted a former director of the hospital, surrounded by his patients. Current inmates found the painting hilarious.

Anne was no longer nervous, although the lecture, like every Tuesday lecture at the Salpêtrière, was a sell-out. Raked benches were packed with men and women in fashionable garb – representatives of the beautiful world that inhabited the same city as Anne, but floated above her, on a different plane of existence. Some would doubtless be notable; there was usually a sprinkling of painters, actresses, courtesans, novelists . . . even politicians came to see the show. Massed together, they made a kaleidoscope of scarlet, black, yellow and green, and they generated a cacophonous twittering, punctuated by the occasional squawk. It was the closest Anne ever came to the higher ranks of Parisian society.

She let her attention float upwards, like the cigar smoke that gathered under the lights. She had worried that she wouldn't be able to do it anymore, but already she felt its approach: that odd sensation of being drifted away from her body; a thin, stretched feeling. Something dark and ominous was looming to her right, and she smelt a familiar burning smell. The hard ball climbed into her throat, gagging her, but he had told her not to worry, and she wouldn't. There was nothing to worry about; nothing . . . Jospin's voice grew pale and tinny, but she held on to it as to a rope – a rope that became thinner and thinner, until it was no more than a pulsating thread of sound.

There was a tremendous bang behind her, and she remembered nothing more.

4

In Passy – a carriage ride across Paris from the Salpêtrière, but a world away by any other measure – another young man, also foreign, was on trial; not in a court, but in a library. Flames hissed in the grate, silver and porcelain gleamed on the mantelpiece, the lamplight was soft. It was a room made for ease and tranquility, but Ellis Butterfield felt neither. It took effort to sit still, and to keep his gaze from straying to the decanters that glittered on a sideboard. His uncle was drinking a cup of tea. Ellis resumed his defence.

'Yes, but it was a misunderstanding. They arrested anyone who was remotely involved, but it was all a fuss about nothing.'

'I do not call shouting obscenities at a police officer "nothing",' said his uncle. 'And you broke the nose of one of the other men involved.'

'Well, heavens! He was hurting the girl he was with – throttling her! Anyway, he hit me first.'

'The police officer?'

'No . . . I assume you asked me here to give my side of the story, so if you would let me do so . . .'

The petulance in his voice made him cringe. Ellis sat back – difficult, since his tall frame was folded into a small, low armchair – and smiled at his uncle as though they were two men of the world. The trouble was, his uncle was not a man of the world – he held himself above it, mingling with lesser mortals only when his duty required. Ephraim Quine, spare, neat, abstemious and important, waved his hand at his sister's son – his blood relative, but one who had inherited none of his rigorously modulated qualities.

'Well – I had gone with some friends to a café, and we were minding our own business when a fellow at the next table started shouting at the girl he was with. Then he grabbed her by the throat and began to throttle her.' He was gesturing with his hands, half risen from the chair, the better to dominate his invisible victim. 'We told him to stop, and he insulted us. So I took hold of his arms to pull him off, and – well, one thing led to another.'

His memory of the evening was a kaleidoscope of bright, dirty fragments, but he knew he had been joined in the fray by Michel and Gustave, while Yves had remained at the table, his face drawn with worry, trying to remonstrate while flesh collided with flesh.

Ellis made his face as innocent as possible.

'You had been drinking?'

'Well . . .' How to explain his life to a man who spent his evenings drinking tea? 'We'd had a drink or two – wine . . . The fellow with the girl was drunk.'

'So there was – what? A rumpus?'

'Hardly a rumpus – a scuffle! Someone must have found the police officer. And, because I was the only foreigner, they decided to blame me for the whole thing.'

'I gather a window was smashed.'

'I don't know how that happened. You know how it is in the heat of the moment – things get out of hand. If they're saying it was me, it is only because they think I'm the one most able to pay for any damage.'

Ephraim's face was the picture of a man who had never let things get out of hand.

'But you laid hands on the police officer.'

'I . . .' Ellis formulated his words carefully. 'Some things were said – not by me – that were deliberately provoking to an American.'

'Be that as it may. My information is that you were, I quote, "extremely drunk", you broke a man's nose, punched another man – an innocent bystander – and threatened a policeman, calling him an insult I don't wish to repeat.'

'I was being manhandled—'

'I'm informed it took three men to drag you off him, and you did not stop shouting obscenities until you were in the prefecture.'

'That is . . .' Ellis gazed at his uncle, hurt. 'That's to throw the most prejudiced light on the thing. I mean, yes, I'd had a few drinks, but I was not "extremely drunk". The fellow with the girl was really hurting her, so I tried to stop him, whereupon he attacked me and I defended myself.'

Ephraim frowned. Ellis knew he had disturbed the tranquility of his uncle's library – a serious crime.

'The woman wanted to press charges against you.'

Ellis felt his mouth drop open. 'The *woman*? For what?'

'She claimed that you, ah, molested her, ah, person.' Ephraim motioned with one hand towards his chest, his eyes on the ceiling.

'That's absolute rubbish! You can't believe I would do such a thing!'

Squirming somewhere at the back of his mind: a picture of the harpy coming for him with a raised, broken bottle, a snarl on her face; another of her on the ground. Was it a second later? Had he done it?

'I did not molest her, Uncle. Good God! She took against us fighting with her fellow, but she knew it was his fault—'

'Ellis, don't become excited. I am concerned that you have a tendency to overreact. This is not, after all, the first time, is it?'

Ellis was silent. It had always been impossible to best his uncle. Simply by walking into his house, Ellis felt in the wrong; he was too large, too noisy, his gestures too wild; merely taking up so much space made him guilty of myriad nameless crimes. (It hadn't helped, that time he had fondled a jade lion from the mantelpiece, replaced it while answering a question, which had led, in some scientifically incomprehensible way, to the lion falling on the hearth and losing a paw. His uncle had sprung from his chair with an actual yelp – the only involuntary action Ellis had ever seen him make. 'Oh! It doesn't matter . . . It's all right, Ellis. Leave it!' his uncle had cried. He gave a ghastly smile and said, with hideous gaiety, 'Ha! We won't talk about how much it's worth!' But, thought Ellis, mortified, you've just done precisely that.)

In the silence of his humiliation, the maid arrived, followed by Ephraim's pet Siamese, Circe. She rubbed herself against Ellis's shins, before leaping into his lap. Grateful for the distraction, Ellis stroked her and was reminded that the knuckles on his right hand were still raw. He tucked them out of sight.

'Uncle, please believe me; I'm dreadfully sorry to have embarrassed you. But I did not do what she is saying. If anything happened to her, it could only be because she threw herself into the melee.'

Ephraim tapped his fingers on the arm of his chair. 'I believe you, Ellis. I've had words with a few people, and the charges have been dropped. But, even to put yourself in that position, as a foreigner and, I'm afraid, as my nephew – you simply must be more careful.'

'I know. I'm sorry.'

'You are twenty-eight. An age at which most men are firmly established in a career. An age at which many men contemplate settling down to family life.'

Ellis allowed his gaze to land on the bookshelves behind his uncle's head.

'Yet you, despite being qualified for a noble profession, and being more than able, persist in wasting your talents dabbling in this bohemian life. You know how it hurts your mother.'

His mother: so long suffering, so put upon, so relentlessly bullied by his father, as long as he was alive. Mention of his mother made Ellis's neck prickle and his throat tighten.

He looked at the cat, purring on his lap. Dear Circe, you do exactly what you want. You want to sit on my lap and you do it, even though your master probably thinks you are an indiscriminate whore. He felt her vibrate under his hands, and said, 'I was never suited to medicine. Poetry may not save lives, but it does matter, most of all to me. Writing poetry doesn't hurt my mother. It is only letters to her that do that, if they pass on rumours that misrepresent my life.'

Despite his warnings to himself, Ellis made a violent gesture. The Siamese escaped to the safety of the fireside.

'She writes to me constantly, begging me to find something for you, something in a more reliable line.'

'I can support myself—'

'You have your late father's legacy.'

'Yes, I am independent.'

'You claim independence, yet you invoke my name when you are in difficulty. The prefecture might well have charged you, had I not used my influence, and that would have damaged me as representative of our country.'

It was a miracle it had taken Ephraim this long to allude to his position.

The other night, Ellis had been determined not to mention his uncle. But when the policemen were dragging him towards a cell, Ellis's resolve crumbled. The stench of the corridor, the prospect of being incarcerated all night, or longer, got the better of him and he cried, 'You'll regret this. My uncle is the American ambassador to France!'

The policemen glanced at each other, derision warring visibly with inklings of doubt.

Michel Blasi, being led down the corridor behind him, said, relief clear in his voice, 'He really is. Think what your superior would say, if he heard you'd arrested such a prominent foreign citizen.'

Shortly afterwards, Ellis and Michel were free men. They rejoined Yves and Gustave outside. They tried to make light of the incident, but each avoided the others' gaze.

'What's that?' asked Yves Michaud, and Ellis had looked down, shocked to see blood dripping from his fingertips on to the cobbles. He could not think how it had happened.

Apologies offered to his uncle, promises made, Ellis listened as the fire popped with a small, satisfied sound. Circe washed herself.

'You won't change your mind? I have trained Madame Noyer in the arcane secrets of English tea. I find that it helps me sleep.'

Ellis thought it politic to accept. Ephraim smiled.

'I've had a letter from your mother. She begs me for my opinion of you. What am I to tell her?'

Ellis laughed. 'She never changes. Do I look unwell?'

His mother was mousy and delicate, fearful of every passing indisposition. She had been terrified of losing her son to one of the fevers that swept the Eastern Seaboard during his childhood, but Ellis was strapping and fair, a born athlete who never succumbed to anything more serious than asthma. He had (he was aware) a blond, rather brutish handsomeness that turned heads anywhere he went. In no respect did he take after the slight and careful Quines.

'You do not. But it would mean so much to her if you were to lead a more settled life.'

Ellis laughed. 'She's waiting for me to give up and go home with my tail between my legs.'

Ephraim allowed him a grimace of agreement. 'If you were to go back to medicine, that would make her very happy. Or, if you won't consider that, we could always find a place for you at the consulate.'

'Thank you. But I have work. In fact, I have two poems being published in a very good periodical, *Revue Noire*. It comes out next month.'

'I'm delighted to hear it.'

'I know they may not be your cup of tea, but the editor has been most encouraging. I wrote them in French.'

'Oh?'

'It frees one, somehow, as though you jettison your old habits of thought along with your old language. Anything seems possible.'

'Is that so? Well, put me down for ten copies.'

*

Outside the ambassador's residence, Ellis drew in lungfuls of damp air. He put a hand on his neck – the skin was hot and he felt raised welts where hives were already breaking out. Conversations with his family often brought on a physical symptom of distress. Just reading one of his mother's letters could bring on an attack of asthma.

It was a mild evening and he decided to walk back to his room in the Batignolles and save the omnibus fare. His grazed knuckles were sore, his ribs ached where they had been punched and an insistent throbbing came from the wound on his arm. He had been terrified lest blood started leaking from his sleeve in his uncle's library. Thank God, it hadn't.

The thought made him giggle with slightly hysterical relief. He had sustained the injury either when they crashed through the café window, or, possibly, it had been the horrible minx, who, on seeing her man set upon by Ellis and his friends, broke a bottle and threatened to slash their faces. Ellis remembered almost nothing of that part of the evening, so could not have said either way.

5

Rumour had it there were more rats in the Salpêtrière than patients. During the day, they rustled along wainscots and skittered across floors: blatant, squeaking, hunting down the smallest morsel of food. At night, they became bolder and climbed on to bunks and ran over the sleeping women, who were so accustomed to it they barely flinched.

Anne lay on her bunk listening to the breathing, grunts and moans of the women around her. Tiny claws ticked on flagstones. Lithe little bodies traversed the laths inside the walls and scuttled between joists. She slept in a dormitory in the basement of the hospital, one of sixty women in regimented rows of beds. She reached a hand over the side of the bed and touched her fingers to the floor: gritty, damp, cold. The thought came that perhaps the floor was not solid: there could be cellars that no one told you about, secret and ancient. Down here, with floor and walls of stone, you knew you were in the oldest part of the hospital, and that was very old. They were close to the Bièvre river – the open sewer, which dived underground on the other side of the boulevard and headed in their direction. It debouched into the Seine a little further east, so it likely flowed under these very stones. They said that a patient from the hospital had thrown herself into the Bièvre and drowned. No one could say who she had been, or when it happened, but everyone knew it was true.

Maybe this unease was just the aftermath of Dr Jospin's hypnosis.

Every muscle in her body ached. She didn't remember what had happened during the demonstration, but she had woken, as always, to the ache and the lingering smell of burning. She didn't know what he had done with her in front of all those people. He never told her. She never asked.

Jospin treated his patients with scientific rigour. He looked at them, measured them, prodded them with implements. He stuck needles through hands and placed electrodes on tongues. He pressed magnets to skulls, and ether-soaked cloths over mouths. He drew tables and diagrams. The women who passed through his hands were recorded, annotated, drawn and photographed. He would do anything for his patients. He would even insert his hand inside a vagina to quell a recalcitrant ovary – a difficult, unpleasant manoeuvre, but sometimes the only way to bring a patient out of her seizure. Anne knew he was passionately interested in women's disease, just not in what they had to say.

Hippolyte Mazade was different. The medical student had asked Anne questions; he wanted to know about her. At first, she didn't know how to answer. She had already been at the Salpêtrière for ages – at least five years – when Hippolyte arrived to study under Jospin, and the idea that anything she had to say would be of interest to one of 'them' was hard to believe. It took some persuading on his part before she would accept that it was not a trick. But he convinced her: they were the same age, twenty, and there was an innocence about Hippolyte; his gaze did not scorch her as most people's gaze did. He wanted to know about her father, who had arrived in Paris as a young man, worked in the glove trade and married a Parisian servant. They had that in common too – her father had come from Haiti, while Hippolyte's grandmother came from Saint Martin. 'They call Saint Martin "the Island of Women",' he told her, but when she asked why, he didn't know. The closest either of them had come to the Antilles was a seaside holiday in Brittany (him). As for Anne, she had never been further west than the Bois de Boulogne.

Anne remembered her father with a huge, simple love, but, when she was eleven, he died. Her mother had taken work as a live-in maid and could not keep her daughter. Hippolyte wanted to hear about the convent school where Anne spent the next four years of her life. He was interested in the punishments they meted out. Anne had been locked up, beaten on her hands and feet, denied food. She showed him the scar on her left palm where the strap had cut too deep. The Sisters said she was possessed and called a priest to have her exorcised. They threw holy water in her face.

'What had you done that was so wicked?' he asked, but he smiled to show that he was joking and did not really believe she was evil.

'I was angry. I tried to be good, but I was always losing my temper. I hit one of the Sisters.' It embarrassed Anne to remember her childhood temper.

'There must have been a reason for your anger. Why did you hit the nun?'

Anne felt ill thinking of it. 'She said I was wicked. She said my soul was as black as my face.'

Hippolyte's face was grave. His skin was lighter than hers, no darker than an Italian's, and most of the time people didn't even know he was Creole, but he understood how that hurt.

'That was wrong of her. You are not wicked, Anne. Nor is your face black.'

Anne looked at the floor. He was so nice, sometimes she couldn't bear it. If she allowed him to look into her eyes, it was as though his gaze looked all the way down into her soul. It didn't burn, but it felt uncomfortable in a different way.

'Your face is beautiful. Your skin is . . .' He tilted his head, considering.

Desperate for him to stop before he said something worse, Anne cried out, 'She said the fiery chariot would carry me away to hell!'

'Hmm.' Hippolyte sat back and stared down at his notes. 'Was this fiery chariot anything like the visions you see before you have an attack?'

No one had ever suggested that before. As usual, when Anne was frightened, she said, 'I don't know.'

In the convent, Sister Bonaventura had painted a dreadful picture of the chariot of hell, which was driven by a demon with blazing eyes, and drawn by beasts with two heads and vast, leathery wings. To prove it was real, she opened a leather-bound tome and showed the pupils a woodcut; the crude lines had a dreadful power. Bonaventura was a fount of instruction: tales of monsters spilled from her mouth – dragons, devils, blind, black worms. Every river and pond had its resident horror; every misdemeanor a bespoke punishment. In her lessons, folktales and Bible stories were boiled up into one terrifying brew.

The Sister was also a walking checklist of good and evil. Answering back to a Sister was evil. Losing your temper was evil. Talking or laughing too loudly was evil. Running was evil. Basically, everything Anne did was bad. The Sisters wanted her to embrace the nature of her name saint, who was gentle, meek and loving: the patron saint of mothers and childbirth, of grandmothers and of housewives. Also, teachers and childless women and, for some reason, miners and metals. Also, sailors. Also, more interestingly, storms. Anne wasn't sure what this ragbag of interests added up to. She didn't much care about grandmothers, since she had never known one. What did she care about mothers either, for that matter? Her own couldn't wait to get rid of her. Saint Anne seemed a receptacle for too many things for any one of them to be really effective. The Sisters said it was because her womb was the source of so many riches – including all the gold and silver in the world. Anne had asked, 'What about lead?' and was beaten on the soles of her feet. Anne prayed for help, for her behaviour to be more pleasing, but she must have done it wrong for her prayers went unanswered. She tried and failed to like Saint Anne, and wished her name was Françoise like her best friend, as Francis was the patron saint of animals. She was enchanted by his calling the birds his sisters, and by his advice that, if God granted that wild animals eat you, you should lie down and let them get on with it.

'Anne?' Hippolyte said. 'Anne? What are you thinking about?'

Anne said, 'My father brought me a black and white kitten. I loved her more than anything.'

Hippolyte said, 'That sounds nice. What happened to her?'

'When I went to the Sisters, my mother couldn't keep her. She said she gave her to some neighbours, but I don't think she did.'

'Why not?'

'I asked about them – what was their name, and how many children they had, and what did they feed her – but she said she couldn't remember. I don't think they existed. I think she drowned her in a bucket.'

Over time, Hippolyte got her to talk about the thing. Anne had never told anyone about the thing. When she was fifteen, the Sisters sent her back to her mother. In the convent, her temper had not improved. They said she was wilful and difficult. They were not convinced the exorcism had been successful.

By this time, Madame Petitjean was working in the house of a jeweller. Her employer was very kind and agreed to take Anne into the house as a scullery maid. She soon realized that her mother was having relations with the employer. He was unmarried, Anne's father was dead, and her mother said there was nothing wrong with it. Her mother wanted Anne to call her Pauline instead of Maman, and scolded her if she forgot. She tried to treat her daughter as an equal, someone with whom she could share secrets. Anne didn't want her mother's secrets; she told her awful things – like what the employer did to her in bed – and boasted about the trinkets he gave her. When Anne didn't respond in the right way – which was always – she grew cross. She told Anne she took after her father – cold and hard. Anne didn't remember her father as cold and hard, but she hoped that she was like him and not Pauline.

Hippolyte said, 'When did you last see your mother?'

Anne didn't have to think. 'Three years ago.'

'She doesn't come to visit you?'

Anne shook her head.

'Where is she now? Is she still in Paris?'

'I suppose so. She had a baby with that man.'

Hippolyte said, 'When was this? Anne? Anne! Oh, dear me—'

She remembered nothing until she woke up, lying on her back. She'd had a seizure. Despite this, Hippolyte pursued the subject of her past.

'You remember, Anne, you were telling me about your mother and your employer. You said she had a baby with him. Then you had a seizure.'

It was a week later. Anne nodded, eyes on the floor.

'I had just asked when this was. Did anything else happen around that time?'

Anne knew exactly what had happened, but the hard ball was lodged in her throat, making it impossible to speak. Hippolyte gave her a piece of paper and a pencil. She put the pencil to the paper, but her fingers had turned to clay. She pressed the lead into the paper as hard as she could and dragged it towards herself, tearing the paper in two. She knew she would be punished for this.

'All right, it's all right,' Hippolyte said instead. 'Don't worry, Anne. Shall I tell you what I think might have happened? Your employer took advantage of you. And your mother wasn't able to stop it.'

Anne had been forming the words for weeks, determined to rid her mouth of them as you would spit out a worm.

'She made me.'

Hippolyte's eyes widened. 'Your mother made you . . . ?' He didn't even know how to say it.

'She said I must, or we'd have nowhere to live.'

Hippolyte's pen scratched at his notes.

'That's . . . um . . . Do you remember when you had a seizure for the first time?'

'The next day. Then, most days.'

'Did anyone call a doctor?'

'They did, because I kept breaking things. They said I couldn't work anymore, because I was too clumsy. So I came here.'

Hippolyte nodded. 'I'm so sorry, Anne. I can tell you, you are not alone.'

'Not alone?'

'Many women who suffer from hysteria have a similar sad tale.'

'Dr Jospin didn't . . . doesn't . . .'

'Dr Jospin doesn't have the time to take detailed histories of every patient in the hospital. His interest is in curing your symptoms. He believes that, one day, science will reveal a physiological lesion in the brain that is the seat of hysteria. In the meantime, finding the cause is perhaps less important than curing the illness.'

Anne's hand went to her head, as though she might feel the fault through her skull. 'But you . . .'

Hippolyte lifted his shoulders and glanced towards the door. 'We have yet to find a physical trace, as you find traces in the body of someone who has died of cholera or tuberculosis. I wonder whether hysteria, which behaves like no other disease and leaves no trace on the body that we can find, may have more subtle causes.'

Anne said, 'The last time I saw her, she came to a lecture I was in. She brought *him* with her, to watch.'

Hippolyte wrote this down. In his notes, she was always 'Honorine', or sometimes, simply, 'H'. When he looked up again, his eyes bore the look she found so troubling: warm and searching.

'Did you speak to her?'

'It was as though they thought they hadn't done anything wrong.

She thought I should be pleased to see them. She was angry because I wouldn't kiss her.' Her voice trembled. Her breaths came in hisses. 'I couldn't speak.'

Hippolyte was delighted by her progress, but, as her symptoms reduced in severity and frequency, she thought she became less interesting to him. She was like a book they had all read; now they knew the ending, they could put her back on the shelf. After a period of not being summoned to take part in the Tuesday lectures, she understood that she had been replaced.

It was around the same time that Hippolyte showed her the photographs. There were hardly any mirrors in the Salpêtrière: tiny, contraband slivers were passed around among the women, jealously kept and rarely seen. Anne didn't much care what she looked like, as she didn't like being looked at, and when Hippolyte opened the folder, she didn't immediately understand that the photographs were of her.

'This is me? No – you're making fun of me!' The girl in the photographs had skin that looked luminous against the dark background.

'Of course it's you.' Hippolyte was amused at her reaction. 'They were taken when you were in a hypnotic trance.' He smiled shyly. 'You're beautiful, are you not?'

Anne frowned. Compliments were payment in advance. But the girl in the pictures *was* beautiful. She didn't know what might have happened next, but a doctor walked in, causing Hippolyte to grab the photographs and slide them out of sight. The doctor made a curt remark; Hippolyte stammered excuses.

Shortly after that, Hippolyte came to find her. He was leaving the Salpêtrière to work in a hospital north of Paris. He was upset and his eyes blazed unnervingly. He promised to come back and see her. He told her she was important to him. He cared about her, he said.

That was two years ago. She had not heard from him since.

*

All night long, in the dormitory, there were noises. Wails. Weeping. Cries of anguish, of fear, even of pleasure, were normal. Anne listened to the darkness. Despite the number of warm bodies, it was always cold, and there was a pervasive stench of armpits, menstrual blood and urine. The smell of burning was also strong, but she knew that was just her illness.

She had once said to Hippolyte, 'You say that the burning smell is a trick of my mind. But what if there really was a fire, and I didn't wake the others because you told me it wasn't real – and everyone died?'

Hippolyte smiled. 'An intelligent girl like you, Anne, knows that fire is more than just a smell. You would hear sounds; you would see smoke. You would feel heat. You would wake the person next to you and ask them if they experienced those things too. And, if all of those were present, then you would be justified in waking the dormitory.'

'The person who sleeps next to me is mad, so how could I trust her?'

Hippolyte laughed. 'I see I can teach you nothing about rhetoric.'

After he explained the word 'rhetoric', Anne's next thought was, what if her hallucinations changed to include all of those things? But, over the next few months, the blackouts, the hallucinations, the periodic muteness that had afflicted her ever since *the thing* – they all became less frequent. It was strange; she had grown used to them. If she was no longer a hysteric, what was she?

6

Two years before, when Lawrence left his home in the Canadian back-woods, the city of Montréal had seemed bewilderingly vast: a teeming hive of people and noise. Paris was many times bigger. Creamy cliffs of stone were riddled with apartments, all crammed with people. At night, constellations of artificial light mocked the darkness. There were warrens of streets with doorways that led to staircases, to courtyards and then more staircases: a million rooms, stuffed with humanity. He thought the word 'million', but could not envisage what he was thinking.

In Canada, he had grown up in a hamlet by a great inland sea. Even in Montréal, you always knew that this was a town surrounded by water. Here, it was the city itself that was like the sea: a frozen ocean of stone. Sometimes, he had to walk to one of the bridges over the Seine, just to let his eyes rest on the far distance, and breathe. He thought of the water beneath him flowing to Le Havre, where he'd disembarked last October, then out into the Atlantic, and on and on, until molecules of it might lap against the wharves of Montréal, or even touch the shores of his childhood home. It comforted him to think this.

Lawrence felt he was adapting to his metropolitan habitat, but he was still uncomfortably aware of his humble beginnings. Towards the end of May, he took an omnibus to the Batignolles, in the north-west of the city, on his way to that most Parisian of events: a *salon*.

He was invited by a man he'd met in a café. He'd chosen the *Zouave* in Montparnasse with care, because it was a known meeting place for artists, and his ambition was to become one. He frequented the place for weeks, reading newspapers, casually eavesdropping on the (surprisingly boring) conversations, before his plan bore fruit and he began to make a friend. He was hampered by his shyness, but Yves Michaud's gentle courtesy disarmed him, and he was thrilled to find that this man – who looked more like a lawyer than a bohemian – was a professional painter. He was well spoken and cultured – clearly from a wealthy family – but he did not boast of his background or achievements. On the contrary, there was something unworldly about him, a modesty that Lawrence found appealingly un-Parisian. Most charming of all, he seemed to find Lawrence worthy of interest, and Lawrence was duly flattered.

Every Wednesday evening, Yves opened his studio to friends. This was Lawrence's first foray into artistic society and he desperately hoped to pass muster. He told himself he was shielded by his foreignness – the French could not discern his class or education, or lack thereof. And Yves liked him, seemed to view him as someone exotic and interesting. He was drawn to Yves; he thought there was a sympathy between them, but he could be wrong – one could always be wrong. Or he could be found wanting by Yves' friends – exposed as an upstart farm boy, uneducated, quintessentially dull.

He climbed six flights of stairs to the top of the building, drawing nearer to the sounds of laughter and the smell of pipe smoke. Though the door was ajar, he hovered on the threshold until Yves spotted him and came over, his smile genuine and warm.

'Lawrence, you're here! Welcome!'

He found himself in a noisy, crowded room, although the studio was a large attic that filled the top floor of the building. Yves led him over to a table and gave him a glass of wine. With one hand on his shoulder, he said, 'Don't mind them. They're all good fellows, and they can't wait to meet you. None of them has met a Canadian before.'

Yves introduced him to another painter called Michel Blasi, and made Michel promise not to abandon Lawrence while he ran out for more wine.

'Honestly,' Michel said, when Yves had gone, 'only Yves would leave his own party to run errands. He could perfectly well afford a servant, but he won't have one on principle.'

'What principle is that?'

'The equality of man. He thinks he should shift for himself, although he's richer than any of us. His family owns property all over the south.' Michel spoke with envious gloom. 'Never mind the principle of giving work to someone who needs it. But no, don't listen to me. Yves is the dearest, most generous fellow I know. Alfred can't afford a studio at all, so Yves lets him share this one for free.'

He pointed out Alfred Quinet, a small, foxy man, in conversation with the only woman present: a pale-skinned girl with flame-coloured hair. Her name was Séraphine Bignon, and Lawrence gathered, from the careless way Michel spoke about her, that she was his girlfriend. There were only about a dozen people in all, he realized, as he looked around him. The studio was beautiful; it had huge windows, in front of which were two easels and a divan. The furniture was opulent; there was even a piano in the corner. Lilac walls were hung three or four deep with paintings, and more canvases were stacked wherever there was floor space.

Michel introduced him to Alfred.

'Are these paintings all Yves' and yours?' Lawrence asked.

'Most of them. This is a recent one of mine.'

Lawrence looked at the canvas and was glad to be honestly complimentary. It was a scene of farmland and woods, with a play of light that seemed to shimmer before his eyes. It was the most powerful piece on the wall. He realized that Yves was the more conventional painter, although he assured himself that there was talent in his compositions and harmonious colouring. He had to concentrate to follow Alfred's heavy accent, which became more difficult as the volume of talk around them rose. Someone sat down at the piano and began to hammer out a tune with more gusto than skill.

'For God's sake, Ellis – we can't hear ourselves think!' Alfred shouted.

The man at the piano turned around and grinned at the room. He changed to a slower tune, but kept playing while talking to a couple of the guests. A big, fair man with a vinous glitter in his eyes, he spoke in loud, heavily accented French. An American. Lawrence was instantly on his guard. He avoided other English speakers where possible. English speakers judged him, asked questions about his background and education. Or they asked where he was from, and, when they found he wasn't from anywhere they knew (a good, conversation-worthy place like New York, or Dublin), they lost interest. Hearing that carrying voice, and seeing the way its owner tipped wine down his throat, Lawrence resolved to avoid him.

'Are you a painter, Monsieur Harper?'

It was the girl, Séraphine, her expression friendly and ironic.

'No. I'm a photographer's assistant.'

'That's a relief! We don't have to talk about painting – unless you want to.'

'No, no. I'm afraid I have aspirations to paint, though. Do you?'

'Not at all. It's a hard life – it's bad enough being attached to one.'

'Oh, you're—'

'With Michel. Yes.'

'You're a model, I believe?'

'At times. It's convenient for an artist to have a model who will sit for him for free.'

She grimaced, and he laughed. She made him feel at ease, but he was disconcerted when he raised his eyes to see, on the wall opposite, a painting of what was surely the same girl, naked on a divan. She followed his gaze and grinned.

'Yes, that's me,' Séraphine said, unabashed. 'Yves did that one. That one is me too, but you can only tell by the hair, huh? It's one of Alfred's.'

She pointed at a spot above Lawrence's head. He turned to see another version of the girl, or some girl, lounging on an unmade bed.

'Ah – yes. They have quite different styles, don't they?'

Séraphine leant towards him and lowered her voice. 'Michel goes on about Alfred's talent, but all his women look the same to me. He makes me look just like Camille, only with red hair.'

'Who's Camille?'

'His girl.'

Lawrence looked at the picture, hoping he appeared interested but not prurient. There was vigour in the painting, but the brushstrokes were so loose that any trace of individuality had been lost.

'It's beautiful. The way the light falls on the . . .' He waved his hand, at a loss for an appropriate word.

She laughed. 'Exactly. It looks like a body with a little head stuck on top. And he's made me look fat! Yves makes me look like me.'

Lawrence nodded. In Yves' painting, Séraphine was clearly recognizable. There was, though (he had to admit), something a little off about the right leg.

'Do you sit for many artists?'

'Not now. Just Michel and his friends.' She leant towards him. 'When I sit for Alfred, Yves pays me. He's so kind.'

'Even though Alfred has a girl?'

She shrugged. 'She's no good for that, at the moment. She's gone to the country to have a baby.'

'Oh.' Lawrence was taken aback. 'And, er, Monsieur Blasi doesn't mind?'

'You're talking about me.' Michel arrived by her side. 'Is he asking you to pose for him?'

'No, he's not. We were discussing how Alfred makes all his models look the same.'

'Séraphine is a philistine. She would have us all make portraits that look like photographs.'

'Not at all!'

Séraphine pulled a face, they all laughed, and that was when it happened – the thing that made Lawrence lose the thread of conversation, from which, that evening, he never quite recovered.

The painting hung above the studio door, which was why he hadn't noticed it until now. It showed a riverbank at the height of summer. In the foreground, green water reflected overhanging willows, and waterlilies flecked the surface. The bank gave way to trees, meadows and a distant factory chimney. On the bank stood the figure of a man, his back to the painter, but half turned, in the act of casting a fishing net. He was starkly nude, feet planted solidly apart, the muscles of the back, thighs and buttocks painted with vigour, attention and skill. The figure was easy, muscular, graceful – with as much beauty and power as any athlete in the Louvre. But this was no mythic figure; the half-turned face was full of individual life, and it bore a fashionably trimmed, Second Empire moustache. It was signed, *Yves Michaud*.

Over the course of the evening, Lawrence was introduced to the rest of the guests, including the rambunctious Mr Butterfield. They spoke in French, as if equally reluctant to acknowledge any similarity or kinship. Lawrence gathered that he wrote poetry, and was nephew to the American ambassador, which Lawrence – heir to nothing and no one – counted as another mark against him. Mr Butterfield did not ask him where he came from, nor who his people were; he was as little interested in Lawrence as Lawrence was in him.

All evening, Lawrence was intensely aware of Yves moving around the room. He stood apart in this company, as he had stood apart from the bohemians in the café. Half a head taller than anyone else, his spare frame was soberly dressed, and his bony face and heavy-lidded eyes gave him the look of a tired saint. Unlike the others, his voice never grew loud, his laughter never coarse. Lawrence observed who he talked to, how close he stood to them, whether he touched an arm. He was the perfect host, never staying too long with one person, always looking for an empty plate or glass. There was something tender and protective, almost avuncular, in his behaviour to his friends. When he came back to Lawrence, he was as charming as before, but then, Lawrence wondered miserably, wasn't he the same with everyone? What was a painting, anyway?

Yet his gaze continually strayed back to the fisherman; he studied the figure, compared it with Yves' nude of Séraphine. They were recognizably by the same hand, but with thrillingly different results: the feminine was conventional and somewhat inert; the masculine full of a tension that seemed to shout directly to him. Yves never referred to any of his paintings, and Lawrence did not dare ask him about it, but every time Yves was beside him, the warmth in his eyes and voice made his heart race. He tried to be nonchalant and witty, carelessly attractive. He tried not to drink too much, in case he gave something away.

7

Even after living in Paris for three years, Ellis Butterfield felt as though his life here was not quite real. His existence was like a rehearsal for some other way of being – he had the sense that, if he just kept at it, he might eventually arrive at a state where people believed they had a right to exist.

He remembered when his life had last seemed real, but that was before the war, when he was still a medical student. As soon as he passed his exams, he left Dartmouth and joined the staff of the Union military hospital in Washington. He learnt to amputate fast and cleanly; there was no other requirement for his skills. Almost half the wounded died. A bold stroke – removing a leg above the knee before gangrene could spread from a ruined foot – that was what counted as success.

It was not the way he had envisaged his adult life beginning. There was a certain technical satisfaction to be had from plugging a leaking wound, or performing a neat resection, but Ellis realized that, whereas his colleagues were capable of separating the work they did from the men they did it to, some flaw in him meant he lacked that ability. He focused on legs, arms, parts, avoided looking at their faces while in surgery, but making the ward rounds left him in a state of near collapse. At twenty, he had to look into the eyes of soldiers even younger than he was, or – which was worse – the eyes of men the age his father would have been, and see their terror, or their gratitude for a clean stump, or their terrible, unmerited trust.

At medical school, he honed a capacity for alcohol that earned him the respect of his peers. He drank because he liked it, and because he found that shyness and nervousness were soluble in wine. It was a magic cure for his asthma, hives and upset stomach; for boredom, anxiety and loneliness. Sober, he felt dull. After a few drinks, he was witty and happy, so much so that people wanted to be around him. He was so good at it, it was practically a talent in itself. In Washington, he drank to numb himself against the horrors of what they were doing. To begin with, he drank only when he finished work; then, increasingly, before.

After the war, his mother could not understand why he did not want to continue his medical career. For a year, he scared her by doing nothing other than writing some unsatisfactory poems, which he never showed to anyone. Then he told her he was moving to France.

'I keep thinking of what your father would have said,' she said, dabbing her eyes.

His father, who died during his first year of college, had been a doctor for over thirty years.

'Why would he have said anything?' said Ellis, more roughly than he meant to. 'People go to France. I'll probably come back. It's not for ever.'

He was impatient. His mother was a timid woman with not enough to fill her days. If she had ever been anything else, he didn't remember. She wanted Ellis to move back home and run a doctor's surgery in the next block. She had scouted suitable locations.

'What will I do without you?' she asked, tears brimming in her eyes. Ellis was her only child. As if that was his fault.

He shrugged, aware that he was being cruel, but unable to stop himself. 'Aunt Bertha is not far away – you needn't be lonely.'

'Oh, Bertha!' Mrs Butterfield did not like her sister-in-law. Ellis didn't like her either, but he was twenty-four and he felt life passing him by.

Mrs Butterfield gave a brave little smile. 'Forgive me, my darling. But you are all I have left in the world. What if I were to move to Paris too?'

Fortunately, her doctors advised against the long sea voyage (admittedly, doctors had their uses), so Ellis escaped. His mother wrote to him almost weekly, and he wrote back, much less frequently, burnishing this official version of his life to emphasize the rewards of writing poetry, enhancing the charm of his lodgings and the virtues of his friends; omitting everything else.

The morning after the salon, Ellis was meeting a friend of Yves Michaud's, a man called Gustave Daudel. Gustave was an art critic, and he had promised to show Ellis one of the most interesting sights of Paris. It was a brilliant morning, one of the rare days when he actively relished the feeling of unreality. He was not really Ellis Butterfield, American poet in Paris (surely a made-up personage) – he was a character in a play, but today the play felt like a comedy rather than a tragedy, with the promise of laughter and pleasure around the corner. Sunlight polished the top hat of a man walking in front of him and twinkled off his silver-topped cane. A woman passed in a dress of succulent green. A play with excellent costumes. And the smells – such detail in the set dressing! – the sweat and manure of horses, the reek of sewage that pooled in gutters, successive wafts of garlic, bread, urine . . .

Even as he enjoyed this whimsy, part of him was ashamed. He feared himself to be a creature entirely made up of feeling. That had been his undoing as a surgeon. He was constantly swept by enthusiasms and sympathies that could pass as swiftly as they arrived. He was unsteady, when he should have been firmly moored in his confident, American self. The joke was, people looked at him and saw nothing but the confidence with which he armoured himself; the hail-fellow-well-met roisterer was his most successful role.

Ellis stooped to enter a dark interior, almost blinded after the brilliant dazzle of the day. He was in a wine shop near the Jardin des Plantes, where Gustave, despite being avowedly bohemian, was, as always, on time.

'Monsieur Butterfield!' Gustave stood and shook his hand. 'Is it not nasty outside – so horribly bright and cheerful?'

'Monsieur Daudel. Good to see you. I have been trying to imagine what you have in store for me. Could it be something to do with the animal kingdom?'

'Bravo. But the animal kingdom is a large one. Have you ever been to the menagerie? No? Capital. We will start there. But then I have something really unusual to show you. Did you go to Yves' soirée last night? I had to show myself at the Lazary for a new play. I was expecting the usual drivel, but it wasn't too bad, and that always takes longer to write up.'

Ellis laughed and replied that he had.

'Was it amusing? Anything to report?'

'Oh, the usual crowd. Although Yves has a new friend. A Canadian fellow, very young, very serious and disapproving, like all Canadians.'

'Ah. Perhaps one of these moody young men Yves picks up from time to time. They moon around until they become sick with frustration.'

Ellis was surprised into momentary silence. 'I couldn't say as to that. I hardly spoke to him. We ended up arguing about religion, as far as I recall. I think Michel might have been angry with me.'

Gustave shrugged. 'He'll get over it. But you have managed, otherwise, to stay out of trouble? No more brushes with the police? No more harpies brandishing weapons?'

'No. I'm a reformed character.'

'Say not so! I'll have to see what we can do.'

After a couple of glasses of eau de vie, they entered the park. It was a glorious day, the zoo was busy with nurses and children, and couples strolled along winding paths.

'You know what Monsieur Hugo wrote about this place? He called it a miracle of civilization. Without leaving Paris, you can travel to every realm of the world and see its wonders.'

They stopped in front of an enclosure where a mountain of mottled flesh stood in a puddle of water.

'What you should know,' said Gustave, 'is that this monster is Kako the Terrible. He has killed not one, but two of his keepers. This is no rumour: it was in *Le Figaro*.'

'How did he do it? Did he sit on them?'

'He charged them and gored them with his fangs. I'm hoping to stimulate your imagination,' said Gustave. 'Poets must be nourished with experiences. I want to take some credit when you become famous.'

'I'll bear that in mind.'

'Hugo also spoke of the edifying contrasts on offer.' Gustave indicated a pudgy child standing with its nurse in front of the railings that surrounded the enclosure of the wolves. 'Here, we see absolute innocence contrasted with extreme brutishness.'

Ellis peered into the enclosure. Only one wolf was visible, and its demeanour suggested not so much brutishness as pathological detachment, or illness. It stood, panting in the heat, its back sunken, its shoulders bony. Its yellow eyes stared beyond the onlookers. Ellis found something about that gaze familiar: he had seen such a look in the eyes of men broken by their experiences of battle.

Gustave rapped his cane against the railings to attract the animal's attention. It did not move by one iota. 'Hugo is an idiot, of course.'

'I thought you fellows liked Hugo.' Ellis had heard both Michel and Yves – they were republicans, of course – speak of him in approving terms.

'Oh, Michel thinks he speaks for the common man. But the common man is less concerned with political reform than with filling his belly, his glass and his pipe.'

At the rotunda, they watched a keeper throw bread to the elephants, who picked up the rolls with graceful trunks and tucked them into smiling mouths. The elephants were popular and, after a minute or two, it became tedious to be jostled by the onlookers. They walked on to the cat pavilion, where it was quieter; on such a day, the animals were torpid in their concrete cells.

'This one,' said Gustave, in front of a cage whose label announced its inhabitant was a panther, Nero, 'used to belong to an actress. She kept it as a pet and took it for walks on a leash, until, one day, while walking in the Bois de Boulogne, it savaged her. She was so badly mauled that she had to retire from the stage and can now only leave her house wearing a veil to hide her scars.'

Ellis stared into the gloom, where a black shape was stretched out on the floor. It didn't look very big. Just then, the panther turned and stared at them, its eyes two points of light in the darkness. It snarled so softly that the growl was no more than a breath.

'Consider the nature of a beast. A panther is savage, whether it lives wild in the jungle, in the apartment of an actress, or in a cage at the zoo. A creature cannot change its nature.'

'Some animals can be tamed. Wolves are savage, but dogs are loyal and loving.'

'Oh, come! Dogs are not wolves.'

'They are descended from wolves. Perhaps it's just that change is slow and gradual.'

'You are provoking. I was going to go on to talk of the nature of men, whether we are capable of change, even improvement. But now you've ruined it.'

'You mean, could a critic ever evolve into a poet?'

Gustave laughed. 'Or vice versa. Come on. If we're late, they won't let us in.'

After the sun's glare, it took their eyes a while to adjust. The amphitheatre was large, full of rustling and whispering; a drone of suppressed excitement. Tiers of seats were packed with fashionable Parisians, including a number of women. Ellis looked questioningly at Gustave as they squeezed into some free space, but he only smiled, turned to survey the audience and raised his hat to a couple of acquaintances.

The lecture began. The small, dynamic man in charge – Dr Philippe Jospin, Gustave told him – brought out a succession of women and conducted them through a series of extraordinary behaviours. The women were patients in the psychiatric hospital; all were ill with a range of bizarre symptoms; and all, he went on to demonstrate, were highly suggestible hysterics.

The first woman, 'Madeleine' – Ellis suspected this was not her real name – had suffered from inexplicable seizures for ten years. Jospin put her into a catatonic trance by flashing a light in her eyes, then proceeded, to the accompaniment of gasps, to push needles through her hands. She stood in front of the audience with her eyes open but face slack, apparently unaware. Jospin turned her hands in all directions; the audience could see the needles protruding from either side. He withdrew the needles with a flourish and again held up her hands for inspection; there was no blood. The audience murmured and applauded warmly.

The next exhibit was 'Therese': an older woman, who appeared truculent and suspicious. After placing her in a trance, Jospin told her that there was a mouse running around her feet. She yelped with terror, lifted her skirts and finally climbed on to a chair as the audience rocked with laughter. When they'd had their fun, he told her that the mouse was gone, and, instead, there was a most beautiful scene in front of her: a meadow full of flowers, the sun shining gently on her face, and she felt extraordinarily happy. The woman's face changed from an expression of terror to one of radiant bliss. Jospin turned to the audience as if to say, *You see? I am not cruel.*

He induced a series of spectacular convulsions in 'Sabine', a young girl so pale she appeared to be made of silver. At the end of her turn, he made her hold out her hands and commanded her to show the audience what was on her palms. He explained that she suffered from religious delusions, and Ellis saw what appeared to be blood well in her palms and drip on to the floor. Women gasped – some crossed themselves – and men grumbled. He felt anger. The poor creature was mad, of course, but this Jospin was a charlatan. Ellis had attended some odd demonstrations when he was a medical student – including, once, a spirit medium – but this went beyond anything he had seen. Yet he was gripped. Ellis realized that the women on show were known to many of the audience – had perhaps been seen more than once, like a favourite actress.

The last woman to appear drew a similarly heightened buzz. 'Honorine' was a striking, tall girl, with tawny skin and a halo of dark hair. First, Jospin lit a taper and waved it under her nose, then an assistant smacked two pieces of wood together behind her head. There was no change on her face, but she fell back into the arms of two waiting men, her body stiff as a plank. Her feet were placed on the seat of one chair and the back of her head on another. Jospin demonstrated, to almost everyone's satisfaction, that there was no support under the woman's body; she was held by the hysterical rigidity of her muscles. His assistants brought weights, which they placed on top of her. The woman appeared to be asleep. No strain was visible on her face. The murmurings grew louder and more incredulous as the pile grew higher.

'There is a rod under her back!' cried a young voice.

'Please, monsieur, come down here. Come . . .' said Jospin, seeming delighted at the interruption.

The young man came to the front of the hall and was invited to pass his hand under her body to see if he could detect a hidden means of support. He did so with unnecessary thoroughness and declared himself more than satisfied. There was much laughter.

Ellis could not contain himself. 'He's a plant, surely,' he hissed to Gustave, who gave him a look.

The assistants removed the weights piece by piece, and, when the woman was unencumbered, Jospin had a mattress placed beneath her and told her that she would, at his word, become relaxed. In an instant, whatever power was holding her vanished, and she crumpled on to the mattress. Jospin brought her to her feet and turned her to face away from the audience. He lowered the neck of her chemise until her back was bare. The atmosphere in the auditorium was electric; there seemed to be a collective holding of the breath at this sudden exposure of skin.

Jospin held up his forefinger and traced something on her bare back. There was a long silence, and then a growing swell of noise as redness appeared on her skin where his finger had touched. Ellis and Gustave were near enough to see that the skin was erupting into raised, red swirls and curves. They read *P. Jospin*, and the day's date. The theatre erupted.

They filed out into the sunshine, the crowd chattering about what it had seen.

'Stimulating, was it not?' said Gustave.

'Certainly. It's extraordinary what people can be induced to believe.'

'You're a sceptic.'

'I trained as a doctor. I know what makes people bleed. And it isn't hysteria, or . . . or hypnotic suggestion, or whatever he's calling it.'

It was said more violently than he'd intended, and he saw Gustave's face close.

'But, certainly, it's an amazing spectacle. Most thought provoking. Is it always this popular?'

'It's quite a fixture on the social calendar. Jospin may be a showman, but he is also a highly respected doctor. In fact, I'm not sure whether to be offended on his part!'

'I'm sorry. I can't help speaking my mind; you must know that, by now.'

'You must admit, they are attractive, some of those women.'

'Without doubt.'

'My pick of the bunch would be the last one. One can just imagine . . . I say, are you all right?'

Ellis had stopped, one hand on his chest.

'Yes . . . I'm—' He struggled to breathe.

'Are you sure, old fellow?'

Ellis found he was stooping over. An intense pressure was squeezing his ribcage. Air whistled in his throat.

'I'll be . . . Just . . .'

Unbidden, his mother's face came to mind. The vice around his ribs tightened. Gustave was looking at him with concern. Ellis was swept with his usual, impotent fury. How ridiculous, how unmanly to be at the mercy of this affliction, like those poor women: the puppet of some capricious power.

'Need drink . . . brandy.'

'Of course.'

Tentatively, Gustave put an arm around his back and helped him down the road to the nearest bar.

8

Throughout June, the weather was unusually hot and dry. The planes and chestnuts cast welcome shade along the banks of the Seine, but their leaves were already dusty. The river shrank, revealing successive tide marks. Mud in gutters dried to reeking crusts. From the country, there were reports of droughts and crop failures.

The animals were torpid, which meant the zoo visitors resorted to ever more outrageous methods to provoke them to activity. The big cats tended to stir only towards dusk, when they became agitated: hissing, coughing, grunting. Watching Marguerite pace the length of her cage – seven steps took her as far as she could go – Victor tried to think of ways to allow her more freedom. It was impossible. Even four strong men holding her on taut ropes could not have controlled her outside the cage – and what sort of freedom would that be, for a queen?

Sometimes, when he worried about the animals in his care, he reminded himself of the miserable lives led by the city's working beasts: the thousands of horses, the mules and oxen. Not to mention the ratters and guard dogs, and then there were the half-starved strays, the feral cats . . . Suffering was everywhere. One's sympathy ran dry.

He turned a corner, and the worsening smell meant that he was nearly home. His neighbourhood always smelt, but the heat made it worse. There was a horse market near his building, which wasn't too bad, but there was also the filthy Bièvre – the last open stretch of the river before it disappeared underground. It never dried up entirely, but it had shrunk to a brown, oily slurry. People said that, if you dipped so much as a finger into the Bièvre, your skin would turn black and slough off. Victor had to cross it on his way home – a familiar route, and one he trod with a heavy heart.

He loved his job, but he was lonely. He'd lived in the same two rooms for almost a decade: bachelor's rooms, spartan and devoid of the comforts that a female companion would provide. He was a professional man, not bad-looking, as far as he could tell, and he did not understand why he was condemned to such a monastic existence. He was no brute – he was a gentle man who deserved some kindness, but he did not know how to find it. He was too fastidious for the street, too tongue-tied for the salon. If only his work had led to opportunities for meeting suitable women, but Papin, his superior, was old and unmarried, and the keepers were not of his class.

Victor arrived home and toiled up the stairs, feeling the temperature rise with every floor. His rooms were under the roof, as they were cheapest, but he sweltered in summer and froze in winter. He could have afforded something more congenial, but he was saving money (for what?), and the Rue Poliveau was only a couple of blocks from the menagerie. It was so close that he had been woken in the night by the rumble of thunder, only to realize, with a thrill of paternal pride, that it was Tancred giving his splendid roar. And sometimes the quiet of the night was torn in two by a throaty snarl – that was the voice of Marguerite.

At the southern end of the menagerie stood the Hotel Lagny, a mansion that had stood on the site ever since the park was the Sun King's Jardin du Roi. For many years, it had housed the offices and salons of Director Lapeyre, and those of the director and superintendent of the Natural History Museum. To the left of the front entrance, a flight of steps led down to a cellar door. Victor had only once been through that door, which led to some filthy storage rooms, and then (although he himself had never ventured further) into a warren of tunnels that dated back to the Middle Ages, when the district was quarried for its white stone. Victor had his modest office in the hotel, and this was where he arrived early this morning, after another night when it was too hot to sleep.

The sun poured down a hard light, outlining every detail with brilliant clarity, igniting sparks in every drop of dew. The sky was a pure blue that presaged no relief from the heat, but, at six in the morning, it was perfect. Victor best loved the zoo when it was empty, when there were no shouting children or jeering crowds, just the sense that he was alone with the animals, and that the world outside could not reach him.

Not this morning.

'Monsieur Calmette!'

There was urgency in the voice. The head keeper, Robitaille, was hurrying towards him.

'Monsieur Calmette, it's Olga. She's ill. She won't get up and hasn't touched any food. Pierre's been in with her, and she's not reacting at all.'

Victor followed him to the lynx's cage, where the animal lay with her back to the bars. Her eyes were open, but the pupils were unresponsive, her breathing barely noticeable. She let Victor feel her abdomen without moving.

'It looks like poisoning,' he said.

'That's what Pierre thought. She was fine yesterday, but now . . .'

Pierre wrung his hands in distress. 'It was so busy yesterday; you know what it's like. We try to watch everyone, but it's impossible.'

'I know. I know. It's not your fault, Pierre.'

Robitaille poked around in the debris on the cage floor. He cursed softly, bent down and picked up a fragment of blue paper – the sort used by butchers to wrap their wares. They exchanged looks.

'I'll try an emetic,' Victor said. 'Can we get her into the shelter?'

The lynx was the smallest cat, and the men managed to lift the animal on to a sack and carry her into the shelter.

'Check the other cages. Maybe we should dose them all.'

He had a terrible vision of Marguerite lying in a heap, the light in her eyes dimming. He ran to see her, but she looked perfectly all right.

There was a rumbling noise and he looked around to see something like a black tent trembling towards him – a bizarre cloth contraption built over a barrow, being pushed by a young man. Oh God, it was the photographer with his mobile darkroom. It had slipped his mind: today it was the turn of the big cats to be photographed for the infernal series of postcards. This ludicrous idea of Lapeyre's . . . Victor found it offensive; as though the animals were nothing more than simpering girls to be ogled in private. He advanced on the young foreigner, whose smile died when he saw the look on Victor's face.

'You cannot do this today – I'm sorry, Monsieur Harper. It's not possible. You will have to come back another time.'

'Has something happened?' Monsieur Harper's face showed concern, but also stubbornness. On previous occasions, Victor had noted his diligence; it reminded him of himself when he was starting out, eager to prove himself.

'One of our cats has been attacked.'

'Attacked? My God. I'm sorry—'

'So, you see—'

'I understand. How did it happen?'

'Sometimes a visitor gets it into his head to throw poisoned meat through the bars. Excuse me, monsieur.'

Victor left Harper and the barrow standing in the path. The youth was inoffensive, and he had been instructed to facilitate his work; Victor shouldn't have told him what had happened, but he was unable to stop himself.

When he visited the cats later, he saw the girl from the bear pit, and a small spurt of pleasure lightened his bitter mood. She was standing by the tiger's cage, her stillness marking her out among the drifting crowd of onlookers. None of the other animals had been attacked. Marguerite had torn her way through a lump of horse meat and was licking her paws and whiskers, her eyes roaming over the faces in front of her as if they didn't exist. The crowd began to thin, moving on to watch a pacing, snarling Nero. Victor and the girl stayed, and he saw her register his glance. He found himself telling her about Olga.

'People do that?' Her brow creased with anger. 'How can they? I suppose people are capable of anything.'

'Yes. Anything that can be imagined. But why anyone would want to hurt a beautiful animal like that, I don't know.'

'Will she recover?'

'I fear not. We do our best to protect the animals, but people are endlessly wicked. The cages used to be merely bolted, but people stole the animals, so we had to install locks.'

'They *stole* the animals? Why?'

'Particularly monkeys. As pets, I suppose. I don't know. Someone once got into the zebras' enclosure and mutilated one of them. In such a terrible way . . . Like with Olga – just pure spite.' He shook his head. 'Now, there are guards at night, but when the zoo is busy, we can't prevent them from . . . doing things.'

'How terrible.'

'Apologies, mademoiselle. I shouldn't have burdened you with this. It's part of our job.'

'No!' The girl shook her head and Victor experienced a moment of grateful sympathy. She felt as passionately as he did.

Together, they watched Marguerite washing her face. Suddenly she stopped, paused, and seized her tail between her teeth. Sometimes she *was* just like a giant house cat: pernickety, aloof, playful.

'You won't let anything happen to her?'

'No. I care about all the animals here, but I think I love Marguerite the most.'

'Because you looked after her?'

'I suppose so.'

They stood in silence for a minute.

'You like coming here?'

'When I can.'

'Well . . . It was good to see you again, mademoiselle.'

She nodded, without turning her head.

The lynx died towards dusk. Monsieur Papin performed the post-mortem. There was a laboratory behind the pavilion, with discreetly high windows. The body of Olga was stretched out on the marble table, and Victor and Robitaille watched as Papin sliced through her soft fur.

'What do you expect to see?' asked Robitaille. He was taking the lynx's death particularly hard. He had been at the zoo for a quarter of a century, since he was a young man, and he treated his charges with as much care as he gave his children.

Papin grunted. 'I won't know until I see it.'

Ignace Papin had been at the zoo even longer than Robitaille. He was a tall, stooped man of uncertain age. His hair was still dark – suspiciously so – and his face unfashionably clean-shaven. A misanthrope, a cynic, unmarried, with (it was said) an enormous private income, his superbly tailored coats almost disguised a pronounced curvature of the spine. He didn't need either his salary or the grace-and-favour house in the menagerie grounds, and occasionally Victor wished that Papin would painlessly remove himself so that he, Victor, could take over. But mostly he was glad to work for a such a gifted diagnostician, one who was utterly dedicated to his charges.

Victor assisted at the post-mortem, weighing and recording each organ as Papin handed it to him. He had dissected countless beasts after deaths both natural and unnatural, but some animals, some deaths, no matter how he tried to remain impartial, got under his skin. Olga would let him rub his knuckles over her head while she purred like a giant kitten. She was exceptionally beautiful.

As Papin probed the contents of the stomach, he exclaimed, and withdrew something in his forceps. 'What's that? My God – a fishhook!'

Victor caught his breath. He saw Robitaille's face twist with anger.

'Here's another . . . three, four. The poor creature, she must have been in agony.' Papin rarely showed emotion, but his face held a look of pain and sorrow as he dropped the fishhooks into an enamel bowl.

'Diabolical!' This from Robitaille. 'I would kill them. Slowly. The guillotine would be too quick.'

Papin concentrated on probing the red mess of the guts. 'And they call animals brutes,' he said quietly. 'That's why I didn't become a doctor. I prefer to have patients one actually wants to save.'

9

When Lawrence first moved in with the family Lamy, knowing no one in the city, he sometimes accompanied them to Mass. He wasn't Catholic, but he enjoyed the painted interior of the church, the shuddering votive flames, the drowsy ceremonial. It was a far cry from the bare kirk of his youth and the minister who promised him eternal torment for his secret thoughts. Most of all, he was drawn by the crucifix, the body of the plaster Christ so exposed and beautiful that he was unable to look away. One Sunday, he turned from his rapt contemplation to find Ernestine gazing at him, the expression in her eyes unreadable, and he looked away, his face hot with shame. After that, he told Madame Lamy that he'd found a Protestant church to go to. He had, but he never went.

A few days after the soirée, Lawrence received a letter from Yves, offering to show him more of the city. He read it over breakfast with the Lamys, his face carefully still, hoping no one would guess at the way his heart leapt. Madame Lamy glanced inquisitively at him, although she was tactful enough not to pry. Ernestine was absorbed in a fashion magazine and paid him no attention.

The following Sunday, Lawrence, early, dawdled by the kiosk outside the Gare Saint-Lazare. He surveyed the unappetizing array of sweets on offer and attempted to engage the vendor in conversation. She stared silently through him, so he pointed to a tray at random.

She took his money and grunted, her sunburned face surrounded by a grubby, pie-crust frill.

At last, the station clock struck nine and he sauntered inside. Almost immediately, he saw Yves, standing by the ticket office, tall and slender, as debonair as ever. He had bought their tickets, and led Lawrence to a platform where they boarded a train.

Yves promised to show him a side of the city he had not yet seen. Lawrence stared out of the window, a sudden shyness making him unable to look Yves in the eye. How quickly this had happened. At first, he'd wanted Yves as a friend and guide to the world of artists; the other night, a new, thrilling possibility had opened up and he was shocked by how much he desired it. Never had he felt such affinity for a relative stranger, at the same time as such admiration for his personal qualities. Seeing Yves with his friends made Lawrence aware of how good he was, how like some pure-hearted knight from a tale of courtly love. It was alarming; it was almost too much. He wanted desperately not to ruin things.

The circular railway, known as Paris's 'little belt', ran just inside the city walls, looping through suburbs where the new stations, like white temples, perched above their surroundings. They passed through villages that, until recently, had no truck with the city. They passed beet fields and vegetable plots, an old woman in black, tending chickens. A ragged plot held some ancient vines, next to it a half-built row of houses, then a handsome hunting lodge from another century. Most of the roads were still dirt, rutted by cart-wheels, and a fine dust covered everything. Lawrence was grateful for the changing view from the windows; it kept Yves from examining his face too closely.

They got out at a station on the western side of the city, walked to the nearest bastion and climbed up to the path that ran along the top of the city wall – the great serpentine mound that coiled around the city. Grass grew on the summit and on the inner slopes. On the outer face, a stone wall plunged thirty feet into a trench, beyond which the ground rose gradually. From this vantage, they could see for miles. The horizon wavered in the heat, smudged by woods, nicked by spires. Stretching from the foot of the wall was a wide strip of wasteland, in which the scattered ruins of buildings stood like stumps of teeth. Trees had been cut down. It looked as though something terrible had happened here.

'This is the Zone,' Yves said. 'They demolished everything that was too near the wall.'

'Why?'

Yves smiled. 'A defensive measure, to keep out the barbarians who might otherwise creep up on us unawares.'

'Are we in danger from barbarians?'

Yves looked at him in mock reproof. 'Parisians think so. Mind you, the feeling is mutual. Paris is not popular with those who live in the countryside. Perhaps cities never are.'

'Where I grew up, cities were another world. Toronto or Montréal didn't seem real, let alone Paris. They were places of escape, ever since I could think about the future.'

'Escape – yes. I suppose a city is like a beautiful woman. Everyone is aware of her, and thinks of her either with covetousness, or pride, or disapproval—' He broke off and laughed at himself.

'You make it sound a terrible fate.'

'To be a woman? Or to be beautiful?'

'Both, perhaps. I'm thankful that no one has reason to think of me in those terms.' He felt a warmth rise in his face, and turned his head, so as not to see if Yves glanced at him.

Below them, a cart was drawn up at the gate, where a customs official and the drover were in heated conversation. They seemed to be arguing, but both men's accents were so strong, Lawrence could not understand.

'I get more used to accents, but slowly. Your friend, Monsieur Quinet, for instance: I found his quite difficult to follow. Where is he from?'

'From the south – not far from where I come from, near Montpellier.'

'Really? You sound nothing like each other.'

Yves smiled. 'Well, I had the dubious benefit of being sent away to a good school, whereas Alfred is the son of a poor widow. It is only by a miracle that he managed to come to Paris and study. He has such talent. I feel it is up to all of us to help him any way we can.'

'You seem to help him a great deal – with the studio, I mean.'

'He's a genius, in my opinion.' He sighed. 'Seeing Alfred paint, and knowing my weaknesses . . .'

'Must you compare yourself to him?'

'A fair question. But we share a studio, and I know talent when I see it.'

'His work has freshness . . . a sensuality, I suppose. But I found also a kind of brutality. The painting of Mademoiselle Bignon, for example – it's powerful, but there was no sense of her as an individual. Whereas your painting of her – it had her character.' He glanced away, and then, as if the thought had just struck him: 'I thought your fisherman was a fine thing.'

'Thank you. It's not too bad. I haven't done anything like that for a while.'

Lawrence felt this as a blow. 'Is it a scene near here?'

'No. It's the river near my parents' house. Painted in the open air. But you're right – nothing I've done since coming here has been . . . When I'm at home, I can't wait to get back to Paris. But here, where I am really free, I seem to have left something behind.' Yves laughed and shook his head.

Lawrence took a deep breath. 'I thought it was timeless – the figure is like a Greek athlete – yet, at the same time, completely modern. The contrast of the man fishing, like an ancient innocent, but then, the factory in the background.'

'Yes! That's what I was trying to get – that echo of a classical scene, yet now, united by the timeless action of the body. That's how they still fish. They stand on the riverbank and cast their net. It's splendid.'

'I've been going to the Louvre to sketch. I love the ancient galleries. Particularly the Greek sculpture.' He stopped, half afraid; waiting for Yves to respond.

Yves laughed. 'And you warn me of the danger of comparing yourself to others!'

At the end of the day, they loitered outside the station. Lawrence hoped for a further invitation. He was about to suggest a drink when Yves seemed to shake himself and said that he felt inspired to work on one of his paintings.

Lawrence smiled quickly. They said goodbye with mutual assurances of friendship and, on Lawrence's part, confusion.

A couple of weeks passed and he was again invited to spend Sunday with Yves. This time, they would take the train into the countryside east of Paris and walk from the station to the river. Yves knew a guinguette where one could lunch and hire a rowing boat. When the day came, it was stiflingly hot, and it felt as though half of Paris had had the same idea – a noisy crowd descended from the train, all of them heading for the waterside. Yves promised, after lunch, they would go somewhere quieter. When Lawrence asked him where, he said, with a smile that made Lawrence's heart gallop, 'You shall see.'

Over lunch, they talked about their families. Lawrence described how his parents had emigrated from Ireland to Canada, only to die of ship fever, whereupon he was adopted by Scottish farmers near Lake Huron. He had been too young to remember his real parents, too young to feel the victim of tragic circumstances, and his adoptive parents were kind and decent. He was probably better off – only the very poorest Irish emigrated.

Yves was enchanted. 'What a romantic story! Reborn in the wilderness – like the beginning of a heroic adventure.'

Lawrence laughed in surprise. To him, his upbringing was the dullest thing in the world.

Yves gestured at the diners who filled the tables on the riverbank, or picnicked on the grass. They were surrounded by talk, laughter and the music of an unskilled quartet.

'To live in the wilderness, where wild beasts roam . . .' He laughed. 'To a dweller in this over-civilized metropolis, it sounds like heaven. You must miss it.'

Lawrence shook his head. 'Not really. The last thing it is is romantic. It's endless, hard work. There's too much wilderness.'

'I would have thought there could be no such thing. I imagine a great silence.'

'There is that.'

'There is some wilderness in France, in the mountains, say, but people live everywhere – villages, hamlets; the countryside is full of them. I would love to go somewhere truly wild. I'd love to paint that. Perhaps that's what I need.'

'There are beautiful places back home, of course. But in winter the snow can be higher than your head and you can't go anywhere. It imprisons you. It's so cold, and it lasts for months, till you think you'll go mad.'

'All right, I grant you that. But the summers—'

'The summers are beautiful. And the autumns. It's just the size of it, somehow. Forest that goes on and on and on. The same trees. The monotony of it. From where I grew up, it takes three days to get to Montréal. Before the railway was built, it took two weeks. Such vastness – it crushes the spirit.'

'But you must miss your family. Your mother?'

'Yes, sometimes,' said Lawrence. 'Of course.'

Yves waited for more, then said, 'I miss my family dreadfully. Especially my sister. She's like the other side of me. Do you have brothers or sisters?'

'No.'

Yves looked sympathetic. 'Well, they can be very irritating. They tend to point out one's flaws.'

'Do you go home often?'

'Quite. The country round our home is beautiful. But, if I stay too long, they start trying to marry me off.' He said it with a laugh.

'Would that be so bad?' asked Lawrence, and he too laughed.

'Oh, I'm too old and set in my ways.'

'Good heavens!' Now, his laughter was genuine. 'How old are you?'

'I'm twenty-seven. You may laugh, but my hair is starting to fall out. It's terrible. And I'm almost penniless. No, I have chosen to dedicate my life to art.'

After lunch, they hired a rowing boat and set off down the river. At first, they were one of an armada of boats, and there was much splashing and showing off, and good-natured jeers between one boat and another, but, as they rowed with the slow current, the river grew quieter.

'That is the Island of Wolves,' said Yves, shipping his oars and indicating the bank on their left. Many boats had pulled up to the shore, and couples walked on paths amid the trees.

'Does that mean there were wolves there?'

'I suppose there were once. Now, the only dangerous animals wear top hats and waistcoats, and their prey is the female of the species. I propose going on a little further, if you can bear it?'

'Gladly,' said Lawrence.

They shed hats, jackets and waistcoats, and rowed in their shirt-sleeves. There was not a breath of wind on the water, and Lawrence was soon aware that his shirt was soaked and clinging to his back.

He was embarrassed that Yves should see him in such a dishevelled state. Nevertheless, he matched Yves' rhythm and they slid swiftly over the water.

It seemed that the river was unfurling from beneath him – a glistening scarf of green silk, opaque and mysterious. They passed more guinguettes, the banks crowded with tables, then the river took a long, wide curve, and peace fell as diners were replaced by woods of willow, oak and alder. They left behind the sounds of people, until there was just the hollow rattle of rowlocks, the purling of oars, and water dripping from the blades. The river narrowed and branches almost met over the water, casting a green shade filled with lit, dancing specks.

'This island we're coming up to now,' said Yves, after a while, pausing to catch his breath, 'is called the Island of Love.'

Lawrence almost dropped an oar. He wasn't sure if Yves was joking.

'Unfortunately, it's rather popular as a result, but, if we go on to the next one, we may find a nice quiet spot. If you are not tired?'

'I could go on for hours,' said Lawrence, meaning it.

He put his back into it, enjoying the effort; it helped to quell his excitement, and the fears that flickered under his mind's surface, like the fish that made dark movements in the water. He allowed himself to be lulled by the rhythm: the glide of the boat, the watery accompaniment, the presence of another so close to him. He could almost imagine that what he so much wanted to happen had already happened . . . He rowed in a blissful sense of ideal companionship. He almost didn't want to stop, because he didn't know what would happen then. As he thought this, he lost the rhythm, and his oar knocked against Yves'.

'Oh, I'm sorry. How clumsy of me.' He fumbled to right his oars, instantly hotter – were that possible – with embarrassment.

'No matter. I was just thinking how well you row. My shoulders are aching. That looks like a good spot, perhaps? Over there?'

Lawrence turned to see a small, wooded island ahead of them. Yves let the boat glide closer, until they saw a clear stretch of grassy bank, and guided the boat to bump gently against it. Lawrence caught hold of a branch, and Yves made the boat fast.

They got out and grinned at each other. From here, they could see no buildings, no people, no sign of human life.

'I need a swim, after that. Phew, I'm out of practice.' Yves sat on the grass and unlaced his boots, then began to undress, looking out over the water.

Trying not to stare, in blinks, Lawrence registered his long, white body, the sharp contrast of black hair rising from groin to navel, before Yves leapt into the water with a gigantic splash. Lawrence folded his clothes with care. Behind him, he heard Yves surface.

'Aaah! It's fine!' he cried. 'Are you coming?'

The water was deep, even at the bank, and dark. Lawrence could see nothing below the surface. He slithered off the bank; one foot met soft mud, then nothing, and the cold rushed up his body. After rowing, plunging into the cool water filled him with euphoria. He swam a few strokes away from the bank, splashing and gasping.

'Good?' Yves laughed with pleasure.

'Good!'

Lawrence dived under the surface. Underneath, the water was green-gold and murky with silt, but he saw Yves' long, white legs kicking a few yards away, the tender stem of his penis waving in the water. Lawrence surfaced, pushing the hair out of his eyes. He let himself float, face up, legs hanging down into the fishy darkness, stirring his arms just enough to maintain buoyancy. The sun came through branches in broken shafts and pierced his half-closed eyelids, combining with the effects of wine until he was aware of little except plash, dazzlement, coolness; the water cradling his body, the surface meniscus licking at his mouth.

Lawrence was torn with longing. Should he swim closer and brush against a limb, as if by accident? What if he were to duck his friend in a playful show of high spirits? Yves floated nearby, eyes closed. With his beard, his slender limbs, his closed eyelids, Lawrence was reminded of the Christ in Saint-Germain-des-Prés. Better not to break the dreamy spell; not yet.

Lawrence floated and tried to let go of everything, tried to let himself become one with the river creatures, existing without thought or intention, content to lie in the dappled shade and drift with the current, waiting for something to happen.

10

Ellis woke from the nightmare soaked with sweat, the vice around his ribs threatening to squeeze the life out of him. He hauled himself to a sitting position and scrabbled for the towel that hung over the end of the bedstead. It was the only thing that helped during an attack: pulling on the towel at arms' length somehow opened a narrow channel through which he could suck air into his lungs.

It took several moments to push away the horror and rebuild the room around him: there was the window, the curtains, the table . . . the noise from the street, the sound of the concierge's wife, Madame Gigoux, cleaning the landing with bad-tempered zeal. The mop slopped wetly against his door, a noise he loathed – it made him think of a slobbering animal – but it was better than the dream. It had been the one with the young soldier who didn't understand that Ellis had just amputated both his hands; he held up the stumps, his face changing from confusion to shock, and he began to scream. In the dream, Ellis was both looking at the boy from the outside and experiencing his horror, both perpetrator and victim. The screaming wouldn't stop. Sometimes the dream ended with him attacking the boy with a bone saw, just to shut him up. He would wake not knowing if it was a real memory, or a warped echo (not the last part, he had never attacked a patient with a saw). All he could do was hold on to the towel, clench and relax his hands, and breathe: in, one, two, three, and out, one . . . two . . . three. He knew this foe; he no longer thought it would kill him. It just had to be outwitted – managed with stubbornness and misdirection and cunning.

Everyone had been so proud of him for his war work, especially his mother. He should have been proud of himself, they said, but he wasn't. He was too tired, then too sickened. Too sad. Drinking numbed all that, and helped him to sleep, at first. Now, it no longer worked like that. Or rather, like last night (he barely remembered last night), it gave unconsciousness, but it could not grant him peace.

At length, the pressure on his chest relented and Ellis was able to release the towel. He got up slowly and drew the curtains, opened the window and breathed in the morning air. He looked down at himself in the sunlight: the only mark on his body was the scar on his arm from that ridiculous brawl. His wholeness was a jibe to all those who had passed under his hands.

He washed from head to toe, relishing the small shocks of cold flannel on his skin, each one driving the nightmare further into the past. Then he stood at the window, eyes closed, renewing himself in the sunshine. It was one of those bright mornings which made him glad to have his attic room on the hill, from where Paris spread out beneath him, glittering with enticements.

Everywhere was downhill from Montmartre, which was an advantage when you set forth in the morning, but a curse when struggling home at night. Always susceptible to signs and omens, Ellis gained confidence that today was going to be a good one: a musician was playing a song he liked; a flower-seller called out to him, and, when he smilingly shook his head, she shrugged and said, 'When she sees you, handsome, she won't need a flower.' He cherished the compliment, cheap as it was. It was one with the brightness of the morning and the promise of a long, soft twilight to come – the sort made for idling on a terrace with a cool glass of wine.

*

Ellis made his uncle's residence in good time. Inside a parcel were half a dozen copies of *Revue Noire,* the magazine that contained two of his poems. He was particularly proud of one: a meditation on letters from across the sea, although couched in such metaphorical language that it could be interpreted in several ways.

He was shown into the parlour at the back of the house that served as a waiting room, where an elderly gentleman already sat, wearing a look of disapproval. Ellis greeted him cheerfully, perhaps too cheerfully – the man looked put out, as if he assumed that they must have met before, but could not remember how, or where. Ellis sat down to wait. His uncle had invited him, but, twenty minutes after the appointed time, he had still not been summoned. He had arrived early – this could in no way be seen as his fault!

His uncle's secretary, James Warburton, put his head around the door and summoned the sour man, who was a *Monsieur le Ministre,* and raised his eyebrows at Ellis in the faintest possible signal of recognition. Ellis countered with a curt nod.

Left alone, he took out a copy of the *Revue* and struck an attitude, legs elegantly crossed, leaning on one elbow, as he reread an article that was heavily critical of the Emperor. Perhaps he should warn his uncle about the political slant. Ephraim disapproved of Louis-Napoléon, although probably not to this degree, and certainly not in this sort of language. He gave in to the temptation to turn to his best poem and look at it again: '*Mots d'Ailleurs*'. The editor had been most complimentary . . .

Another black-clad gentleman joined Ellis in the waiting room. He also appeared to be in a bad mood, and Ellis barely bothered to greet him. When James Warburton returned and apologized to *Monsieur le Comte* for keeping him waiting, Ellis could contain himself no longer. He stood up and interrupted, crossly and rather loudly: '*Mr* Warburton! A word, if you please.'

'I'll be back in a moment, Mr Butterfield,' said the secretary, with a glare.

Ellis made up his mind to stoke his indignation. This was an insult, they were underlining just how little Ellis's time was worth, compared to their own.

He stood in front of the window, looking out at the garden. Among yellowing box hedges, he caught a flash of movement: Circe, Ephraim's cat, was stalking through the shrubbery. The air was drowsy and wind-less, busy with the creatures of summer. He began to turn over some phrases in his head, something about the denizens of the air, as much a city full of differing desires as a city of men, but instead of being anchored to the earth, they were free to rise as high as . . . as what? Something modern, like a hot-gas balloon . . . He watched a gossamer seed head drift up and out of sight. A streak of speed – the Siamese leapt into the air and swatted at a bumble bee, which nevertheless escaped. He forgot to be annoyed.

'Mr Butterfield, please accept my apologies for the delay. The ambas-sador is terribly busy and I'm afraid—'

'Oh, really! He invited me, Mr Warburton; I've come all this way expressly, and I'm not leaving until I've seen him. This is no way to—'

'I was just going to say, Mr Butterfield, that he can spare you a few minutes. If you come now . . . A *very* few minutes. Events on the international stage . . . things are moving very fast. The assistant to the Minister for Foreign Affairs is here and, really, the ambassador shouldn't be taking time away from . . .' He spoke while leading Ellis down the corridor to his uncle's office.

Now, Ellis was aware of the atmosphere of tension. The secretary's face was drawn and his voice sounded hoarse. He rapped on the ambas-sador's door, opened it without waiting, then shooed Ellis inside.

'Ambassador, I'll be back in five minutes. I will try to put off *Monsieur le Deputé*, but he is impatient.'

'Uncle . . .'

Ephraim looked grey and exhausted.

'Ellis, I'm sorry, but I can't spare more than a few moments. Today, of all days.'

'Why? What's happened?'

Ephraim sighed, and gazed down for a moment. 'I suppose you will read it all in the evening paper. There has been a vote, the deputies have ratified it. France has declared war on Prussia.'

11

Lawrence had been in the studio all day, during which time all the heat of the house had risen up and became concentrated under the eaves. It was like breathing a warm, viscous fluid. When he came downstairs for dinner, he was tired and irritable.

'Lawrence, dear, have you heard the news?'

'How can he have heard, Maman?' said Ernestine from her chair. 'He has been upstairs in that awful oven.'

'What news?' said Lawrence.

'It seems we are at war. It's in *Le Figaro*. Look.'

Lawrence took the proffered newspaper, but his head ached too much to focus on the newsprint.

'Not that we need worry, really,' said Louise Lamy. 'It will all take place far away, and of course we will win. But still . . . We went to the Rhineland once, didn't we, Serge? It was lovely. A shame to think of all those soldiers trampling over it.'

Lawrence ate in silence, but not because he was especially worried about the war. A week had passed since he had swum in the Marne with Yves. Six days, in which he had turned over every word and glance, every gesture and signal, searching for what was meant, what was wanted – or not – and still he wasn't sure.

Yves had been first to climb from the water and stretch out on the grass. Lawrence pulled himself up on to the bank a minute later, his skin numb with cold. Yves lay on his back, eyes closed, drying himself in the sun. Drops of water pearled on his white skin and glittered in the dark of his beard and pubis. He was long limbed and graceful, his rib cage visible under the skin. Lawrence looked away with an effort, sat on the grass next to him, not too close, and lifted his face to the sun.

'That was good,' murmured Yves.

'Yes. Now I'm cold.'

Lawrence hugged himself and rubbed his arms briskly: surely a clear invitation? Yves didn't move, or open his eyes, so, after a moment, Lawrence lay on the grass on his back. The sight of his stained fingers against the skin of his upper arms disturbed him. If he stretched out his hand, he could have touched Yves. Although he was sure that Yves was of his own inclination, he felt too strongly the possibility that Yves would recoil, perhaps simply from innocence, or shock. Like tentative lovers the world over, Lawrence resorted to subterfuge. He pretended to sleep; he rolled on to his side and contrived his hand to fall near the other's body. The hand lay, half curled in the grass, and Lawrence, peeking through his eyelashes, thought it looked like the hand of a demon. He could not reach out that blackened hand to touch Yves' pure skin.

After a while, his spying revealed that Yves' mouth was open, the breath rough in his throat. He was asleep. Lawrence watched in disbelief, but it was so. He told himself that it was hot, they had drunk a lot of wine, they were tired with rowing and swimming. But his throat swelled with misery.

He rolled on to his stomach and pillowed his head on folded arms, letting the heat, the smell of hot grass, the sound of bumbling, zooming insects lull him into stupefaction.

He awoke when Yves gently shook his shoulder.

'Lawrence? I didn't want to disturb you, but I'm worried you will get sunburned. I burn terribly.'

Lawrence lifted his head and turned his stiff neck. To his dismay, Yves was dressed. The skin of his back felt tight. The sun had moved and shadows crept across the grass towards him. He was embarrassed to be naked while the other was not.

Yves gazed over the water. 'We should head back. It will take longer against the current.'

There was a remoteness in his voice that was quite different from his earlier ease, and made Lawrence scramble to dress himself, hiding his semi-tumescent genitals. He could not think that he had done anything to annoy – had he, without knowing, given off some signal to provoke displeasure?

Rowing upstream was hard work. They returned the boat, walked to the station and boarded the stuffy, crowded train. Lawrence tried to lighten Yves' mood with impersonal chatter. He told Yves of the difficulties of photographing the animals in the menagerie – a project he had begun, so far with limited success.

'At least they are not vain about the results, unlike some of our human subjects. We recently had a sitting with a regular client – I believe you could call her a *grande horizontale* – and all the plates had to be destroyed as they did not meet with her approval.'

'Really?' Yves looked at him with a wan smile. 'Am I allowed to ask her name?'

Glancing about the carriage, where most of their fellow travellers seemed to be sleeping, Lawrence lowered his voice. 'I'm probably not supposed to say, but I know you are discreet. It was Blanche Fleury.'

'La Fleury? I once saw her on the stage, in *Phèdre*. She was marvellous.'

Lawrence looked out of the window. They were now passing through the city walls. 'I should like to see her act.'

'Her performances are rare now, I believe, but you should.'

Lawrence waited for Yves to suggest they go together, but he did not. He fell silent. Yves seemed lost in thought. The train came to its terminus. Lawrence cast around for something that would rekindle their earlier intimacy, but could not hit on the right note. He had restrained himself from the slightest demonstration of his feelings – was that the fault?

When they passed once more into the late sunshine, Yves turned to him with a strained smile. 'Well . . .'

'Thank you for a beautiful day.'

'Thank you for accompanying me.' Yves took a step back, nodded, turned to go, then turned back. 'Wait – I'm sorry, my friend; I must apologize for my bearish mood this afternoon. I have rather a headache, that's all, but—'

'That's quite all right. I understand.' Lawrence's voice was hectic with relief. 'All that sun – and rowing.'

'And I'm used to neither.'

In a rush, Lawrence said, 'I was afraid I had tried your patience.'

Yves looked at him, his eyes pained. 'You could never try my patience. I'm just –' he shook his head – 'a little out of sorts at the moment. Please, forgive me.'

'There is nothing to forgive.'

'Are you feeling quite well, Monsieur Harper?'

Ernestine derailed his train of thought. She was giving him one of her disconcerting stares.

'Oh, a headache, that's all.'

'I'm not surprised, in this heat. I hope you're not going gallivanting about in boats tomorrow. It cannot be healthy, in this weather.' Madame Lamy was suspicious of fresh air and exertion. 'I never feel well in such heat. Perhaps, for the Emperor, it is the same, and now . . .' She grimaced eloquently.

Ernestine looked at her mother. 'You think we're at war because the Emperor is feeling liverish?'

'Well, who knows? I'm sure it has an effect. But, Titine, I swear *you* have never looked so well. You should wear your lilac-grey to Mass tomorrow. It is just the thing in hot weather.'

After dinner, unable to face the heat in his room, Lawrence went for a walk. Every street thronged with people; every café was open, blazing with light and roaring with talk. Drinkers overflowed on to the streets and gathered on corners. He caught a sense of fervid glee: strangers in conversation, bonded by their approval of the Emperor's bold stroke; the henpecked old dotard had at last stepped up to the mark! They laughed at the prospect of French troops setting up camp in Berlin; they shouted insults about the enemy. In the atmosphere of impromptu festivity, their blood heated by sun and wine and national fervour, groups of revellers sang the banned anthem of the Revolution, of watering the land with blood.

Lawrence turned down a side street, away from the lights and noise, until he smelt the powerful reek of animals, and realized he was by the menagerie. Even here was the sound of carousing: a band of men were larking in the street, singing and shouting. At first, he could not distinguish words, but, as they came towards him in a ragged line, strung out across the road, as if to sweep up anyone in their path, he deciphered the refrain, chanted over and over: '*Vive la Guerre!*'

He retreated into the shadows. The men – boys, he saw now; none could have been more than seventeen – passed without seeing him, bawling, '*Aux armes, citoyens! Aux armes! Marchons à Berlin!*'

Out of the darkness behind him came a sound that made his blood freeze and his scalp prickle: a long, guttural roar that rose in volume, swelling until it drowned out the singers, who, one by one, fell into an awestruck silence.

12

On Sunday, as usual, the Lamys walked to Mass. Saint-Germain-des-Prés was a convenient distance from their house and attracted a smart congregation. This was important because Louise longed for Ernestine to be married, and, if one is concerned with the happiness of others, one must leave no opportunity unexploited. She did not want her daughter to marry because she believed that marriage and mother-hood were a woman's only destiny, but because she wanted her to be as happy as she was in her own marriage.

Louise had met Serge when he was apprenticed at her father's printing business. Although a deaf mute (and thus cheap), he had trained at the National Institute with painters and sculptors, and was quick and clever, and curious about new technologies, like the daguerreotype just then coming into fashion. Louise had had a few suitors by then, but they all liked to talk more than they wanted to listen, and she had ideas of her own. She was intrigued by Serge, who clearly had much more going on in his head than he let on, and had such a merry smile besides. She asked him to teach her the language of hands, and she enjoyed having this secret means of communication as they worked together. She had not realized how subtle it could be, how you could make jokes. Even so, she was surprised to find that she had fallen in love with him – it took a proposal from another man to make her realize what a grey prospect life without Serge had become. Her mother was appalled – despite her Creole background, she was a raging snob – but Louise, even when young, was a force to be reckoned with. And look at them! It was, she often said, the best decision of her life.

There were a few suitable young men in their congregation, and a greater number of not-so-young men, and Louise went out of her way to cultivate the families concerned. There was a small difficulty, admittedly, in Serge's deafness, and that his profession of photographer wasn't quite . . . Foolish, of course, but it was, perhaps, not one of the most respectable careers. The wives with whom she chatted so pleasantly after Mass treated Louise cordially, but there was always the faint suggestion that the Lamys – and therefore their daughter – weren't quite as good as they were. Perhaps this was what her mother had feared, although, to look at Titine, no one would ever guess that her great-grandfather had come over from the Antilles. Louise herself, when she was young, had known what it was to be dismissed because of her colouring, but, once her hair turned silver, no one any longer seemed to notice, or care. She believed that she didn't mind on her own account, but, for Ernestine, she burned with injustice.

Recently, Louise had been taking particular pains with one Monsieur Ranvier, a widow who couldn't be much over forty. He owned a large and successful butcher's shop on the Rue de Rivoli, which was patronized by several top restaurants, and he was, in her opinion, not unpleasing to look at. A wealthy wife had died over a year ago, leaving him with a young son and a comfortable legacy, and Louise was aware that he wouldn't be on the market for ever.

She called her daughter over. Ernestine was always beautifully turned out, and today she was wearing the lilac-grey which so suited her colouring. Among the flushed and perspiring congregation, Ernestine appeared delightfully cool, and Louise noticed how Monsieur Ranvier's eyes lit up when she joined them. Then, after only a minute or two, Ernestine cut him off with barely an excuse, and went to talk to someone else. Ranvier, on the brink of an anecdote, paused, and

Louise detected a wounded look in his eyes. She explained that Ernestine had complained of a headache that morning – the heat, and the news, so trying . . . and he nodded sadly.

They walked home in silence. When they reached the house, Louise rounded on her daughter.

'You embarrassed me, Titine. Walking off like that from Monsieur Ranvier – it was positively rude!'

'Oh, Maman, why don't you say what you mean? You want me to act the coquette with him. You even tell me how to dress! *I* was the one embarrassed. You are no better than a— I don't even want to say the word!'

'Titine!'

'You would have me encourage a man like that, when there is no point.'

'I don't want you to act the coquette; I want you to be polite to our friends. And I don't know what you mean by a "man like that". Monsieur Ranvier is very nice. He has an excellent business, a fine figure and—'

'He is twenty years older than me!'

'Must I remind you that you are no longer a young girl? I don't know what you are waiting for, miss – a banker? A viscount, perhaps?'

'Why are you cruel, Maman? It was you who encouraged me to educate myself, who told me that there is more to life than marrying the first man who comes along.'

'Monsieur Ranvier is not the first man! He's not even the tenth man! You are too choosy and time is no friend to a woman.'

'Good God! This morning we are at war, and you talk to me of butchers!'

'The war is hardly going to affect us, Ernestine, whereas—'

Ernestine swept out, before Louise could formulate an argument in favour of butchers – who might, she thought, do rather well in a war economy. She looked up to see Serge come into the dining room. He looked sympathetic.

Louise sighed. 'What are we going to do about her? She's so prickly. You'd almost think she didn't want to be married.'

Serge signed, 'There is nothing we can do; our daughter is grown up.'

'Don't shrug like that. Why is she angry all the time? Is it our fault?'

Louise had suffered three miscarriages before Ernestine, and they'd found it hard to deny her anything – until she grew up and started complaining that their business demeaned her. There were limits.

Louise signed, 'I wish you would talk to her, Serge. She listens to you.'

Serge signed that such delicate matters were the preserve of a mother.

'All very well for you,' she signed back, her hands blurring with speed and annoyance. 'You never say anything, so you can't say the wrong thing.'

Back in the autumn, when Lawrence Harper had presented himself at the studio, Louise decided to offer him the post even before she saw his painting. She thought him very personable, and he seemed so nice: he spoke quietly, and he had the gift of listening intelligently. When she left him upstairs and came back to the shop, she took the accounts ledger from Ernestine and made out the entry for a half-day's work. Without looking at her daughter, she said, carelessly, 'Well, I rather think we've found someone for the post.' But, despite Louise's warm feelings towards the young man, romance had refused to blossom.

The previous year, Louise's hopes had centred on Lawrence's predecessor, Edouard Duchamp. He was a steady young man, if somewhat stolid, and Louise and Serge were fond of him. He and Titine had formed a cordial friendship, and Louise allowed herself to dream of a wedding. After months of this, yet with no hint from either of when they planned to move things forward, Louise could restrain herself no longer.

'So, Titine – it is almost as though Edouard is one of the family. I keep wondering if you are going to have, perhaps, something to tell me?'

Ernestine, winding the watch that was a present from her father, did not lift her eyes from its face. 'Why would I have anything to tell you?'

'Oh, come. When a young man and a young woman spend so much time in each other's company, people naturally begin to wonder if there is an understanding between them.'

'People? You mean, you and Papa.'

'I only wondered . . . you seem to get on so well, and he's such a nice young man. You go for walks! You went skating!'

'We went skating once. If you want me to tell you something, I'll tell you this: I find Monsieur Duchamp a bore.'

'What an unpleasant thing to say! He's quiet, I know, but . . . Anyone can see that he is devoted to you. What's more, he's a frequent guest at our table, and your father and I regard him almost as one of the family. One day, we will retire, and our dearest wish is to pass the business on to someone we know and trust. Have you thought of that?'

Ernestine gave a short laugh. 'You will do as you please, Maman, as always.'

'Titine, we just want you to be happy!'

Ernestine stared at her, a bitter smile twisting her mouth. 'You understand nothing, as usual.'

'How can I understand when you never tell me anything?'

Louise was at a loss. If her daughter had thrown herself on her bed in despair, she would have understood. If she had sobbed and raged, she could have consoled her – but Ernestine, that complicated mystery, never gave her the opportunity.

She would have been astonished to learn how passionately Ernestine had desired the very thing she herself hoped for. Ernestine was only too aware of the advancing years – what woman is not? Despite her words, she had nursed a passion for Edouard Duchamp. She knew he was dull, but she forgave him because . . . well, he was handsome, and he had a charming way of smiling, as though he had a secret that he would, one day, share with her. They made a handsome couple; they drew admiring glances when they walked in the Luxembourg. Then there was the work: long hours in the studio, Ernestine working on the sets, while Edouard printed photographs.

Ernestine liked to work. Studio Lamy photographs were known for their detailed artistry, and a good part of that was down to her eye for designing and dressing the sets. Louise had also taught her the art of colour tinting – at first, she worked on portraits, but, when she was twenty-one, her parents revealed to her the seamier side of their business. They were not ashamed of it, so why should their daughter be? But Ernestine was mortified.

'Did you really not know?' Louise had asked, smiling – she could be quite coarse, at times.

Ernestine was speechless with horror – how dare she smile! Of course she hadn't known. She felt stupid, as well as soiled.

She loathed the erotic postcards. She argued that it was degrading, shaming – unsuitable for a respected artist like her father, who'd had work accepted by the Academy. In answer, Louise opened their accounts, which showed that the postcards made more money than all their other work put together. Dirty postcards had paid for her exclusive education (perhaps, in retrospect, that had been a mistake); now, they paid for her fashionable wardrobe, for the theatre, for holidays at the seaside.

She kept her counsel and waited for Edouard to declare his love. She knew of her parents' hope that she would take over the business; naturally, this would be with a man, who would, just as naturally, be her husband. The combination of Ernestine and the studio was surely an attractive proposition. She let herself imagine what it would be like, when she and Edouard had taken over the business – the changes they would make. In her diary, hidden from prying eyes, she practised signing, *Madame Ernestine Duchamp*.

Then came one evening the previous summer. Louise asked Edouard if he was planning to take Ernestine to the *fête champêtre* in the Bois de Vincennes. Ernestine had mentioned it to Edouard, and received the impression that he intended to take her – to the point where she had planned her outfit. But, that evening, Edouard recoiled. He stared at the table, and there was a tinge of pink on his cheek when he answered.

'I'm afraid I shan't be able to, madame . . . mademoiselle. I have promised to visit my aunt with my mother. She isn't well. In Poissy.'

Ernestine froze in the act of transferring a forkful of dinner to her mouth.

Her mother said, 'Oh, I'm sorry to hear it. Please give her my best wishes. Has she been ill long?'

'About a month,' said Edouard. 'It was just a cold, but she has become run down.'

Ernestine had never heard of an aunt in Poissy. She turned to him with a smile. 'You must let me give you some of my tisane. It is famous for colds,' she said.

'Thank you. You're very kind,' he said, but didn't quite meet her eye.

It had not occurred to her that Edouard had the brains for deception. Whereas, before, her love had been lightly tinged with condescension, she now discovered a perverse thrill in self-abasement, and adored him. That his secret was that he loved another was terrible, but his deviousness somehow made him even more desirable. After all, it was not as though anything had been *said*.

He never affirmed that his affections were engaged elsewhere, but, after that evening, he was evasive and distant, which was all the proof she needed. In response, she was insouciant, taking more pains over her hair and costume than before. She would not let him see her suffer. Most of all, she could not let her mother know. Humiliation she could endure; pity would be unbearable. A few weeks later, Louise asked that excruciating question about their future. Soon after, Edouard handed in his notice.

When Ernestine was sent to boarding school, she had admitted in all innocence that her father was a photographer, and that her mother helped him. The other girls stared – their fathers were lawyers and deputies, and the idea that a mother might work was extraordinary. They didn't know about the postcards (nor did she, then); it was bad enough that her parents were artisans. The teasing was without mercy. Cleverness could not save her. It might have helped if she was pretty, or cheerful, but she was too awkwardly aware of her parents' oddities – she wouldn't even let her father come to the school, hid her fluency with her hands.

Ernestine knew what had gone wrong with Edouard: he did not see her as a suitable wife because she knew too much about the desires of men, even though, in her conduct and her person, she was as pure as any man could wish. Her social advancement was rooted in filth, and, for all her accomplishments, she was tainted. Education had made her aspire to a life she could not hope to achieve. It was her parents' fault.

13

The inhabitants of the zoo might have been oblivious to the war in the east, but they were affected by the heat and drought. The keepers went back and forth with buckets of water to cool the animals, which led some to complain that the creatures were treated better than they were. Pierre, Robitaille's young protégé, volunteered for an infantry battalion and disappeared in a wave of sentiment. As a single man who could choose his destiny, he was more envied than otherwise.

The price of meat rose by the day, and green fodder was increasingly scarce. As plants and grass withered, finding foodstuffs for the herbivores became more difficult.

In the middle of the night, three cubs were born to the bears Clovis and Aino, but before dawn one was killed and eaten by its grown-up brother. Victor and Robitaille kept a watch on the big cats, but no further atrocities were committed. Perhaps the citizens of Paris had turned their surplus malice towards the human enemy. Certainly, the crowds who thronged the zoo seemed cheerful; there was a new spirit of camaraderie in the air. But plans to import a pair of red pandas from the zoological garden at Berlin were, under the circumstances, quietly abandoned.

On her day off, Anne went to the zoo and stood by Marguerite's cage for a long time, but, this time, something was different. Over the past few weeks, she had come to expect the assistant veterinarian to appear; perhaps she looked forward to their talks about the animals. He was the first man since Hippolyte Mazade who actually listened to her. But today there was no sign of Victor Calmette. She did see the keeper of the cats, a man Monsieur Calmette had introduced her to, so she knew his name was Robitaille. She debated whether to speak to him. He nodded a greeting to her.

'Monsieur Robitaille?'

'Yes, mademoiselle?'

His voice was nice and quiet, but she kept her eyes on the ground, just in case.

'Do you know whether the veterinarian is here today?'

'Yes. Monsieur Papin is here. What is it about?'

'Oh. I meant . . .' She felt herself blushing – although, like most people, he probably didn't think dark-skinned people could. 'I meant Monsieur Calmette.'

'No. He's having a day off today. What do you want to know?'

He said it so simply and naturally that Anne was flooded with gratitude. She had never thought about it, but of course Monsieur Calmette must have a life outside the zoo. Beyond that, she did not speculate, because why should she? It was none of her business.

'Are you going to get another lynx?'

Robitaille looked towards the empty cage, and sighed. 'Well, what with the war and everything, no one knows what is going to happen. The powers that be don't tell us keepers. I'm sorry, mademoiselle, I can't tell you more than that. We'll have to wait and see.'

Marguerite lifted her head and swivelled her ears. She seemed to be listening. Her tail switched back and forth in a purposeful rhythm, as if she were sending out a message.

Robitaille stayed and they chatted for a few minutes about the cats. Like Monsieur Calmette, he didn't ask awkward questions; he spoke to her as if she were like them – a person who was interested in and cared about the animals. She felt a flush of pleasure. What if Jospin could see her now?

Robitaille touched his cap. 'Well, mademoiselle – I'd better be getting on. I'll tell Monsieur Calmette that you were asking after him.'

Anne opened her mouth to protest. Then she stopped herself. Why shouldn't he know? He was her friend.

'Thank you, monsieur.' A thought struck her. 'But the zoo will still be open? The war won't change that, will it?'

'I don't suppose so. We haven't heard any different.' He nodded to her and left.

Anne turned back to Marguerite, who gazed at her and blinked slowly. For a moment, there was no one else in sight, and Anne was conscious of such peace and completeness that she hardly dared breathe.

For her, the thought of the zoo being closed was almost too terrible to contemplate. Beyond that, the fact that her country was at war did not affect her. She could not imagine a life in which it would.

14

On Wednesday evening, Lawrence again boarded the omnibus to Yves' studio. He hadn't had a chance to speak to him alone since their parting at the station, with its rekindling of his fragile hopes. He was determined to be more resolute; he would linger until the end of the evening, until everyone else had left. He must know.

The street door was locked, but prolonged knocking brought the concierge. 'Messieurs Michaud and Quinet are not here,' he said, in response to Lawrence's enquiry.

'I'll wait for them. They are always at home on Wednesdays.'

'Not today, monsieur. They're not coming back.'

'What? You mean – this evening?'

'No. They've left town. Gone.'

Lawrence leant one hand against the wall.

'You must be mistaken. Monsieur Michaud didn't say anything to me about leaving town.'

The man shrugged. 'Monsieur has gone home to his family.'

'When? We're speaking of Monsieur Michaud – the tall gentleman, with black hair.'

'Precisely. He left yesterday. He said goodbye to me, right here.'

'But – but Monsieur Quinet . . .'

'Had already left.'

Lawrence struggled for words.

The concierge seemed to take pity on him. 'I expect he has written monsieur a letter. The post is terrible, these days.'

Lawrence walked blindly, desperate to get away, but it was impossible to go home. Something led him towards Montmartre, where he wandered the hillside almost at random, and, when he had put enough walking between himself and the street where he had received such a shock, he entered a bar.

He found a corner and sat down. After his third glass of a powerful spirit poured from an unlabelled bottle, he felt a treacly numbness steal over him, wrapping him in layers of indifference.

The obese woman behind the counter, who had met him with a basalt stare when he first came in, seemed to warm to him. She came to top up his glass unbidden, leant on the table and looked at him. 'These days, huh?' she said, in a voice as mineral-tough as her eyes. 'What a world we live in. What a world.'

Lawrence nodded.

'You're too young and handsome to be sad. For me, sadness is natural – I am old and fat. Youth and beauty should be happy, because it won't last! Has she broken your heart? It'll mend soon enough, *mignon*.'

Lawrence shook his head; speech seemed unnecessary.

'No? But, yes! Forget her. You'll find someone else in the wink of an eye. You don't believe me now, but, when you get to my age, you'll see what you have lost. Make the most of it. I've lived a life, and I know.'

She gave a grating laugh and returned to her counter. Lawrence noticed that every customer was on his own and seemed as sunk in private gloom as he, but he was webbed in the viscous embrace of the spirit, and signals from the outside reached him weakly, at one remove. His body seemed to eddy in space, rather than moving of his own volition. The woman came and went, poured liquid into his glass, barked out some more comments – laughed her laugh that was like a saw dragged through wet wood – until, at some later point, he found himself outside in the warm, moonlit night, and walking – eddying – along the street. He reached an intersection he didn't recognize – a star of streets whose rays seemed to offer equal promise, or lack thereof – and, taking one, found himself in an ill-lit road that led along the wall of a graveyard. He observed the thought that he probably shouldn't be in such a deserted place after dark, so he turned around. He passed a man loitering on the pavement behind him, crossed another road – he didn't seem to have retraced his steps precisely, but never mind – and stumbled on an uneven paving stone.

He became aware that he was being followed. He didn't think too much of it – it wasn't that late, there must be people around. He didn't know exactly where he was, but he was sure that soon he would rec-ognize some landmark. He turned downhill, since downhill always took you, eventually, to the river.

'Hey,' said a voice near his shoulder. 'Monsieur! Are you lost?'

Lawrence glanced over his shoulder and saw a dark-haired, fresh-faced youth. There was something about him that made him think of the country, although he was not in a state to analyse the reason; the man's accent, his high colour, his clothes – in the greenish glow of a street light, nothing made a distinct impression.

'Are you looking for something, my friend?'

He used the familiar *tu*.

'No, thank you.' Lawrence waved him away, and reflexively put his hand to the pocket where he kept his money. He kept walking, but the youth walked apace.

'I think you are. Perhaps I can help you.'

The voice was rough – another accent he found hard to follow. Lawrence knew this was the man he had passed at the cemetery; he must have been following him for some time. At least he didn't have much money left, so . . . Then he realized, with a prickling, thrilling shock, that money was not what the man was after.

'What's your name?' asked the youth, and Lawrence found an answer on his tongue, surprising him: 'Rossignol.'

In French, the word meant 'nightingale', but *rossignol* was also the word for a skeleton key, and he had secreted the fact at the back of his mind, apparently, for just this purpose.

'Oh, a nightingale? Monsieur Nightingale!'

The man had a hand on his sleeve and Lawrence allowed himself to be halted. He faced the youth and looked in his eyes. He had a long, loose mouth and a sparse beard; he was no older than Lawrence, but already had a look of hard usage. He was too raw and bony to be handsome, but the look in his eyes made Lawrence's blood surge with amazing force.

'Do you sing by night?'

'No. But I pick locks.'

Lawrence found himself shunted into a dark opening that led into a high-walled yard. He smelt the comforting reek of horses, but could see nothing. His foot kicked through soft muck. Giving himself up to the idea that he was probably going to be robbed, he found his arm twisted behind his back and the youth tried to turn him to face the wall.

'No,' said Lawrence, and it was as though another person – Rossignol – found the strength to twist back and take the youth by the arm. He put one hand on the back of his head and then they were kissing deeply. The youth tasted of wine so sour it could have been vinegar. Lawrence was so drunk he didn't have to think. Not thinking, he felt the youth kneel in front of him in the dirt, felt fingers pull apart his fly buttons, felt him pull his erect cock out into the open.

'*Putain*,' said the youth, and something else that Lawrence didn't catch.

He was engulfed in the hot mouth and, as his head tipped back, he saw the rectangle of paler sky, dusted with stars that shed no light here in the yard. He closed his eyes, felt steely agricultural fingers kneading his buttocks. He gritted his teeth, but then he was spending, clinging on to the youth's hair for grim death.

'Jesus Christ,' he breathed. He shouldn't have said that, of all things. His heart was hammering and his voice unsteady. It had only taken a minute.

'Shit, you were ready for that.'

The youth stood up, panting, wiped his mouth and unbuttoned his trousers.

'Well, Monsieur Pick-lock,' he said. 'My turn.'

Next morning, he woke up oblivious to anything but the several pounds of pig iron that had been left in his skull. The maid, Lisette, who had come in with the hot water, gave a little scream.

'Oh my God, what happened?' Her hand was at her mouth.

Lawrence peered at her through gluey eyelids. 'What?'

'I'll fetch madame.' She thundered downstairs.

Lawrence levered himself out of bed and shuffled to the washstand. He looked in the mirror. It was a shock. He had a dirty cut on the side of his face, not deep, but blood was smeared on his cheek and forehead – and on the pillow, he saw when he turned around. He had no idea how it had happened. What on earth . . . ? He couldn't remember— God, the youth – the man, the yard . . . But he had not robbed him – they had gone their separate ways, with a brief 'Goodnight' and an awkward handshake. Surely he would remember being robbed? And – miracle – there, on the table, were the few coins emptied from his pocket the night before.

Madame Lamy came in, panting from her rush up the stairs, uttering cries of concern. Lawrence sat on the bed and apologized. She insisted on examining his head, dabbing at his face with a wet cloth. She exclaimed over the bump on his forehead.

'But are you all right? Does it hurt? What on earth happened? Let me look.'

She was sitting on the bed next to him, her hands holding his face, turning it this way and that.

'I think it's my own fault.'

He was hideously embarrassed, conscious that his breath must stink of eau de vie, if not something worse. All he could think to say – probably truthfully – was that he'd had too much to drink and had fallen. He was sorry to be late for work. He was sorry about the bloodied bed linen. She probably wanted him to leave. He could pack his things and be out by the afternoon . . .

'What on earth are you talking about, Lawrence? I don't want you to leave. You're one of the best assistants we've ever had. And we like you – hadn't you noticed? What an idea! Or is there something else?'

He shook his head, which hurt, looked at her and felt grateful tears prickle the back of his eyes. 'You don't want me to leave?'

'Of course not. I've heard that some foreigners are thinking of leaving Paris. We hope, Serge and I – we hope that you aren't planning to go.'

'No. I'm not planning to go. Thank you, madame. I'm very grateful . . .'

'You're always welcome here, Lawrence. For goodness' sake. There's no one in the studio this morning, so there's no hurry. When you've got yourself cleaned up, go and have some breakfast. No, no, leave the bed – Lisette will see to that. Coffee is downstairs, when you're ready.'

She left the room and Lawrence carefully wiped his face, revealing a bruise on his cheek, a swollen and darkened eye, as well as the scrape. Nothing serious. He was lucky. Doubly lucky: Madame Lamy really was a darling.

The conversation with Yves' concierge seemed to have taken place weeks ago. The pain that had run him through like a spear was dulled and distant. He knew it was there, ready to engulf him if he allowed it, so he would leave it alone, not touch it, not think about it; let the layer of overproof indifference congeal around his heart, sealing it off from further harm.

15

A week passed. It became noticeably quieter at Studio Lamy. Fewer people came in for portraits, and Lawrence detected a changed atmosphere in the streets and cafés. It was as though Paris was holding its breath – there was a suppressed excitement, a drawing together that made people eager to talk and pass the time; but there was also hesitation, as people waited for something to happen, for things to begin.

Today, something *had* happened – a small thing in itself, but it had thrown him into disarray. At breakfast, there had been a letter by his plate, and the sight of the handwriting made him feel faint. He put it in his pocket, and, as soon as he could go upstairs to his room, he slit the envelope and took out the single sheet.

It was dated a few days ago, from somewhere he had never heard of. Yves had written,

My dear Lawrence,
Forgive me, I beg you, for leaving town so abruptly. I am very sorry for it, but it was necessary to see my family, and somehow I did not know how to tell people. I beg your pardon. There was something I had been turning over in my mind, something important, and that necessitated returning home. I have made up my mind to enlist in our local battalion of the 4th Zouaves.
This may seem a peculiar course of action to you – and to most of my friends, I think – but I know that I cannot remain in a studio,

dabbling in paint, while my country is at war. In Paris, everyone seemed sanguine about the outcome, but here in the country it is a different story. There is trepidation, even fear. Others may do as they will, but I must follow my conscience. Of course, when it is all over – which I pray will be soon – I will return to Paris and to the pursuit of art – at least, as far as that is within my power! I hope and trust I will see you then, my dear Lawrence.

I know that our friendship is not of long duration, but I value it highly. I feel – unless I am mistaken – that you understand me better than friends I have known for years. I had been thinking of asking a favour before I left: I would like very much that you sit for me – I think I have the perfect thing for you! I hope this does not seem too much of an imposition, and of course the decision is entirely in your hands.

Until such time as we meet again, I pray for your health and good fortune.

I remain, very affectionately yours,
Yves

Lawrence read and reread, memorizing each word. He hid the letter in a book and placed it beside his bed. He took it out again.

It was overwhelming – *unless I am mistaken* – what else could that mean? It wasn't overwhelming – it said nothing. He was ecstatic, then fearful; full of hope one minute, the next chastising himself for an idiot. He replaced the letter inside the book, but all day his thoughts ran back to the hiding place; at lunchtime, he made an excuse to go and read it again. Yves was his friend; he could be sure of that, at least. Was he deluding himself to imagine that it said more? He tried not to think about it. He thought of nothing else.

Paris did not have long to wait for things to begin. Within days, the French army had crossed the border into Prussia and struck a stunning blow, taking the town of Saarbrücken. When the news reached the capital, there were celebrations in the streets. Lawrence was jubilant with relief – if victory was to be as quick and crushing as this, perhaps Yves would not enlist at all.

Three days later, on Sunday, he went out in the morning to buy newspapers and headed, as usual, to the Zouave, where Yves and his friends had gathered. When he saw the headlines, a chill slid down his spine. In the café, he found Michel, Séraphine, Gustave and Ellis Butterfield huddled around a table. The place was half empty, and the talk was intense and gloomy. Everyone was trying to absorb the news: after Saarbrücken, where the French army met no resistance, there had been three terrible defeats, one on top of another. Towns he had never heard of were suddenly the most important places in the world. No one could quite comprehend it. Séraphine could not hold back the tears. Michel tried to comfort her, assuring her that her brother, a soldier, wasn't involved – neither his regiment nor its leaders were mentioned.

'An early setback, that's all,' said Michel. 'Another whole army is on its way to the front. Things will turn around. You'll see.'

A group of men came into the café, talking in loud voices. One, a tall, heavily whiskered man, brought his fist down on the counter with a crash.

'We were betrayed!' he shouted. 'There are spies everywhere! Yes, even here – Germans and their allies are listening to our talk and passing on our secrets.'

Lawrence smiled – the man was clearly the worse for wear. People muttered.

The bearded man surveyed the café and pointed at their table. 'There's one!' he yelled, and the knot of men swarmed towards them, knocking over a chair.

Lawrence stared in disbelief, looking around to see whom he had meant. Then the men were surrounding their table, pressing close with the carelessness of the very drunk. Alcohol and sour sweat reeled off them. The bearded man had his hand on Ellis's arm, and was trying to drag him from his seat.

'Look, a German!' he shouted. 'Here's a German – a dirty spy!'

Customers turned to stare, expressions changing from irritation and bemusement to something darker.

'I'm an American, for God's sake,' said Ellis. 'American!' He tried to brush off the man's hand, but the drunk clung on, his knuckles white. 'Go home, you fool. You're plastered.'

'Stand up! We'll show you how we treat spies round here.'

The others began shouting and remonstrating. Ellis stood up, his face hard. He launched himself at the bearded man, and Gustave leapt up and pinned the assailant's arms behind his back with ruthless efficiency. The man struggled, but, held by two sober men, was quickly overpowered. Between them, they manhandled him towards the door. Lawrence, on his feet, was shoved in the back by one of the others and turned to push him away. The man went down like a sack of coal.

In another minute, it was over. Lawrence saw Gustave outside, holding Ellis by the arm, leading him away from the attacker. The drunkard's followers had lost their bravado with their leader, and the café owner shooed them out the door and they shuffled off. Ellis and Gustave came back inside. Ellis was breathing heavily and glowering. Gustave appeared coolly unaffected.

'Come on, Butterfield, sit down. There are idiots everywhere. No sense in being disturbed by them.'

Ellis sat back down. Lawrence and Séraphine blotted the spilt coffee with newsprint. Michel, who hadn't moved from his seat throughout, refilled his pipe. Gustave called for more coffee, and brandy.

The café owner came up to them. 'What a to-do,' he said gruffly, staring at Ellis. 'Well, are you a German?'

They all denied it vehemently.

Ellis said stiffly, 'I am an American, my name is Ellis Butterfield and my uncle is Ephraim Quine, the American ambassador to France.'

The owner looked taken aback. 'Oh. Well. One has to be sure. And, you know, you could be, to look at you.'

Ellis stared helplessly.

The café owner bent and polished the table with his cloth. 'I apologize for the disruption, gentlemen, lady. I'll bring you more coffee.'

He also brought eau de vie. 'On the house.'

Ellis thanked the others for their swift actions. Gustave gave an ironic bow.

'And you, Monsieur Harper – you put paid to that fat fellow like brushing off a fly.'

'I think he was so drunk he just fell over,' said Lawrence, with a rush of pride.

'But, seriously,' said Michel to Ellis, 'you should be careful. You do look like a German. And your accent doesn't help.'

'What on earth am I supposed to do about it?'

'Can't you get some papers from your uncle?'

'What if I *were* German,' Ellis went on. 'What would you have said then?'

Michel frowned. 'You have to understand, we are at war. Our friends and families are fighting. Frenchmen are dying.' He flicked his hand at the newspapers. 'If you were German, I could not sit at table with you.'

Séraphine glared at Michel. The silence became uncomfortable. Lawrence wanted to alleviate it, but there were few times he had felt his foreignness so keenly. It was as though an invisible barrier had descended, separating Ellis and him from the others. Soon, Ellis made his excuses to leave.

Lawrence left too and caught up with him outside. 'Mr Butterfield! Ellis! Wait a minute.'

The American turned to him with a scowl.

'I'm sure it's only that Michel is worried about Séraphine and her brother. And Yves.'

'Perhaps, but I don't want to stay where I'm not wanted.' Ellis smiled bitterly. 'I've lived here for three years. But, when it comes down to it, a foreigner is a foreigner, and we're no longer welcome. At least, I'm not.'

'I don't think it's that. I don't know what it's like to be at war – you do, of course – I guess it strikes at your very core. If the worst came to the worst, they may be forced into it. We're only bystanders. I doubt he meant it.'

Ellis shrugged, his eyes on the ground.

Lawrence said, 'Do you mind if I walk with you for a while?'

'Be my guest – if you can bear to be seen with a German spy. We'd better keep our damn foreign voices down.'

They found a café on the far side of the Luxembourg – a place that looked too bourgeois for the expression of violent sentiments. Ellis called for wine and poured two large glasses. The first he swallowed in a single gulp, and refilled his glass. There was still a dark gleam in his eye.

'I know Michel is a good fellow at heart, that's why I was surprised by what he said.'

'The news was a shock. I felt it like a blow, and it's not my country.' Ellis grunted.

'Michel is right – it's early days. Things can change; it could all be over soon, and we will be sitting in the Zouave, looking back on it.'

Ellis stared into his glass. 'I wouldn't bet on it.' He glanced around them. 'At the risk of being accused of sedition, or whatever it is, there's not a lot of confidence in government. My uncle sees people, you know, ministers and so on, and it doesn't look good. Quite a few Americans are packing up.'

'But why? The war is hundreds of miles away.'

'Because they reckon that, before too long, the Prussians will be at the gates of Paris.'

Lawrence was silenced. He looked at the families in their Sunday clothes, at a father adding a drop of wine to a glass of water for his son. Next to them, an elderly couple ate lunch in companionable silence. A mother and grown-up daughter, in matching outfits, whispered together.

'Is that what your uncle thinks?'

Ellis shrugged. 'He doesn't commit himself, but I'd say he thinks it's a possibility.'

'If that happened, would he leave?'

'God, no. He's responsible for the Americans who are still here, and he's also looking after the Germans, since their ambassador has scuttled off to Berlin and left them.'

'What about you?'

Ellis gave a strange smile. 'I don't know where I would go.'

'Not back to America?'

'No.'

'I wouldn't either. Go home, I mean. I love my work. I feel . . .' Lawrence thought of Yves.

'You feel – at home?'

'I suppose so. There's more freedom here.'

'You think so?' Ellis looked at him frankly, and Lawrence hoped he wasn't blushing.

'I grew up in the backwoods. People are . . .' He shrugged.

'Yes. Simpler to be away from family and their expectations.'

'Do you feel at home here?'

Ellis didn't speak for a moment. 'As much as I do anywhere. So, we are stuck here, whatever happens.'

To Lawrence's surprise, Ellis laughed, and his face changed, became mischievous and merry.

'I don't mean to be gloomy. There is no point worrying about the worst that can happen. Even if it does, so what? The Emperor will sue for peace and French pride will take a good drubbing – which would, frankly, be no bad thing.'

Afterwards, they walked through the Luxembourg, where the grass had turned yellow, and their feet on the gravel paths raised zephyrs of fine dust. The lake was a stagnant puddle. Lawrence felt unsteady, although he had not drunk as much as his companion. Ellis's voice was a little louder than before, but he seemed otherwise unaffected. They talked easily and lightly, avoiding the subject of the war.

When they reached the river, Lawrence could see the American's spirits were sinking again. To make up for his former aloofness, Lawrence gave him one of his cards. 'We should meet again.'

'By all means.'

'You will still go to the Zouave?'

Ellis grimaced. 'I don't know. Perhaps.'

'Next Sunday? Say you will. I'm relying on you!'

'All right, then.'

They shook hands, and parted.

16

Throughout September, the hot, dry weather continued. In the east, within the space of a few weeks, France lost several battles to the Prussians and was no longer an empire. She was now a republic, and a lot of people were happy. Well, not happy exactly – France had lost, for the time being, but there was a pause, a breathing space, while France went about raising a new army. It was only a matter of time before they were victorious. Or not – it depended on whom you were speaking to. The Emperor was languishing in a Prussian prison. He had surrendered Sedan – unforgivably, as other cities, like Strasbourg and Belfort, to say nothing of the rest of France, still held strong. But somehow Sedan was the key. The Empress, like the rest of Paris, was furious. She, with whatever staff remained loyal to the tattered Bonapartes, fled the Tuileries, leaving her jewel boxes upturned on dressing tables, clothes tossed on the floor and meals half-eaten. It was rumoured she had escaped France dressed as a madwoman.

Anne had heard this rumour and didn't believe it. She couldn't imagine the Empress (a woman she had never seen) dressing in one of their rough frocks. Surely her royal face would mark her out, whatever she wore? But then, all sorts of previously unimaginable things were happening. An army of Prussian soldiers was marching on Paris – only days away, they said. There was going to be a siege. Everyone had to pull together. Thousands of ordinary Parisians had joined the National Guard and were being drilled in parks and on boulevards, rifles bristling from shoulders. There were sheep in city squares, and the Bois de Boulogne was a sea of livestock. You heard country accents all around – people arrived from the east, fleeing ahead of the invaders. It was also said that these invaders were decent and well behaved, tall and blond, with excellent uniforms.

Anne knew these things because of her friend, Monsieur Calmette. Being a regular person, he read the papers (newspapers, always discouraged in the Salpêtrière, were now forbidden), and they talked about what was happening. He had asked her to call him Victor, and she allowed him to call her Anne. No one ever called her Mademoiselle Petitjean, and this did not strike her as significant.

Today, her favourite bench near the cat pavilion was empty, and she sat down, fluffing out her skirts to take up more room; if she was lucky, no one would sit near her. Then, she could sit back and tilt her face to the sun. The zoo had been quieter since the war began. Victor said a lot of people had left to go to their country houses, as they did every August, but this year they hadn't come back. Anne wasn't worried about the siege, because Victor said that the Prussians would wait outside the walls until there was an agreement, then they would go away. Paris was stuffed with food and the walls were trebly fortified. She could not imagine how a siege would affect her life: she never left the city anyway, so what difference would it make?

She sighed, but it was a sigh of contentment; she was alone, the sun was warm, she was surrounded by the warrior spirits of Marguerite, Irma, Tancred and Nero. Their presence reminded men that they were weak, vulnerable creatures, with no defences against being crushed and savaged and bitten, and she found that a comfort.

'Anne. How good to see you. Are you well?'

She opened her eyes and Victor was there. He was smiling. These meetings tended to follow a pattern: she would ask him about the animals' welfare, and he would tell her, seriously, and in detail. Once told a thing, she never forgot it.

'Today, I have a proposal for you, if you are agreeable?'

She didn't react. It sounded bad, because anything surprising was bad.

'I would like to invite you to tea.'

Anne felt alarm. 'Where?'

The tigress looked on with sleepy, amber eyes, and tilted her head as if she too wanted to know.

'Don't worry, you don't need to be dressed up. It's here, in the zoo. I would like you to meet my colleague, Monsieur Papin. I'm sure you will like him.'

Anne was less sure, but couldn't think of a way to get out of it. She followed him through the park, to a gate in a high wall. Behind the wall, a row of dark trees obscured whatever lay beyond. It felt secret and enclosed. Victor opened the gate slowly, saying, 'Please take care where you step; there are a few rabbits in here.' Sure enough, Anne caught the startled scuts of several fawn bodies bolting away from them. There were more than a few; there were scores of them. Everywhere she looked there were rabbits. She started to laugh.

Victor stared, smiling. 'I've never seen you laugh before.'

Immediately, she stopped. 'What are they doing here?'

'It's something Monsieur Papin is trying. Come and meet him.'

Anne was shown into a large, gloomy house, crowded with things. It smelt strange – not unpleasant, but not like anything she knew. As her eyes adjusted to the shadows, she made out paintings on the walls, vases on shelves and mantels, side tables covered with sparkling, shining objects. Everywhere she looked, there were things she wanted to examine, but there wasn't time. A housekeeper who led them through doors and corridors muttered incessantly in what sounded like no language Anne could name.

They were shown into a room where the curtains were drawn against the sun, and she was introduced to Monsieur Papin – a tall man in very elegant clothes. He got up from his chair with a curious, corkscrew movement, and Anne saw he was older than she had first thought, and that he had a twisted spine. He greeted her with great courtesy.

'Mademoiselle Petitjean, this is indeed a pleasure. Please, sit. I have ordered tea; I hope you will join us in taking some refreshment.'

Anne sat on a stiff-backed chair, too awestruck to speak.

'Monsieur Calmette has told me a little about you, and I have been badgering him to bring you to meet me, so this is all my fault.'

Anne was rigid with fear. What did this mean?

The housekeeper came back in, still muttering, bearing a tray with a pot of drinking chocolate and an array of beautiful patisserie that made Anne's mouth water.

'You must try one of each,' said the old man, seeing her eyeing the tiny cakes. 'I am very fond of cakes myself. I always have some at this time of day.'

Anne glanced at Victor, who smiled and nodded, so, before anyone changed their mind, she took three of the exquisite confections. The smell of freshly baked butter and sugar made her dizzy with greed. She was afraid she might actually growl.

'This is one of my favourites,' said Papin, holding up a nugget of golden pastry with a glossy, caramel lid. '*Un puit d'amour*. I always have to watch out for the middle; I have had many a mishap.'

Anne watched as he bit into it, revealing a cache of oozing red sauce. He dabbed his mouth with a napkin and looked down to see if he had spilt any on his shirt front.

'I rejoice: no serious damage.'

Anne thought him the most extraordinary person she had ever met. They worked their way through the cakes, which had jokey names like 'well of love', or 'nun's fart' – a bun filled with sweet cream. She ate as daintily as she knew, concentrating on not making a mess, but, in spite of all her care, a gobbet of cream escaped from her fingers and fell – horror of horrors – on to her skirt. Anne froze, not daring to look up. She had ruined it. She wished she would die. In the same second, Papin gave a yelp and dropped his cake into his lap.

'Oh dear, I suppose it was too good to last,' he sighed, and busied himself with his napkin, then looked up. 'Ah, mademoiselle. I'm so sorry. I have led you into misfortune.'

He laughed and passed her another napkin, and she wiped up the mess with trembling hands. They finished the cakes without further mishap.

'Now, I want to ask you something, Mademoiselle Petitjean,' said Papin, and he proceeded to quiz her about her love of animals.

She put down her plate, and, on her favourite subject, she found it easy to talk. Her voice, which had been no more than a whisper, came back to her, and she asked him why there were so many rabbits in his garden.

'They should be in cages, but they persist in burrowing under the netting. You are, I'm sure, aware of the coming tribulation – the siege that everyone is talking about? Well, we have been stockpiling food for the zoo animals. But, not knowing how long the blockade will last, I thought it wise to begin breeding rabbits as an additional source of food. I apologize if that distresses you.'

Anne shook her head. 'I should have thought of that. But what about the herbivores? Won't finding fodder for them be difficult too?'

'Indeed. I am hoping that rain and cooler temperatures will mean the grass grows again. I have petitioned the director of the Jardin des Plantes to turn over the park to growing forage, but –' he glanced at Victor – 'there are conflicts of interest. Perhaps I am unduly cautious. Most of those I speak to are entirely sanguine about the preparations.'

He leant over and tugged a tasselled rope that hung by the fireplace.

'Monsieur Papin is most concerned about the animals' welfare,' said Victor. 'The animals are lucky to have such a dedicated guardian.'

'Monsieur Calmette is too kind – he too is dedicated to his charges, if not quite as impartial as one would sometimes wish. You, I'm sure, remember the fate of our poor lynx, Olga?'

'Yes.'

'Monsieur Calmette wished to guillotine the persons responsible for such cruelty.'

'I would have done more,' said Anne. 'To torture such a creature – it is worse than anything.'

Papin smiled. 'I, too, think such wanton cruelty is beyond redemption.'

The housekeeper shuffled in and mumbled something. Anne could not make out a word, but Papin listened and nodded.

'Thank you, Sophie,' he said, as she cleared away the cake dishes. 'I hope you'll forgive me, mademoiselle, but I have a proposition for you – a business proposition. You are absolutely free to say no, and we will say no more about it.'

The room suddenly seemed colder. Of course, this was all too nice to be real. There had to be a cost.

'There is no reason to be alarmed,' said Victor. 'Monsieur Papin and I have been talking. Things are about to change, and we are going to need help. We were wondering whether you could help us – and, at the same time, perhaps, we might help you.'

Anne stayed as still as she could.

'Monsieur Calmette has told me a little of your past life and your current situation. I do not need to know the rest, but I imagine you have known hardship.'

Anne looked at her hands gripping the napkin, and her throat closed. But there was something about Papin – perhaps his obvious frailty – that meant she did not fear him.

'We wondered whether you were quite happy in your situation at the hospital, or whether you would like to come and work here, as my housekeeper. I am sending Madame Innocent to my house in the country. She is elderly, and not as well as she should be, and, despite my assurances, she is mortally afraid of the Prussians. I will stay, of course. The animals will need my, and Monsieur Calmette's, attentions more than ever.'

Anne glanced towards Victor.

'You don't have to answer right away. Think it over. Of course, you will want to know the hours, the pay and so on. I have taken the liberty of writing it all down.'

He pushed an envelope towards her. Even the envelope was amazing – made of a heavy, creamy paper, with a rich, smooth texture unlike that of any paper she had encountered. It lay on the table in front of her.

'Does he mean it?' She spoke to Victor in a whisper.

'Of course. Madame Innocent is going to the house in the Limousin, along with some of Monsieur Papin's collections, which are valuable.'

'A precaution only. Probably unnecessary. I can afford to indulge myself, so . . .' He shrugged.

'I assure you, Anne, and I have worked with him for over ten years, that Monsieur Papin is a fair and kind employer.'

'Oh, I know,' Anne said with vehemence. 'I mean . . . I don't know. I mean, yes.' Something struck her. 'But, if I don't work on the wards, I don't think they'll let me stay in the hospital. I've no savings.'

'You would live here, of course. I can show you the room where Madame Innocent has been living. I do not lack for space, as you see.'

'Here?' It seemed unreal. 'You mean, in the zoo?'

'Well, yes.'

Anne couldn't prevent the smile from breaking out. Papin smiled too.

'But then, when it's over – I would go back to the Salpêtrière?'

'No. I am offering you a permanent position. Madame Innocent has more than earned an easy retirement. I would like you to stay.'

Anne stared at the envelope. There was her name written on the front, in an elegant hand. Even the ink was rich and glossy. She picked up the envelope, unfolded the paper inside, read the words written there and looked up. There must have been some mistake.

'But, monsieur – I live in the *hospital*. For women who—'

'Yes, we know.'

'I don't understand. If you know about me, how can you . . . ?'

'I confess, mademoiselle,' said Papin, 'that I am acquainted with Dr Jospin of the Salpêtrière. I have taken the liberty of speaking to him, and he recommends you in the highest possible terms.'

Anne was conscious of a torrent of feelings. She recognized, among them, suspicion and anger, because they had gone behind her back and they had discussed her. And fear, because what if Monsieur Papin had seen her in a lecture? What if he knew things about her she didn't know about herself?

Was what they had done wrong? And was that any different from her life of the past few years, as a subject to be written about and photographed and hypnotized. It was the same – and it wasn't. They were asking her what she wanted, and they were waiting for her decision.

She was so unused to wanting something, she didn't know if this was what it felt like. The prospect of choosing made her feel dizzy. She could say yes, and her whole life would change. She hardly dared breathe, but, when she did, she couldn't smell burning, just the rich, faintly spiced scent of the house.

17

Having trounced French forces in the east and made the Emperor a prisoner of war, the Prussian army was closing around Paris. Soon, the city would be surrounded, but, within the walls, the mood was defiant. Paris was a fortress. Paris was prepared. The surrounding country had been stripped of food, which was packed into Paris's warehouses. The city walls were trebly fortified. The Champs de Mars, the Luxembourg, the Tuileries gardens – every open space was an arsenal. The National Guard set its new recruits to learning drills and building earthworks.

Taking a trip to inspect the fortifications was the current craze. Ernestine professed herself uninterested, but, one Sunday, after Mass, Monsieur Ranvier invited her to join him for the afternoon to see them. At a low point, she agreed – anything was better than going drearily home with her parents, and he had his own carriage. They were chaperoned by his elderly mother, who was morose and fearful, but Ernestine was surprised how much she enjoyed herself. From the fortifications at the Porte de la Muette, they drove into the Bois de Boulogne so that she could admire the astonishing numbers of sheep and cattle, spreading to the horizon in a black and white flood.

'So, you see,' he said, smiling, 'we shall not run short of meat.'

He was sanguine at the prospect of the siege, and calmed his mother's fears. To Ernestine, he was polite and respectful; he asked her opinions and professed himself impressed with her answers. He said she was very brave, as well as knowledgeable. At one point, she intercepted a glance between Monsieur Ranvier and his mother. She gathered that she was approved of, and was pleased. She had thought she would not care.

When he dropped her off at the Rue des Ciseaux, he asked if he might see her the following Sunday, and she conceded that she would be at Mass as usual. Then she took a deep breath and prepared to face her mother's questions.

The next day, Ernestine visited her dressmaker in the Faubourg du Temple. The next time she saw Monsieur Ranvier, she wanted to appear in something new. It showed that she was taking him seriously. It showed respect. Despite wars and besieging armies, life went on. It did not do to let standards slip.

Her dressmaker, Madame Lecointe, was a rare find, but Ernestine was careful not to give too much praise. Aristocrats, and those former schoolmates who aped them, might pay no attention to the price of things, but she was enough Louise's daughter to relish a bargain. Perhaps, though, family of Monsieur Ranvier would not need to think of such things. They might even shop for dresses on the Rue de la Paix . . .

Climbing the stairs, she was surprised by a familiar voice – more surprised still to hear the beseeching note in it before it broke into sobs. She hesitated, but it was too late; the door opened and a figure rushed out, almost cannoning into her.

'Oh!'

It was the studio model, Fanny Klein. She would have dashed past had not Ernestine's skirt effectively blockaded the staircase.

'Why, Fanny!'

'Mademoiselle Lamy!'

'Heavens, Fanny – what on earth is the matter?'

Even in the dim light of the staircase, Ernestine could see that the model's face was lopsided and swollen. Since hearing the news that she was expecting a baby, they had not seen her at the studio for a while. Fanny stared at the floor, shaking her head.

'Nothing, mademoiselle. It's nothing.' She tried to smile, but tears made gleaming trails down the misshapen cheek.

'But what has happened to you?'

'Oh, nothing. I fell and banged my head, that's all. Silly.'

Ernestine sighed. It was perfectly plain what had happened.

'So, you come to Madame Lecointe?'

'Only to . . .' Fanny drew in a shuddering breath. 'To ask for work, because . . .' She gestured towards her face, and choked down a sob.

'Well, well. There's no need for these tears, Fanny.'

Fanny shook her head.

'Other than that, are you well?'

A stupid question, but manners demanded it.

'Yes . . . That is, no.'

She began to cry again, so piteously that Ernestine had no choice but to take her arm and walk her out to the street. Fanny carefully pulled down her veil before stepping into the daylight, but it could not entirely hide the swelling, nor the bruises. Having committed herself thus far, Ernestine did not feel she could abandon her. Ignoring Fanny's protests, she swept her into a nearby café. In the dimmest corner, Fanny sat with her back to the other customers and kept her head lowered. Ernestine ordered cups of hot chocolate.

When the chocolate was served and Fanny had to lift her veil, Ernestine felt a lurch of horror – her face was hard to look at. Fanny had always seemed so cheerful and happy – smiling and blushing when Louise teased her about her new husband – but this, too, was marriage.

'Raymond – Monsieur Klein, I mean – was upset because he was laid off from his work, and I could not earn, and . . . then I miscarried.'

Ernestine found herself putting out her hand and touching the girl's arm. Fanny had been modelling for the Lamys for over two years, but this was their first real conversation.

'I'm sorry to hear that, Fanny. Still, what's done is done.'

'I wish you had not seen me like this, mademoiselle.'

'Nonsense. You'll be right as rain in no time.' She made herself smile before glancing away. What messes some people got themselves into – surely avoidable, if you kept your wits about you. She herself would never—

'It's just, I don't know what we'll do,' Fanny said. 'Things are very hard at the moment.'

'Monsieur Klein – is he working now?'

Fanny's shoulders slumped and she shook her head slightly. 'It's not his fault. So many employers have left Paris, and normal building work has all but stopped – he's a tiler, you see. I've been looking for sewing work, but I can't find anything, and Madame Lecointe was cross with me for going there. She had a client and she saw me and—' She dissolved into tears once more.

'Well, that's unfortunate, but, come, I'm sure something will turn up.'

Fanny hung her head meekly. She made Ernestine think of a whipped dog. Ernestine heard her mother's voice in her head, scolding her. Louise was very fond of Fanny. Even worse would be her father's judgement. She felt for her purse. Secreting a note in her gloved hand, she touched Fanny's arm.

'Oh, no, mademoiselle, I couldn't possibly—'

'My mother would never forgive me if I did not insist.'

'Oh! Oh, thank you! I will pay it back as soon as I can, of course. You're so kind, Mademoiselle Lamy – you're an angel!'

Seeing Fanny's expression of amazed gratitude, Ernestine regretted giving her so much. Still, she could always get her father to reimburse her. She would not ask him to. She would simply mention what she had done.

After she had extricated herself from Fanny's cloying gratitude, she returned to Madame Lecointe's to negotiate the new dress, but she didn't enjoy it as much as she usually enjoyed discussions of fabric, shade and trim. If giving to the needy was good for the soul, why did she feel soiled, as if the girl's squalid circumstances were clinging to her?

She held a blue moiré up to the light, and thought of Monsieur Ranvier's attentive politeness. Would he ever lose control of himself like Fanny's husband? She could not believe it – he seemed a gentleman through and through. Her mother liked him, and she was usually a sound judge. Was he capable of raising his hand to a woman – more specifically, to her? She thought not. She compared the moiré to a mauve bengaline. She thought she would rather like to see him try.

18

The last shards of sun blinked through the trees and their shadows reached towards where Ellis stood by the French windows. All he could see around him was pleasant and green, all he could hear was birdsong. The air smelt of grass, warm earth and rosemary.

An unexpected consequence of the war was the newly hatched truce between Ellis and Ephraim, now that his uncle had bigger things to worry about than an errant nephew. Ellis tried to remember what it had been like when war had broken out at home. 'His' war, he called it in his mind. He had been in the middle of his medical studies, and the prospect of fighting seemed very far away from student life. He knew where he had been and with whom when the news broke: a professor interrupted his lecture to impart the news, and class was dismissed. Ellis and his great friend, B., wandered outside, discussing it, without really knowing anything. He could picture the weather: chilly and bright, with drifts of late snow banked up by the roadside. He could picture B.'s face. He thought they had been excited at the prospect, but trying to remember how he felt was like looking through glass at people whose voices he couldn't hear. Even now, with an invading army poised to encircle Paris, it was impossible to imagine anything uncivilized happening in this drowsy garden.

His uncle came back into the room after yet another summons from Mr Warburton, even though it was a Sunday.

'Ellis, forgive me asking, but have you written to your mother? In a few days, there will be no post in or out, and she worries about you so.'

'I have. I've told her that there isn't the slightest cause for concern. You'll still be able to communicate, surely? You have channels.'

'For diplomatic communiqués. You haven't changed your mind about staying?'

Ellis laughed. 'It's not that easy to get rid of me. Everyone says there'll be no danger. The trains are packed with Englishmen arriving specially to see the fun. A friend of mine has let his apartment to a journalist from London. He is going to be a "siege correspondent" for his newspaper.'

Ephraim frowned. 'I don't see how he is going to correspond with anyone when there is no mail service.'

'Through his embassy, I suppose.'

'The British embassy has left Paris. The only member of staff still here is a concierge.'

'Oh? Where have they gone?'

'To Versailles, like most of the embassies. Whether that will be safer is a moot point. Come with me; I have something to show you.'

Ephraim led Ellis through the garden. In the parterre, the central bed had been stripped of its rose bushes, and in their place was a large structure of wood and wire. A flock of chickens made soft, crooning noises as they scratched the bare earth. Ellis laughed.

'Here's something I thought I'd never see: you, a farmer! Have you told my mother? She'll be tickled.'

'Hardly a farmer. But, with all the refugees to feed, we have to think ahead. That's the rooster. Handsome fellow, isn't he? We will be self-sufficient in eggs.'

They passed through a gate into the orchard, the remnants of a much larger one that had existed before the house was built. Long grass surrounded the ancient trees. In the twilight, there were plaintive moans from a herd of goats crowded into a makeshift pen. Ellis leant over the fence and scratched the head of the nearest goat. It glared at him from an unsettling, oblong-pupilled eye.

'Where did you get them?'

'Madame Noyer arranged it. She has relatives.'

'And all this because of the siege?'

'We have to think of those who are coming to us for help, and it's as well to be prepared. Of course, we will pick all this fruit before we let the goats roam.'

'Do you think this is necessary? The square at the end of my street is crammed full of sheep. Everywhere I look, there is food and provisions.'

'I hope it isn't. But that is no reason not to be prudent. You or I have no cause for concern, but there are others less fortunate, like the poor Germans who have been turned out of their homes, or refugees arriving in Paris from the east.'

'Most of my friends have left – mostly to go and skulk in the country. They're not Parisians, so I suppose they don't feel the same way about it. Alfred Quinet has suddenly discovered a desire to paint seascapes. But, you remember my friend Yves Michaud – the painter I told you about? He has done the heroic thing and enlisted.'

'I recall you wanted me to meet him. I hope I may, some day.'

'Of course. Michel Blasi, too. Michel has joined the National Guard.' Ellis paused to break a switch off a sapling, and he swished the long grass with it. 'I was thinking of doing the same thing. I don't see why I shouldn't write poetry and serve in the Guard at the same time.'

'I'd have thought that someone with your experience would be far more useful in one of the ambulances. I know a Dr Snow who is setting up an American ambulance. Why don't you let me put you in touch with him.'

Ellis sighed. 'It's been too long. And I was never very good at it. Besides, if and when the Prussians do get here, the government will have to sue for peace, won't they? Isn't it just a question of terms?'

'But the terms are everything. The government has sworn not to cede an inch of soil, but the Prussians have the upper hand. Why would they be magnanimous?'

'Why wouldn't they?'

'That may have been possible initially, but the government's insistence on raising new armies and all their talk of an *attaque à outrance* is unlikely to provoke mercy.'

'They've humiliated France, trounced the army and destroyed its empire. Isn't that enough?'

Ephraim snorted. 'That is not for you or me to decide.'

Back in the formal garden, the Siamese cat was sitting on the gravel, gazing at the hens, who seemed oblivious to the danger.

'What a temptation! You don't think there's any chance she'll find a way in?'

'No; Jacques assures me the coop is impregnable. They don't seem afraid, do they?'

The ever-present Mr Warburton emerged from the French windows and waved a piece of paper. Ephraim excused himself to meet him.

Ellis picked up the cat, who gave a musical yowl.

'You're my favourite,' he said. 'Yes, you are.'

She stretched her claws through his shirt front, pricking his skin. Her eyes were a mesmerizing shade of turquoise, fixed on his, as if she had something of importance to communicate. He should get a cat, he thought. It would be nice to come home to a living creature – something to curl up with, other than a bottle.

Dust from her paws besmirched his coat. He put her down, brushed at the dust, then noticed his uncle standing alone outside the French windows. Even from this distance, Ellis could see his posture was different. He looked old. Feeling a twinge of alarm, Ellis went to him.

'Is something wrong?'

Ephraim shrugged. 'No, it's nothing.'

'Maybe I should go. You're busy.'

'My dear boy.'

This shocked Ellis more than anything else. His uncle had not addressed him as such for years.

'Uncle . . . come inside.' He took Ephraim's arm and led him into the sitting room. 'Please, tell me. I won't repeat anything you say, I swear.'

Ephraim sat down and passed a hand over his face. 'Oh – that was a telegram. The French ambassador to Washington – a man I liked and respected –' he stopped and cleared his throat for an inordinate amount of time – 'has died.'

'I'm sorry to hear that. I'll ring for some tea – or some brandy?'

'Tea, thank you.'

Ellis felt relief. 'What happened? Was he sick?'

Ephraim gave a wintry smile. 'No. Well, perhaps, in his mind, although I always found him to be the soundest of thinkers. Prévost-Paradol was very intelligent, very measured – yet . . . apparently, he wrote a letter predicting this terrible French defeat. Then he shot himself.'

From *La Voix*, 8 October 1870:

A great crowd gathered to watch the launch of the hot-air balloon carrying Monsieur Gambetta, with dispatches for the government in Tours. As his chariot rose into the ether, the Minister of the Interior unfurled the Tricolore and waved it above the masses, who responded with cheers of 'Vive La Republique! Vive La France!' All who witnessed this stirring sight cannot fail to believe that fortune will once again turn in our favour.

From *Times of London*, 19 October 1870:

The City of Light is now a drab place. The theatres are closed, and cafés dimmed. Your humble correspondent has joined the Parisian Guard, the civilian militia which takes men from all walks of life to defend the city. In its ranks, bankers and artists rub shoulders with plasterers and rag pickers. Paris being the hotbed of Republicanism that it is, your correspondent is a mere foot-soldier who takes orders from his battalion sergeant, previously known to all as the district's fish-seller!

From *Le Figaro*, 1 November 1870:

BLACK MONDAY. Yesterday saw an attempted coup at the Hôtel de Ville. Disorderly groups of National Guard, inflamed by Jacobin orators, marched upon the seat of government and handed over a list of demands, chief among which, in ominous echoes of the Terror, was the formation of a 'Committee of Public Safety'. A drunken mob invaded the chamber, and in the ensuing chaos our elected deputies feared for their lives. Order was eventually restored by the police and a loyal battalion. The Red ringleaders have been arrested and imprisoned in the Mazas.

From *Le Cri du Peuple*, 2 November 1870:

Every promise made by the government in response to demands of the 31st has been broken. They promised to hold an election; they have reneged on it. They promised not to punish the people's leaders, whose only 'crime' was to try and negotiate a compromise; yet, today, Eudes, Pyat and Blanqui are imprisoned. They promised to continue the war against our Prussian aggressors, yet they are planning an ignominious surrender. Even M. Adam, Chief of Police, has resigned in protest against this government's perfidy.

19

The last communication that Lawrence had had from Yves was a brief note before Paris was cut off at the end of September. In it, he joked about the poor quality of the food, the living quarters, equipment and training. In spite of that, he was happy; his battalion was full of excellent fellows and spirits were high. They had seen no action and were desperate to engage in real fighting. Yves included, on the single sheet, a self-portrait, with an overgrown beard and enormous boots, at which a rat nibbled.

The letter tormented Lawrence. He was disappointed by the impersonality of it, jarred by the repeated use of 'we' instead of 'I'. He was torn by jealousy of the 'excellent fellows' with whom Yves lived in such proximity, and tortured himself: what if Yves met someone who 'understood' him better than he did?

He told himself that a soldier's letter could not be otherwise, but from his misery it was apparent that he had invested a great deal in the vague promise of Yves' previous letter. He read the letters side by side, the older worn to the softness of cotton. It said nothing, really. He hesitated to reply, thinking of the likelihood of his letter being intercepted and read by strangers who might laugh, or sneer. Then he began to write, only to wake up the next morning to find that the encirclement of the city was complete, and they were now cut off from the rest of the world.

When the balloon post began, Lawrence rushed to add the letter, and one for his mother, and joined the crowd watching the balloon take flight from the hill of Montmartre. It struck him as a desperately unlikely vessel: a basket the size of a cupboard, no higher than his waist. The balloon itself was a great bag of varnished cotton – a patched and dirty thing that looked as though it had been lying in a shed for years. Its burner roaring, the bag swelled with gas until it rose, tugged at its mooring ropes and the basket began to lurch off the ground. The pilot climbed in and squatted among the sacks of mail. He was lifted by the blind urgings of the balloon, waved, blew kisses to the watching women, and then the whole creaking contraption was untied from its mooring posts and rose swiftly, swaying and spinning in the late September air. Wonderful, yes, but wildly unstable and vulnerable to Prussian bullets. The crowd cheered, applauded, sighed, gasped, the collective gaze pulled after it as it drifted westward.

A woman standing next to Lawrence claimed the job was so dangerous that pilots were drawn from the ranks of condemned men in La Roquette. Someone else said they were sailors.

'How do they steer?' he asked the proponent of the sailor theory.

'They cannot steer, monsieur. They go where the wind blows them.'

'So, they just hope it blows in the right direction?'

This drew a hard stare. 'You're not French, are you? Where are you from?' The man narrowed his eyes in suspicion.

'Canada . . . Montréal,' said Lawrence. These days, it was dangerous to open one's mouth around strangers.

'So you say . . . How do we know you're not a spy for the Prussians?'

Lawrence resisted the temptation to ask the man the same question. He held up his hands and tried to melt imperceptibly into the crowd. After a moment's glaring, the man turned back to follow the diminishing globe as it became a thumbnail, a dot, a memory printed on the white sky.

'Pilot' was a misnomer; the man in the basket could no more affect the course of his craft than could Lawrence, standing on the ground. He wondered whether his letter would reach its destination. It seemed such a small chance, but then, all his hopes rested on vanishingly small chances. He was as much at the mercy of forces beyond his control as the man in the balloon – or Yves, in an army camp somewhere in France, waiting to be told his fate.

He became used to siege time. When you know nothing, when there are no letters and no news, time slows to a maddening crawl. After the dry summer, the trees shed their leaves early. It grew cold, then colder. Tempers were short. The inhabitants became used to the background grumble of artillery from the outlying forts, but outside the walls nothing seemed to change. Inside them, there were anti-government demonstrations, and new newspapers sprouted every day. Everyone had an opinion on how the siege could be broken, but nothing made a difference. Every day was the same as the one before, the only change the rising cost of food and the growing anger of the besieged.

Milk was the first thing to run out, and breakfast coffee was now served black. Lawrence didn't mind much, but Madame Lamy pointed out that it was a terrible thing for the children. He had been to the Bois de Boulogne in September, when its grass was invisible under the sea of cattle – he could not imagine they would eat their way through all those animals in the foreseeable future. One chilly Sunday in November, he made another trip to the Bois, this time with Ellis Butterfield. They were shocked to see it thinly populated with a few scrawny sheep searching in vain for a blade of grass, the earth grazed bare, the woods destroyed – so many of the old trees had been felled for fuel.

He and Ellis were the only ones of their set still meeting at the Zouave. The only other friend still in Paris was Michel, who had volunteered for the Guard. Lawrence hadn't seen him for weeks – he imagined him busy parading in uniform, or engaged in target practice, like the recruits he had seen in the Luxembourg gardens. Nor had he heard anything of Séraphine. One evening, Lawrence walked to where Séraphine lived with her family, on a hill near Père Lachaise Cemetery. He found the whole family in a tiny apartment: Monsieur and Madame Bignon, Séraphine and her younger sister, Paulette – and Michel, surprised and delighted to see him. When he was introduced, Séraphine's parents pressed him to stay to dinner.

Madame Bignon and Paulette made another place at the table, and Séraphine saw to the stove. Lawrence sat as they worked, feeling awkward. Meeting Séraphine and Michel in the Zouave or at Yves' studio was one thing. He'd assumed that they lived, albeit in the cheaper eastern districts, very much as he did. The evident poverty distressed him.

Michel was in his Guard uniform. His battalion was based nearby. It wasn't too bad, he said, but there wasn't a lot to do other than rifle drills and guard duty. At first, the novelty had been charming; now, he found it tedious. He had not laid eyes on a Prussian. Regular troops manned the bastions on the city walls, and the outlying forts. So far, the invaders were content to sit just out of reach of the French artillery and starve them out.

'Half the battalion spends its guard duty in a wine shop. Not me, but, in a way, I can't blame them. The boredom drives you mad. At least they pay something, and, since no one's buying paintings at the moment, I thought I might as well.'

'You've given up your studio?'

'I sublet it to a family who arrived before the siege. I think they wish they'd stayed at home. Séraphine's parents are kind enough to put up with me.'

He smiled at Séraphine's mother, who patted him on the shoulder.

'Michel is so good to us. He brought us this rabbit, and, with the price of meat the way it is, that's a blessing.'

She ladled out plates of stew. There was plenty of wine, but Lawrence was aware that she had given him an unequal portion of the meat, and that one rabbit does not provide anything like enough for six people. Séraphine and her sister protested they weren't hungry and insisted on tiny portions. He cursed himself for not choosing a more tactful time to visit, but he had not thought. As the evening wore on, the impression of scarcity weighed more heavily upon him.

'I feel ashamed of dropping in like that. I should have brought something. I didn't think . . .'

Michel dismissed the idea with a wave of his hand. He had brought Lawrence to a local bar while the women cleared away dinner. 'Oh, no – they were thrilled. They would have been mortally insulted if you hadn't stayed. They'll talk about your visit for weeks.'

Lawrence grimaced, but Michel was serious. Food prices were soaring, unemployment and hunger were growing, but everyone agreed that the worst thing about the siege was the boredom. For weeks there had been no news, and, in the vacuum, rumours bred like flies. In the last few days, Lawrence had heard that the Prussian Prince had died; that Britain was entering the war; that snails were being trained as spies; that there were tunnels dug under the city ramparts . . . Nothing was verifiable, and most dissolved as quickly as they appeared, to be replaced by something more outlandish still.

'You bring them food?'

Michel shrugged. 'A chicken costs five days' wages, and Monsieur Bignon has no work, so I do what I can. A mate breeds the rabbits. He was smart; he bought a pair weeks ago, and now he charges ten francs a carcass. Wish I'd thought of it.'

'But you are well – and Séraphine?'

'Oh, we're fine. Séraphine just worries terribly about her brother. He's in the army, but we don't know where. Haven't heard a thing – not that that means anything.'

'No. So – you won't have heard anything from Yves, I suppose?'

He laughed a little, at the absurdity of the idea. 'No. I thought he was crazy when he joined up; now, now I think I envy him. Being stuck here, with nothing to do except march up and down – honestly, it drives you up the wall.'

20

Fanny unwrapped Louise's parcel and exclaimed with pleasure.

'It's too kind of you, madame! Raymond will be so pleased. We haven't had beef for weeks. I haven't even seen it since . . . I don't know when.'

Fanny didn't mention the money that was folded into an envelope. When Louise had first visited, after Ernestine reported her troubles, Fanny protested that she could not accept any more financial help. But that was before the price of meat doubled; before butchers' windows filled up with dogs, cats and horsemeat, and the prices doubled again. Now, they both pretended that the envelope wasn't there. Louise smiled at her. She noticed a fresh bruise on her wrist, but said nothing. What was the point? Fanny crowed with delight over a tin of cherries and told her over and over that they didn't need meat; they could get by on vegetables and bread.

'Oh, come, Fanny. Now that we— Oh, I haven't told you the news! Ernestine has just become engaged – yes, I know! – to a Monsieur Ranvier.'

'Oh, madame, that's wonderful! I'm so happy for her. You must give her my warmest congratulations.'

Fanny looked truly delighted. Louise felt her heart go out to the girl. She was such a dear.

'How did they meet? Please, tell me all about it. I love happy stories like that.'

'Oh, well, she met him at our church, you know, in Saint Germain. He's very nice – a widower, with a young son, and he owns the smartest butcher's shop in Paris. On the Rue de Rivoli, no less.'

'Rue de Rivoli? It's not the one with the blue awnings – and the gold – the big one?'

'Boucherie Ranvier – yes, that's it.'

'My goodness, it's so beautiful! I always look in the window when I go past. They lay out the meat so that it looks like jewels.'

'Yes, it's beautifully done. Beautifully priced, too – but that's where this came from. He's been very generous to us.'

Fanny picked up the joint of beef and gazed at it in wonder. 'It's almost too good to eat.'

'Nonsense. You can have steaks and make a nice stew with the leftovers.'

Fanny stroked the packet. 'It's so nice to hear that Mademoiselle Ernestine is happy. And meeting in church – so romantic!'

It was cold in the kitchen, but Fanny made no move to add wood to the small fire. She said she was getting a little sewing piecework, but so many ladies had left Paris that demand was low. And those who remained – well, with the price of meat the way it was, even the well off had to cut corners.

The street door banged, followed by heavy footsteps on the stairs, at which Fanny jumped up and added some sticks to the fire. A minute later, the apartment door opened. Fanny stood up as her husband came into the kitchen.

'Raymond, you remember Madame Lamy, from the studio? Look what she has brought us – a joint of beef from the butcher's on Rue de Rivoli! And a wonderful cheese. And a tin of cherries! Isn't that kind? I'll make a clafoutis – you know how you like that.'

Raymond Klein greeted Louise gruffly. Fanny moved the best chair nearer the fire for her husband, and he sat. She fetched a bottle and a glass, and he filled his pipe. Monsieur Klein was undoubtedly good-looking in a saturnine way, with hollow cheeks and haunted, dark eyes, but he sat in gloomy silence, while Fanny kept up a flow of chatter.

'Fanny was telling me that you have joined the Guard, monsieur. How smart you look in your uniform, doesn't he?'

'He does.' Fanny smiled. 'It suits him.'

'How do you find the life?'

'It's all right. The best I can hope for at the moment, I suppose.'

'What did you do today, darling?' Fanny asked.

'Same as we always do – what do you think? March around. Stand guard. Now, the commander says they want us to stick broken glass to the top of the wall. What do they think the Prussians are – cats? And I have to put up with their teasing. Would you believe, madame, that they call me a Prussian, just because of my name?'

Louise made her excuses and left. She felt sorry for Fanny. In a way, she even felt sorry for the husband. But what could she do about it? He was the man Fanny had chosen, so there it was.

The district where Fanny lived wasn't a good neighbourhood for cabs, and she began to think she might have to take the omnibus – something she hadn't done in years. A sharp wind blew from the east, making fallen leaves scrape the pavement at her feet.

Despite the cold, Louise felt hot and sticky by the time she had walked to the Place du Trône. Normally, she would have hailed a cab by now, but not a single cab had passed her. In fact, now that she thought about it, the usual din of iron-shod hooves and iron-bound wheels was eerily absent.

Under the lights of a café, she saw a crowd of men in Guard uniforms drinking and laughing. Why weren't they at home with their families? She felt vulnerable and conspicuous. She drew her scarf tighter around her bonnet. She would just have to keep walking – the quickest way home was past the prison, and, if she kept to the main streets, there was bound to be a cab before long, surely?

The boulevard stretched away ahead of her, taunting her efforts to make progress. There was something dispiriting and inhuman about these huge, straight thoroughfares. They weren't made for an elderly woman to walk along at night. There was no shelter from the wind, and the far end never seemed to get any nearer. Her feet were aching. What had happened to all the cabs? She looked up just then and saw a sign pointing to a side street, bright and newly painted: *Butcher – equine, canine, feline*. Was that where all the horses had gone? Louise muttered an obscenity – that was how upset she was.

Now, Ernestine was going to marry a butcher – but he wasn't like *that*, of course. And he owned the business, he didn't actually . . . She tried to ignore the ache in her hip and thought instead about her daughter's sudden engagement. After spending a number of Sunday afternoons with Monsieur Ranvier, Ernestine had announced the news in a matter-of-fact fashion. Louise and Serge, not really daring to hope, had been amazed and delighted. Louise had embraced her daughter, both laughing and crying (she had to admit) with relief.

Since then, she had tried to discern a difference in her daughter's spirits. Surely Ernestine was finally happy. Was she in love? He was nearly twenty years older than her, but he was kind and respectable, and had kept his trim figure. Perhaps the siege had brought her face to face with her mortality. Louise couldn't tell, and Ernestine did not choose to share her feelings. Throwing caution to the wind one day, Louise leant on the counter while Ernestine was bringing the ledger up to date.

'It's so exciting to think about planning a wedding, isn't it?'

'Well, it won't be until after this is all over,' said Ernestine, her eyes on the columns. 'We want to do it properly.'

'Oh, no, of course. But, still . . . I know that I've sometimes annoyed you in the past by speaking of these matters, but I am delighted to see you happy, Titine. We both are. It's all we've ever wanted for you.'

Ernestine granted her a small smile. 'I know, Maman.'

'Monsieur Ranvier is a good man. We like him so much.'

Ernestine frowned at an entry in the ledger and lifted her pen for a moment.

'And, of course, you love him.'

There was a tiny pause. 'Of course.'

Louise ploughed on. 'Love is a strange thing. Sometimes you don't fall head over heels in a rush. It starts quietly, but grows all the deeper for it – that's how it was with your father and me.'

'Hmm.'

'It's funny, isn't it? To think that you didn't even like him to begin with!'

'I didn't dislike him. I didn't know him.' Ernestine examined the pen she was holding, as if considering its usefulness as a weapon. 'Do you mind? I'm in the middle of a column.'

Louise rarely touched her daughter, but now she put her hand over Ernestine's.

'He's kind and considerate. That is much more important than looks and excitement. Love is the best thing you can find in this life. I'm so happy that you have found someone you love, and who loves you.'

For a moment, she thought Ernestine was going to explode. Her eyes glinted, her lips tightened, but she simply said, 'Yes, Maman, I feel blessed.'

21

Anne was not afraid of the dark, but tonight, as she opened the gate from the garden on to the Rue Cuvier, she felt a lurch of unease. She couldn't see the buildings on the other side of the street. It took her a few moments to work out that the street lights had gone out. Paris had run out of gas.

Anne thought. She knew the way to the bakery on the Rue des Ciseaux; she had been there every morning since her job started – and, recently, as the bread queues started earlier and earlier, every night. Directly overhead, through a rift in the clouds, a single, bright star shone. It occurred to her that it could not be so bright and not have a name, but she didn't know such things. She set off through the dark streets. It was three thirty in the morning.

The lamp inside the bakery shed little light on the queue. Anne joined the end, just another dark shape bundled in a coat and shawl, stamping her feet against the cold. This morning, she noticed something: certain women, on arrival, greeted a shape in the queue ahead of her, went to talk to them, and melted into the queue, so that it grew as much ahead of her as behind. Those behind her also noticed the interlopers, and one shouted at the latest comer: 'Hey, you – there's no saving places, here! It's first come, first served. Why should you go ahead of me, who was here first?'

'Mind your own business! I was here earlier – I had to go and get something. I'm coming back to the same place.'

'You lying bitch! You were not here earlier – and what about her, huh?'

Frustration simmered. Anne listened. She knew those women were lying.

She was angry and upset by the time the shop doors opened. The queue shuffled forward, and loaves began to fly out the door. There were arguments as some were denied the amount they wanted. But most silently took their bread and scurried off, heads down.

After twenty minutes, Anne was just reaching the shop when the baker came to the door and shouted, 'That's it! No more bread! We have pastries and pies, but no bread. If you want bread, you'll have to go elsewhere.'

Most of the women behind her shouted or swore, but drifted off to look elsewhere. Anne and a few others hung on. What would happen if she went back to the house without the bread and pastries that Monsieur Papin liked? She would lose her job, most likely. But now the other bakeries would be empty too.

By the time she got to the front of the queue, tears had made itchy tracks on her cheeks. There was nothing behind the counter but a few pastries.

'Two loaves, and half a dozen pastries, please.'

'Are you deaf? I said there was no more bread – not a single loaf. All gone.'

'You must have something left.' It came out in a whisper. 'It's for Monsieur Papin, the direct—'

'Doesn't matter if it's for the Pope himself. There's none left.' He made a gesture of finality with his hands.

Anne leant forward in desperation. 'They cheated, those women – they jumped the queue ahead of me!' She even looked into his face, she was that desperate.

The baker rolled his eyes. 'What am I supposed to do? Tell the Guard, if you can find them. Be earlier tomorrow. Next!'

'Wait! Give me half a dozen.' She pointed a trembling finger at the pastries.

Outside, two women stood chatting, and Anne recognized one of the queue jumpers and her friend. Loaves jutted insolently from under their arms. Servants, like her. But they were successful servants, who knew the tricks. They weren't going to lose their jobs. Anger flared in her. For a moment, she considered something reckless.

The older woman noticed her fixed look and sneered. 'Too slow, huh?'

She lifted her eyes to meet the woman's and knew that, without even trying, the look was in her eyes. The woman took a step back.

'You cheated,' Anne said.

The younger turned to the other. 'What was that? Did it speak?'

The other shrugged. 'Don't think so. Just jungle noises.' They laughed and began to move away.

Anne was rooted to the spot. She couldn't focus; everything shimmered with furious light. She felt rage splintering off her in black, glittering shards. She thought of Marguerite and how she could crush the women with one blow of her paw. She imagined blood spraying into the cold air, staining the snow in long gouts . . . But she wasn't at school now. She wasn't a patient anymore. She thought of Monsieur Papin, who didn't care about her past.

She was such a bad servant, she couldn't even buy bread. She felt sick taking her failure back to the house. Lucie, Monsieur Papin's cook, tutted, but supposed she could make some rolls. Anne said she would go earlier tomorrow. And, amazingly, that was all. Anne went to light the fire in the dining room and take up the hot water. Her anger died down, but the humiliation smouldered on.

For years, Anne had dreamt of escaping the Salpêtrière. Now that she had, she was surprised to find that she missed it. Mainly, she missed Marie-Jo and Lisa, but she also missed the camaraderie of the ward girls; she missed that sense of being hidden and protected from the outside world. Life had been hard in the hospital, but life was hard on the outside too.

She had no complaints about the job itself. Monsieur Papin was an easy employer, and the house was beautiful. The best thing about it was that she could walk through the zoo when it was closed. She could sit in front of Marguerite's cage at night, and no one stopped her. But, at first, she couldn't sleep. She had never had a room to herself. Her life had begun in a crowded apartment; then she was at the nuns' school; then at the house where her mother worked, where she had slept in a cupboard with another girl. Then the hospital. That was her life.

Here, she had Madame Innocent's old room, where she slept in a mahogany bed. There was a soft mattress, a feather quilt. She frequently got too hot and had to kick off the quilt in the night. But it was the silence that bothered her most. There were no snores, or farts, or groans; no gasps or cries; no talking, no lovemaking; not even the sound of breathing.

The smell of the house was camphor, she learnt, and cloves, and dried lavender that lived in bowls, and wax polishes that smelt good enough to eat. There was one that smelt of almonds, another of oranges.

As well as her bed, there was a washstand, a cheval glass (astonishing to be able to see all of herself at once), a wardrobe and chest of drawers. There was a shelf for her things, although she didn't have any things. Her wardrobe was so sparse that Monsieur Papin took her to a dressmaker to have clothes made that would be 'suitable for her new position', as he put it. Her new dresses were plain and dark, but of warmer, finer stuff than she had worn before.

Then there were curtains that she could draw over her window – a window she could look out of and see the sky. There was even a clock on the mantelpiece: a weighty chunk of marble with brass handles, topped with a rearing, brass horse. She liked the horse, with its spiky, gilded mane and its friendly, predictable tick.

Her duties were to help Lucie, the cook, and keep the house clean. This was more complicated than cleaning the hospital. Many of Monsieur Papin's treasures had been sent away to the country, but the house was still full of dainty things and she couldn't just crash about with mop and bucket. The chairs and tables had legs of rare, fragile woods. Even the feet were beautiful – carved into smooth pebbles, or fashioned like the paws of tigers. She rubbed them lovingly with the wax that smelt of almonds.

She laid fires and cleaned hearths. She took monsieur his hot water in the morning and left it in his dressing room while he could be heard coughing in his bedroom. She ran errands – to the fancy grocer's on Rue de Rivoli, for example, where prices for the things monsieur liked – tinned oysters, or peaches in brandy – were unbelievable, but they were still available. Or she would go to one of the Right Bank butchers, who still had proper meat when the neighbourhood butchers had nothing but horse and dog. There was no milk left in Paris, no fish. There was a black market for vegetables: certain shops employed those desperate enough to climb over the ramparts at night and grub around in the Zone for potatoes or onions, while dodging Prussian bullets. A cabbage cost two days' wages. A chicken – Anne saw one in a window on the Rue de Rivoli – cost twenty francs.

Victor Calmette and Monsieur Papin came back to the house when they finished work. Victor looked, usually, tired and worried. Monsieur Papin smiled when he came in. They ate supper together, for all the world like a peculiar sort of family.

And, every day, when it grew dark, Anne fed the rabbits in the garden. This was her favourite part of the day. She watched the funny little creatures hopping around in the twilight. She scattered grain and added peelings or the outer leaves of cabbages. They thrived. The rabbit babies were so sweet. Of course, they did not live long, although she had nothing to do with that side of it. She tried not to think about why they were there.

22

Like every café in Paris, the Zouave was a shadow of its former self. Instead of staying lit up into the small hours, it closed at ten in the evening, when the gas was shut off. During the day, the interior was dimmer than ever; the lamps were lit only when darkness fell. It was also freezing; one's cup of coffee, one's brandy, pipe or cigar were the only sources of warmth. The bread tasted of sawdust, the coffee was watery and bitter, but there was no shortage of customers. Many men found their jobs had disappeared – employers had fled, businesses shut down to ride out the crisis, and the demand for labour dried up. Most customers wore Guard uniforms – they came in when their shifts had finished, or before, since there was so little to do. It was cheaper to sit in the Zouave over a few glasses of wine than to buy firewood. It was cheaper to drink than to eat.

Lawrence and Ellis kept their voices down. Like everybody else, they were swaddled in coats and scarves. They bought different papers every week; so many had sprung into being since the siege began, this was easier done than not. No one expected hard news or solid facts in these sheets, but there was a great hunger for opinion, gossip, speculation – anything that filled the void. They debated whether any of the stories were true and which was the most far-fetched.

Lawrence said, 'When I was young, we lived so far from anywhere that the news was always days late, and it was never about us.'

Ellis smiled. 'When you were young!'

He liked to tease Lawrence about his youth. Lawrence had not felt so conscious of it, or of his lack of education, among his French friends. Speaking English again, he felt exposed, particularly with Ellis, who had been to a good school and a famous college. He frowned at his paper.

'It says here that they are recruiting ladies for a battalion called the Amazons of the Seine. They're to be armed with hat pins dipped in prussic acid. That can't be true, surely?'

'Prussic acid for the Prussians? Why not? It's no crazier than most of the plans in here.' Today, Ellis was reading *Le Combat*, a reliable fount of virulent scandal.

'What does your uncle say?'

'All we talk about are goats and hens. The great news this week is that his cat murdered one of the best layers. He's given her to me so that she can't commit any more atrocities.'

'Are you allowed to keep a cat in your lodgings?'

'I've no idea. Probably not.' Ellis shrugged with magnificent unconcern. 'I don't suppose I shall be evicted at the moment.'

'Don't cats need milk and so on? How do you feed it?'

'She seems happy to eat whatever I eat.' He made a face at Lawrence. 'She is a victim of the siege. Like the rest of us, she has to make do.'

Michel rarely came to the Zouave anymore, taken up with his guard duties in another part of the city. Their other friends were even further away. Alfred had married Camille and taken her and their child to Brittany. Gustave had spirited himself off to the south-west. As for Yves, Lawrence could only imagine.

He expended much effort in trying not to think about him. He knew there could have been no reply to his last letter. If Yves had written one, it would be languishing in the provinces somewhere. *If* he had written. Last summer belonged to another life. Now, each morning brought a hard frost, and the thought of lying on sun-warmed grass was risible. He still thought of it, but his threadbare longing was tainted with self-reproach. He felt certain that he would not have been rebuffed – and what if he had? His heart would have been wounded, but he would not be suspended in this limbo of not knowing.

Among the rumours was one that Gambetta had won a victory over the Prussians at Orléans. Perhaps the tide had turned. Another said that there was going to be a great push out of Paris in the next few days to join up with troops advancing from the south. Maybe soon, it would be over.

Ellis turned over the final page of newsprint, which was so poorly made it disintegrated in his hands.

'I might start a paper. I could make up any amount of nonsense and people would pay for it. Look at this – someone is talking of releasing the lions and tigers from the menagerie to run amok among the Prussians.'

'I saw that one. I suppose, if you report what someone has suggested, there is no way of being wrong. Or you could start your own literary magazine. Are they still publishing poetry, nowadays?'

'Well, not in here. The *Revue Noire* folded after two issues. The editor is talking of starting up another paper, but his printer has joined the Guard, or he has run out of money. Always some excuse!'

Despite the jocular tone, Ellis didn't meet his eye. A couple of weeks ago, with an uncharacteristic display of diffidence, he had shown Lawrence a couple of his poems. Lawrence read them, but they seemed puzzlingly obscure. He said that he had never studied poetry, so was not qualified to pass judgement, but mouthed something complimentary, which Ellis greeted with a wooden smile. It felt like a test he had failed.

When they had tired of the awful coffee, they walked out into the grey afternoon. Pins of icy drizzle stung their cheeks. The sky looked heavy, without definition.

Buildings appeared uninhabited: there were no lights in the windows, no smoke issued from chimneys. They gravitated towards the river, with its ragged tonsure of trees. The Seine retained its sombre magnificence, but even the swollen current seemed lifeless. There were no boats. Crossing the Pont des Arts, they saw a rind of ice clinging to the banks and the bridge piers. Fishermen sat, grim and motionless, on the banks.

Drawn by lights burning in the Louvre, they went inside – a promise of warmth that was not kept. The museum now opened once a week. Many works of art had been shipped to the provinces for safe keeping, and there were few paintings on show.

'God – I haven't been here for months,' said Lawrence. 'I used to come on Sunday afternoons, and draw.'

The sculpture halls were among the few rooms still open. The only other visitors were two women, sketching. The women wore hats, scarves and fingerless gloves; it was colder inside than out. But there was something soothing about being in the presence of these works. The room held a host of statues, many with missing arms or feet, even heads. But they exerted a mesmerizing spell. These muscles would never waste, this skin would never sag; they were immune to deprivation, as to time. They had endured many wars; they would doubtless endure this.

Through an archway, Lawrence saw one statue he had drawn over and over: a dreadfully damaged Apollo. Despite missing both legs and hands, the marble features suggested radiant calm. The torso was thick and manly, with a faint suggestion of rib arch under its smooth armour of muscle. There was a slight curve to the belly, down to the modest genitals (how did the sculptor make marble look *soft*?), and it bore a wound on the left ribs, a rusty blemish, like dried blood. It was that, and the shallow indentation that led from throat to navel, that made Lawrence feast his eyes on it as if he could never get enough.

He was pulled into its orbit – it was only a beautiful thing, like the Aphrodite to his left. He paused in front of her, until Ellis had definitely taken note. The Apollo stood among a cohort of lesser statues, all beautiful, all serene, their blind eyes wide and dreaming. The Apollo had not been diminished by its damage; it was, if anything, ennobled.

Ellis had not spoken for a while and Lawrence wondered if he were bored – or did he find this masculine beauty distasteful? Was this how Ellis had felt when Lawrence failed to respond appropriately to his poems? He determined to show that – in this field, at least – he was not a philistine.

'I've often thought these ancient statues are all the more perfect for the parts they are missing. When you look at French attempts to replicate classical sculpture, like Julien or Magnier, they are so accurate, so slavishly complete, yet they somehow don't have the same confidence . . .' He looked at Ellis. 'I say, are you all right?'

Ellis didn't answer. His face was contorted, as though from pain.

'Ellis? Are you ill?'

Ellis shook his head and turned away, but not before Lawrence thought he glimpsed tears in his eyes. He was horrified, uncomprehending. Ellis stumbled to the nearest wall and leant against it, gasping.

'What's the matter? Let me help you.'

Ellis shook his head again. 'Asthma,' he managed to say at last, and Lawrence heard the breath whistling in his throat.

'Can I fetch something?' Lawrence tried to think of something useful. 'Water? There's a bench over there; come and sit down.'

Lawrence helped him to the bench, where Ellis sat heavily, bent forward, gripping the seat with both hands.

'Should I look for a doctor?'

Ellis shook his head. 'I – am – doctor,' he panted, and Lawrence saw he was trying to smile. 'Just need a . . . drink.'

Lawrence looked around to see the women staring at them and whispering. After a moment's discussion, they moved away.

'I can't do anything to help?'

Ellis held out his hands, and made Lawrence understand that he was to take them in his.

'Pull.'

Lawrence took the outstretched hands and leant back, until he was exerting a steady pressure. There was no noise but the dreadful, high-pitched wheezing of Ellis's chest. Lawrence had seen asthma attacks before, but not one as severe as this. He tried not to show that he was frightened.

'Is this all right?'

Ellis merely grunted.

Lawrence could only see the crown of his head, with its whorl of blond hair, and the way it grew in three distinct points down the back of his neck. He pulled steadily. His arms started to ache, and Ellis gripped his hands so tightly they hurt. He sucked in air as if through a straw, with great effort.

In a wine shop near the museum, Ellis swallowed three brandies in the time it took Lawrence to finish one. Gradually, his face lost its waxy pallor.

'You look better. How do you feel?'

'All right. I'm sorry you had to . . . Such a damn nuisance.'

'Don't be sorry. It's not your fault. What causes it?'

'I don't know. It chooses the most inconvenient times. It's usually worse in winter.'

'Is there no medicine for it?'

'Only this.' He held up his glass. 'The great cure-all.' He emptied it and gestured for more.

'I could see you home.'

'God, no. I've taken up more than enough of your time. I'll be all right in a while. Perfectly all right.' He turned around and gestured impatiently at the barkeep, then said peevishly, 'Really, I wish you would go. I'll sit here for a bit, then I'll go home. I'm no sort of company.'

It was a dismissal. There was a look in his eyes, a feral glitter, that gave Lawrence pause. This was the man he had first seen at Yves' studio: unpredictable, belligerent, fuelled by a chaotic energy. It was with relief that he left.

Lawrence was annoyed with himself, afraid that in the museum he had appeared gauche, trying to show off. At the same time, he resented Ellis for commandeering so much of his day, even by accident, and having the nerve to be ungrateful about it. He wondered whether he should avoid him in future – it was only the siege that had thrown them together, after all. But, the fact was, Ellis was the only friend he had left. He felt very alone.

In the Place Dauphine, he heard children's voices under the trees. Whispering and giggling. A woman's voice: 'Be quiet and hurry up. How much have you got?'

Lawrence loitered in the shadow of one of the trees. He discerned movement in the twilight, a patch of white that could be a woman's fichu. He heard the crack of a branch, giggling, whispers.

'Someone's watching. Hurry!'

Lawrence walked away. On the embankment, he noted that the odd, lopsided silhouettes of many of the trees was due to their missing branches.

He trudged down the street, hearing only his own footsteps. It was true, what Madame Lamy had said the other day: there were far fewer cabs. So few horses left to pull them. He felt something cool brush against his cheek, the stroke of a tiny feather. Then another, and another. Sparkling cold. He looked up: pale specks whirled towards him, alleviating the darkness. It had begun to snow.

23

The snow cast a welcome veil over the squalor in the menagerie. Things were falling apart; the zoo could no longer afford to pay the staff, and, despite closing the gates to the public, despite changing the locks on gates and cages, some miscreants had broken in and stolen a gazelle. People had the ingenuity of desperation. They were eating cats and dogs, sparrows, rats. Papin bought horsemeat on the black market to feed the big predators. Victor thought this was reasonable. There were thousands of horses in Paris; only one tigress.

He stopped by Marguerite's cage every day, and, now there were no visitors, he talked to her out loud. The tigress would stare into and beyond his eyes with her crystalline gaze, and Victor was filled with the conviction that she understood – not what he said, but somehow the sense of it – that they shared some feeling.

Spared taunts and stares, the rattling of canes on her bars, she seemed peaceful. She paced her cage less often, she roared less. Most of her time was spent reclining on the filthy concrete, her immaculate pelt all the more dazzling by contrast, her front limbs arrayed before her like royal robes. She was the still centre of the zoo, the nucleus of their solar system. Her gaze was as steady and relentless as the sun.

The other cats seemed more affected. Irma was snappish and irritable, Tancred lethargic and occasionally vicious. Nero, more nervous than ever, would work himself into a frenzy – he would spring at the bars of his cage, hurling his entire weight at the iron, then twisting as he dropped to the floor with shocking grace. He tore the air with his rage.

The staff were managing to feed them: there was still horsemeat to be had, at a price, and Papin's rabbits, and there was a network of men in the neighbourhood who sold them the carcasses of stray dogs and were asked no questions.

Victor was relieved that Marguerite was tranquil. She seemed to enjoy watching the falling snow; it was as though it put her into a trance. Equally entranced, he would sit and stare at her until he was frozen stiff.

He was summoned to a meeting with Papin, Director Lapeyre and those members of the board of governors who had not fled the city.

'Gentlemen,' began Lapeyre, 'under the circumstances in which we find ourselves, and, of course, contrary to our wishes, we must concede that it is not possible to maintain the menagerie as we would wish. I am forced to the conclusion that, if we wish to save any of the animals, we will have to sacrifice others. Perhaps Messieurs Papin and Calmette could draw up a list.'

They had been hedging around this subject for some time.

Papin pressed his fingertips together. 'Monsieur Directeur, none of us knows how long the siege is going to last. It could be over in a few days. It would be an unforgivable tragedy to slaughter half our animals, only to find that it had been unnecessary.'

'But this last attempt to break the siege – complete and utter shambles!'

The governor was referring to the events of recent days, when a combined force of National Guard battalions and regular army troops had tried to break the blockade. With the Devil's own timing, the river broke its banks, the troops floundered, and it became apparent from the dazed and wounded men who staggered back into Paris that nothing had been gained. There was no army from the south waiting to relieve them. The Prussians, entrenched in their positions, repulsed the French attack and punished them cruelly. The makeshift hospitals – the theatres and churches of former days – were finally full.

Papin said, 'Nonetheless—'

The other governor, an ancient *comte* Victor had never seen before, made a guttural noise that indicated disagreement. 'We cannot know – precisely! You say it may be over tomorrow. I reply it may last until Christmas, or beyond! Paris is running out of food. Even the estimable Monsieur Papin cannot provide horsemeat when there are no horses. I have only one horse left for my gig. I have had to forgo my carriage altogether. We must all make sacrifices.'

'And how is your table, Monsieur le Comte?'

'What?'

'Are you forgoing meat? Are you dining off rats?'

The director raised his hand. 'Monsieur Papin is upset. He will withdraw that last remark.'

'I will not.'

'It is insulting to equate the Comte de Bicêtre with the beasts in the zoo!'

'There is food, as we all know. As long as we have money, there is no need for the animals to starve.'

The director hit the table with the flat of his hand. 'We cannot afford to pay black-market prices for the quantities that we need, leaving aside the question of whether that would be the right thing to do. When there is so much hardship among the people, how would it look? The herbivores will starve before long, anyway. This is the only solution that is both sensible and humane. I expect your cooperation.'

'By choosing which animals to sacrifice?'

'I do you the courtesy of asking. If not, I'm sure Monsieur Calmette will oblige.'

Papin did not speak again until the meeting was over. Then he scribbled a few words on a piece of paper and pushed it into Victor's hand. 'See to it,' he said.

Victor unfolded the paper. The hierarchy was as apparent as it was inevitable. The stars of the menagerie were to be saved. The list of the doomed was made up of small, dull creatures: the lemmings and agoutis; the meerkats; then, the more common antelopes. There were no visitors to see they were no longer there.

That evening, Victor took Anne to one side. He had been turning over the words all day.

'From now on, the zoo is completely closed. I'm afraid you cannot walk through it any longer.'

'Why?'

Since the gates were shut to the public, Anne had continued to pass freely through the menagerie. He knew that she visited Marguerite. He dreaded telling her the reason, but could see no way to avoid it.

'There is not enough fodder. The rabbits can't breed fast enough. We can no longer buy meat. There is little enough food for people . . .' He paused, waiting for her to agree, but she didn't move so much as an eyelid. 'And so . . . we have to make choices.'

She stared a fraction past his face. He watched. Anne was an intelligent girl; she must have been aware of the situation.

'Which?'

'We will save Marguerite, of course, and the other cats. The bears and wolves . . . and so on.'

'What about the elephants, and the giraffe?'

He didn't want to go into that. 'We have enough dry fodder, for the time being.'

'And sacrifice?'

He told her. Her face had its mask-like appearance: a graven sandstone image, obsidian eyes.

'You understand that we have to do this, don't you? We have no choice.'

*

By and large, Anne's appointment as Papin's housekeeper had been a success. Papin liked her; eccentric himself, he did not mind eccentricities in others, as long as they did not impinge on his comfort. The feeling that he had helped Anne gratified Victor. But, each night, after dinner, he walked home alone. He climbed the stairs to his freezing rooms in the Rue Poliveau, to spend the evening in silence and solitude.

He thought of Anne when he lay in his bed. He had not done this before. He had appreciated her striking looks from the first, but it was impossible to think of Anne as just another pretty girl. He liked her way of talking and her way of seeing things, which was unlike that of any woman he had met. She wasn't a flirt, or a shrew, or a drudge, and, despite the hardships of her life, she had a strange dignity. She carried herself as if she had temporarily left off her crown.

It should have been easy. Before the siege, when they had met on her days off, there had been a sense of intimacy. He thought they understood each other, that she looked forward to seeing him. Now, he saw her every day, but had not come to know her better. She no longer smiled at the sight of him. Could it be that she took him for granted? Had he been a fool to help her?

A few days after the sacrifices began, he waylaid Anne outside the dining room.

'Oh, Anne, I thought you might like to visit Marguerite? I could take you in at lunchtime tomorrow, if you liked.'

Anne stopped; almost, but not quite, raising her eyes to his.

He added, 'I know you must miss her.'

The next day, he waited for her at the gate. He saw her take in the empty enclosures, the unnatural quiet. At the pavilion, Anne stood in front of the tigress's cage. Marguerite crouched, tearing into a lump of meat on which scraps of brown fur were visible.

The tigress glanced up from her meal and paused, looking straight at Anne. Victor held his breath. It seemed to him that his thoughts travelled to the tigress, and through her, to the woman next to him.

'She recognizes you,' said Victor, whose heart was pounding. 'Do you see?'

Anne held the railings, just looking.

'She looks well, doesn't she?' said Victor.

Anne nodded.

'I won't let anything happen to her,' he said. 'You know that, don't you?'

Anne nodded again.

'And you know that – well, you know I think of you as a friend.'

There was a slight but perceptible stiffening in her body.

'And I hope that you have come to think of me in the same way.'

There was a silence and Victor felt as though all the air was being sucked out of him.

Then she licked her lips and said, 'Yes.'

'It's just that, recently—'

'Monsieur!'

Incredibly, infuriatingly, Robitaille was hurrying down the path towards them.

'Monsieur! There you are. It's the director . . .' He looked at Anne doubtfully. 'Hello, mademoiselle.'

Anne nodded to him.

'Excuse me, but he wants to see you right away.'

Victor stared miserably at the tigress. 'Yes, of course. Well, I will just see Mademoiselle Petitjean out. Then I'll come.' He nodded to Robitaille in such a way as to indicate that he wished he would disappear.

Robitaille looked shyly at Anne. 'She's looking well, isn't she, mademoiselle?'

'Yes.'

'We won't let anything happen to her. As long as there is breath in my body.'

*

That night, Victor made an excuse to Papin and went for a walk. He couldn't face Anne. Underfoot, the snow had hardened to a glassy crust and, at every step, he felt cold strike through the soles of his boots. The Seine had frozen and snow lay on the surface. He made out figures crawling on the ice. The skin of his face felt stiff.

He found himself in the old streets of the Temple. The few shops that were still open cast the only light. Now, you heard passers-by before you saw them – hacking coughs and stumbling footsteps announced a presence. He kept walking blindly. At last, he sat down in a small café and ordered a bowl of stew. These days, one didn't ask for details. It tasted disgusting, but it was hot, and there was plenty of wine.

After he'd eaten, he walked again, trying to outpace his sense of having failed. If he were a different man – if he had been more forceful – could he have bent Anne's will to his own? Was she worth it? Wasn't she, in the end, too strange, too difficult? Not her fault, but not his either . . .

When he was young, his father had counselled him: 'When you're on the horns of a dilemma, think of the most admirable person you can, and ask yourself, what would he do? There will be your guide.' As advice, it was singularly unhelpful. He couldn't think of any man who was entirely admirable; different people were admirable in different ways, but they all had faults. And besides, he didn't know what any of those individuals would do in his predicament – all cases were unique, but Anne was the most unique of all.

He tripped over something and nearly fell. Recovering, he put out a hand and met part of a human being. He had been too absorbed to notice that someone had fallen into step beside him.

'How cold it is, isn't it?' said a girl's voice. Victor discerned a figure with her arms wrapped around herself against the cold. In the dark, he couldn't tell her age, but the voice was young.

'Looking for company, monsieur?'

'I haven't got much.'

'I'll do it for a loaf of bread.'

Victor stopped outside a lit window and turned so that the light fell on his companion. He saw a pale little face, the eyes wedges of darkness. Quite pretty, perhaps in her late teens. Although shabby, there was something respectable about her.

'I don't have bread, but I have . . .' He fumbled in his pocket. Impossible to ignore his arousal, it had been so long. 'Twenty sous.'

In the dim light, the face underwent an extraordinary convulsion, an eruption of naked greed. She could not have expected so much. He almost recoiled.

'I know a place nearby.'

'How do I know someone is not waiting there to rob me?'

A panicked look washed over the pinched face. 'I wouldn't do that! I wouldn't share it! I swear!'

Even if he had not believed her, he would have gone with her anyway. She appealed strongly to him and he could tell she was not a whore – not in the normal run of things. A decent girl, a seamstress, probably, or a laundress.

'What's your name, little one?'

She hesitated before saying, 'Paquerette.'

She took his hand in an icy paw and led him around a corner. A quiet, narrow street; a thin strip of greyish sky above, even less light. Through a black opening, they passed into a small court surrounded by high walls. Victor quailed at the thought of open sky above, snow on the ground. He regretted not insisting on a room, not looking for someone else, not bargaining harder – but the girl pulled him to her, and he knew he would go through with it.

She hoisted her skirts and, after some blind probing, he found his way into her dry, meagre body. She moaned, her breath warm and sour against his neck. As he thrust, her head knocked against the wall and bumped his collarbone, the cold invaded his clothing and snapped at his flanks. He tried to fix the image of Anne's face on his closed eyelids, but she eluded him. The girl gasped again: a pretty noise he found exciting. The thing was soon done.

He let go of her arms and the girl withdrew into the darkness. He could feel her impatience as he fumbled for the money, but he felt a rush of gratitude towards her, even tenderness.

'There's a café near here – they serve stew and bread for fifteen sous. It's not bad.'

He wanted her to think well of him. She might even hope that he would come and find her again . . .

The coins were gone from his hand. Before he had finished straightening his clothing, he was alone in the yard.

24

Over Sunday lunch, Charles Ranvier opined that the government would soon surrender to the Prussians. Everyone knew that food stocks were running low, and, short of an unprecedented victory by French troops from outside Paris, there was no other possible outcome. Surrender might take a few weeks, but it would come. He smiled at the Lamys, who were sitting around his table enjoying a joint of roast pork.

His young son, who never looked Ernestine in the eye, frowned and dug his fork into the tablecloth.

Charles laughed. 'Théophile is distressed by my lack of belligerence. But, as I keep telling him, one should not equate patriotism with blind, unrealistic optimism. We will have to take what comes. And, never fear, I have made provision for all outcomes.'

Ernestine's parents nodded sagely, but no one asked what he meant. She looked at her fiancé sitting at the head of his table and wondered what it would be like to be married to him. Would he expect her to sleep in the same bed, as her parents did, even though they had plenty of rooms in their house? She found it impossible to imagine being intimate with him. She *had* imagined intimacy with Edouard, had craved it . . . Perhaps that would come, as her mother implied. She hardly knew the man opposite her. She had allowed herself to be courted because, in her situation, what else was she going to do?

When he proposed, she had accepted him with little hesitation.

Guessing what was coming, she had already marshalled the arguments with brutal clarity. What was the likelihood of meeting a man more to her taste, yet also in a position (and of the inclination) to propose to her? Unknown, but, judged on the last few years, slim. Could Charles Ranvier afford to keep her in style? Certainly. Could she influence him? She thought so. And the clinching argument: would living with him be more or less bearable than continuing to live – a failed, aging spinster – with her parents?

Her refusing him was no more likely than a French victory over the Prussians. Ernestine too was a pragmatist; she did not equate marriage with blind, unrealistic romance.

It still took her a conscious effort to address him as 'Charles'. She diligently reminded herself of his better points: he ran a successful business, he was clever at seeing opportunities, he had quite good taste (which she would improve). He'd confided to her that he harboured ambitions of public office, which did not displease her. And, although she acknowledged that it was shallow, she liked that he showered her with gifts. The value of his affection was an impressive sum that she could display to anyone who cared to ask.

On the other hand, sometimes his deferential manners drove her to extremes of irritation. When he turned to her and asked her whether she would like to walk in the Tuileries or in the Luxembourg, she had to bite back the urge to snap, *You decide; you're the man, for heaven's sake.* It was at times like this that thoughts of Edouard Duchamp welled up in her mind, the beautiful surface covering banal mediocrity. It was cruel that he still haunted her, but she allowed herself the luxury of thinking of him, painful though it was. He was hateful and deserved to be hated. Charles Ranvier, at least by comparison, deserved to be loved. Since when did that have anything to do with it?

A couple of weeks ago, he took her on a mystery outing that ended at a jeweller's in the Rue de la Paix. He wanted to commission a necklace.

Ernestine had no objection to that; it was what a good fiancé did – not just talk of devotion, but demonstrate it in hard currency. But, there in the shop, under the nose of the beady-eyed assistant, Charles seized her hand and almost shouted, 'My dear girl, it was not so long ago that I thought my life was over. I could see no prospect of happiness, other than that of watching my son grow up to be a man. But, for myself, I saw nothing. And then I met you, and you allowed me to love you. Your love is a miracle.'

Ernestine's eyes darted to the assistant. True, he was busy putting trays of diamonds back into locked drawers behind the counter, but surely he was listening? She blushed – not with emotion, but with embarrassment.

She knew her fiancé was a jumped-up shopkeeper, just as she knew that she was an aging spinster with a beaky face. It was just that the overwhelming emotion she discerned in her lover was not adoration, but relief. He put on a good show, but that was what it was – a show. There, in the shop, she swayed, momentarily dizzy, and was provided with a chair. She assured Charles it was just a passing faintness. She did not say she had experienced a sudden vertigo at the course she had embarked on: it terrified her that this was what she had settled for, but she had. There was no turning back.

In the carriage on the way home – by this time, horses to pull them were rare, so she did appreciate it – she looked down at his hand, holding her hand in its lace glove, on the seat between them. He cherished her, treated her like a princess . . .

She had the odd sense that she was looking at herself from else-where and, as the wheels jolted over a hole in the cobbles and the carriage springs yelped, she dug her nails into his palm, and said, 'Oh!'

'Ahh!' His hand tensed under her nails, but he did not let go. 'Are you all right, my dear?'

'Oh, yes. Just thrown off balance.'

He patted her hand. 'Really, the roads get worse and worse.' He shouted to the driver to be more careful. 'You've given me quite a jab!'

'Oh, did I?'

He opened his hand and held it out – a row of red marks showed where her nails had bitten into the skin.

She looked at him with innocent eyes. 'I'm so sorry, dear.'

She lifted his hand to kiss the palm with a brush of her closed lips. She had no idea what had prompted her to do such a thing, but she felt a small, keen jolt of pleasure.

25

The Boucherie Ranvier took up half a block behind the Hôtel de Ville. Warm light spilled on to the pavement, and it was common for a crowd to gather outside the window, goggling through the condensation, their breath forming a pall in the icy air. The shop was famous for the artistic deployment of its wares. Joints, cutlets, ribs garnished with paper frill; galantines, tarts and sausages nestled on blue paper; all arranged in the form of, say, a spray of flowers, a swirl of arabesques, a geometric pattern. The previous Christmas, the window dressers had outdone themselves with a stunning tableau: there had been a landscape of liver and steak, a stable of *boudin blanc*, a manger of kidneys, a ballotine ass. The Holy Family were shaped from terrines and presiding over all was a star-shaped pie. This year's display was more modest, but the business did not seem to be suffering. The shop was crowded with prosperous customers, while the less well off made do with the view from the street.

Lawrence was curious to see the business belonging to Ernestine's fiancé. As he stepped inside, he looked at the price list on the wall behind the counter and quailed. If you had money, there was no privation: here was beef, in a dozen different forms; here were pâtés, pies and such a mouth-watering array of charcuterie that he felt dizzy. A chicken cost thirty francs, and, in the centre of the display, a turkey – a pimply, mauve monster – was on offer for a hundred. A hundred francs!

Lawrence had lived on a restricted diet for weeks. He was

overwhelmed with such hunger that, though he tried to focus on the price list, he couldn't think straight: there were words he could not make sense of. What did *Cuissot de Loup* mean, in this context? And *Perroquets,* for heaven's sake?

A snowy-whiskered gentleman was taking his turn at the counter.

'Come, thirty francs for half a kilo of camel's hump? It had better be good, at that price!'

'It's very good, monsieur. Our chef recommends roasting or braising it in red wine. It is very tender, very juicy.' The man behind the counter bunched his fingers and kissed them.

'Hm.' The man appeared to reflect. 'And the haunch of antelope?'

'Very tasty, but a little tougher. It benefits from slow cooking. That is reflected in the price, as you see.'

So it was true. *Cuissot de loup* was a haunch of wolf. *Perroquets* were parrots. *Chameau* was camel. Last summer, Lawrence had spent over an hour photographing the camels at the Jardin des Plantes. There was a pair: Cleopatra and César, brought from Egypt only a year before. They were dopey, mischievous creatures, who made him laugh. Cleopatra was the better subject – her white coat contrasted strikingly with enormous dark eyelashes. She was inquisitive, snaking her long neck over the fence, mumbling at his face and the camera with agile lips, glancing at them from heavy-lidded eyes . . . A parcel of meat was handed over the counter. Was that a piece of Cleopatra? His stomach rumbled.

Culling the animals made sense: meat was terribly scarce, people were starving – but not these people! For forty francs a kilo, he could buy antelope haunch (noble blackbuck, or one of the absurdly pretty gazelles?). He could afford one mouthful of camel, or two mouthfuls of ostrich. Parrots were fifteen francs apiece. There was kangaroo. Then, the more expected creatures: cat and dog (specifically, loin of spaniel), both a relative bargain at twelve francs a kilo. Sparrows were three francs apiece, whereas stuffed larks were six . . .

'What's your pleasure, monsieur?' The assistant behind the counter was as pink and plump as his wares.

'Good evening, monsieur,' said Lawrence. He had less than seven francs in his pocket. 'Where does the camel come from?'

The man looked startled. 'From the menagerie, of course.'

'Of course. Is it, er, any good?'

'It's delicious. Our chef recommends roasting it or braising in red wine. It's probably the best of the unusual meats here. Well, either that or the kangaroo, but there's hardly any of that left. It's been really popular. I could do a kilo of kangaroo steak for twenty-five francs.'

'And the wolf?'

The butcher shrugged. 'To be honest, I haven't tried it myself. But I'm told that, if you've had dog, it's not far off.'

'I see. You haven't got any of the big cats?'

'No. Between you and me, I don't think there would be much demand. But you never know . . . Drop in again next week – who knows what we'll have by then?' He leant forward confidingly. 'There's talk of buying an elephant in time for Christmas.'

'Right.' He looked despairingly at the display. 'I'll take two hundred grams of the pâté – that one there.'

The butcher turned the label on the cheapest slab of pâté. 'This one? It's horse, flavoured with juniper and rosemary.'

'Yes, thank you. No, that's all.'

The Siamese had made herself at home. If Circe thought she was slumming it, it didn't seem to perturb her. She spent her days curled up on Ellis's bed, or sitting on the windowsill, staring down at the humans in the street. When Lawrence arrived, she padded up to him, sniffed at him delicately, then turned her back.

'It's all right, you pass the test,' said Ellis, laughing.

Ellis was recovered from his dark mood of their last meeting. His answer to Lawrence's note enquiring after his health had been penitent and friendly. He begged Lawrence to visit; he was unable to come to the Zouave for the foreseeable future. He would explain all when they met.

'I'm sorry you were concerned. I've been so busy, I didn't even think of it, to be honest. I should have written to say thank you for looking after me that day. I'm a bear when I get that way. It makes me mad to be so helpless – but I shouldn't have taken it out on you.'

Lawrence shook his head, meaning the apology was unnecessary. Ellis looked tired. He still gave the impression of being too large for such a small room, but some of the brash, assertive sheen was dulled. Lawrence liked him the more for it.

Ellis poured two glasses of wine and handed one to Lawrence. Bottles, empty and full, stood in ranks in the corner.

'What's been keeping you so busy?'

'Ah. Yes.' Ellis smiled and looked down. 'I've been coerced into going back to proper work. I'd forgotten how exhausting it is.' He made a comical grimace.

Lawrence duly laughed. 'When you say "work", what—?'

'I'm working as a surgeon. In an American hospital. My uncle was involved in setting up an ambulance station on the Champs Élysées, and I couldn't really refuse to help. What with so many wounded after the last *sortie*.'

'It's wonderful that you're doing that. Admirable.'

Ellis shook his head. 'I didn't have much choice. The whole thing's a mess. We've got two hundred wounded, and we turn away more all the time. The poor devils end up in some makeshift hotel or in a private house, and that's as good as leaving them out to rot.'

Lawrence took a swallow of wine. 'There seem to be hospitals all over the place. Half the churches near us have been taken over. Madame Lamy is helping in one.'

'Is she? Good for her. And Mademoiselle Lamy too?'

'Oh. No.' Lawrence was amused by the idea. 'She's too busy planning her wedding.'

He watched as Ellis emptied his glass and took out a cigar. He found it impossible to imagine him with a scalpel in his hand. Saving a life. It was too great a shift.

Lawrence handed over the pâté and told Ellis about the Boucherie Ranvier. The Siamese jumped off the windowsill, came to Lawrence and rubbed herself against his shins.

'Such a tart. She smells the pâté.'

Lawrence scratched the sand-coloured head. 'You leave her here all day?'

'Yes. She's very civilized. More than some friends I've known.' He unwrapped the pâté and inhaled its scent with a groan. 'You'd better hold this, otherwise she'll have it. I have something to add to your offering.' He knelt on the floor, reached under the bed and took out a box. Inside, wrapped in newspaper, were half a dozen eggs.

'My God. Where did you get them?'

'My uncle's hens. They're supposed to be for the refugees at the embassy, but I thought I deserved them. They're not working as surgeons – although one of them is a professor of rhetoric.'

Lawrence laughed. He hadn't eaten an egg for weeks.

'I can make an omelette. It's my only culinary skill.'

'Oh, God, yes.'

Ellis poked the small fire into life and broke the eggs into a pan. Lawrence's mouth watered fiercely – he would have happily swallowed them raw. They ate the omelette and pâté with sawdust-flavoured bread, and washed it down with quantities of claret. The makeshift meal tasted divine.

Circe wove patterns around their legs, uttering urgent yowls. Ellis gave her the last little piece of his pâté and she jumped on to his lap. He was lying on the bed, propped on some pillows, while Lawrence had the armchair by the fire.

Leaning back with a satisfied sigh, Lawrence said, 'I dream about nothing but food now.'

'So do I.'

'Can you imagine, a chicken costs thirty francs? And people are gathering round the window to stare at meat they can't afford. They seemed happy just to look at it.'

'I can't tell you how tempted I've been to steal one of my uncle's chickens. The only one they've eaten is the one Circe killed. Such a waste; it couldn't possibly feed forty people.'

'That's how many refugees he has?'

'That's just at the residence. There are more at the embassy. And dozens he's had to turn away. Circe is my refugee.' He picked up the cat and pressed his face to her furry body. 'Yes, you are, gorgeous. The residence has a big garden and orchard, where the chickens and goats are kept. They have to mount guards every night to stop people breaking in and stealing everything.'

'I suppose it's no more peculiar to eat a camel than a sheep. But I felt like I knew the camel. It made my gorge rise.'

'I'd eat a camel in a moment,' said Ellis, stroking the cat, which had settled itself in the valley between his thighs.

'If you have a spare thirty francs, you can, but you'll have to hurry. And you've seen the elephants, haven't you? The butcher said they might be buying one for Christmas. The thought of eating one of them . . .' He shook his head. 'I mean, people *love* those elephants. You'd think that would count for something.'

Ellis shrugged, but gently, so as not to disturb the cat. 'I suppose people are starving.'

'The starving are not buying meat at Ranvier's.'

'Lawrence! I didn't know you were a Red.'

'I'm not a Red. But—'

'I'm joking.'

Ellis was right: there was no point getting worked up about a place like Ranvier's. This was still Paris.

'I wanted to see it because Mademoiselle Lamy is engaged to the owner. He must be making a fortune. But one of the elephants! It would be like . . . like eating le Rouquin, or someone like that!'

Ellis laughed. Le Rouquin was a much-loved comic actor – so famous that his mere entrance on stage brought a storm of applause.

'I know what you mean. Elephants do seem to have characters. They look as though they are smiling. But they're not really smiling. Are they, sweetheart?' Ellis looked down at the cat, from which emanated whirrings of pleasure.

Lawrence found his gaze fixed on her, and on Ellis's hands, rhythmically stroking the sleek body. The Siamese stretched out her front paws and gave Lawrence a look of triumph. He swallowed the lump that had come to his throat and looked away. He cast about for something to fill the silence.

'I wonder where Yves is now.'

What had made him say that?

'Yves? Mm. I wonder. The worst thing about this work is wondering, What if someone I know comes in? Not that I know many people – but Michel, say.'

'I wish I were able to do something as important.' Lawrence was dismayed to hear his voice sound so pompous. His tongue felt awkward in his mouth. He had been at ease with the previous Ellis, the rambunctious Yankee that, if he was honest, he had slightly looked down on. Ellis the surgeon made him feel feckless, young, useless.

Ellis said, 'I'm sure Yves is fine. Well – I expect he's cold, hungry and bored, like the rest of us.'

Lawrence wanted to agree, but couldn't. He is only saying it to be kind to me, he thought. Why would he say that, unless . . . God, I have not thought about Yves for—

The fire popped. Lawrence finished the wine in his glass. Ellis's glass was also empty and he made to rise, but Lawrence stopped him.

'Don't move. Circe looks so comfortable.'

Lawrence poured wine into Ellis's glass and refilled his own, added the empty bottle to the others on the floor and stood by the window, peering out through the curtains. Snow was falling again.

How suddenly things shift: a shudder deep below the surface, and the landscape is irrevocably changed. He tried to conjure his well-worn images of Yves, but they refused to coalesce – there was only a formless sense of him, ethereal and out of reach. The opposite of Ellis in every way. Ellis drank too much, talked too loudly in his atrocious accent, played the piano badly. Lawrence had never thought him handsome, or only in a crudely athletic way. Not his type, at all.

But, when he looked at the man on the bed, he noted the length of his legs, the large, well-formed hands, the glinting blond hair, the rather fleshy features, now contorted into a yawn; the way the Siamese cat nestled her head, teasingly, into his groin.

It would not do, Lawrence told himself. It really would *not*, yet he couldn't help but look at the cat and know, with a plummeting feeling, that he would give a year of his life to be in her place, under those hands.

26

For reasons that were obscure, the Lamys' maid left before Christmas. She gave no notice, but one morning there was no warm water for washing. Shivering, Lawrence splashed his face in the near frozen contents of the jug that had stood overnight, and went downstairs to find the Lamys in a state of disarray. Ernestine was combing her wardrobe for missing items. They had searched the kitchen, the drawing room, the dining room, even the shop, but nothing seemed to be missing. Louise was more upset than angry.

'What if something has happened to her?' She said this over the breakfast that the cook eventually brought up with much grumbling. 'Perhaps she met with an accident.'

Serge shook his head and signed. Ernestine said crisply, 'If she'd had an accident, she would hardly have packed her things. And why should something have happened? She probably found a new post. Monsieur Ranvier says that lots of people are looking for staff at the moment.'

'But Lisette has been with us for years! She was like one of the family. To creep off like that, like a thief, not saying anything. I don't mean to say that she is a thief—'

'Maybe we just haven't noticed what she's taken. Cook said her husband is in the Guard. Perhaps she has gone to be a *cantinière*. Maybe she's one of those women who follow the troops into battle with a barrel of brandy.'

'Titine, don't be ridiculous.'

*

Lisette's desertion came on top of everything else, and Louise felt she was coming to the end of her tether. This morning, she struggled to hold back the tears. Since the disastrous attempt to break the blockade at the beginning of December, there had been wounded soldiers in the streets, men with red crosses on their arms, uniforms embellished with bloodied bandages. The sounds of suffering leaked out from the private hospitals that had sprung up on every block. Sometimes these were houses whose master or mistress had decided to take in a couple of lightly wounded, almost as a hobby. Louise was volunteering in their church as a nurse's aide, and she had seen things she would never forget. The Grand Hotel at Opéra, previously famed for its opulence, was now notorious for another reason: for a hundred metres around this largest of emergency hospitals, the smell of death turned the stomach.

Everyone was short-tempered and gloomy, depressed at the prospect of Christmas under such privation. They'd thought the siege would be over long before now, but the year was about to turn and things looked worse than ever. All the water in Paris was frozen: puddles, fountains, even the Seine. The streets were grey with soiled snow. No one talked of anything but how cold and hungry they were. And, everywhere there were people, there was the staccato dirge of coughing. Telltale spots of blood in the snow. People were dying of pneumonia. Louise read about outbreaks of smallpox and cholera that had caused hundreds of deaths. It was so sad. Mostly in the poor districts and no one you actually knew, but still.

This morning, the papers were full of rumours of another *grande sortie*, which was going to smash through the Prussian lines at an undisclosed location, or to the north, or to the east, depending which paper you read. But also, the government was going to instigate bread rationing. At the Comédie Française, an actress had received, instead of flowers, a lump of cheese, and had wept with joy.

Louise worried about Lawrence Harper. She noticed that, of late, he seemed sad, and it pained her that he did not seem minded to confide in her. She had thought and hoped, at first, that she was like a mother to him. But slowly it crept up on her, this acknowledgement of the tenderness she felt for him. She knew she should be ashamed – it was a joke everyone knew: the ugly old woman, the handsome young man. The worst sort of crude, offensive joke. But she didn't want to stop looking at him – at his hair, his hands, his skin. – and, when she did, she couldn't help wondering what caused his sorrow. She could have asked, but she didn't, because she was afraid of what he might say.

After Lisette walked out, and to smooth things over with Cook, Lawrence volunteered to queue for the bread. Getting dressed in the middle of the night and walking out into the freezing dark was a shock. He thought, If Lisette had to do this every morning, no wonder she left.

He was the only man in the queue, and kept his eyes on the ground, but, even so, he became aware that the woman in front of him was both unusual and familiar. Her appearance was so striking, he couldn't be mistaken. It was the woman he had seen, months ago, at the zoo: the girl whom Ernestine had appraised, before concluding, 'Striking, but the wrong type.' Lawrence had looked around, curious, and caught a flash of large eyes and dark hair. For that second, she had looked daggers at him, but in that look was an imperious grace. He could imagine her as Joan in armour, a warrior saint, but, when he suggested it, Ernestine had said, 'A Creole Saint Joan? Ha! And, believe me, men don't want to look at angry women.'

Lawrence allowed his thoughts to follow a familiar path back to the night in Ellis's room. He gave himself licence to think, What if he had put down his glass and crossed to the bed? His eyes would meet Ellis's with that pure jolt of recognition: the look that says, *I see you.* So addictive, it was worth any risk. He would take Ellis in his arms.

He allowed himself to imagine the scrape of golden stubble against his lips, the heat of his mouth and the feel of that athlete's body, bigger and heavier than his; the weight and muscle of him.

His heart jerked and his blood responded. It warmed him to think of it; no harm in thinking. He thought, I will get over this. He had made a promise to Yves. Unspoken, but a promise nonetheless. This unruly passion was an aberration, like the bread made of beans and dust: an artefact of siege. All he had to do was endure until the longing and tenderness died. He could do that; he'd done it before.

'You're a long way from home, aren't you?'

The voice was insinuating. Lawrence looked around, terrified that his thoughts had been discerned. The speaker was a guardsman – one of a pair patrolling the bread queue – but he was looking at the girl next to Lawrence.

'You're dark and lovely. You must find it a bit cold here. What's your name? Eh? What's the matter? Cat got your tongue?'

Only a slight stiffness in her bearing betrayed that she had heard anything.

'Too good to talk to me, are you? Don't you speak French, my girl? Hello! Do – you – speak – French?' He leant towards her, his tone becoming louder and more derisive.

The girl stared fixedly away from him.

'Monsieur, can't you see she doesn't want to talk to you?'

The guard wheeled to face Lawrence, then reacted with pantomimed surprise. 'Oh, excuse me, *madame*! I don't think I was addressing you. But what's this? A man? Or is it? I can't really tell.'

Lawrence felt himself grow cool and hard as a blade; did the moron think *that* would hurt him?

The guardsman turned to the queue, inviting laughter. He was a tall, heavy man – a bully, used to getting his own way. He veered back to Lawrence. 'What are you, her . . . husband?' The pause was deliberately insulting.

'No. But you should respect her wishes. Why don't you leave her alone?'

'And you know her wishes, do you? It seems to me it's nothing to you if I talk to someone. I'm here doing my job. You're a foreigner, aren't you?'

Lawrence cursed inwardly.

'Maybe you're both foreigners? Two foreigners, queuing up for our bread!'

There was a swelling murmur of discontent from those near enough to hear.

'I'm not a foreigner.' The girl spoke without looking at anyone. 'I have a right to be here. And so does he. He's a photographer. He works right there.' With a jerk of her head, she indicated the frontage of the Studio Lamy.

'A photographer? Oh ho! And how does a girl like you know a photographer, I wonder?'

The crowd responded with titters.

'I think we can guess, huh?'

'That's not so,' said Lawrence.

'Oh? It's not so? Not *so*?' The guardsman looked him up and down and made a rude noise with his lips. But perhaps the respectability of the shopfront disconcerted him, or he reached the conclusion that there was no more sport to be had here. He went back to join his colleague. The queue was distracted by a light inside the shop. They remembered why they were here.

'Thank you, mademoiselle,' said Lawrence, in a low voice, as the queue began to move. 'How did you know I work there?'

She was silent for a moment. 'I saw your photographs of the zoo animals. I work for the chief veterinarian.'

'You were there, that day, weren't you? Last summer. By the lions' cage. I never quite managed to photograph the black panther – not well, anyway.'

She made a brief, affirmative movement.

'It's sad, what's happened there. About the animals, I mean. Monsieur Calmette seemed very fond of them.'

She looked away. 'But it's necessary, if any are to survive.'

'I suppose so.' But Lawrence was puzzled. 'I'm sorry, I don't quite understand. How does that help any of the animals survive?'

'Some must die to feed the others.'

'Oh, you mean, for the money?'

'The money?' She shook her head impatiently. They were shuffling forwards. 'What money?'

'Well, I don't know – but I meant the animals they are selling to the butcher's on Rue de Rivoli – I suppose it's for money to buy fodder?'

She stopped so suddenly, he bumped into her. She barely seemed to notice.

'Why do you say that?'

'There's a butcher's on Rue de Rivoli that is selling meat from the zoo animals. I was there the other day. Boucherie Ranvier. Have I said something out of place?'

Anne forgot how cold her feet were. She forgot how angry she had been at the guardsman. She even forgot about the man next to her. She moved forward, bought her loaves and walked away from the bakery without looking back.

She walked to the Jardin des Plantes as fast as she could. In her shock, she wondered if his story was really true, because how could such a horrible thing be true? But why would he make it up? Anne was familiar with Ranvier's shop; it was one of a number of places she had visited to buy delicacies for Monsieur Papin, but, it was true, she hadn't been sent there for some time.

She dropped the bread on the kitchen table and picked up the jug of hot water Lucie had put out for Monsieur Papin. She climbed the stairs and walked along the corridor to his dressing room. She stood, holding the jug. Steam rose from its mouth. She heard Papin coughing through the adjoining door. She saw herself walking through the door and dashing the scalding water in his face. She pictured his shock and pain. But what if sacrificing the animals was not his decision? There were others behind him – the zoo director, the governors – shadowy men Anne had never seen, but had heard talk of, whose word was law.

When she went shopping, she decided to see for herself, and craned through the window to read Ranvier's price list. There it was: cuts of bears and wolves. There was elephant's trunk. There was giraffe's neck – Pépin's neck; gentle Pépin, with his beautiful, mild eyes. Anne trembled with horror. Her mouth filled with bile and her sight blurred with tears, but she persevered to the end of the list: dogs, birds, rats . . . No panther there, no lion, no tigress. No Marguerite. Thank God, there was no Marguerite.

She watched through the glass as smart customers at the counter smiled, their mouths opening and shutting, grabbing their parcels of flesh with greedy, murdering hands. People pushed past her as they went in or came out and she didn't even notice. Didn't they care that they were eating Clovis and Pollux and Pépin? They did not.

She had hoped the young foreigner was somehow mistaken, but now she knew. These people were not eating the animals out of desperation. They were plump and well fed. She watched one woman leave the shop with her purchases; she looked like a cook. No, perhaps not her choice. It occurred to Anne that she should speak about this – but what would she say? And to whom?

On her way home, she passed a church doorway where sat an old woman, dressed in black, so hunchbacked that her head seemed to grow out of her chest. She held one hand outstretched to passers-by, invoking Saint Anne to bless her with alms: she was hungry; she was blind; she had no family, nowhere to sleep . . . The plaintive whine went on and on, but the saint (who could, presumably, have showered the beggar with gold if she felt like it) did not appear to be listening. Not even humans merited alleviation of their sorrows, so why should beasts be treated any better?

Anne knew about suffering. She knew about cruelty. But she had believed the zoo was a place of sanctuary – for the animals and also for her.

Saint Francis, Saint Francis – how could you let this happen?

No answer came. Anne was not surprised. She didn't believe in saints anyway.

27

Ellis exhaled for a count of five. He shrank his consciousness to his right hand, the almost hairless piece of flesh, the tip of the catlin. It was a simple procedure: a lower-limb amputation, something he had done countless times in his previous life and three times in the past week. There were red streaks creeping up from the mangled foot, so he felt with the inside of his wrist for where the feverish heat stopped, for healthy flesh. A clean, firm incision; the blood welled. By now, he had stopped looking around for Swan's nod of approval.

The nurse swabbed away the blood and Ellis went on cutting. He tied off the major blood vessels, cut down to the bone. He pulled back the skin and muscle like a sleeve, screwed on the retractor and scraped the periosteum from the bone. He weighed the bone saw in his hand, placed it – breathe in, breathe out – and began to saw. Sweat ran into his eyes. He was faster than he had been, but not as fast as Swan and the others. He ground his teeth as he sawed, although he did not know this. Bone severed. Flesh cut away. The nurse took the leg in both hands and disposed of it. A file, to smooth the cut bone. The retractor, unscrewed. Needle, to finish. When it was done – muscles sutured into place over the end of the stump, the healthy skin sewn into a tidy parcel – only then did he dare glance at the face of the man on the table. Barely a man: a boy, seventeen or eighteen, his face calm with ether dreams. Not as handsome as the marble Apollo in the Louvre, but luckier, the statue being a quadruple amputee and this boy losing only his left foot.

Ellis sighed and blew out his cheeks. He glanced questioningly at his regular nurse, an elderly nun from the Order of Ursulines.

Soeur Débarras checked the watch pinned to her apron. 'Just under eight minutes, Monsieur Butterfield,' she said. She had seen many more amputations over the years than he had.

Ellis grimaced; better than it had been, but not fast enough.

Next on their table was a heavy, hairy man with shell splinters in his arm and side. Cutting, probing, tweezing. Then a crushed hand. Then a knee disarticulation, the lower limb already severed by a shell fragment with remarkable precision. Then a foot that had lain out in the snow for forty hours, toes already black with frostbite . . .

And on. And on.

The operating theatre at the American hospital was set up in the ballroom of a mansion on the Champs Élysées. It was the length and breadth of a tennis court, with immense windows at either end that gave on to snow-covered gardens. The tables were lined up under crystal chandeliers; the backdrop to their cutting was ornate painted plasterwork, and a double row of mirrored panels, fifteen feet high, reflected light on to their work. The carpets had been rolled up and rubber sheets laid down, but still the parquet floors were stained with the effluvia from damaged bodies.

Swan, the chief surgeon, took on the really challenging cases: the compound fractures; the torn abdomens; the cases of gas gangrene. Most died, but the few who survived owed their lives to his stubbornness. He was wonderful to watch; his hands moved without haste, but at lightning speed. Ellis felt ham-fisted in comparison. But he couldn't allow himself to dwell on that. He discovered that he could keep going from day to day if he made his mind blank – a smooth plane across which only the most banal thoughts wandered: what they would be given for lunch, the softness of his bed, the prospect of wine.

His uncle was delighted. Ellis knew this because he had received a letter saying so – more effusive than any letter he had got from him since school. He'd not seen Ephraim in person since being summoned to his residence at the end of November and being told that Dr Swan was in desperate need of surgeons, especially those with war experience. Ephraim could think of no reason why Ellis would refuse this call to duty. Swan was there in the room, a grizzled, laconic presence, clearly produced by his uncle to put additional pressure on the wastrel nephew. Ellis protested that it had been five years since he had practised and he feared he was no longer competent.

'Well, son,' said Swan – his accent a disconcerting Southern drawl – 'if you can hold a scalpel and tie a ligature, and you've worked under army conditions, then you are better qualified than many of my staff. So, let's try it and see. What do you say?'

Ellis thought back to the last months of the war, when his terror of making the first cut had become so great he could only overcome it with large doses of bourbon. How could he admit that to this man? Swan was so relaxed and confident; in any gathering of men, his tally of lives saved and pain alleviated would be unbeatable. He stuck out his hand, and narrow grey eyes seemed to look deep inside Ellis and read everything that was there. Unable to resist, Ellis put out his hand and they shook.

Oddly, his fears of not being able to do the job were unfounded. Even odder – there was a curious benefit. His asthma attacks had been worsening since the outbreak of war, culminating in the attack in the Louvre in front of Lawrence Harper, but, since starting work at the hospital, the attacks had almost entirely abated. Strange, because they usually became worse with cold weather. Now, he trudged between home and hospital through snow-covered streets, and the cold did not strangle him.

He stopped thinking about poetry completely. When he tried to force his mind in that direction, it refused to respond, was sluggish and earthbound. His intelligence, such as it was, had migrated to his hands. Also, he was always tired, unable to concentrate enough even to read, but the tiredness felt hard-earned and virtuous. It was a long time since he had felt virtuous.

For his first few days in the hospital, he was intimidated by the nun. Soeur Débarras had been a nurse for more than thirty years. She had treated the wounded of the uprising of '48; she had seen victims of every kind of accident. The railways were the worst, she said. Lord above, when the railways came, it was like a plague. The things we saw – people crushed, burned, cut clean in half . . . The amputations had tripled. She crossed herself. Good preparation for the carnage inflicted by shells.

Since then, Ellis had grown to like her. She was methodical and skilled. She was equally calm in the face of terrible agony and the most shocking obscenities, but beneath the serenity lurked a mordant wit. She made him laugh. He told her about the cat he had inherited from his uncle. Soeur Débarras also had a cat, or rather the Order had one – a mascot stray, as he understood it. Some of the nuns called it Minou, but she, she whispered to him, called it Lucifer.

Ellis nearly dropped his scalpel. 'Good heavens! Why on earth?'

'He is as black as sin. He is utterly selfish and amoral. He cares for no one but himself.'

Ellis grinned. 'He is a cat.'

'Yes. Cats are devilish creatures. At least, this way, we can keep an eye on him.' She smiled, betraying affection. 'Of course, he gets away with murder.'

She asked Ellis if he was married, or affianced. He said no and she looked at him askance. He realized some explanation was expected for this unnatural state of affairs.

'There was someone, back home, but . . .' He shook his head, as if the memory was too painful to go on. It was what he always said.

'You should marry,' she told him. 'Men need to marry.'

He smiled. 'Ah? And why is that?'

'My dear young man, do I really need to tell you? You lead a lonely life, here. Your family is far away. Your friends – so you tell me – have left Paris, or you hardly see them. Everybody needs somebody to care for, even more than they need somebody to care for them. Without loving, the soul shrivels to dust. And, apart from the benefits to you, Monsieur Butterfield, remember this: for every man who does not marry, one woman is left in despair, or in disgrace.'

Ellis was startled, but not entirely witless. 'But you are neither,' he said, with a teasing smile.

'How do you know?' she said calmly, which silenced him.

At the end of each shift, his back ached, his hands ached, his eyes throbbed. He ate a meal in the canteen, lit a cigar – wine and cigars were still abundant and cheap, thank God – and walked home. The intense concentration required by the work left his mind an exhausted blank, which in many ways was a relief.

Tonight, he climbed the stairs of his building and put the key to the door of his room, only to discover it was unlocked. He frowned; it wasn't like him to forget such a thing. As he found matches for the lamp, he made chirruping noises to call Circe – he'd smuggled a piece of pie from the canteen to share with her. But, tonight, there was no yowling, no light brush of her body against his legs. Ellis turned up the lamp, peering under the furniture, but she wasn't there. Could he have left his door open this morning? He was sure he had not. He opened the window and shouted and whistled, then left it open as he went downstairs to hammer on Madame Gigoux's door. After a wait, the concierge's wife opened the door and blocked it with her body.

'What is it, Monsieur Butterfield? It's late.'

'I'm sorry, madame. But Circe – my cat – has gone, and my door was unlocked. Have you seen her? She's a Siamese cat, almost white, with brown paws and ears. Very blue eyes.'

Madame Gigoux shrugged. 'I have not seen a cat. Surely monsieur is aware – tenants are not allowed to keep pets. To lock up a cat – it's not natural, is it?'

'I didn't know that. I'm sorry, but I'm looking after her for my uncle. She belongs to him – the American ambassador, you recall? I keep her locked in so that she doesn't bother anyone. That's why I don't understand how she could have got out.'

'Perhaps you left the door open when you went out this morning.'

'I know I locked the door this morning. And she was definitely inside. Besides, even if I had, a cat cannot close a door, and it was closed when I came in just now.'

Madame Gigoux stared at him. 'Everyone makes mistakes, monsieur. Even, I am sure, Americans.'

There was a burst of laughter from an inner room – Monsieur Gigoux, and someone else. Ellis smelt some sort of stew, meaty and savoury. It stirred his taste buds and a terrible thought came to him.

'Madame—'

'I bid you good night, monsieur.'

The door shut with a click. Ellis stood outside, breathing as if he had been running. He was trembling with rage. He had the urge to barge in and examine what was in their pot. Unreasonable . . . No reason to think . . . Perhaps Circe had escaped – but how?

Upstairs, his room was ice cold, but he could not bring himself to close the window. He wedged one pane open, leaving a Siamese-sized gap, and put the pie on the floor below it. He quickly drained a bottle of wine, then lay down in all his clothes, under a pile of blankets.

By morning, fresh snow had blown in through the window and made a feathery drift on the floor. The pie was shrouded in frost. There was no sign of the Siamese.

28

On the morning of Christmas Day, Lawrence walked across the river. The snow would have muffled the hoof beats of horses and the grinding of cab wheels, but there were no horses and no cabs. It would have been quite silent, apart from the distant grumbling of the artillery.

Along the banks, trees had not only been cut down, but their roots had been grubbed up, leaving a row of dirty scars. On the Quai de la Mégisserie, children scavenged. A girl of about twelve was in charge; she carried a stick on her shoulder in the manner of a rifle and yelled commands at the others, who scraped in the snow for twigs, or burrowed for scraps of root. There were shouts of triumph and screams of laughter. Despite their miserable occupation and the intense cold, they seemed to be enjoying themselves. It was the ninety-ninth day of the siege.

Lawrence wore his best coat, and had done his best with cold water, brush and sponge to smarten his appearance and remove the evidence that, due to lack of fuel, none of his clothes had been properly laundered for a month. He had polished his boots, dabbed himself with cologne and spent far too long at the mirror trying to feel handsome, worrying that the pimple on his cheek rendered him grotesque, telling himself he should not care.

He did not notice the girl until she was right in front of him. She wasn't much older than the girl on the bank, and she stopped, forcing him to turn aside and walk around her, tightening his grip on his cane.

'Merry Christmas, monsieur! Merry Christmas!'

Startled by the laughter in her voice, Lawrence looked around and caught the girl's eye. A mistake. He saw her grin.

'Merry Christmas,' he mumbled, reluctantly.

She kept pace with him, a skipping, sideways gait, so that she could keep her eyes on his face.

'Handsome monsieur! Where are you going on this day of days?'

Lawrence sighed. 'I've no money on me.'

The girl made a derisive noise. 'Yeah. With that beautiful coat, and that cane! I bet that's silver.'

He felt sorry for her; she was so stunted, thin and white faced, as though she lived in a cellar and ate scraps. Despite her wizened appearance, her voice was mellow and deep – as husky as a pipe smoker's.

'Since it is a special morning, monsieur, the morning our Lord was born, I'm going to give you a present.'

Lawrence muttered something unintelligible.

'But it's something special! Hey! Do you think I'm a bad person? You hurt my feelings, monsieur.'

Reluctantly, Lawrence said, 'No.'

'No! You see! I am Minette, and I give you the chance to meet my sister.'

'No, thank you.'

'Ah! Don't speak too soon. She's just turned sixteen. She's really pretty. Blond hair, blue eyes. Plump as a peach. I know what you're thinking, but she's not at all like me. I'm the runt. I got the brains in the family; she got the beauty.'

'I'm in a hurry.' Lawrence shook his head and walked faster, but he couldn't help smiling a little. There was something strangely likeable about this appalling creature.

'But, monsieur – look!'

She flung out her hand and he turned to see, parked in a side street, a sway-backed horse, a closed cab, and a black-clad scarecrow hunched on the driver's seat.

'She's in there. Waiting for you.'

'I'm going to be late,' he said.

'One turn around the block – that's all you'll need. My brother drives the cab, and I breathe on the windows so no one can see in.'

'No.' He made his voice firm, but almost smiled again, it was so absurd.

'Just come and have a look. Until you've had her, you don't know what heaven is.'

He shook his head and frowned, walking away.

'Please, monsieur . . . we're desperate. It's the only way we can eat!'

He kept walking. Probably there was no one inside the cab – just the brother, or whoever the accomplice was, with a knife. A cold hand clutched his arm.

'Cunt like velvet.' She brought out the words with dreadful, hissing relish.

Lawrence tugged his arm away, his face burning in the cold air. He had an impulse to raise his cane and bring it down on her head. He walked quickly away, stabbing the snow with his cane, and this time she did not follow.

'Faggot!' she yelled after him, quite cheerfully. 'Auntie!'

In his hurry to get away from her, he trod in something unfortunate, but didn't dare stop to clean his boots until he'd put several blocks between them. He felt soiled through and through. She had made him – of all men! – feel complicit in her filthy trade. The girl and her family probably were starving, but so were thousands of others.

He'd had mixed feelings about accepting Ellis's invitation – Christmas lunch at the American consulate – but it was a public occasion, and there would be free food. Since the evening in Montmartre, when he'd been ambushed by desire, he had tried to force his thoughts back towards Yves. He dwelt on the day they had spent on the river. He reread the letter in which Yves was so affectionate. He tried to imagine his gentle friend in the snow, in battle, but it was impossible. His memories were worn so thin that Yves seemed more a creature of myth than a man.

His nerves were wound as tight as violin strings as he walked into the *hôtel particulier* where the lunch was taking place. He was overly conscious of trying to keep his face carefree, affecting the good-humoured nonchalance of a man about town. A servant advanced and took his coat, hat and cane, leaving him empty-handed and defenceless.

He was directed into a salon full of people. It was a motley gathering and his ear caught various accents: German – perhaps refugees from the embassy – American, English and others he couldn't place. Strangers' eyes slid over him without interest, looking for someone familiar to them, or someone important, and he was neither. He couldn't see anyone he knew. He hoped Michel would be here, and Séraphine, but most of the guests were older – deracinated foreigners like himself. His gaze roamed the room, seeking Ellis, yet half dreading to find him, and, when he caught sight of the fair head rising above the crowd, he felt a lurch in the pit of his stomach.

Ellis looked to be deep in conversation with a white-haired man, and Lawrence did not want to interrupt, so he made his way over to the windows which overlooked a courtyard. He took a glass of champagne from a passing waiter. He drank from it, looked around and caught the eye of a man with a moustache.

'Merry Christmas, monsieur,' said the man, in Parisian French, bowing his head.

'Merry Christmas,' replied Lawrence, raising his glass in a toast.

'Wonderful to have a party like this to come to, is it not?'

'It is, yes.'

'My name is Prestat.' He held out his hand and Lawrence introduced himself. 'I'm very pleased to meet you. You're an American, I think? Though your French is excellent; you have hardly any accent.'

'Thank you. Actually, I'm Canadian. From Montréal.'

'Ah, that is why. We are a gathering of many nations here. Ambassador Quine is kind to think of those who are far from home.'

'Yes. Well, I've never actually met him. I—'

'I think that is true of many of the guests. It's an annual tradition, this party: every Christmas, he invites many foreigners to this beautiful consulate. It used to be the mansion of the Vicomtesse de Valvert . . . You know who she was? She was a mistress of Louis XV.'

'Oh?'

'One of many, of course. But that is our French royalty.' He chuckled. 'Do I shock you, monsieur?'

'Oh, no,' said Lawrence.

'I'm always happy to make the acquaintance of visitors to our great city – especially those from the New World. I think you have much to teach us. Your morals are so much higher than ours.'

'Oh . . . well . . .' Lawrence could think of nothing to say to this.

Talk turned to the siege and their prospects of deliverance. Prestat was well informed about the doings of those in government.

'What is your connection with the ambassador, Monsieur Prestat?'

'I have had the honour to help him out once or twice on certain legal matters.' The man leant confidingly towards Lawrence. 'I admire your country greatly, but not all your countrymen are of high morals. It's no secret that Monsieur Quine is burdened with a troublesome relation. I have had to advise him, on occasion – drunken brawls, an unsavoury business with a woman. Arrests, even! Tsk. But none of us can choose our relations, can we?'

'No, quite so.' Lawrence's initial thought was to wonder who this was. Ellis had never mentioned another relative in Paris.

'He's one of these young men who fancies himself a poet. Which is all very well, but does one have to behave like a wild beast to prove it? I suspect that he is like most of these bohemians who have no worldly success, so make their renown instead through shocking behaviour. I think, if one has no talent, one should just give it up, not drag one's relatives into the mire. But perhaps I have spoken too harshly. Are you, perhaps, a poet, monsieur? Oh dear, I fear I have offended you!'

'No. I work for a photographer.'

'Ah. I'm all in favour of modern technologies. Where would we be without the hot-gas balloon? Even worse off than we are now!'

Lawrence made his excuses and walked away. He had forgotten how wary he had been of Ellis when they first met, how surprised that Yves had chosen this man for a friend. With piercing suddenness, a picture of Yves came to mind. How could he have so betrayed him, even in thought? Lawrence seized another glass of champagne and hid in the thickest part of the crowd. He was ashamed of himself for his faithlessness, but also for failing to claim Ellis's friendship in front of the gossiping lawyer. He swallowed the champagne, then a hand landed on his shoulder. Ellis was by his side, large and beaming.

'There you are! I've been looking everywhere for you!' His eyes shone and there was a flush high on his cheeks. They shook hands. 'I was afraid you weren't coming. I hardly know anyone here. I invited Michel too, but he's on duty. Come, I'll introduce you to my uncle, if I can find him . . .'

He took Lawrence by the arm and led him through the crowd. At one point, Lawrence saw the lawyer again, now talking to a jewelled and powdered woman, and his eyes met Lawrence's over her shoulder. Seeing him with Ellis, Prestat's eyes narrowed and the corners of his mouth twitched. What it meant – anger, embarrassment, dislike – Lawrence did not know, but he felt as though he had taken advantage of his friend.

'I have no influence over the seating plan,' Ellis was saying, 'so I apologize in advance if your company is boring, but at least the food should be good.'

Smells of roasting meat wafted through double doors at the end of the salon, and the attention of the guests swung in that direction. Lawrence could smell garlic, wine and – was that lamb? Surely, there were mushrooms . . . He scented the air, his senses keen as a blood-hound's. His mouth watered so hard his cheeks hurt.

Lawrence saw the lawyer again, sitting a few places away from him. Part of him wished he hadn't come, but he knew that the prospect of a good meal outweighed any other consideration. Finer feelings counted for nothing. Where food was concerned, the siege had turned them all into animals.

29

Inevitably, the zoo animals' fate became known. It was reported in the papers, sniggered about in cafés, whispered in classrooms.

The zoo's director and governors justified it on the grounds that, since they could not guarantee the survival of the animals, they had to think of their future – the zoo might as well profit from them while there was still meat on their bones. They did not put it quite like that. Victor and Papin were furious, but it was out of their hands.

As for Anne, well, no one ever knew what Anne thought; she did not rage or weep, but she was more silent and distant than usual. Victor watched her. He waited for a glimpse of her eyes and tried to read what lay behind them. At last, he stopped her in the corridor.

'I know you are upset about the animals, Anne. We all are. Monsieur Papin is distraught. Throughout his life, he has devoted himself to their care, and there was nothing even he could do.'

She was silent, her eyes fixed on the wall over his shoulder.

'You know they give us orders. We are only employees. We have to do as we are bid – just as you do. You didn't mind about the rabbits, did you?'

'That was to keep others from starving.'

'Are people not more important than animals?'

'People buying meat at thirty francs a pound are not starving.'

'I don't know what you would have me do.'

There was a long pause, then she said, in a low voice, 'Refuse.'

'Refuse? Anne! I would lose my position, and then what?'

'What if they tell you Marguerite is to be next?'

Victor had asked himself the same question. Marguerite and the cats were still in their cages – hungry, thin, angry. The crocodiles and sundry reptiles were holding on, as was Kako the hippopotamus, whose reserve price was so astronomical it had deterred even the Boucherie Ranvier. The little birds, too insignificant even to kill, had been abandoned to their fate.

'I promise I will do everything in my power to prevent that.'

'But you just said you had none.'

Victor felt a wave of anger wash over him. He wanted to seize her by the arms, make her look at him, at least. 'How can you not understand? This is the way the world is, Anne! We have to be practical. You hurt me with your intransigence.' He looked at her downcast eyelids, trying to guess her thoughts.

'Do you want me to leave, monsieur?'

She understood nothing, least of all him.

'No, I don't want you to leave. Besides, Monsieur Papin is your employer, not me.'

'Does he want me to leave?'

'No, I . . . Your leaving is the last thing I want. I wish you would look at me! I wish . . .'

She almost did, then – her eyes flickered towards him in surprise, but she would not, *would not* look straight at him. Absurdly, Victor felt tears prickling his eyes. She was so stubborn; she refused to see him as an equal, and he no longer knew what this meant, whether she held him to be above her, or . . .

She was hard as quartz, as unknowable. He was at a loss; he would never be able to pierce her armour.

'It's the war that is doing this – to us, to the animals. You see that, don't you? We are all its casualties.'

*

Papin surprised Victor by suggesting they invite Anne and Lucie, the cook, for a small Christmas party to cheer them all up.

The men tried their best to make it a happy occasion. When they had eaten a roast chicken, a chocolate cake with tinned cherries, and some elderly cheese, Papin opened one of his special bottles of champagne – the only part of the meal that was redolent of life before the siege. He poured them each a glass and unfurled himself as far as his spine allowed.

'We are living through remarkable times. Sacrifices have been demanded of us all. Some of them have been painful. We are under siege, but the hardship will not last forever. It is Christmas Day, and I want us to remind ourselves of all we have to be thankful for. We have enough to eat, and a warm place to live, and we have Anne and Lucie, to whom we are very grateful. We are sensible of all that you do for us, *mesdames*.'

'Hear, hear!' said Victor.

Papin raised his glass to Anne and Lucie. Anne bobbed a curtsey. Lucie gave an embarrassed smile.

'Now, we have something for you both.'

He looked at Victor, who went to the sideboard, opened it and took out some presents. He was nervous. He had taken a risk.

Lucie had a length of cloth and a new hat. Anne too had a present of cloth, but Victor had bought her something else, something he had found in a shop of curios. It was a book of travels in the Antilles, with hand-tinted engravings. It was long out of date, but there was a chapter on Haiti. Victor thought the pictures wonderful; the colours were so rich and bright, he could scarcely believe they existed. Anne had never been there, but surely an account of her father's homeland would mean something to her? Surely she would feel warmly towards the man who gave such a thing? He watched her face as she unwrapped the paper, a tiny frown etched on her brow. She opened the book carefully and gazed at one of the illustrations. It seemed to dawn on her gradually what it was. She turned to the title page. Then she closed it and thanked them both, her eyes still downcast. As usual, he could not tell what she thought of it, whether she appreciated the thought behind it – whether she was happy at all.

30

Lunch outlasted the daylight, and Ellis and Lawrence were among the last to leave, stealing as much food as they could carry. They stole towels in which to carry their spoils and tied them into unwieldy parcels. Lawrence was numbed by champagne and brandy. His brain told him a sharp wind was buffeting his face, but he did not feel the cold. He stumbled along in the snow, one foot in front of the other, more or less. Behind him, he heard Ellis laugh.

'What?'

'You look funny.'

'Funny? How?'

'You nearly walked into that lamp post.'

'I did not.'

Lawrence hadn't noticed a lamp post. He would have noticed, wouldn't he, if he'd nearly walked into it?

'Mr Harper, you are drunk.'

'Yes, I am. So?'

'Me too.'

'I know.'

They both laughed. It was a delightful drunkenness, a cocoon against darkness and cold. Lawrence felt wanton and giddy, warmed by the enormous lunch and the prospect of giving gifts. But it was a long walk to the eastern edge of Paris, and the muscles of his arms were complaining. They stopped in a doorway to put down their bundles.

Ellis lit a cigar. 'Maybe we should find a cab. It'll take hours otherwise.'

'A cab? Are you crazy? Have you seen a single cab today?'

'No. I guess there aren't any, it being Christmas. Or omnibuses.'

'I saw a cab this morning, but it wasn't for hire . . . God – I'd forgotten.'

'Forgotten what?'

Lawrence told him about the young girl accosting him on the street. He flushed, recalling it; even in the cold, his face burned with embarrassment.

'She was a foul creature. Just a child. She seemed to be enjoying it. And what she said . . .' He shook his head.

'What did she say?'

Lawrence couldn't bring himself to repeat it. 'Words you don't want to hear in a child's mouth.'

Ellis gave a shout of laughter. 'How puritanical you sound! You're so . . . Canadian.'

'What on earth does that mean?'

'Oh, you know – nice and polite and bashful. It's a compliment.'

'No, it isn't.'

'Sorry. It's just that you're . . . surprising, sometimes. Especially given what you do for a living.'

'What I do? I do what I'm asked. I'm just the assistant.'

'Think how many men would kill to be in your shoes; all those lovely girls . . .'

'It's not like that. It's hard work.'

Lawrence was annoyed by the sly amusement in Ellis's voice. He began to feel cold. He stamped his feet, hoping Ellis would hurry up with the cigar. They shared the meagre shelter of the doorway, and the smoke stung his eyes.

'She said, "*Une chatte comme le velours.*"'

'Oh.' Ellis blew out a stream of smoke. 'Well? Were you tempted? Go on – admit it!'

Lawrence looked at Ellis in sincere horror. 'You wouldn't ask that if you'd been there.'

He bent to pick up his parcel and hunched his shoulders as he set off against the wind. He heard again the girl's jeering, '*Tapette!*' He wondered if Ellis was thinking the same thing. The back of his neck felt hot.

'Hey, wait. Lawrence! I've been in Paris too long. Nothing shocks me.'

Lawrence slowed his pace until Ellis caught up with him.

'Well, I was shocked. You don't expect to hear that from such a young girl.'

'These children, they're feral. Barely human.'

'I felt sorry for her, though. She looked starved. And she was sort of . . . funny. That was partly what was so awful. She made you like her, and then – that.'

They stopped again, to retie the towels. Lawrence found that a fruit tart had crumbled to sugary rubble. Ellis took a swig from an opened bottle and passed it to Lawrence. Lawrence drank, then said, carelessly, 'Do you have any relatives in Paris? Other than your uncle, I mean.'

'No. Why?'

'I met a man today who was talking about a relative of Mr Quine's. I just wondered . . . if there was someone else.'

'Oh?' Ellis sounded guarded. 'Who was this?'

'I think his name was Prestat. A lawyer.'

Ellis let out a short, bitter laugh. 'Oh, him. I'm sure he had nothing good to say about me. You want to know if what he said was true?'

'No, it doesn't matter.'

'No?'

Lawrence shrugged uncomfortably. 'He was just gossiping.'

'My uncle and I don't always see eye to eye. He has a position to uphold and I suppose, on occasion . . . Remember that day in the Zouave? People pick fights with me. If you look different, people don't like it.'

Lawrence thought, It's not just the way you look.

'I've never done anything I wasn't provoked into doing. I know I'm an idiot sometimes. I get carried away. Is that what he said?'

Lawrence hesitated. 'He said . . . something about a woman.'

Ellis sighed. 'Once, a girl in a dance hall accused me of molesting her, because I tried to stop her man from strangling her, and he attacked me. She came for me with a broken bottle and I may have pushed her over.' He took another swig from the bottle. 'Michel was there; you can ask him.'

Lawrence shook his head.

'I'm not always proud of myself,' Ellis said. 'Are you?'

'No, of course not.'

'So, go on: what are you not proud of?'

'Lots of things.'

'Come on. Name one. You have to, now – you know the worst about me.'

Lawrence sighed. Nothing came to mind – that he could say out loud. He knew with certainty that this was not the worst thing about Ellis. To fob him off, he finally said, 'I once went with one of the studio models.'

Ellis stared at him for a moment, and then burst out laughing.

'Why is that funny?'

Ellis drained the bottle and threw it away. It landed in the snow with a dull clink. 'It just is.'

In Ménilmontant, they were welcomed with open arms and cries of amazement that they had come so far in such terrible weather. The Bignons had long finished their Christmas meal, and were sitting around the table, playing cards and drinking wine.

'Behold, two wise men!' shouted Ellis from the doorway.

'Two fools, you mean,' said Michel, as they shuffled into the crowded kitchen. Melting snow dripped from their trouser and coat hems, even from their hair. Icy air rolled off them. They pulled bottles of wine from their pockets, and untied their damp parcels to reveal pies, cheeses and tarts in various states of disrepair.

'I think this was a cherry tart, when I started.'

'My God, but this is wonderful! What a marvellous Christmas present. You're so kind, both of you.' Madame Bignon had tears in her eyes.

They were all on their feet, practically drooling, eyes shining with greed.

Séraphine laughed. 'Oh, my goodness, Maman, look! Champagne!' She picked up a bottle. 'Is that Gruyère? Oh, I could kiss you.' She flung her arms around Lawrence and kissed him on the cheek.

'Hey . . .'

'You too, of course.' She kissed Ellis more circumspectly.

'Have you just come to molest my girl?' said Michel, but he too embraced them.

It was a relief to thaw out in the Bignons' undemanding company. Lawrence glowed with pleasure. From the way they attacked the leftovers, he discerned that their own meal had been frugal. They ate and talked, and even the taciturn Monsieur Bignon was beaming. Ellis was at his most genial and expansive. Lawrence wondered if he had been forgiven for bringing up his misdemeanours. He had known perfectly well that the troublesome relative was Ellis; he hadn't needed to ask.

For years, Lawrence had placed every man he met into one of two categories, almost without thinking: maybe, and never. Well, there were also those men whose flamboyant manners left no room for doubt, but such men scared Lawrence, or repelled him. On the few occasions when he had ventured to places in Montréal where men of similar tastes gathered, he noticed that they did not seem to interest each other. He understood, while also finding it absurd, or sad. They frightened him because, of course, *he* was not like that, and he could not think that such a life awaited him. He had stopped going because his youth and appearance made him the focus of an attention that was too over-whelming to be flattering. He felt like prey – something to be caught and devoured. He had to learn a subtler, riskier language, picking up cues while giving nothing away. Even then, you could be wrong. He had been sure of Yves' nature, but not of his courage (perhaps courage was the wrong word). Gustave Daudel he had placed, fairly quickly, as a maybe. Michel, obviously, was a never. But, somehow, even after the evening in the Batignolles, he had failed to categorize Ellis at all.

When the candles were guttering in their holders, Lawrence and Ellis made to leave. Madame Bignon looked out of the window. 'You boys can't go out in this – look at it!'

Snowflakes swarmed against the glass.

'It's no worse than earlier.'

'You're crazy. It must be minus ten degrees out there.'

They were urged to stay, but brushed away the offer. There was no room for them to sleep there anyway, unless they lay down under the kitchen table.

Outside, a buffeting wind blew ice crystals into their faces no matter which way they turned. Fresh snow overlaid the ice and made the going more treacherous. After they had trudged along in silence for a while, slipping and falling, Lawrence turned to Ellis and took him by the arm.

'This is madness.'

'What?'

'This is madness! Come back to Rue des Ciseaux. You can stay in the studio. It's much nearer than your place. It'll take you hours to get home.'

Ellis's face was screwed up against the snow. 'Really? Would that be all right?'

'Of course. There's the studio ... lots of room. They won't mind.'

*

Lawrence had a key to the back door, and he let them inside. They stood for a moment in the corridor, brushing snow off their clothes; it was a relief to be breathing still air.

Ellis spoke in a piercing whisper: 'Are you sure this is all right?'

'Oh, yes. Madame Lamy is a dear. She won't mind a bit. You could even leave by this door in the morning and no one would know. I doubt anyone will go up to the studio tomorrow.'

He led Ellis up the stairs, pausing on the landing to listen, but the house was silent. He had the sense that they couldn't have woken the sleepers if they tried.

In the attic, a faint greyness bled through the snow-covered skylights. Lawrence felt his way about the room and lit an oil lamp.

'You don't have to worry about disturbing the Lamys. The only room on the floor beneath this one is mine.' All the same, he spoke in a low voice. He knelt in front of the stove and fed it with kindling.

'There's no need for that,' said Ellis. 'I'll be fine.'

'You'll freeze up here otherwise.' Lawrence twisted scraps of newspaper into knots and lit a match.

'You still have coal?'

'We've been burning props and backdrops up here. Here, hold this.'

Lawrence gave him the lamp while he selected a Romanesque temple from the dwindling stack of flats. He braced it against the wall and stamped on it to break apart the struts.

'You won't need that?'

'I was never happy with it. There's a divan over there. And rugs and shawls in that corner, with the costumes.'

Ellis lifted the lamp and swung it around to look at the studio, sending shadows bounding over piles of props and equipment.

'Why are there so many mirrors?'

'They're used to direct the light.'

Ellis swung the nearest mirror to and fro, examining the effect. He touched the harness hanging from the ceiling and grinned.

'Dare I ask what this is for?'

'That? Oh, we hardly use it. It's more for painters, to support the model if they have to hold a difficult pose for a long time – like, if they're meant to be flying, or standing on one leg, that sort of thing.'

Ellis leant on the harness and swung against it. 'I had no idea you had so much fun.'

'I'm mostly in the darkroom.'

Lawrence fed broken struts into the stove. The smell of turpentine spread through the studio.

'There's more wood here, and you can burn the canvas too, if you're desperate. It smells a bit, but it's not too bad.'

'Where's the darkroom?'

'In there.' He stood up and showed Ellis the door to the darkroom. He opened it and they surveyed the shelves and bottles, the trays, the racks, the strings for hanging prints to dry.

'It looks like a laboratory.'

'That's what it is. More science than art.'

Lawrence searched through the pile of costumes for warm coverings. Most of the fabrics were gauzy, diaphanous – hardly the thing to keep out the midwinter cold – but he found a woollen shawl embroidered with gold thread and held it out. 'Take this.'

Ellis draped the shawl around his shoulders and struck a dramatic pose. 'Admit that you come up here and dress up from time to time.'

Lawrence laughed. 'I've never been up here at night before.'

'Really?'

Ellis tossed a piece of organza over Lawrence, so that it fell around him like a veil. Lawrence pulled it around his shoulders. One of the mirrors was nearby, a slice of light angled so that it caught their image. In it, their two figures were silhouetted. The shawl's gold threads glinted, but their faces were in shadow.

Ellis put his arm around Lawrence's shoulders and addressed the glass. 'I am the Bey of Constantinople, and you are my chief of spies.

Or – no –' he picked up the paste tiara and placed it on Lawrence's head – 'queen of the harem.'

Lawrence looked at the reflection, at the slighter, veiled figure which seemed pliant, to meld itself into the larger. He felt a jolt of queasy rage and tore the veil from his head. There was a teasing smile on Ellis's face.

Lawrence stepped away to pick up the rugs he had gathered. He went to lay them on the divan. He felt like a maid.

'That's wonderful. Thank you. You're not angry? I didn't mean anything by it.'

'I know. Of course I'm not angry.'

To prove it, he stood next to Ellis again and they both regarded their reflections in the mirror. Ellis seemed to attract light: his blond hair, the golden shawl. By contrast, Lawrence was shadow. They could have been two strangers.

'Thank you for doing this. And for everything.'

'I should thank you. You invited me to lunch today.'

There was a pause during which neither moved or spoke. Lawrence allowed himself the luxury of not thinking. He was too drunk and too tired. Ellis might have said something else, or he might have said nothing – Lawrence could not remember. Each moment uncoupled from the one before it, as though, every second, his existence began anew. He gazed into the tilted glass as the taller figure, the one that glistened, put his hand on the shadow's neck and pulled its face towards him.

31

Lawrence leant against the wall outside the dining room, waiting for the throbbing in his head to subside. He debated whether to creep past and breakfast elsewhere, but that would only provoke curiosity. Weighing into his decision was his raging thirst, and a hangover so crushing he doubted that he would get very far. His eyes refused to open properly. He finally pushed the dining-room door and found Louise there alone.

'Lawrence, there you are! I see it was a late night! I hope that means you enjoyed your Christmas as much as we did.'

He smiled and murmured in reply. He cherished the hangover as a charm against her questions.

'More coffee.' Louise rang the bell, and then stood up. 'Bother, I keep forgetting about Lisette.'

'Oh, please . . .' he said, but she had already gone.

He sank into a chair, his elbows on the table, and propped his head on his fingertips. His skull felt as if it were made of something heavy and fragile, but worthless: a badly made pot. His whole body trembled; his liver complained that he had swallowed poison.

'God, those stairs! Imagine how trim I would be if I had to do this all day.' Breathing heavily, Louise put the tray with a pot of coffee and some bread rolls on the table. 'You do look pale, dear.'

'It's just a headache.'

'Cook has freshened up the bread a bit – I'm afraid it's the best she could do today. But there is good news. Tomorrow, we will have a new maid! You'll never guess who it is . . . Fanny Klein is coming to work for us – as a maid, I mean. It'll just be for a while, I expect, until things settle down, but that will be nice. I must say, it'll be a relief to have help again.'

Lawrence picked up his cup with a hand he couldn't prevent from trembling.

'Poor thing. You must have had a good time, last night.'

'Um . . . I went to Ménilmontant with a friend, and we . . . Well, it was snowing so much, and he lives in Montmartre, which was . . .'

What was he saying? Eventually, he managed to explain about walking to Séraphine's after the lunch, and that Monsieur Butterfield had stayed the night in the studio. The sooner he said it, the more innocent it would sound, he hoped.

'I hope it was all right to offer, madame. The weather was so bad . . .'

'Of course it's all right, Lawrence. And you were going to call me Louise, remember – that is your Christmas present to me. Last night was atrocious. I was relieved we were home before it started in earnest. Could your friend not have stayed to breakfast? It would have been nice to meet him.'

'He had to go to work early. He's a surgeon at the American hospital.'

'A surgeon? Goodness me, how wonderful.'

Lawrence nodded. Saying Ellis's name caused him inner turmoil; he was flooded with warmth, something swelled in his chest, a thrill that edged on panic. He put down the roll he was holding – he hadn't worked out what to do with it – and took a sip of coffee.

'To think, a surgeon! Is he young? How old is he?'

'Er, about twenty-eight, I think.'

'So young! He must be very brilliant.'

Lawrence was surprised and enchanted. Was he? He had never thought of Ellis as brilliant. Louise was looking at him brightly, agog for more information, but Lawrence could not think of a single thing to say that would not arouse suspicion.

Fortunately, Louise was in that mood where she could more or less carry on a conversation by herself. He focused on the bread on his plate and tore off a piece. It was slightly damp, with a disturbing, vestigial warmth. He tore the morsel in half, to make it more manageable. His eyelids seemed to be sweating. It was a relief that carrying out a simple task like drinking coffee took so much concentration; there was no room for other thoughts.

Ernestine came in and sat at the table with a sigh.

'Dear, how is your head now?' said Louise. 'We have another invalid on our hands. Poor Monsieur Harper is not feeling well either.'

'Oh? Sorry to hear it. It's no better.' Ernestine poured herself a cup of coffee and, picking up a roll, looked at it with distaste. 'Is this what Cook has given us for breakfast?'

'It was all she could find. Things will be back to normal tomorrow.'

'Well, I'm not going to eat this today.' She dropped the roll on the table with a thud.

'I'll tell Cook to make some pancakes, shall I?' Louise sighed and stood up. 'Lawrence, I expect you'd prefer pancakes too.'

'Oh, I'm fine, thank you. I'm not really—'

'Oh, come, but when they get here . . . Titine, I hope you will make allowances for Fanny while she gets used to us. It's very good of her to agree to come at such short notice. And she will fetch the bread for us, so that is a blessing.'

Ernestine made a noise that could have signified anything and opened a magazine. The wind rattled the windows like an importunate beggar. Lawrence rolled a piece of the bread into a pellet and placed it in his mouth, where it lay on his tongue, as inedible as a piece of wood.

'What did you do yesterday, Monsieur Harper?' Ernestine didn't raise her eyes from the magazine.

Lawrence choked down the pellet. 'I went to a lunch at the American consulate. And then to a friend's house.'

'Ah?' She looked up. 'I think a friend of Monsieur Ranvier's was at the consulate.'

'There were a lot of people there,' said Lawrence.

'A lawyer,' she went on. 'What's his name? Prestat. Jean-Antoine Prestat.'

Lawrence felt cold. He was trying to think – he must have given the man his name. 'One is introduced to so many people, but one doesn't really talk to them at these events.'

'Well, you move in elevated circles, monsieur. Whom do you know at the consulate?'

'No one. Well, not there, really. I . . . er . . . A friend . . . of a friend is the ambassador's nephew.'

'Oh? What's his name?'

'Monsieur Butterfield,' he said, with a feeling of despair.

Should he mention that Ellis had stayed in the studio last night? Or would that be making too much of it? He could no longer judge which facts were innocent and which might point to the unsayable truth. He lifted his cup and dropped it on the table, where it spread a grey stain over the cloth.

'Oh, goodness! I'm terribly sorry.'

He truly didn't know if he had dropped it by accident or on purpose.

After the ordeal of breakfast was over, he was relieved to crawl back to his bed. It was pleasant to lie in a darkened room with a sheet over his head, hidden from the world – except for Louise, who would climb the stairs every couple of hours with a cup of tisane, or to ask if he needed anything.

'You really don't need to come all this way up again, madame. I will sleep and then I will be fine.'

'Are you sure? You looked so pale and shaky earlier. I was worried.' She smiled down at him, put her hand on his forehead and declared that it was cooler than earlier.

'Quite sure. I'm feeling better now. Just tired, and . . . you know.'

'Oh, I know. I was young once.'

Before she went out, she looked at him with such tender concern that he was flooded with guilt.

Left alone, he was free to dwell on the events of last night. There were things he remembered vividly, and blanks that, try as he might, he could not fill. One of the blanks was what he had intended when suggesting Ellis come back here; another was the point at which the studio had ceased to be a place of shelter and became something else. But Ellis had begun it, of that he was certain. Ellis put a hand on his arm and left it there, drew Lawrence to him. He did not remember awkwardness, just a blurred progression from one moment to another: the sight of figures in the mirror, then the feel of Ellis's hand on the back of his head, caressing, firm. The heat of his mouth and breath. They had kissed and caressed each other, undressing and finding refuge under the heap of shawls on the divan. In the fragile capsule of warmth, they climaxed quickly in each other's hands. Nothing needed to be said.

Had he fallen asleep immediately? He remembered nothing more until, at some point in the night, he awoke to feel Ellis's body pressed against him, one arm flung over him. Expecting demands, his heart galloped, his earlier decision that he would not give too much of himself crumbling in the certainty that there was nothing he would not do. But, after a minute, he realized that Ellis was sleeping, his breath rasping hoarsely in his ear. Then he moaned: a wordless, frightened cry.

Lawrence took hold of the hand that was curled loosely in front of him. 'Ellis?' he whispered, and the panicked breathing changed, slowed, became more peaceful.

Lawrence murmured into the darkness, 'I'm here.'

*

When he awoke again, it was because Ellis had moved. His warmth was replaced with a brutal onrush of icy air. Lawrence groaned.

'I have to go. I'm due at work.'

It was still dark. The stove had gone out. Lawrence was pinned to the bed by the weight of rugs, by a crushing headache. 'What time is it?'

Ellis fumbled to light the lamp and opened his watch. 'Gone six.'

He sat on the edge of the divan. Lawrence propped himself up on his elbow, his skin shrinking from the cold. His nose was blocked, his tongue felt like a dry sponge. He was desperate for water. Ellis sneezed, picked up his underwear and began to turn it right side out.

'I'll help you tidy the place.'

'It's fine. I told you, Madame Lamy won't mind a friend staying the night. Especially last night.'

He looked at Ellis's back, his skin gold in the lamplight. He watched the flexing of shoulder blades and muscles as he pulled on his under-shirt. The shoulders were wide, his long back tapered to an unathletic softness at the waist – a stubborn roll of flesh that Lawrence longed to reach out and grasp. His back was a marvel . . . In front of his eyes, it vanished under his shirt, cloth strained over ropes of muscle as he bent to pick up his necktie. He pulled on his trousers. He hadn't looked at Lawrence once.

Lawrence reached for his own clothes. Skin disappeared under coverings, obliterating any trace of what had passed between them. In another minute, they were simply two men, fully dressed.

'Do you want some water?' Lawrence rushed to the darkroom without waiting for a reply, struggled to find a receptacle. A glass beaker looked clean enough. He filled it, came out and held out the glass.

'Thanks.' Ellis drained the beaker in long swallows, coughing to clear the phlegm from his throat. He buttoned his coat and patted his pockets. 'My coat smells of cheese.'

Lawrence laughed too much. 'What time do you start?'

'About eight. Hopefully it was quiet last night.'

'Wonder if there's been more snow.'

'Soon see.'

Lawrence combed his fingers through his hair and smoothed it back off his face. It felt stiff and tangled. His mouth tasted bad. He wondered if the sight of him was as disgusting as he felt.

He was preparing himself for all that had passed between them to disappear into the fog of a drunken evening, never to be spoken of, and was surprised when Ellis put a hand on his shoulder and squeezed it for a moment that seemed longer than a simple friendly gesture. But he still didn't look at him.

'I'd better go.'

'I'll come and let you out.'

He led the way down the stairs. Never had there been so many steps; never had they made such spiteful creaks. They crept down as quietly as possible, neither of them speaking. It took forever. Lawrence unlocked the street door with a guilty stealth, and Ellis stepped out into the cold. Fresh snow whitened the ground, but there was a wan streak of grey overhead.

'Doesn't look too bad,' Lawrence said.

'No. Thanks again. Well – I'll see you.'

'Yes.'

Ellis smiled then, caught his eye briefly, and raised his hand in a sort of salute, before walking away.

Lawrence raced back up the stairs, hangover be damned, and did not stop till he had examined every piece of cloth under the lamp, scrubbing what might have been telltale stains from a length of cotton drill (or might not, but he couldn't take the risk), and replaced the shawls and rugs with the other props. He picked up the tiara from where it had fallen on the floor and piled it with the other trinkets. They seemed more tawdry, less convincing than ever. He checked the divan again, smoothed his hand over it. Surely that was enough?

When, at length, he was convinced, he extinguished the lamp, crept downstairs to his room, undressed and collapsed in his own bed, tossing and turning to make it look as though he had been there all night. Even with the blankets and quilt over him, he shivered, and could not get warm again.

32

Anne first noticed the girl in the queue just after Christmas. She was about her own age and had the sort of pleasantly pretty face that both men and women smile upon. The next time she saw her, she thought, No, she's beautiful; you just don't realize right away. On another morning, she walked out of the bakery behind her and watched as she went to the door of Studio Lamy and went inside. Anne saw a candle spark to life inside the shop, then vanish, wavering, into the interior.

After that, Anne found she was seeking her out. There was something about the girl that reminded her of Odile the Saint, at the Salpêtrière. They were both like candle flames; you wanted to stare at them, wanted to draw near. It was why Odile was such a success at the Tuesday lectures – she was back as star billing, Anne had heard. But also this girl was not like Odile at all. She looked to be the opposite of mad, if there was such a thing.

Anne got the shock of her life when the girl spoke to her.

'My goodness,' she said, having just arrived, rather out of breath, and taking her place behind Anne in the queue. 'I thought I was going to be late this morning!'

Anne was startled, because it sounded as though she was resuming a previous conversation. Also, it seemed an odd thing to say when you lived next door.

The girl indicated the studio with one hand. 'I work there, but I have to come from home, and it takes nearly an hour.'

'Oh,' said Anne. She wanted to say something else, but nothing came to her.

'Do you have to come far?' asked the girl.

'No. Just from the menagerie.'

The girl stared into her face, then burst out laughing. 'I'm sorry. That just sounded funny. Of course, you don't mean the zoo, just nearby. I pass it myself, on the way.'

'I did mean the zoo. The chief veterinarian's house. I work for him.'

'Oh? I didn't know anyone lived there. Do you like animals?'

Anne was beginning to wish this girl wasn't quite so friendly, but words just tumbled out of her mouth.

'Yes, I do. Especially the big cats.'

'They're beautiful, aren't they? I like them too. But I feel sorry for them, stuck in those little cages. The way they walk up and down, they look like they're dreaming of their home in the jungle.'

'Only the panther lives in a jungle,' Anne heard herself say. 'The lions live in great open grasslands, and – and – the tiger comes from mountain forests.' She stumbled in her eagerness to impart her knowledge.

'My goodness, you know a lot.' But the girl didn't sound cross at being corrected, more that she was genuinely interested. 'It must be a fascinating place to work.'

'Yes, it is.'

'I work in the photographic studio, here. That's interesting too. My mistress is so nice. You can't imagine a kinder employer. My name's Fanny Klein, by the way. But call me Fanny.'

Anne saw a hand extended towards her, and took it. 'Anne Petitjean.'

'Happy to meet you, Anne – may I call you Anne?'

Fanny kept chatting – Anne heard about Fanny's husband, Raymond, who was in the Guard, and about the studio itself. Fanny told her, to Anne's astonishment, that she posed for photographs with her clothes off. Anne didn't know what to say, but Fanny just laughed.

'Oh dear, I hope you're not shocked. Raymond always says I talk too much.'

Anne shook her head, her thoughts rushing too much for speech.

Fortunately, at that moment, the door of the bakery opened, and the queue began to move.

They bought their loaves, and she said goodbye to Fanny, who smiled and said, 'Till tomorrow!' from the doorway of the studio. Anne found herself smiling in return.

She was pleased with herself, but all those words left her feeling exhausted. She was stirred up, as if all the blood and fluid inside her was roiling and crashing about, rather than flowing peacefully on its appointed course.

Did this mean she had made a friend?

It was three months since she had left the hospital. She often thought about the friends she had left behind. She worried about them, whether they were still being well looked after. The last time she had been to see Marie-Jo and Lisa, they said they were fine. No, they weren't cold; yes, they were getting enough to eat – but their eyes went round like saucers when she described her shopping trips to the Rue de Rivoli. She even thought about lying when they asked if she got to eat any of the pastries she bought for Monsieur Papin, but lying was too hard, and she mumbled that she did get to eat a few leftovers, sometimes.

Marie-Jo gave a groan. 'You have leftovers! Oh my God! Oysters!'

When they weren't talking about food, she was being questioned about her relationship with Victor Calmette.

'You can't tell me, in all this time, he's never tried anything,' said Marie-Jo.

Anne shook her head. 'Really, he hasn't.' Her eyes went to the floor.

'He sounds like a gentleman,' said Lisa. 'You need to give him some encouragement!'

'Oh, no, I don't—'

'I'm serious. Look, you need to think about your future. You don't want to end up like us – back here? If he's a decent man, make sure he'll look after you.'

'He's barely spoken to me since I started work there. Why would he . . . ?'

Marie-Jo shook her head, tutting. She and Lisa exchanged a glance.

'Because you're a pretty girl, for one thing. Don't make that face! And you've got class – God knows how, after living in this dump for so long, but you do. Three: he got you out of here. Why would he do that, if he didn't like you? For heaven's sake, he must like you a lot. He'll want to marry you, or at least . . . you know.'

If it had been anyone other than Marie-Jo, Anne would have walked away in a fury of embarrassment. But she loved Marie-Jo.

'Don't you like him?'

'I don't know. I mean . . . I like him, but not . . . like that.'

'My God! Who needs "that"? Who cares about "that"? Do you think he's a good man?'

Anne nodded.

'Well, then. And, if he's really not biting, what about the old rich one? That might be even better.'

After that conversation, she could not help thinking about Victor, which she generally tried not to. In effect, she had lied to Marie-Jo, because she did think Victor liked her, and that feeling only intensified when he gave her the book. As soon as she opened the parcel and saw the rich leather binding, the exquisite engravings, she felt panic. It was too nice. It weighed on her heart.

What would Fanny think? The advice from Marie-Jo and Lisa was all very well, but they were – well, they were hardly experts on men, and they lived in a lunatic asylum. Fanny was a young woman who was happily married. She had always lived on the outside, and you could just tell that people thought well of her. She couldn't have been more normal.

Anne took a roundabout route home. She liked walking at night; she felt protected by the darkness, rather than otherwise. She passed the Church of Saint Médard, which she liked because it was famous for the miracle of the barking nuns. Médard was often invoked at the Salpêtrière, being the patron saint of lunatics. And vineyards, and brewers, and prisoners, and barrenness in women, and the weather, and toothache . . . As so often the way with saints, he was a regular jack of all—

The sound turned her to stone: a high whine that became a scream. She was just about to cross the Bièvre river where it turned eastward. Even though she had never heard one so close, she knew what it was: a Prussian shell. They had been shelling the outer forts for months, but that was a distant rumble everyone was used to. Not dangerous. They weren't supposed to reach . . . Not here. But it was here. She couldn't run – where would she run? She flinched, and looked up – saw something like a streak of lightning fall to earth. A sharp tearing, a giant hiss, and she saw without understanding . . . a shining pillar of white erupted from the surface of the Bièvre, not ten metres away. It grew to the height of the rooftops, wavered, hissing, then melted away with a long sigh. Anne saw the hole punched in the ice, the black water smoking gently. She tried to run. It was going to explode any second. This was how it would end.

Seconds crawled by. The smoke cleared. The stinking Bièvre, which had gulped down so much rubbish over the years, had swallowed the shell whole. Anne looked around – surely a window would open and someone would lean out, exclaiming . . . Someone must have heard the scream, seen the gleaming pillar? Closed shutters gazed back.

She hadn't even dropped her basket of bread. She wondered if she was ill again, if it had been a hallucination, a hysterical vision. But she felt strangely ... all right. She could move; she could walk. She could hear her breathing and her footsteps. And it had definitely happened: there, where the ice was broken, the black water undulated and steamed – a pot just under the boil.

33

Soeur Débarras had just handed him a needle and catgut when the crash came. They all froze, then the roar died away in a long, angry rumble. It was loud – close enough to make the chandeliers tinkle, closer than anything they'd heard in the hospital. Ellis couldn't move. For a second, he was back in Washington, under Confederate attack.

'Come on, it's at least a mile away,' drawled a voice. It belonged to Meehan, a surgeon who had spent most of the American war in field hospitals, operating to the sound of gunfire. There was a slackening of tension, a ripple of laughter, murmured prayers from the Sisters.

Ellis opened his eyes, breathed out and began suturing. His hands weren't shaking too badly.

'The wind must be from the south,' said Soeur Débarras. 'Sometimes it sounds closer than it is.'

Even so, they all knew, the impact had been closer than the ring of forts outside the city walls. Much closer. Ellis concentrated on closing the wound. Before the next patient was brought in, there was another explosion: crack, growl, the long exhale of shock.

Swan came in towards the end of the afternoon and surveyed his staff calmly.

'Well, they're shelling inside the city now,' he announced. 'The Prussians have taken Châtillon and moved their artillery up there. Montparnasse seems to be the limit of their range. From what I gather, there's not much damage. One of the shells landed outside a café. They took some casualties to Val de Grâce, but it's all south of the cemetery. The furthest north was in the Rue d'Enfer.'

'Where was that? Which café?'

The chief surgeon shrugged. 'I don't know. I'm reliably informed that we're in no danger here. So, for the time being, we carry on.'

Swan's face was haggard with exhaustion, but his voice was reassuring. He patrolled the room, hands behind his back, exchanging a few words with each surgeon, making the odd joke. He stopped by Ellis's table and watched as he put in the last stitches of a knee disarticulation.

'Isn't this the fellow from the Opéra?'

'Yes.'

A surgeon in the Opéra hospital had removed the man's foot a week earlier, but necrosis had set in. The man's mother brought him to the American hospital in a cart she dragged herself, with her neighbours, as red streaks spread up his calf like branches of an evil tree. Ellis had just sawn off the whole lower limb. Swan gave an approving nod.

By the end of his shift, Ellis's chest was ominously tight. He wasn't the only one shaken by the bombing, but his infirmity was an added curse. He worried that others sensed his weakness and despised him for it. Soeur Débarras hadn't helped; she looked at him and told him to go home.

'You look tired, monsieur. Christmas did you so much good, but it has all worn off now. Go home and rest. You'll be all right there, you're well out of harm's way.'

'What about you, Sister?' She had never told him exactly where her convent was.

'We'll be all right.' She smiled. 'The Lord will protect.'

On being pushed, she admitted that her home, the Couvent des Angelines, was near the Luxembourg.

'But that's not far from Montparnasse.'

'It's far enough. And very many people live in Montparnasse, and further south. It is those poor people we should be concerned for.'

'Won't you be worried?'

'I'm too old to worry.'

'Well – let me walk you home, at least. Please.'

'I shall not, monsieur. What nonsense!' She chuckled.

'Sister, I'm going that way anyway. I have a friend who lives nearby. I want to see if— make sure they're all right.'

She allowed him to accompany her and another of the nursing Sisters across the river. On the Left Bank, the streets seemed the same as ever – dark and quiet, with the crunch of ice under their boots. Occasionally there was a flash of white light in the distance as a shell fell on Montparnasse, or on Montrouge. The Sisters calmly named the districts as each shell exploded: that one was Montsouris; that one must have landed near the Gobelins.

They encountered an elderly couple hurrying in the opposite direction and stopped them to ask for news.

'We were visiting friends in Croulebarbe, when a bomb fell only a few blocks away. The noise! And the building on fire! My God . . . what are we all coming to?'

The woman crossed herself. They were returning to their home in Château d'Eau; some people had already started fleeing the southern districts, heading across the river, where they believed they would be safe.

Ellis had managed not to give much thought to what had happened on Christmas night. It was not that such occurrences were commonplace for him, more that his work was so tiring, so all consuming, that he barely thought at all. It was easy – necessary – to push aside anything external to the job: inconvenient memories; fruitless speculations. Only in the moments between falling into bed and falling asleep would memories of Lawrence's skin wash hotly, sweetly, over him. Whether it would be repeated, what it meant, he managed not to wonder.

He told himself that Lawrence was perfectly all right. He would have been working today. But the café where Yves' friends used to meet was very near Val de Grâce. It wasn't Sunday, but still . . .

He had to stop at this point; his chest so tight that he shuffled into the nearest bar for a brandy. Customers crowded around the counter, talking about the shelling. Stories and rumours flew: one man had seen a fire engulfing a building near the Catacombs, another had heard of a man being sliced in two, just walking down the street. Whole streets of people were packing up and leaving for the northern districts. Well, if they had somewhere to go, that is.

When he reached the Rue des Ciseaux, everything looked normal. The Studio Lamy and its neighbours had such a respectable, permanent air, it was hard to imagine a shell daring to fall on them. Glimmers of light showed at the curtained windows above the shop. He felt a little foolish for having come all this way. His ring at the door was answered by a young woman in a maid's uniform.

'Good evening, my name is Monsieur Butterfield. Is Monsieur Harper at home?'

'Monsieur . . . ?'

He repeated both names.

'Ah, Monsieur Harper. And you are . . . Excuse me, Butterfield? Yes, he is here. Shall I . . . ? Come in, yes. Please, excuse me.'

The maid seemed unsure of herself, then fled ahead of him up the stairs. Ellis waited in the corridor. There was no reason to have worried. He had not been worried, it was just that his stupid asthma would not let him go home without making sure. He looked up to see Lawrence coming down the stairs, a quizzical smile on his face.

'Ellis – it is you! I thought Fanny might have made a mistake.' The door behind him was open and voices could be heard inside.

Ellis made an elaborately casual gesture. 'I had an errand to run nearby, and, after the shelling, I thought I'd drop by, just to—'

'Well, how good to see you. Come in.'

As Lawrence showed him into the drawing room, Ellis felt the brief, deliberate pressure of a hand on the small of his back. There was no time to return it, but it made him extraordinarily glad.

'Madame Lamy, Mademoiselle Lamy – may I present Monsieur Butterfield.'

Ellis bowed and shook their hands.

'Ah, the surgeon! Monsieur Harper said you took shelter here the other night – I was sorry you could not stay to breakfast. We are happy to meet you now, even under these trying circumstances.' Madame Lamy had bright black eyes and an engaging manner.

The daughter was reserved; she gave him a chilly smile and a limp hand.

'How thoughtful you are!' exclaimed Madame Lamy, when he had explained the purpose of his visit. 'Of course, we can hear it –' she waved her hand at the window as another roar came from the south – 'but we haven't seen anything. Apparently, there was a fire near the Catacombs . . . Have you heard anything?'

Ellis related what Swan had said about Montparnasse Cemetery being the limit of the guns' reach.

'Well, that's a relief. That's what Monsieur Lamy thought too.'

'Maman! How can you say that is a relief when Monsieur Ranvier's house is almost at the cemetery?'

'Well, not really, Titine. And he won't have been there today, anyway. I'm sure we'll hear from him soon.' She turned to Ellis. 'We're waiting to hear from my daughter's fiancé. Obviously, it is a bit of a concern.'

'And what's to stop the Prussians moving forward again? We don't know what's going to happen.'

'The gun emplacements will be on high ground,' Ellis ventured. 'If they have captured a French fort – Châtillon, I gather – they will stay there. There would be no profit in firing from lower ground.'

'How can you know that?' Mademoiselle Lamy persisted.

'I can't know for certain, but—'

'Monsieur Butterfield was in the American war, mademoiselle – in Washington,' said Lawrence. 'He has experienced this sort of thing before.'

'There you are, then!' said Madame Lamy. 'That makes perfect sense.'

'If you give me Monsieur Ranvier's address, I could go to the house and make enquiries . . .' Lawrence looked questioningly at Ellis.

'Yes, we should do that. I just walked two of the nursing Sisters to the Couvent des Angelines – it was perfectly quiet and calm down there.'

'Oh? That's not far from his house. It's Rue Notre Dame des Prés.'

'I'm sure that's not necessary, Titine. Messieurs—'

'It's no trouble. I could do with a walk. What do you say, Ellis? It won't take long to walk there, will it?'

They cut through the warren of streets north of the Luxembourg gardens. Periodically, there was a flash of light in the sky: another explosion to the south. The rutted ice had melted and refrozen so many times, it was as hard as rocks.

'Where were you, when it began?'

'In the darkroom. I broke a plate. Were you operating?'

'Yes. Of course, we're further away, there. The consensus is that there's no danger, as long as we stay north.'

'You really think they won't move closer?'

'That's what they say – you know, men who know more about these things than I do.'

'Are you all right? Do you want to stop for a bit?'

Ellis stopped. His breathing was audibly laboured, but, in his gladness, he had barely noticed.

'Sorry. Damn it. I could do with a drink. Have we time?'

There was time. They found a bar – a small place, with bare tables lit by candles. To walk inside, into the light, felt like stepping under a spell of protection. Lawrence ordered brandies and they stood at the counter. The *patronne* and the other customers were friendly. Being under attack lent them a solidarity in which even foreigners were accepted. They exchanged rumours. Ellis related what he had heard about a man being sliced in two. A customer said that the first shell had fallen in Rue Lalande, near the entrance to the Catacombs. Some buildings had been damaged, some people hurt – not that badly, they thought. There was general agreement that the shells were falling south of the cemetery and were not much of a threat.

They left and skirted the Luxembourg gardens. There weren't many people on the streets, though figures showed at lit windows, peering out in the direction of the bombardment. The shelling grew louder as they walked south, but, in the Rue Notre Dame des Prés, which curved away from the corner of the Luxembourg, all was calm. Ranvier's house was a large, handsome building, with the shutters closed and no light showing. There was no damage here; they had yet to see any sign of damage. Lawrence knocked on the door, but there was no reply.

'Well, the fiancé's house seems perfectly all right. Monsieur – what's his name?'

'Ranvier.'

'Ah, yes, the camel killer.'

Ellis lit a cigar. He and Lawrence stood in the entrance to a carriage yard. Shells were falling every few minutes; they could feel the shocks, faintly, underfoot. He didn't want to go back.

'Isn't that a fire over there?' Ellis pointed to a pulsating glow in the sky, that traced the outline of rooftops.

'Yes, I think so.'

'Do you want to go take a look?'

Lawrence hesitated. 'I suppose I should get back before too long.'

'Yes. Of course.'

Still they stood, watching the uneven glow.

'They don't want us to sleep. They've had enough of waiting.'

Ellis, who was also waiting, felt Lawrence put a hand on his arm. They hadn't touched since that brief pressure outside the Lamys' drawing room.

'It'll take you hours to get home. Why don't you come back, stay the night? Madame Lamy will be angry if I let you go.'

'Oh, well, I—'

Another shell exploded in La Glacière. White light flowered over the rooftops: a burst of dry lightning.

Lawrence pulled him backwards into the darkness of the coach yard. This shell was no nearer, but the air in the yard seemed momentarily squeezed, shuddering within its walls. Their mouths collided and they held on to each other. Ellis dropped his cigar and they grappled in the darkness, treading on each other's toes, breathing hard, bodies pressed together in a shared, sudden hunger. He could barely see Lawrence's face in front of him. He felt a voluptuous pressure against his groin, then Lawrence fumbling to undo his fly buttons.

'Aah, what if—?' he managed to whisper, before Lawrence's tongue stopped his mouth.

He gave himself up to being pleasured, quieting his breathing as much as he could, but he came fast, with a violent, clenching spasm, and a thin choking noise escaped him; it felt as though all his strength flooded out into Lawrence's hand, leaving him empty and insubstantial. His knees buckled and he collapsed back against the wall. Lawrence leant into him, his forehead against his cheek, then he felt lips press against his neck, his jaw. He turned to kiss him again, slower this time. When he groped for Lawrence in turn, Lawrence held his hand.

'Come back,' he said.

Ellis leant against the wall, panting. This Lawrence was thrillingly unfamiliar: commanding, unexpected. A man who took advantage of dark places.

Another explosion came, and the tremor was palpable. He felt the vibrations in his own body, and in Lawrence's where he was pressed against him.

'Come back with me.'

By the time they returned, the Lamys had heard from Monsieur Ranvier. He was safe on the Right Bank, although worried about Ernestine. He wanted to move his fiancée and her parents to a hotel further north, as long as the attacks lasted.

'We're practically on the river. We wouldn't want him to go to all that expense for nothing. You should go, of course,' said Madame Lamy to her daughter. 'We can't have him worrying about you.'

Lawrence and Ellis related what they had learnt about the shelling, and the safety of Monsieur Ranvier's house. Madame Lamy insisted that Ellis stay.

'Thank you. I'll have to leave early to get to work, but that's very kind of you.'

'Nonsense. We're more than happy to meet any friend of Lawrence's. You must promise to come to dinner another time, so that we can meet you properly. Mustn't he?'

In the spare room, Ellis sat on the bed, listening to Madame Lamy's footsteps descending the stairs. No matter how tired he was on getting home at night, it was his habit to drink a bottle of wine before turning in. It helped to soften and smooth any parts of the day that were too jarring. He doubted he could sleep without it. As for what he was contemplating before that . . . the brandy he had drunk in the bar was too little, too long ago. He waited, his heart thudding with anticipation and nerves. He would give his right arm for a drink. Then, outside the door, there came a creak, a soft tap. Lawrence came in noiselessly.

'Are you all right?'

'Yes.'

They both spoke softly.

'Tired?' For the first time, Lawrence too seemed tentative.

'Well . . . I don't know if I'll sleep.'

The noise of the shells still came, but it was dull and monotonous, already receding into normality. Lawrence sat beside him on the bed. In the lamplight, his face open to scrutiny, and sober, Ellis didn't know how to behave.

'I like your Madame Lamy.'

'Yes, she's wonderful. I was lucky to end up here.'

The dipping mattress impelled them towards each other. Lawrence placed a hand on his thigh and rubbed it slowly. 'You're cold.'

'Of course, she's in love with you.'

'Don't be silly.'

'It's true. Don't tell me you haven't noticed.'

'She's friendly and kind, that's all.'

The hand that was caressing his thigh slid up to his groin. Ellis closed his eyes and took a deep breath. 'What if they hear?'

'They won't. Not if we're quiet.'

The hand was now massaging his erection. It was too much – terrifying to be at this point still sober, as if his body was out-racing his mind and there was nothing he could do about it. Every time he had had sex, without exception, he had been drunk.

He felt Lawrence's breath on his cheek, his face brush against his, then turned to find his open mouth. Lips, tongues, teeth. How deftly Lawrence took control, as if the thought that there could be any alternative to this was absurd; now, he slid to the floor, tugged down Ellis's pants and buried his face in his lap. Ellis leant back on his hands with a groan. He didn't know what he had done to deserve this. When he was on the brink of climaxing, the hot mouth pulled away. Ellis looked down with a gasp. Lawrence reached up and put a hand over his mouth, looked teasingly at him.

'Be quiet. Or I'll have to stop.'

Ellis hadn't noticed that he was making any noise. He lay back and pulled the pillow over his mouth. Vulnerable, with his feet tangled in his pants, his mid-section exposed to the cold air, he gave himself up for the second time, moaning prayers and imprecations into the pillow.

Lawrence sat back on his heels and wiped his mouth.

Ellis emerged from under the pillow, panting.

'God. That was lovely.'

Lawrence grinned. Ellis caught at his hand and pulled him towards him.

'What do you want?'

'Anything.'

Ellis began unbuttoning Lawrence's shirt, but it was too cold not to hurry. They tore back the icy covers. Lawrence peeled off his clothes, gold-skinned in the lamplight as he pulled the shirt over his head. His body was boy-lean and smooth. He was beautiful, and quite unembarrassed. His confidence was as unnerving as it was exciting.

'I haven't done this . . . that often. So . . .'

Lawrence, kneeling on the bed, smiled down at him. 'So? I mean it: anything.' He joined him under the covers.

In the tent of blankets, Ellis kissed the taut skin of his chest and stomach. He'd forgotten how healthy skin felt, what delight there was in touching a body that didn't need to be mutilated to live. He stroked hot skin, felt the strong, springy limbs and found the hard, glossy head. Lawrence smelt salty and sharp, like crushed pine needles. He drew in a deep breath as Ellis sucked him, but was otherwise silent. Ellis consciously tried to do what Lawrence had done to him, hoping he would be good enough.

In the narrow bed, they were pressed against each other from shoulder to toe. Ellis pulled the blankets around them both. He listened for horrified footsteps, an outraged pounding on the door. Nothing happened, just Lawrence sighing against his shoulder. Ellis reached out with his free hand and fiddled with the lamp beside the bed. Eventually, he managed to extinguish it.

'Are you worried about the Lamys' oil supplies?' Lawrence asked.

'What if someone came in?'

'Why would they? People don't wander round, barging into other people's rooms at night.'

'You did.'

Lawrence laughed softly. 'I did. I should go back to my room.' But he didn't move, just snuggled against Ellis, his hand lying on his chest. 'In a minute. You're so warm.'

'So are you.'

Ellis listened to Lawrence breathe. He slowed his breaths until they were in unison. Then Lawrence spoke from the darkness.

'How did you know?'

'How did I know?'

'What made you so sure? The other night. Was it obvious?'

'No.' Ellis thought of Yves, and what Gustave had hinted about his friendships with young men. He wasn't going to say that name. 'When I asked you what you were ashamed of – and you said, going with one of the models.'

'You didn't believe me?'

'It's not that. But who would say that was something to be ashamed of? It seemed such a funny thing to say; I don't know—'

'So, because of that, you knew?' Lawrence sounded put out.

'Not exactly. I suppose I knew before. I was fairly sure. And then, you invited me back here.'

'Because of the snow!'

'Oh, of course. The snow.'

In the distance, another shell exploded. The sound was soft, but spine-tinglingly clear. It made you tense, listening for what might come after . . . But the reverberations rolled away into quietness.

In Washington, Ellis had seen the Union artillery at work. He could picture it: the gun crew going about its routine, sponging the breech, drying, loading the shot, seeding the case, aiming, priming, pulling the lanyard; each man slotting in and out of place in practised, thoughtless harmony, a man–metal machine; the shell flying away in a beautiful feather of flame. He had looked on with awe at such trained, efficient precision, because they were on the same side. You could admire it, almost forgetting what the result would be.

Lawrence shifted his limbs against him, and Ellis felt the kick of a renewed erection against his thigh. The warm hand strayed from his chest down to his belly, moving in lazy circles, and he grew against that hot, slithery presence. He turned, the bed creaking, so that they were face to face, feeling the brush of skin against skin, the sweet shock as cock met its twin. His heart was beating so hard, he thought Lawrence must hear it; the room was so quiet, his breaths were bellows. In the dark, they kissed, the other's mouth a sheltering cave, a well for his thirst.

34

More than once, Victor had lain awake counting bombs. At first, there had been around three hundred a night; now, it was closer to four hundred. They fell at one-minute intervals, for hours. He tried pulling the pillow around his head, he tried stuffing wax balls in his ears, but neither helped. He could muffle the noise, but he couldn't block it out altogether. Every evening, around ten o'clock, his mind would start racing, and his heart would accelerate with a sickening bound as he waited for the first explosion. Each night, he knew it was coming, but also he would think, Perhaps tonight is the night it will end. Sooner or later, there would be the first crash, the first lurch of the heart. The later the Prussians started, the greater the suspense, but if for some reason he lost track of the time and was not prepared, that was worse. Coming out of the blue, the blast felt like a physical blow. He would have called it intolerable, except that he had no choice.

The remarkable thing was the way people grew used to the bombardment, and many were positively blasé. True, the shelling did surprisingly little damage. Buildings in southern districts were damaged, fires were started, and you heard lurid stories – people sliced in two and what have you – but it was impossible to know which of those were true. When you looked into it, only a handful of civilians had been killed – far fewer than had died of smallpox or typhoid, or from winter diseases exacerbated by the cold and hunger. Still, he couldn't get used to it. He knew how the noise terrified the animals.

They snarled and cowered in the darkness, or threw themselves against the bars in their frenzy.

At first, they – meaning the newspapers, Director Lapeyre and public opinion generally – said the Prussian guns couldn't reach north of Montparnasse Cemetery. Then, the dome of the Panthéon was damaged; a house in the Rue Mouffetard was hit; the nursery in the Luxembourg lost a year's worth of apple seedlings; a shell even smashed through the roof of the Gare d'Orléans and destroyed three balloons being manufactured there. The station was next to the Salpêtrière – and that was next to the Jardin des Plantes, which held everything that was dear to him.

Like everyone else, Victor and Papin calculated the reach of the guns, drawing angles and lines on a map. From the former French fortress at Bicêtre, shells were hitting the Gare d'Orléans and the districts of Maison Blanche and La Glacière. Further west, the enemy had captured the fort of Montrouge and perhaps the one at Issy as well – that accounted for the shells falling on the Luxembourg and Saint Germain, as far north as Les Invalides. Those Parisians who were defiant were sticking it out, but there were many inhabitants of the Left Bank – those who could afford it, or who had anywhere else to go – who fled the area. Those who stayed left their doors unlocked, so that passers-by could fetch water to put out the fires, or take shelter.

The diagrams had reassured him that the zoo, and the veterinarian's house at its northern end, was comfortably out of range. Even in his attic rooms in the Rue Poliveau, Victor felt safe. He might freeze to death, but that was another matter.

He had a headache behind his eyes. He knew he was not going to sleep. He lit a candle and looked at his watch – it was half past one.

A short while later, he turned into the park entrance. The night was clear and a half-moon cast cold silver light on to the paths, but Victor could have walked them blindfold. He unlocked the gate of the menagerie. The stillness and emptiness of the enclosures was uncanny. Those animals that had been spared were quiet – listless with cold and hunger.

Not the first time he had come to the zoo at night. Not even the first time during the bombardment. Victor made his way to the cat pavilion, his boots ringing on the frozen path, and heard a stirring in the lions' cage. A guttural cough: Tancred. Victor stopped and greeted them, let them recognize his scent. Irma the lioness put her paw against the bars and growled hopefully, her eyes gleaming in the faint light. The poor creature was skin and bone.

'I'm sorry, my dear. I haven't got anything for you.'

Despite the cold, he smelt the rank horseflesh they'd been fed the day before, and the musk of carnivores. Robitaille was the only keeper still tending to them. He and the redundant elephant keeper were the only members of staff left, and between them they looked after all the remaining animals: the cats, the crocodiles, the hippopotamus, the rhinoceros; two wolves out of the original five; the quagga, which looked to be on its last legs. Papin and Lapeyre had discussed putting it out of its misery, but the quagga was the rarest of creatures, possibly extinct in the wild, so they resolved to keep it alive as long as they could. The snakes had gone into hibernation – at least, he hoped they were still alive; it was hard to tell. A handful of the pre-siege population. Presiding over such wholesale slaughter was something he could never have imagined. But at least Marguerite was still here.

The tigress lay against the bars of her cage, head lifted, sniffing him. Victor pulled the scarf more closely around his neck and squatted in front of the railings. A shell rumbled in the distance. The great head moved vaguely, as if seeking the source of the noise.

'It's all right. They can't hurt you, dear girl. I'll never let them hurt you.'

The tigress growled softly. Victor wished he had brought her something, but he had nothing to bring. There was not a scrap of food in his rooms.

Even by moonlight, he could see how loosely her fur was draped over her bones. Hip and shoulder jutted above her flank like mountain peaks. Her ribs were visible. He had noticed the same progression in his own body: lying in bed, his hip bones reared up either side of the shrunken belly, the skin a loose, white tent. His own body disgusted him, but Marguerite's want aroused pity.

He had no idea how long he had been there when he heard a sound: a foot striking a loose piece of ice. He turned and saw a dark shape against the snow-covered path. He lurched to his feet – knees cracking in complaint – and cast around for something he could seize for a weapon, but, before he could move, the intruder saw him and turned away, and he saw the outline of a skirt.

'Anne! Anne, it's Victor!'

The figure paused.

'It's all right. I come to see her too.'

Marguerite uttered a growl.

After a pause, Anne came towards him. 'I'm sorry, monsieur . . . I borrowed the keys. I'll put them back as soon as I return.'

'I'm not angry, Anne. Really, it's all right.'

'I just came by . . . I'm on the way to get the bread.'

'Bread? At this hour?'

'This is when the queues begin.'

'Oh.'

He should have known better – Anne never lied.

'I brought her some leftovers.'

'Oh, good. Go ahead, then.'

Anne took something out of her basket, attached it to the end of her cane and poked it between the bars. Marguerite sniffed languidly, ate the morsel and yawned, as if to say, *Is that all?*

'You've done this before?'

Anne nodded. 'Sometimes there's nothing to bring.'

'Do you always feed her? Not the others?'

Anne shrugged. 'Sometimes the others. But she's the biggest.'

There was an explosion – a loud one. The cats hissed and snarled. Victor went to look in Nero's cage. He was usually the most nervous. Tonight, Victor could neither see nor hear the panther; he must have been cowering in the dark recesses of his shelter. He walked back to Anne.

'I wish I could explain to them that there is nothing to fear.'

Anne said, 'Isn't there?'

'Not from shells. Not here.'

He stole a glance at her, but her eyes were fixed on the tigress.

'Does the noise bother you, Anne? Can you sleep through it?'

Anne said, 'I'd better go. The queue . . .'

He watched her vanish into the darkness and turned back to Marguerite. She was cleaning her whiskers. He moved on and peered into the shadows of Nero's cage. There was no sign of movement, but he was almost impossible to spot at night; only the gleam of his eyes would give him away. Victor squinted with the effort of penetrating the darkness. Nothing. He would come and check on him tomorrow. He thought of Anne walking the unlit streets in this freezing cold. Perhaps he should have gone with her – at least offered his company. Was it safe for her to be out there on her own? Presumably she did this every night . . . When did she sleep?

He would make his rounds of the other animals. He would stand in front of each of them for a few minutes, urging calmness on them, endurance – a little while longer. He was aware it didn't help. But somehow it soothed his own turmoil.

Robitaille was distraught.

'I know I locked up! I always do, messieurs!'

Victor nodded. 'I know you do, Robitaille.' He looked at the director. Lapeyre was furious. Victor couldn't blame him. 'What other explanation is there? The cage door is unlocked, isn't it? A dangerous predator is at large in the midst of a city!'

'With respect, director, we don't know that he escaped,' Victor said. 'It is more likely to be theft. Someone who broke in. He's a famous animal, after all.'

'The lock wasn't forced.'

Victor shrugged uneasily. 'It's been a while since the locks were changed, or it could have been picked. These criminals are so clever.'

'Who would steal an animal like that, at a . . . a time like this?'

'They've stolen them to eat before,' Victor hazarded.

'Then why not take the quagga? There's more meat on that – and a lot less bother.'

Victor didn't know. He was sorry for Robitaille. He knew him to be stalwart, the most reliable man in the zoo. But, also, anybody could make a mistake.

'If the panther has escaped, there will be consequences. What if he harms someone? What if he kills a child? By God, I hate to think—'

'I'll look for him,' said Robitaille, who was almost in tears.'

Lapeyre nodded, dismissing him. He sighed angrily.

'What chance does he have of finding him? A black cat, in a huge city? When there are no lights!'

'He knows the places to look. If Nero is out there, he'll have to find somewhere to hide. He's scared of people, so he'll avoid them as much as possible. He might escape the city altogether.'

Lapeyre snorted dismissively. 'At this rate, there won't be a zoo left at the end of this. Just empty cages. We'll be a laughing stock.'

Victor's heart sank. 'Shouldn't we help look? I can round up some men—'

'And have everyone talking about this? Think, man – we can't breathe a word of it. We'd have a riot on our hands.'

He said nothing to Lapeyre about Anne's night-time visits. The only consolation he could find was that he had already been at the cages when she arrived, and he felt sure, thinking back, that Nero was already gone. And surely, if Anne had decided to free one of the animals, she would have freed Marguerite?

35

Anne heard the front door open. Papin never normally came back to the house before lunchtime. She went into the hall and saw Victor Calmette. Anne had never seen him in the house at this time; she knew it portended nothing good.

'Ah, Anne . . .' he began.

From his face, she didn't think he was angry, but he wasn't smiling either. Probably he was going to fire her for taking Monsieur Papin's keys – had he told monsieur already? She felt cold at the thought. Foolish to have hoped that nothing would happen in consequence. She bowed her head in readiness. Would the hospital even take her back?

'Let's go in here,' said Victor, indicating the dining room, and closed the door after them.

She could tell that he was uneasy about something.

'Anne, I wanted to ask you . . . well, the thing is . . .' He sighed, smoothed his hand over his hair and started again. 'You're not to repeat this to anyone, do you understand?'

Alarmed now, she nodded.

He lowered his voice further, leant towards her. 'Nero, the panther, is missing. His cage was unlocked this morning. He's gone.'

At first, she didn't say anything. It was like being hypnotized, although she could still see and hear. Then she spoke, although it came out as more of a creaking noise: 'And Marguerite?'

'Marguerite is still there. She's fine. All the others are fine. It's just Nero.'

She could feel him watching her and understood what it meant.

'You think it was me.'

'Well, no, I . . . Was it you, Anne?'

'No, monsieur.'

'Of course. That's what I thought – that you wouldn't have done it, I mean. I'm sorry, I just had to ask, after – you know – after last night. Robitaille is looking for him. He thinks it's his fault – I suppose it is possible that he forgot to lock up; everyone is under strain. And the director . . . well! It's a disaster. Either to lose him, or . . . And, if he's loose in the city, what might he do? He might hurt someone. This could finish us!' He wrung his hands.

'Do you want me to look? To help, I mean.'

'No, no. There's no need for that.'

'He should try round the Bièvre.'

'Right. Why do you say that?'

'Lots of smells. The tanneries. And slaughterhouses . . .'

'Of course.'

Victor exhaled a long sigh. 'I'm sorry, Anne, I had to ask.'

'If someone has broken in . . . Is that what they think happened?'

'I don't know. We don't know. There is no sign of force. Pick-locks, maybe? Stolen keys? We haven't changed the locks for too long, what with . . .' He made a helpless gesture.

Anne thought, How could you let this happen? You, who are all they have. At the same time, she rejoiced. She couldn't help it.

All day, Anne thought about Nero. Was he safe? Frightened? Hungry? On her way back from shopping, she walked along the zoo boundary. She knew its paths intimately, had pictured the choices that would have faced him as he slipped out of his cage. Had there been bombs falling? If so, he would have fled from the noise: north, across the river. He would have followed the darkest passages, seeking shelter. He would have followed the smell of blood – plenty of butchers in the old streets around Les Halles. But, if he had escaped earlier, before the bombs fell, she was certain he would have found his way to the Bièvre. Tiny alleyways, overhanging awnings, piles of detritus, endless holes and crannies. It smelt of rotting leather, lye, animal scraps. There were always dead things there. People said there was nothing you wouldn't find in the Bièvre, if you were desperate enough to look.

Nero was secretive, silent, the colour of shadows. Perhaps he could pass through the city unnoticed. He had taken the chance to be free.

That night, around two, she woke without prompting. She lit her candle and steeled herself for the leap from the warmth of her blankets towards the chair where her clothes were waiting. She pulled the clothes on as fast as she could, her skin shrinking from the cold cloth, holding her breath.

Tonight, she got as far as buttoning the front of her dress before the first rumble came. It was such an ominous sound, like the growling of maddened beasts. The first shell she'd heard explode (only a week ago? It felt as though the bombs had been falling forever) had made her heart climb into her throat. That was in the afternoon, during her errands, and she had stopped dead on the street, cringing, her hand on the wall next to her, waiting for darkness to swamp her, the sky to cave in . . . but nothing happened. The shock passed, and she was still standing. She could move. More than that, nobody even looked at her. Other shoppers crossed themselves, turned to the nearest passer-by, with round, open mouths; hands fluttered to hearts. It wasn't just her. She was both relieved and slightly disappointed.

Victor had asked how she slept through the noise. Truth was, these days, she was so tired when she fell into bed, nothing kept her awake. She had changed since she came here; she was used to the soft mattress; she took her privacy for granted. Anne Petitjean was becoming . . . what? Like everyone else?

She stifled a yawn as she crept downstairs, boots in hand, mindful not to wake anyone. She sat down on the last step, laced up her boots and took the key to the house from the hall table. The other key was in its usual place in the top drawer of Monsieur Papin's escritoire. Did that mean that Victor Calmette had not told him about her theft?

The cats were quiet. She went to the panther's empty cage and stared into it. The darkness stared back; it had nothing to say. It just showed you: anything was possible, if you wanted it badly enough. Whether it was a good idea was another matter. How would you know?

At Marguerite's cage, Anne whispered to the tigress, who raised her head, sighed and laid it down on the concrete. Anne peered at her.

'It will be over soon,' she told her, because she had heard Monsieur Papin say so: when the food really and truly ran out – even the black-market stuff – the government would have no choice but to surrender. He'd made it sound inevitable. In which case, what were they waiting for?

Anne took out the third key. She had stolen it a week ago; someone had left it in the lock of one of the cages. It was there, right in front of her, so what else was she going to do? She scraped it softly against the railings.

'What do you say?'

Marguerite's eyes were closed. Perhaps she was asleep. The strange thing was, it hadn't been Anne who had unlocked Nero's cage. It should have been. She had thought about it, and thought about it, and then someone had beaten her to it. But then she wondered if it had been her – something done in a trance, like the things she had done in Jospin's lectures, and she had no memory of it – or if she had thought about it so hard, it had become real.

'Do you want to go?' she whispered.

The tigress didn't move. She seemed tired, uninterested. Perhaps she was right. She could never pass unnoticed in the dull, grey city, that was her trouble. The trouble, and also why she was glorious.

36

At a nearby table, uniformed French officers were entertaining a pair of gaily dressed young women. Their table was crowded with bottles of champagne and plates of food. Lawrence saw oysters, sardines, biscuits; he even caught the ammoniacal tang of foie gras. He swallowed the water that flooded his mouth. They were careless of their plenty.

Not everyone at the table was equally indifferent. Lawrence nursed his glass of brandy and watched with amusement as one young woman, pretty and dark haired, kept up a flow of chatter while deftly conveying morsels into her mouth. If she was trading her vivacity for food, she was striking a hard bargain. The other grisette had realized what was happening and looked sulky, but all the interesting plates had been manoeuvred within easy reach of the dark-haired girl, and the officers were too drunk to notice.

He was so absorbed in watching them, he didn't notice Ellis come in, not until he slid into the chair opposite and signalled the waiter for a drink. Lawrence experienced a turbulent rush at the sight of him. He tried not to stare too greedily, but it had been a week since they had met – days and nights turgid with memories and imagination. But the picture he'd carried in his head clashed with the reality in front of him in small, jarring ways.

'How are you?'

'Oh, you know. Lord, what a day I've had.' Ellis smiled at Lawrence, but met his eyes only for an instant, before glancing around the room.

He looked exhausted: paler than Lawrence remembered, and he was unshaven, the skin under his eyes swollen, almost translucent. Of course, his job was hugely demanding. Lawrence was chastened by the gravity of his friend's work, the insignificance of his own.

'Do you want to talk about it?' he said lightly.

Ellis shrugged, and Lawrence saw that he was drunk. Hadn't he just come from the hospital?

'It never stops. One gets used to it, of course – it's just that I haven't been used to it, not for a long time.' He passed a hand over his face as if wiping away memories and gave Lawrence a savage grin. 'It's not interesting. Tell me what you've been doing.' He leant back, his eyes sliding away too quickly. He lit a cigar. There was something off in his tone of voice.

'Um, not very much. There's hardly any work in the studio, so Monsieur Lamy and I have been going out, taking photographs of the shell damage – or trying to. The Panthéon has been hit – and the Salpêtrière hospital. You know, the women's asylum?'

'God, were many hurt?'

'Apparently no one. But – bombing a hospital!'

'Gustave Daudel took me there last summer, to a public lecture. It was extraordinary. They display the patients as if they were circus acts, and all the beau monde turn out to see it. Some of the women are very beautiful.'

'It's been hit more than once. Can they be doing it on purpose?'

'Who knows . . . Hey! I asked for *eau de vie*,' he shouted at a passing waiter. 'But that's a good idea – photographing it, I mean. These things should be recorded. There were artists everywhere in our war – photographers, too, by the end of it. I don't think I've seen any here.'

'We're hardly the best people for the job. Everyone is so worried about spies. Monsieur Lamy doesn't talk, of course; he just hands out cards if someone challenges us. If I try to explain, they hear my accent and that doesn't help.'

The brandy arrived and became the focus of attention. Ellis poured two glasses, raised his to Lawrence, emptied it in one swallow and grimaced.

He gave a great sigh. 'God, that's better. Have you eaten?'

Lawrence shook his head.

'We shouldn't eat here, it's daylight robbery, but I know where we can get something half decent on the way to my place – if that's still all right, that is.'

He didn't look at Lawrence as he spoke. He sounded so offhand, almost hostile, Lawrence wondered if he really wanted him there.

Ellis drained his glass again and stared around him, taking in the table of officers, now ordering more champagne and oysters. 'All right for some, isn't it?' He jerked his head towards them. 'I wonder if they'll pay for those girls tonight, or maybe the oysters will cover it.'

Lawrence leant forward. 'Shh. They'll hear you.'

'A bunch of these girls comes to the hospital every evening to try it on with the surgeons. They think we're all rich.'

'I suppose, relatively, you are.'

Ellis caught the eye of the dark girl at the table and lifted his glass to her. He grinned at Lawrence. 'Do you think I'm in with a shout?'

Lawrence hadn't expected overt signs of intimacy, but this was going too far. 'You must be hungry. I know I'm ravenous,' he said, smiling to show how little he cared about it, hoping Ellis would take the hint.

'Just thirsty,' said Ellis, summoning the waiter again.

A little while later, one of the officers, getting unsteadily to his feet, stumbled while pushing back his chair and knocked Ellis's shoulder, causing him to spill his drink. The officer giggled. Ellis turned around.

'Damn you,' he said loudly. 'If you can't hold your drink, you shouldn't be allowed in a place like this. *Connasse*,' he added, no less loudly, turning back to Lawrence.

Lawrence saw the young officer's face register, with almost comic slowness, the insult.

'How dare you,' he began, 'a foreigner, insult an officer of the French army!'

One of his friends put a hand on his arm. Another stood up.

'I insist you take that back,' said the officer, his face draining of blood. His pallor could have been as much due to his state of intoxication as to anger.

Lawrence thought the man not much more than eighteen. His cheeks gleamed with soft fuzz. 'Look, it was an accident,' he said to Ellis, then, turning to the officer: 'He's sorry.' But he spoke knowing it was in vain: both the officer and Ellis ignored him.

'I insist you take that back.'

Ellis kept his back to the officer and didn't answer.

'Monsieur . . . You will apologize to me – or I will have to demand satisfaction!'

Lawrence wondered if he was hallucinating. Ellis's expression alarmed him. His eyes, grown narrow, glittered with malevolent satisfaction, almost glee. This is what he *wants*, Lawrence thought, appalled. Ellis stood up and turned to the officer. He towered over him. Whatever was in his eyes made the man step backwards.

Lawrence jumped to his feet. 'Ellis, for God's sake! He's only a boy!'

As the little drama intensified, the dark-haired grisette kept her eyes lowered, concentrating on the table. The other girl seized the moment to stuff an oyster into her mouth.

The young officer looked terrified. 'Honour must be assuaged. The honour of France—'

'This is ridiculous!' Lawrence realized he was the only person still reasonably sober. He gained courage from the fact that the café's patron had noticed the altercation and come over.

'Take it outside, gentlemen. This is a respectable establishment. I won't have trouble in here.'

'That won't be necessary,' Lawrence took Ellis firmly by the arm. 'It was a small accident. No harm done.'

'No harm? He insulted me!' cried the youngster, almost piteously. He looked as though he was about to cry.

Lawrence stepped towards the nearest officer and made his voice as curt as possible.

'For God's sake, take your friend home. My friend is a crack shot. It would be murder.'

The man glanced at Ellis, and Lawrence saw a pinprick of fear in his eyes. Before he had time to reply, Lawrence tightened his grip and dragged Ellis towards the door. He expected resistance, but Ellis allowed himself to be steered outside. The cold hit them like a slap.

'Come. Let's walk,' said Lawrence. He was furious.

'Always wanted to fight a duel,' said Ellis. 'Would be . . . 'n experience . . .'

'Christ.'

'It's Paris – part of the whole – whole, you know—'

'How's your aim?'

He laughed. 'Don't know. I've hardly even fired a pistol.'

'Then it probably would be your last experience.'

Ellis giggled as though this were a great joke. 'Go down in history, at least. Might as well . . .'

Something has happened, thought Lawrence. Something terrible, and he is trying to drown it.

When they finally made it to his room, shells had been falling for more than two hours, but in Montmartre the noise was faint. Ellis stumbled going up the stairs. His anger had calmed, but Lawrence knew that was due to the amount of alcohol he had poured on it, rather than to anything that Lawrence had done.

He unlocked his door and knocked against a chair as he searched for a lamp.

Lawrence looked down for the shape of the cat. 'Where's Circe?'

'Circe's gone.'

'Gone? Back to your uncle?'

'No, I mean gone. Stolen. The concierge took her.'

'Really? But why—?' Even as he said it, he thought of the obvious answer.

'She probably made her into a stew.'

'God. Do you have any reason to suspect her?'

'Plenty of reasons,' said Ellis shortly.

'I'm sorry. When did this happen?'

Ellis was still fumbling with the lamp; after several attempts, he managed to keep a match alive long enough to light the wick. 'Few weeks ago.'

'She may come back. You know how cats are. Maybe nothing's happened to her.'

Ellis ignored him and made his way to the window, where he fumbled among the bottles on the floor, found one and uncorked it. 'Drink?' He held up a glass.

Lawrence hesitated. 'No . . . Yes, thank you.'

He was afraid that, if he didn't, Ellis would drink the whole bottle himself. Before meeting, he had been tingling with anticipation; now, he was sorry he had come. The evening was not turning out as he'd imagined.

'Did something happen today? You seem upset about something.'

Ellis set the glasses on the table and poured sloppily. He stared at Lawrence with lowered head before handing him his glass. 'I seem upset?'

'Ellis, what is it?'

'If I seem upset, perhaps that's because I've killed a man.' He turned away and spoke so quietly, Lawrence wasn't sure that he'd heard correctly. Ellis seemed to be smiling though, so perhaps—

'Is that a joke?'

'A joke? No, unfortunately. Not today, actually. Yesterday.'

'You mean, someone you were op—'

'Someone I was supposed to be saving? Yes.' He finished his glass and poured another. 'Of all the people that I could wish dead – God knows there are plenty – I managed to dispatch some poor, innocent guardsman. He couldn't have been more than twenty.'

Lawrence looked at him, full of horrified pity. He thought of the boy officer in the café. Ellis wouldn't meet his eye.

'That must happen to every surgeon. I'm sure it wasn't—'

'Wasn't my fault? Oh, but the thing is – the unfortunate, the *unavoidable* thing is – it was my fault. I made a mistake, and he died.'

'I'm sure it wasn't like that—'

'You know what you're talking about, of course.'

Lawrence picked up the bottle and refilled his own glass. Ellis threw himself on to the bed.

'So, now you know who you're dealing with. Blood on my hands. Bungler-in-chief. Don't feel you have to stay – might be taking your life in your hands.'

Lawrence stood by the window and parted the curtains. He couldn't see anything outside, beyond a faint line where roofs met the sky.

'I'm so sorry. It must have been terrible. I'll go, if that's what you want. But I want to stay.' He waited. 'We don't have to do anything.'

'But that's what you came for, isn't it? I wouldn't want to *disappoint*.'

Lawrence made an effort not to rise to his goading. Ellis was silent.

'I thought about you all week.'

No reply, but a slight snuffling sound from the bed. Lawrence waited a decent interval before going to him. Ellis had his back to the room, hiding his face with his hand. Lawrence perched on the edge of the bed.

'Will you tell me about it?'

'I'm no good, that's all,' said Ellis thickly. 'I should never have agreed to do it, but they made it seem that it would be selfish to refuse. So I said yes. And now ... Swan regrets it, I'm sure. But there are men like him, who never make mistakes, and there's me, who always does.'

'No, you don't. What about all the men you've helped? All the lives

you've saved because you were brave enough to take on that responsibility?'

'That's the job. That's what everyone does. They don't kill a man
because their hands are shaking.'

'I don't believe that. Everybody makes mistakes. I do all the time.
It only doesn't matter because what I do doesn't matter. Not really.
What did Swan say?'

'He was quite decent about it. Told me to go and get drunk.'

'Well, then . . . homework accomplished! It won't happen again.'

Ellis was quiet for a time.

'It happened before. That's why I had to stop.'

'You mean, in Washington?'

'I got so scared, I couldn't work without a drink. And then . . .'

Lawrence searched for something to say. 'I'm sure Swan knows
best—'

'He doesn't know about that. I should have known I couldn't do it.'

'Stop.' Lawrence put his hand on Ellis's head and stroked his hair.

'Do you know what the theatre nurse said? The nun? She told me
I needed a wife. That all men need a wife, for times like this.'

Lawrence took his hand away.

'People think it's the answer to everything. The way it's meant to
be. And, if you don't, then you can never be a whole man.'

'Ellis, that's something else altogether. You're upset by what's happened, but that's got nothing to do with it.'

'What if it isn't something else? What if they're right?'

'They aren't,' Lawrence said, as firmly as he could.

'You don't know what it's like, year after year. The same questions.
The same hints. The look in their eyes. Even if they don't *know*, there's
that fear you might be . . . *wrong*. My mother. My uncle. Friends, even . . .
Until you start to believe it.'

'I know what it's like,' said Lawrence, stung. 'Of *course* I know. I was
sixteen when . . . when I fell in love with someone. And . . .' He wasn't

sure this was an argument. It was something he never talked about. But, as a distraction, it seemed to work.

'And what?'

'He was a neighbour. He seduced me, and it was . . . I realized there was no alternative. Not for me. I mean, I'd always known, but that confirmed it.'

'Did your family know?'

'Eventually.'

'And they told you that you'd grow out of it.'

'We never talked about it, at all,' Lawrence said.

'So, here you are – running away.'

'I'm not running away.' He was angry. 'I'm not hiding.'

'Sorry. I just . . .' Ellis passed a hand over his face. 'What happened to your friend?'

'He died.'

There was a silence.

'Poor Lawrence.'

'It was a long time ago.'

'He loved you?'

'I don't know. He was married, it turned out – I mean, she lived somewhere else, but he had a wife. And I don't think that made a him a "whole man".'

Ellis sighed.

'What about you? The first time.'

Ellis wouldn't look around. 'It's hard to talk about.'

'I'm hardly going to tell anyone.'

'I had a friend, at college. We were so alike in all sorts of ways. We talked of dedicating our lives to higher things: art and poetry. Not domesticity. He said he despised all that. We wrote all through the war. We were going to go away when it was over, together. Come to Europe.'

Lawrence felt the cold, silken touch of impending tragedy.

'Just after the war, he wrote to say that he'd fallen in love and was getting married. No apology; not even acknowledgement. Nothing. That letter made me feel that I didn't exist, because, if I had existed, how could he have done that?'

Lawrence reached for him, and this time stroked the side of his face. 'Maybe he wasn't brave enough.'

Yves came to his mind – his claim to be too old for marriage, too poor. Lawrence had thought such absurdity was a message for him.

Ellis muttered something unintelligible.

'What?'

'I'm a confirmed idiot. My life has always seemed unreal, somehow. Don't you feel that, sometimes? That nothing we do is real?'

Lawrence had never felt that. He didn't want to say so, so he lay down next to Ellis and moulded himself against him, one arm on his chest. He spoke into his hair: 'You're not an idiot. You're absolutely real. And you're not "wrong".'

Perhaps he was drunker than he had realized. It could hit you like that sometimes, when you changed position, and the waters of inebriation closed over your head. That could have been it. He murmured, 'I love you.'

Ellis went absolutely still, then he took Lawrence's hand, but made no reply.

37

Every night, the shells came. There was a new grimness to life, yet people became used to the growl of explosions, as they will get used to anything that happens day after day. In the streets of Croulebarbe and Maison Blanche, in La Glacière and Montparnasse, where lived no one of importance, the damage was less than it might have been. Parties of Right Bankers even crossed the river after supper to watch the fireworks from a safe distance.

Fanny no longer noticed the noise. She was a sound sleeper, and their apartment in Ménilmontant was quiet. She felt terrible for the poor people in the south, for those who'd had to flee their homes. Fanny wished she could help, but things in her own home were difficult too. There were days when all she could summon up for dinner was a soup made of frost-bitten carrots. She made a palm-sized piece of horse gristle last two days. Raymond never managed to bring home his entire week's pay; when she questioned him – very mildly, she thought – he shouted at her. He had a position to keep up among the men; no one respected a fellow who wouldn't put his hand in his pocket – didn't she care about that? Did she want them to despise him? She didn't ask again.

Fanny tried to get piece work, but that sort of thing had all but dried up. Before Madame Lamy's offer, she'd managed to find a job in one of the new uniform factories. The pay was awful, but anything was better than nothing. After only two days, her husband stormed into the workshop and dragged her out in front of everyone because, he shouted, all the women there were prostitutes. She'd nearly died of embarrassment. Madame Lamy's offer of domestic work had come as the answer to her prayers.

To begin with, Fanny found it exhausting – being a maid was harder than sewing, and an awful lot harder than modelling – but she was quick on the uptake and she grew used to it. The house had a lot of stairs, but, as Sabine the cook said, that was good for the figure; although, to be honest – as Raymond kept pointing out – her figure had shrunk too much already and her clothes were hanging off her. Sabine, initially terse and forbidding, had become quite a friend, and, all in all, the Lamys' house was a peaceful haven. Monsieur and Madame Lamy had always been nice to her, the house was full of lovely things, and the whole neighbourhood was so genteel, she couldn't imagine anything bad happening. It was even more peaceful when Mademoiselle Lamy went to live in a hotel near Opéra, because her fiancé worried about her and wanted her further away from the bombs. Fanny had always been nervous of sharp-tongued Mademoiselle Lamy, and she had found it embarrassing to be serving her breakfast when the woman had seen her in the altogether, from every possible angle.

Taking up the cans of warm water in the morning, Fanny paused before tapping on the door of Monsieur Harper's bedroom. This simple act caused her more anxiety than anything else her job entailed. The other day, she had knocked, counted to five, then opened the door. Halfway to the washstand, she realized the room was empty. Not only that, but by the light of her candle she saw the bed had not been slept in. She looked around. Could he have started work already? She filled the jug on the washstand and left.

She did the same at the door of the spare room, which she had made up last night for the guest. She crept inside, and then, belatedly, caught sight of the two heads on the pillow, one dark and one fair.

She dropped the water can, which landed on the rug with a thud, splashing her shoes.

In her horror, she bent to retrieve the jug, not daring to look around. She heard creaks from the bed, an exclamation. She stood up, keeping her eyes on the ground.

'I'm terribly sorry, monsieur. I'll fetch some more water.'

'It's all right, Fanny.' It was Monsieur Harper's voice. 'Don't worry about it. Please.'

She was almost out of the door when she heard him say, 'So cold last night, it was impossible to sleep.'

'Oh . . . yes.'

She half turned to reply, half saw him propped up on one elbow, twisting around to smile at her. The owner of the blond head hadn't moved. She was so flustered, she closed the door on her foot, her heart hammering with embarrassment.

She had reacted to the oddness of it: the dark head and the fair, so close they almost touched. But, as she calmed down, hurrying back to the kitchen, she told herself she had overreacted. Nothing was strange – or, rather, everything was, in the siege. It was simply as he said: the poor things had been too cold to sleep alone, and no wonder.

She couldn't help but notice, though, with her parting glance, that Monsieur Harper's shoulder, arm and half his chest protruded from the blankets, bare as the day he was born . . . and surely, if you were as cold as all that, you would keep your clothes on?

Later that day, Monsieur Harper called to her as she was toiling up the stairs.

'Oh, Fanny . . .'

'Monsieur?'

She stopped and waited, glancing fearfully at his face. He smiled at her in his usual friendly way. She was afraid that she was blushing.

'I should apologize. I'm sorry to have startled you, earlier. It was so cold last night, neither of us could get to sleep in our rooms. It's like the Arctic, up there.' He gave a short laugh.

Fanny tried to smile. 'Yes, of course.'

'I know how precious hot water is. I hope you didn't get into trouble.'

He was looking at her kindly; his eyes entirely frank and clear.

'No, monsieur. No trouble.'

Fanny hadn't told Sabine anything about it. The only person to go into the spare room later that day was her. She stripped the bedding without looking at it, and the damp patch on the rug was already invisible, so no one was any the wiser.

She had always liked Monsieur Harper, had always found him considerate and respectful when she worked as a model – but henceforth, when they were in the same room, she kept her eyes on the floor.

When she had looked around from the doorway, the way he'd appeared struck her as disturbingly familiar – it was very like some of the poses she had modelled for Monsieur Lamy's camera, while Mademoiselle Lamy would go on at her – 'Twist round more, Fanny . . . No, from the waist . . . Lean into your shoulder, drop your hip; lower the chiffon –' until she was stiff and ached all over. Monsieur Harper had seemed just like that – only the light from her candle made it look as though his skin was covered with gold. He must have spent time outdoors without his clothes. Why on earth was she thinking that? Perhaps it was because his skin had contrasted so with the other man's white shoulder . . . or because the nipple she had glimpsed stood out darkly against his hairless chest? Really, God knew, it was not her place to think about such things.

She had been with the Lamys since Christmas, and Raymond had mostly given up interrogating her when she arrived home. By the time she got in, she was exhausted, and her hands and feet were so numb, it took half an hour of painful tingling before they finally warmed up. Her working day was finished only after she cleared away the Lamys' dinner, and she rarely saw daylight, but this was the compromise they had reached: Raymond would not countenance her living in. He had to get his dinner at the café down the road, but, on the other hand, Fanny didn't have to spend money on food for herself. He complained that he felt like an unmarried man again, coming home to cold, empty rooms. But the money was more than welcome; they had been able to reclaim their best shoes from the *mont de piété*, and Fanny sometimes brought home leftovers from the Lamys' kitchen, and he didn't mind that at all.

The thing that bothered him most was that she might encounter other men during the day. He would make her recount what she had seen and done, who had been in the house, who had visited. She teased him gently – she had learnt how far she could go. He didn't like that a young, unmarried man lived in the house, especially now that Mademoiselle Lamy was engaged to the butcher and out of the picture, as far as that went. Raymond had never seen Monsieur Harper, but knowing he was there was enough; he would ask her whether he talked to her or flirted with her. He knew, he said darkly, what men were like.

'I'm in the kitchen all day. It's only at mealtimes that I see him, and then that's with monsieur and madame.'

'And does he talk to you then?'

'Good heavens! He says, "Good morning" – that's all. I'm the only servant in the house, Raymond. I'm rushed off my feet. I don't have time to hang around and chat to anyone.'

'You weren't always the maid,' said Raymond. 'You used to – you know – in front of him, didn't you?'

'Oh, for heaven's sake, it didn't bother you then.'

'*Then* it was different. Now, you're there all the time. You don't know how men talk about women. About maids. You walk around that house all day – when he has seen you stripped.'

Fanny sighed. She couldn't deny it, so she found herself telling him what she had seen when the blond gentleman had stayed the night. She thought that would set his mind at rest, but Raymond just stared at her, his jaw twitching.

'*Merde*,' he said, frowning and pressing his lips together until they went pale. 'I don't want you working in a place like that, Fanny. I want you to give in your notice.'

Fanny prided herself on never losing her temper – she couldn't bear a shrew – but this time she couldn't prevent herself from rolling her eyes.

'You just said you didn't like the thought of him flirting with me. I tell you I don't think you have to worry about that, and now you want me to leave? For goodness' sake, Raymond!'

'You don't understand: some men go with anything. I never liked you going to that studio. It's an immoral place – that just proves it!'

'He's not like that! Maybe they were cold – it's freezing in those bedrooms.'

'Freezing, is it? How do you know what his bedroom is like at night?'

'Oh my goodness . . .' Fanny let her voice rise. 'Shame on you, Raymond. Monsieur and Madame Lamy are some of the most respectable people I know, and the kindest. Are you saying you don't trust me? Is that it?'

Raymond stared sullenly at the floor. 'No, I'm not saying anything about you. But I don't like you being in those surroundings. People talk, you know . . . and you're my wife.'

'Yes, your wife with a job. Where would I get another like that? It seems to me, either you trust me, or you don't.'

'I didn't say I didn't trust you, Fanny, but a man has to take care of his wife's reputation – you see that. And it's better to be poor than compromised.'

'Oh, is it? Is it better to starve to death? My job pays more than you bring in from standing around in that uniform all day—'

Whatever made her say it? She knew she shouldn't have. Without understanding what had happened, she found herself sprawled over the table, her head ringing. She couldn't quite hear her voice when she said, 'I'm sorry, darling. I didn't—'

The second blow was harder than the first. She must have blacked out, because, the next thing she knew, she was looking at the ceiling, her back agonizingly bent against the edge of the table, and Raymond was gripping her arms with iron hands.

'Ahh . . . you're hurting me!'

He made an inarticulate grunting noise and shook her, and her head thudded on the table. She thought she was going to be sick. He was saying something like, 'See what you make me do . . .' and there was an awful wailing, which was her.

She went limp; it was the only thing to do. The only time she had truly feared him was when she was pregnant. She had fought back – that was why he'd hit her in the stomach and she lost the baby, but he had been very sorry about it, and had cried afterwards.

Her vision blurred and a torrent rushed in her ears. Fanny was afraid this time, not of him, exactly, because she loved him with all her heart and knew that he loved her, but of the rage that was like a wild beast inside him, unleashed and uncontrollable. She pitied him; she knew he couldn't help it; he was as much at its mercy as she was.

38

Since the shelling began, public opinion had hardened around two opposing camps. One, led by the Red press, held that, having come this far, France must never surrender, or all the privation and suffering Parisians had endured would be for nothing. The government was wasting time. It had half a million men in arms, but what was it doing with them? Overnight, walls blossomed with posters calling for the overthrow of the government. The posters were red, unsigned and menacing. The other camp, exemplified by establishment papers like *Le Figaro* and *La Patrie*, hinted that surrender would be inevitable if they did not break out of the encirclement in the next fortnight, unless some outside force arrived to deliver them. The establishment also voiced the fear that surrender would lead to a revolt from the armed Guard members. It would be the Terror all over again.

Both camps had their adherents in Rue des Ciseaux. Louise was a patriot, but a realist. Things had gone far enough, she declared, when bombs fell on churches during Mass. This had happened only once, down in Montparnasse, but she had been very shaken by it. She wanted an end to it all, no matter the cost.

'But would you believe, Lawrence, that our little Fanny is a Red? Or, rather, her husband is. She told me that he thinks the Guard can make a great push and break out to save us, and he said it would be better to die in the attempt than to surrender.'

'Oh?' Lawrence was reluctant, as a foreigner, to put forward an opinion on such an inflammatory subject.

'But what can you expect of a man like that?' she went on. 'All blood and violence, as we know. It makes me shudder to think of it. And all of them armed with rifles!' She gave Lawrence a significant look.

A couple of days before, Fanny had appeared at breakfast with a black eye and was subdued, not her normal, sunny self. She went about her duties stiffly, as if she was in pain. She said she had slipped on the ice and fallen, but she refused to go home when Madame Lamy said they could do without her for the day.

'She said to me, "I'm here now. I'd rather just get on." But, if you ask me, I think she's afraid to go home.'

Lawrence had also asked her what had happened. Fanny answered, without looking up, 'Oh, nothing. I fell, that's all. Clumsy.' She seemed mortified by the attention. Lawrence begged her to be careful. She was shy around him, and rarely met his eye, so he was not the best person to enquire further, but it seemed wrong that someone so close to them was suffering and they could not help.

'Is there nothing anybody can do?'

Louise gave a resigned shrug. 'No. You are good to listen to me. These are women's troubles. I shouldn't bore you with them. Serge thinks I talk too much. But, as I always say, someone in this house has to.'

Louise badgered Lawrence to invite Monsieur Butterfield for dinner. For a few days, Lawrence kept her at bay with talk of how busy he was at the hospital, but Louise persisted, and it was arranged that Ellis would dine with them on the Friday.

Lawrence was afraid that everything had gone wrong between them. Remembering what he had said that night made his skin crawl. Love him? The spectre of Yves looked on with mute reproach. He had been passionately sure of his feelings for Yves, and what had become of them? He told himself that he had said it out of charity, to alleviate

Ellis's distress. But Ellis had remained silent, and Lawrence thought, Well, we will, evidently, politely forget I said anything.

They fell asleep like that, neither wanting to stir things up by moving. On waking in the depths of the night, teeth clacking with cold, they hurriedly undressed, got under the covers and made love, all without a word. Ellis began snoring almost immediately, but Lawrence lay awake, unable to stop thinking. In the morning, both were hungover and sheepish. Ellis apologized for his behaviour in the café, but his spirits seemed recovered.

'There's no need to apologize. Anyone would be upset by what happened.'

'How did you get me out of it?'

'You don't remember?'

Ellis shook his head. Perhaps he had forgotten everything about last night – including what Lawrence had said to him.

'I told them you were a crack shot and that it would be murder.'

Ellis laughed. 'Thank you. I applaud your powers of invention.'

Lawrence just nodded. Ellis might look pale and puffy eyed, but his tone was casual, as if he were shrugging off just another drunken *bêtise*.

On the evening Ellis was expected, they lit a fire in the dining room in honour of their guest. Now that Ernestine had moved to a hotel, the Lamys were even more careful of their dwindling fuel supply. When Ellis arrived, flushed and radiating cold from his walk, Louise apologized for the meagreness of the warmth, and the tallow candles that sent a veil of fatty smoke to the ceiling.

'We're honoured you've come all this way, monsieur. I know how important your work is, and it is so nasty out. We've made up the spare room for you, so you don't have to trek all the way across town in the middle of the night . . .'

She said she hoped Monsieur Butterfield would forgive the poor offerings of their table – which, in fact, thanks to Monsieur Ranvier, boasted a joint of beef. Ellis's eyes lit up with greed when Fanny brought it in and laid it on the table with a flourish, smiling at her proximity to such a glory.

'Where did you get it?' he asked, swallowing, unable to tear his gaze from the meat. 'Are there secret herds of cattle somewhere?'

'Monsieur Ranvier won't tell me,' said Louise. 'But it seems you can get anything if you know the right people. It's rather shameful, of course; I know many people have nothing. But I'm not going to turn it down.'

'I'm very glad you didn't,' said Ellis, laughing. 'I haven't eaten this well for weeks.'

Throughout dinner, Ellis was on his best behaviour. He was attentive to Madame Lamy, laughing at her chatter, listening to her hopes for her daughter's wedding, and included Monsieur Lamy in the conversation, waiting patiently while Louise translated his gestures. Serge brought up some bottles of good wine from the cellar – a burgundy that released wafts of summer when you swirled the glass – and Ellis complimented him knowledgeably. Lawrence basked in the glow of having such a charming, accomplished friend. But it was also disconcerting; he had so rarely seen this side of Ellis, it was almost as if this was a man he didn't know – one who, he couldn't help thinking, didn't take such pains to be charming with him.

Lawrence watched as Ellis's glass was emptied and refilled: he was drinking, but no more than the rest of them. This public, urbane face of his lover made him depressed. Lawrence toyed with his own glass and felt foolish for having taken his dramatics so seriously. Only a few days ago, Ellis had been – or had seemed to be – in a state of wild despair; now, it was hard to imagine. He thought of Yves' quiet dignity with yearning. He felt he could not trust the evidence of his own eyes.

'Lawrence tells me that your uncle is the American ambassador. Forgive me asking – I'm sure you get tired of being pestered for information, but, well, I have to – is there anything you can tell us? Is it certain the United States will not step in to help France?'

'There's no question of it, madame, I'm afraid. More than that, I really don't know. I don't think my uncle is privy to the government's secrets. But I don't mind being asked anything by such a charming hostess.' Ellis gave his most winning smile. 'I can see why Lawrence is so attached to staying here.'

'The American embassy has become a refuge for evicted Germans,' said Lawrence, disrupting the flow of conversation.

'Oh! Goodness me.'

'The United States is neutral, and the Prussians' own embassy has vanished, so there is no one else to look out for them.'

'Of course. One tends to forget that anyone is neutral in all of this.'

'And Canadians are neutral also, of course.' Ellis smiled across the table at Lawrence.

'Oh, it's impossible to think of Lawrence as neutral!' Louise laughed at this and rested her hand briefly on Lawrence's arm. 'Isn't it, Serge? He's almost like a Frenchman.'

Serge nodded and smiled.

'I don't feel neutral,' said Lawrence.

Ellis looked at him, surprised by the belligerence in his voice. He held his gaze as he said, 'Nor do I.'

At the end of the evening, Lawrence did not know what to expect. He sat on his bed, unbuttoned his collar and waited for the creaks and bumps from downstairs to fall silent. He didn't know what he would do then. Beyond an exchange of notes to confirm the invitation, he'd had no communication with Ellis since that night in Montmartre. This evening had been spent in pleasant conversation over a good dinner, but he knew he had appeared graceless next to Ellis, and the knowledge made him miserable. Resentful, even.

Still, the footsteps in the corridor made his stomach turn over, and the door opened. In the lamplight, Ellis was very handsome. He had lost weight over the last weeks – everyone had – and his cheeks were leaner, his eyes dark-shadowed. It made him look older and more distinguished. His smile was warm, but tentative.

'Can you bear my company a little longer?'

Lawrence made a gesture that could have meant anything. 'Are you working tomorrow?'

'Yes.' Ellis closed the door and came into the room, but remained standing. His eyes roved over the sparse furnishings. He wasn't smiling anymore.

'I formed the impression you weren't happy with me this evening. And I thought, Well, I'm not surprised.'

'Why not?'

Ellis sat down on the bed next to him, but not touching. He clasped his hands in his lap.

'I'm sorry about the other night. I behaved terribly. I was a selfish pig.'

Lawrence softened instantly, although he agreed.

'Anyone would have been upset.'

'I know how I get when I've been drinking. It makes me feel better for a while, when I can't face something. Then it makes me feel worse. I'm ashamed of myself. I've hardly drunk at all since then.'

Lawrence didn't know if he believed this, but Ellis appeared sincere.

'You treated me with far more kindness than I deserved. I thank you for that.' He looked down at his hands, unclasped them and spread his left hand on the bedcover between them.

After a moment, Lawrence took the offering, putting his hand over Ellis's fingers. 'You don't have to thank me.'

'I want to make it up to you.'

Lawrence felt the heat surge in his loins, and grinned. 'All right.'

'Since that night, I've been thinking . . . Can I ask you something?'

'Of course.'

'I suppose, you see – I'd thought you might be waiting for all this to be over. You know –' he stared, very deliberately, straight at Law-rence – 'waiting for Yves to return.'

Lawrence hadn't expected that name, nor the shock it gave him. His gaze dropped to the floor; he couldn't help it.

'I thought there might have been something between you and him – at one time, at least.'

Lawrence looked up, met Ellis's eye. 'At one time, I thought, per-haps, but . . . there wasn't.' There was nothing he could say that was more true than that.

'Oh.' Ellis exhaled the breath he had been holding. There was a touchingly hopeful look on his face.

Lawrence made himself smile. 'I'm not waiting for anything.'

He watched as an answering smile spread across Ellis's face. Oh God, thought Lawrence. Is he in love with me? Is this what I want?

He leant forward and they kissed. Ellis's mouth was alive with heat; he tasted of grapes and tannin, the dark wine that made you feel the sun on your skin.

What did he want? He wanted to lick long, velvet strokes up the adorable declivity of his sternum. He wanted to roll his face over the golden-furred belly. He wanted to feel his weight pressing him down. Beyond that, what did he need to know?

39

The latest rumour spread through the city like a disease. Papers at all points on the political spectrum reported it, adding weight with 'credible eyewitness accounts'. The monster had been sighted as far afield as Montmartre and Charonne. It had been surprised plundering graves in the Cimitière du Nord. It had been spotted strolling down the Champs Élysées. It had eaten a child – or perhaps it was a sheep. Most agreed that it was another ruse by the Prussians to weaken Parisian morale. Hunting the 'Prussian monster' became the hobby of bored members of the Guard all over Paris.

The zoo had managed – a feat astonishing to both Victor and Papin – to keep the fact of their missing panther a secret. And because the witness accounts were so divergent – some claimed the monster had wings, or a single, red eye; another said it walked upright; another that it scuttled like a crab – few people had come to the obvious conclusion.

Papin and Victor were called to a meeting by Director Lapeyre.

'There is always the possibility that it isn't Nero. We don't know that he's even alive,' said Papin.

Lapeyre gnawed at a fingernail. 'Yes, that's my hope. The keeper – he found no sign of him?'

'None. But I think the Charonne sighting probably was him. That one said it was like an enormous cat.'

'I'm surprised we haven't been approached by the papers. If we are, our official line is this: Nero died of starvation two weeks ago. It is hardly stretching the facts.'

He looked around the table. Victor nodded. Papin just shrugged and stared out of the window.

Victor had noticed a change in Papin. Since the beginning of the siege, he had aged. His back seemed more twisted; his head sunk further into his shoulders. Food was so scarce that even his substantial means could not procure enough meat for the animals. Irma the lioness had died. One morning, they found her lifeless body in the cage; Tancred, her mate of twelve years, alternately licking her face and gnawing her flank. Robitaille and Victor dragged the carcass away from him and butchered it to share between the remaining carnivores. Robitaille wept that day. He blamed himself for Nero's disappearance; now, no matter what the others said, he blamed himself for Irma's death. Two days after that, Papin finally shot the quagga, unable to bear its pathetic state any longer. Victor thought the chief veterinarian's heart was broken.

He had begun to withdraw from the daily life of the zoo; often, he didn't stir from the house all day. There was no one with whom Victor could share his concern. Papin had never been approachable; now, he was so withdrawn as to be positively forbidding. The only person who might care, that Victor could think of, was Anne, and relations between them were . . . Well, there were no relations to speak of. She was Papin's housekeeper – efficient, largely silent, more remote even than her master.

The more Victor thought about it, the more he became convinced that it was Anne who had freed the panther. It must have been. The thought did not make him angry. He was, rather, envious. With each day that Nero survived in the city, with each sighting of the monster – it could walk through walls, scale buildings, be in two places at once – he felt a secret joy. He, who had worked with wild beasts for years, and who loved them more than anything – he had always followed rules and observed protocols and swallowed insults and been . . . tame.

That afternoon, he let himself into the veterinarian's house and heard the tentative plink of piano keys from the music room. Anne was fascinated by the instrument. He quietly opened the door to see her polishing the top of the piano, and he hated that she jumped when he spoke, as though he were an unwelcome apparition. He apologized for startling her, and suggested that they visit Marguerite, knowing this was the one thing she would not refuse.

The tigress looked better than she had for weeks. She devoured a piece of the quagga meat and washed her paws. She turned her jewel eyes on them and looked in that way she had, that made you feel as though you were under her spell.

'She looks all right, doesn't she?' said Victor. 'Better, I think.'

Anne studied her. 'Yes.'

'There are so many colours in her eyes. Far more than the other cats.'

Anne nodded. 'And they change each time you look at her.'

'It's as though . . . there are whole worlds in there. Maps.'

'Yes!'

She liked that, he could tell. He felt her attention warm to him.

'Is it true what they're saying?' she said. 'Will it be over soon?'

'Well, I know no more than most, but – perhaps. They are talking of this great attack we will make on the Prussian forces. So, either that will succeed, or, if not, then surrender seems inevitable.'

'Monsieur Papin thinks an attack is sure to fail.'

Victor was shocked. When did Papin discuss such things with Anne?

'Well . . . I think Monsieur Papin is despondent. In fact, I've been worried about him. He does not seem quite himself. I wondered, since you are in the house, if you have noticed anything?'

'I don't know that I'm the right person to ask. But –' she seemed to consider – 'I think he's sad.'

'Is that because of the animals, do you think?'

'Well . . .' She hesitated. 'He has told me that he wants to retire.'

For a moment, he was too shocked to speak. Possibilities flared at the corners of his mind.

'You mean – when it's all over?'

'Yes. He told me he doesn't want to stay at the zoo any longer.'

Victor stared. Why would Papin tell Anne, and not him?

'But I don't know that he is decided. You must ask him.'

'Yes, of course.'

'Monsieur . . . He, um . . . He asked if I would go with him, when he leaves.'

Victor felt the void open up beneath his feet.

He would not have had the courage to confront Papin without the knowledge that he had schemed to steal Anne away from him. He found him in his study, covering sheets of paper with his tiny cursive script.

When he bid Victor enter, Papin didn't look up. 'Does this mean more bad news?'

'No. Nothing's happened.'

Papin blotted the last sentence. 'I'm glad you're here, Monsieur Calmette. I've been meaning to speak to you.'

'And I you.'

'Please, go ahead.'

Victor swallowed. 'Mademoiselle Petitjean told me that you are thinking of leaving.'

Papin sighed. He put down the pen he had been twirling between his fingers. 'I should have spoken to you earlier. I apologize that you have heard it in this fashion.'

'Of course.'

'If what I believe is likely to happen comes about, then I do not want to be a part of it. And I think it's time for me to step back, time you had more responsibility. I am aware that not many men would have been as patient as you.'

Victor thought, He means *tame*.

'I'm growing old, and more infirm. I will retire to my country place. These recent decisions have affected me more than I would have thought possible. I am sick of it.'

'I'm sorry to hear that – both that you suffer, and that you intend to retire.'

'I've been meaning to speak of it. But it has been a difficult thing to contemplate. This zoo has been my life. One wants to be certain before bringing it up.'

'Of course. And are you certain?'

'I think so. We will have to see where we stand when all this is over. I want the zoo to be in a position to build up again.'

'What is it you think will happen, that you don't want to be part of?'

Papin leant back in his chair. 'I am no tactician, but I can't see the National Guard getting us out of this mess. It is an undisciplined, drunken rabble, which has failed at every turn. Why should this time be any different? Our surrender is inevitable. And then, I fear, there will be some sort of revolt. I remember the rioting of '48. I'm too old for that again.'

'And the zoo?'

'Oh, the zoo will survive. It will change, of course – and change is a young man's task.'

'Have you spoken with Monsieur Lapeyre about your plans?'

'No. I will speak to him, and I will encourage him to make you my successor.'

'Thank you.'

Victor walked away from the meeting in a quandary. It was good news. He kept telling himself it was good news. Finally – promotion. The money he sorely needed. And this house . . . But the one thing he held on to more than any other was that Anne had not – as yet – given Papin an answer. She said she had not known what to say.

He went straight from Papin's study to the kitchen, half hoping she would not be there. But she was there, so he had no choice but to go on.

She followed him into the dining room. He invited her to sit down. She did so, and he sat too, not opposite her, but at the oblique angle he knew she found less threatening.

'Well, Anne, I come from speaking with Monsieur Papin. Thank you for telling me what he said. He confirms that he intends to leave. And I want to reassure you. Because if, as seems likely, I become chief veterinarian, I would want you to stay on here. You wouldn't have to leave.'

He tried to gauge her reaction. He wasn't expecting smiles and tears of joy, but, surely, there would be something? Her eyes were fixed on the table. After a few moments, she moistened her lips and nodded.

'Thank you, monsieur.'

'I hope that is reassuring to you.'

She nodded again, her face unchanging.

He plunged on, his heart beating wildly. 'I know Monsieur Papin has asked you to accompany him to the country, as his housekeeper –'

She inclined her head again.

'– because he holds you in high regard, and is mindful of your . . . er, your past, and I am sure he wants to ensure your well-being in the future. But I want to say that I, too, want to ensure your well-being in the future.'

'Thank you, monsieur,' she muttered, almost too quietly to hear.

'And, furthermore . . . Furthermore, Anne, I hope you know that I hold you in the highest regard.'

She made a small movement. He was encouraged.

'And so . . . and so I would like to . . . ask you, Anne, whether one day you might consider, um . . . consider becoming my wife. If, of course . . .'

She seemed to be trembling. Was that a good sign?

'If that would be agreeable to you, because it would make me the happiest man alive . . . There's no need to decide now, of course. Perhaps I should not have spoken of this at this time, but, under the circumstances . . . and I don't think it can come entirely out of the—'

'Please – stop!'

'What is it?'

'Please, monsieur. I can't! Not now. I'm sorry.'

She stood abruptly and rushed out of the room.

That night, the dull growl of shells came with the regularity of a giant, beating heart, but, sunk in his misery and confusion, Victor barely noticed.

In the middle of the night, after two months of snow and ice, a warm wind blew in, and he counted the hours listening to melting snow sliding off the roof with heavy sighs, and the insistent, maddening drip from a broken gutter outside his window.

The thaw had other, more serious, consequences. By dawn, an impenetrable fog shrouded the city. The frozen ground turned into a quagmire. It was late January, the date of the much-trumpeted *grande sortie* to the west of Paris, near a village called Buzenval. It was the last attempt to break the siege. Ramshackle Guard battalions were sent into action against the enemy and became bogged down in the mud, held up by lost artillery, blocked bridges, missing horses.

The men who reached Buzenval at dawn had to wait, packs on their backs, for up to eight hours, while various elements of the French forces straggled up to join them. The guardsmen were equipped with outdated rifles, had little training, had never fired a shot in anger. They were plumbers, tailors, printers, machinists. They were clerks, students, painters and shopkeepers. They were pitted against a professional army with state-of-the-art artillery. They went into battle knowing the fate of the country rested on their shoulders, hoping that, after all this time, the Prussians had lost the stomach for a fight. They were mistaken.

From *Le Cri du Peuple*, 23 January 1871:

Yesterday, the 101st battalion of the National Guard, dismayed at the manner in which they had been wasted on the field of battle at Buzenval, marched to the Hôtel de Ville to protest the incompetence of our leaders. They were joined by ordinary Parisians, women and children, who, for the last four months, have frozen and starved for the honour of France. A shot rang out, and, although no one was hurt, the order was given to army troops inside the building to fire on the protesters. And fire they did – into the hearts of innocent civilians, five of whom now lie in the morgue. Women and children were killed by the very soldiers supposed to 'defend' them.

From *La Voix*, 28 January 1871:

Yesterday, Monsieur Favre, of the government of National Defence, signed the peace treaty with King Wilhelm I of Prussia, Chancellor Bismarck and Field Marshal Moltke. An armistice is agreed, and Paris is finally free.

40

Lawrence had to admit that he had, in certain ways, enjoyed living under siege, horrible though it was. He'd grown used to the nightly thunder of shells, and with the uncertainty and the darkness came a perverse excitement. The endless restrictions were, in a sense, freeing. What to do, where to go, how to live – these were no longer questions that anyone had to ask themselves.

He became aware that this was the case in the weeks that followed France's surrender, as Paris struggled to get back to its old self. No one was happy about the way the war ended, but at least it was over. That meant there was fuel again, and food in the shops. Newspapers – proper ones, with news of the outside world – were devoured like food. Street lights came back on and theatres reopened. Parisians who had fled to their country houses came trickling back to open up their homes, count their belongings and bemoan the loss of trees, the shortage of horses, the theft of their garden trellis.

They also faced a constant diet of humiliation. The Prussian army paraded in triumph down the Champs Élysées, watched by Parisians in bitter silence. Afterwards, the cobbles were scrubbed with bleach. On top of that, on top of the loss of Alsace and parts of Lorraine, and the huge reparations the government agreed to pay, a law was passed that ended the moratorium on debts and rents. Parisians were given forty-eight hours to pay what they owed. At the same time, the government ended the daily wage to the National Guard. On the face of it, this was reasonable, since there was no longer an enemy at the gate. But businesses were in less of a hurry to reopen; it wasn't so easy to put an end to hunger and hardship. A relaxation of the fear they had all lived with was replaced with something rank, a sour atmosphere in which other things flourished: resentment, suspicion, blame. People were crazy. It was so prevalent, there was a name for it: the papers called it 'obsidional fever'.

Lawrence wondered if that was what he was suffering from – a complaint he had never heard of, that might have been made up. He knew he ought to be glad that the siege was over, but all he felt was a curious flatness. He was short tempered and bored, and he worried about Ellis, who became engulfed in the medical crisis following the Battle of Buzenval and then became ill. Lawrence missed him and thought of him constantly. Looking back on the siege, he realized he had been happy. His heart had beaten faster – with the danger, with heightened alertness, and with thoughts of someone who he knew was thinking of him.

Buzenval had changed everything. The ill-equipped French were thrown against the Prussians with catastrophic results. Lawrence knew that every hospital was overwhelmed with the wounded, and did not expect to see Ellis in its immediate aftermath, but, surely, after some time, he would reappear? After how much time? He wrote, saying he couldn't wait to see him. Ellis replied to say that he was terribly busy, and, also, he wasn't well. He would be in touch. Something about the tone of the letter struck Lawrence as evasive. Had there been another incident like that one that had caused him such anguish? After nearly a week, he wrote again, trying to hint at his sympathy and concern without naming it outright. This time, there was no reply.

On the night of the Lamys' dinner, he thought he had found what he wanted. He believed Ellis had felt the same. Now, he was forced to wonder if what they had had was just another artefact of the siege, a side effect of the madness, something to be brushed aside and forgotten.

From *Le Figaro*, 27 February 1871:

Now that the majority of the French people have spoken in a national election, brigands from the insalubrious quarters of Paris can no longer hold honest citizens to ransom. The government has put in place measures to quell the sort of dangerous insurgence that took place on 31st October of last year, and 22nd January of this. The revolutionary 'Red' papers have been shut down. Political clubs and gatherings have been outlawed, and moves are underway to disband the swollen ranks of the National Guard. Now the country is at peace, we can no longer countenance half a million rifles on the streets of Paris. Order must, and will, be restored.

41

Ignace Papin promised to stay on in his post a few more weeks. Things at the zoo were still in a sad way, with empty enclosures and missing staff. Some of the keepers came back; some could not be found. One day, Robitaille came to work in tears; he had just received news that Pierre, his young protégé, had been killed fighting in the provinces. Victor was shaken. He had occasionally thought of Pierre through the winter – they all had; he was liked by everybody. They had thought of him, joked about him, wondered idly where he was. Now they learnt he had died at the beginning of November, at the Battle of Coulmiers. For months, his presence had lived on in their minds when he was already dead. Victor felt as though they had been tricked.

After much humming and hawing, Director Lapeyre appointed Victor as the next chief veterinarian. Victor was gratified, if nervous. He knew he wasn't adept at dealing with directors and governors. Papin had a formidable personality, bolstered by the authority bestowed by generations of aristocrats. Next to the director, Victor was acutely conscious of his modest background, his lack of presence. But the main thing, he reminded himself, was that at last his ambition was fulfilled: he was the chief veterinarian of a major zoo and would take possession of the beautiful house in the park. He was a man of substance.

Most of the zoo's surviving inmates picked up. Lapeyre wrote to other zoos, looking for animals to restock the empty enclosures. He found a new lynx, some wolf cubs, a couple of bears. They had already acquired a lioness – a refugee from a menagerie in the south – who moved into Nero's old cage, the one next to Tancred, in the hope that they would become a breeding pair. Victor pleaded the case for a Caspian tiger, but the prospects were not good. Marguerite seemed to be the last of her kind. Out in the wider world, the 'Prussian Beast' faded from public memory. No sightings had been reported for some time. Victor wanted to believe that Nero had escaped the city, but knew it was more likely that he was dead.

Even with his promotion, and now that the threat of the butcher's shop had been lifted, Victor felt little lightening of spirit. Marguerite continued to be listless, and he did not know what was wrong with her. She had become slovenly, something he had never seen before. He sat in front of her cage and spoke to her, but she rarely looked at him. She lay on the floor, her eyes seemingly unfocused, as though she had gone somewhere else. She was only eleven years old, but he wondered, for the first time, if she might be dying.

He was also despondent about Anne. After the awful episode in the dining room, he had not dared raise the subject of marriage again, although he clung to the words, 'not now', that she had uttered. He was afraid even to approach her. At least, as far as he knew, she had not yet given Papin an answer, about going to work for him in the country, either. The uncertainty tormented him, and he despised himself as a coward, but the end of March seemed soon enough to hear bad news, if such it was. The conviction grew in him that his success with Anne, and the life of Marguerite, were somehow intertwined. If Anne accepted him, then the tigress would live. He did not know why he felt this so strongly, but he could not rid himself of the feeling.

Working for Monsieur Papin had been one of the happiest times in Anne's life. What was previously unthinkable – a life outside the hospital – had become real. She was proud of it, and of the fact that Papin liked her. She felt he understood her, without her having to explain. He talked to her lightly and indirectly, and she never felt his eyes fasten on her like greedy little mouths. Now, she was in a quandary: should she go with him to the country, where she had no friends, where there was no Marguerite? She had never been further than fifteen kilometres outside Paris. But, in order to stay, she didn't know what she might have to do.

It was funny: now that things were back to normal, Anne missed the bread queues. For a while, she continued to wake at two in the morning, and it took her a minute to remember that she no longer had to head out into the dark. Sometimes, she dressed and crept out of the house to visit the animals. The nights had changed – not only were they warmer, but street lights reflected off the clouds down into the park. The dark was less intense; when she looked up, she could no longer see layer upon layer of stars. She made her way to the cat pavilion and found Marguerite awake, staring through her bars. She gave a soft, throaty rumble when she saw Anne. That night, she was talkative – grunting, huffing and coughing. Anne squatted in front of the cage and spoke to her, and Marguerite seemed to reply. Her great head was pressed up against the bars, as close to Anne as she could get, and her eyes were fixed on Anne's face.

A few days later, as she was coming out of the bakery one morning, Anne bumped into Fanny Klein. She hadn't seen her for a while, and Fanny's face changed on noticing her – it lit up; that was the only way to describe it. Anne had never known anyone take so much pleasure in everyday moments, like seeing the face of a friend.

'Are you in a hurry today?' Anne asked.

'Not especially. Why?'

'I want to ask you something.'

They walked up Montagne Sainte Geneviève. Anne asked after Fanny's husband, and learnt that things were hard, as the building trade had not recovered and he could not find work. She had formed the impression that Fanny's husband was a rather difficult person.

'I expect things will pick up when the weather gets warmer,' said Fanny. 'They usually do. What about you?'

Anne told her about Monsieur Papin retiring, and the choices that seemed open to her – to go and be his housekeeper in the depths of the country, or to stay with Monsieur Calmette, who had asked her to marry him.

Fanny was excited to hear that Anne had had a marriage proposal. Then she read her face. 'But you don't like him? Is that it?'

'I don't know. Not like that, anyway.'

Fanny smirked. 'Is there someone else you do like?'

Anne shook her head. 'I think I just don't want to get married – to anyone. It doesn't feel right for me. For some people, it's wonderful, of course. Like you,' she added, out of politeness.

'Oh, well!' Fanny laughed. 'As to that – you should only marry if you love him. That's the only reason anyone should get married. As soon as I met Raymond, I knew that was it. I couldn't live without him – but, even then, it's not always easy.'

'Really?'

'Marriage is hard work, there's no doubt about it.' Fanny was smiling. 'Mind you, it's probably easier if you have plenty of money.' She paused. 'Do you like him? Is he a good man?'

'I suppose so. Yes.'

'Yet the thought of being married to him horrifies you?'

'No. It's not . . . horrifying . . .' It was difficult to find the right words. 'I'm not like other people, perhaps. I need to be alone more than I need anything else. The thought of being tied to someone – anyone . . .' She shook her head vigorously.

'Perhaps he'll keep you on as his housekeeper, if you want to stay at the zoo.'

'But what if he doesn't?'

'Then you could go with the other one. Or you could find another job. Anyone would hire you, Anne. Everyone wants servants, now. Or you could do something else. You're clever.'

Fanny made it sound simple. It was an astonishing thought.

They walked on in silence for a minute.

'Listen.' Fanny turned to her. 'Why don't you come to a meeting on Saturday? It'd be after work.'

'What sort of meeting?'

'One where people discuss things – things like marriage, and work. Women get up and talk. About new ideas.' She looked at Anne shyly. 'I don't know if you're interested in political things, but, well . . . it's at eight o'clock, Saturday evening, in the Church of Saint-Jean-le-Pauvre, Rue des Blancs Manteaux. Say you'll come!'

'Oh, well, I don't know . . .'

She saw Fanny's bright, hopeful face.

'But, perhaps, yes, I could.'

42

Ellis met B. during his first week at Dartmouth College. B. was the scion of an old New York family, whose poise and confidence masked an essential shyness. At first glance, he and Ellis – the son of nobody much, never calm, confident only in drink – had little in common, but they quickly became friends. To Ellis, B. was like a better version of himself, a mirror lit by kindest sunlight. His background was wealthier, his education more exclusive, his family more cultured, but they reflected each other back and forth, magnifying their youth, ideals and talents. And B. had loved him, Ellis knew. It was an article of faith to Ellis that their friendship had been perfect. He needed to believe that his soul was capable of such a thing, and nothing else in his life had come close.

That relationship, though consummated, had never been like what he experienced with Lawrence. Those midnight couplings were driven by a need that had to be slaked, but never acknowledged by light of day. The cataclysm of B.'s marriage had proved such love could not last. The aftermath of the war – and of B.'s letter – was a grey nothing. For the first few months, Ellis barely set foot out of doors. His time at home was leavened only by an affair with a young man who worked in the post office. It was addictive, but they had nothing in common; Ellis didn't even like him very much. When he summoned up the resolve to break it off, the man threatened to blackmail him. Ellis laughed, to hide his horror, but nothing came of it.

His lifebelt was moving to France. It held out the promise of a life less straitened, a life where more things were possible. Parisian life *was* permissive compared to home, but the atmosphere of the Second Empire was in many ways frivolous and cynical, and there were aspects of the life – like the places where men went to meet men – that alarmed as much as thrilled him. His upbringing had stronger roots than he knew, and, after his first, heart-in-mouth walks near the shrubberies of the Champs Élysées, he avoided them. He began to feel that there was nothing for him here, either. Nothing, that is, until Christmas night. That intimacy arose from the sort of drunkenness that could be blamed for any indiscretion, then he found he didn't need excuses, either for Lawrence or himself. He was like a man who stumbles and falls in a drunken state, then finds he has picked up a nugget of gold.

After that night in Montmartre, Ellis vowed to cut down his drinking. At first it was easy, with the thought of Lawrence to sustain him. He wanted to be worthy of this: his first experience with a man who didn't close his eyes when he made love. They went to his lodgings in Montmartre, where there was a lock on the door and no servant to surprise them in the morning. It was enchanting to wake and realize he was not alone, to roll against Lawrence's body and know that there was no need to pretend. To kiss in daylight. To be seen.

But then, Buzenval.

Swan organized ambulances to treat the wounded in the field, but Ellis was detailed to stay at the hospital. The field stations were swamped, surrounded by stretchers loaded with crying, groaning men, the surgeons red-eyed with exhaustion. The wounded who could travel, they loaded in carts and sent into Paris, and there too the hospitals were flooded with casualties. The surgeons and nurses worked double shifts, but still couldn't keep up. Ellis stayed at the hospital for six days straight, snatching meals in the canteen and odd hours of sleep upstairs. By the third day, his hands were shaking, and he resorted to nips of brandy to steady them. He wasn't the only one. The skin on his neck and torso broke out in hives; he scratched himself till he drew blood. One morning, he woke after two hours' sleep, feeling decidedly unwell, and, while amputating a man's hand, he was doubled over by an asthma attack. Soeur Débarras had to take over the suturing while he collapsed against the wall, unable to speak.

Someone helped him outside and left him in the hall. He couldn't even climb the stairs. He was on his own for some time, gripping the banisters and trying to breathe, and then Soeur Débarras was there, stroking his hair, and he leant into the black habit, his eyes closed. Then his colleague, Meehan, appeared, and took him off to a nearby bar, where they emptied a bottle of brandy, or perhaps more than one.

It turned into one of those nights when time began to slip and slide, hopelessly out of kilter. He was vaguely aware that there had been a riot, with people gunned down in the street, but he could breathe again, and it didn't seem to matter that much. Sometime later, he found his way home, drank a bottle of wine on top of the brandy, which had been purely medicinal, and passed out.

He woke in sheets that were damp and sticky, and it took him a minute to work out that he lay in a swamp of his own making. With exclamations of disgust, he jerked himself out of the bed. Yes, it was bad: the sheets were stinking, soiled with shit. Cursing, he stripped off his underwear to discover the hives had spiralled around his body and, in places, the skin was broken. Lying in filthy sheets had not improved matters. He washed as best he could with cold water, wincing as he dabbed open sores.

Since the disappearance of the Siamese, relations between Ellis and the concierge's wife had not improved. He kept asking whether she had seen his uncle's cat. He told her how upset the ambassador would be if she could not be found – she had been a present from his late wife. He had no scruples about embroidering the facts. Madame Gigoux denied all knowledge, maintained that she had never laid eyes on the creature – up until the point when he said that he was posting a reward for her safe return. He saw anger sparkle in her eyes, followed by calculation, and then listened outside her door as she shouted at her husband, calling him, he was certain (although it was a stout door), a greedy pig.

Now, as he crept down the stairs, hoping to leave unnoticed, she materialized between him and the door to the street, barring his escape. He was nauseous, had a crushing headache, and was acutely embarrassed by the bundle of soiled linen in his hand.

'Monsieur Butterfield! I have news of your cat! My husband, yesterday – he saw the animal, without doubt! He tried to catch her, but she ran away up the street.'

'Is that so? Madame, I'm late for work. I must . . .'

He held the incriminating bundle behind his back, hoping she wouldn't notice it. But, since the thaw, smells had sprung back to life, and her nostrils twitched.

'Are those my sheets? Where are you taking them?'

'No . . . yes. There's a laundry at the hospital. I don't have time—'

'Tenants are not allowed to take linen out of the house. Laundry is done once a fortnight.' She stared, her eyes narrow with suspicion.

'I'm not asking you to pay for it, so, if you will excuse me—'

Unable to bear another moment of this petty argument, he made to walk past her, whereupon – the astonishing cheek of it – she made a grab for the sheets and the bundle disintegrated between them, revealing brown smears.

Madame Gigoux glared at him with a sort of triumphant contempt.

'And what about my mattress, monsieur? That must be soiled too. It will have to be burned. You will pay for that, of course.'

'Really, this is intolerable! I cannot . . .' He was shouting, even as he realized he had nothing else to say. 'Yes, I will pay for it. All right?'

He stooped to ball up the stinking sheets, his face, his whole body on fire with shame. It was unbearable. He stood, and it was all he could do not to throw the bundle in her face. He stepped towards her, feeling his hands clench so hard his knuckles hurt.

'And you will pay me for another cat, no doubt, since you ate the last one.'

The woman flinched and took a step backwards, her eyes slits of venomous blackness. Her tongue flickered at her lips.

'I don't know what monsieur means. No doubt monsieur is not feeling well, this morning. You can discuss it later with my husband. I'm sure you can come to some arrangement.'

She scuttled back to her apartment and slammed the door.

In the street, Ellis realized that his teeth were clenched and there were tears in his eyes. His breath wheezed in his throat. He would have to take the damned sheets to the hospital – finding a laundress would be impossible – but that would leave him without bed linen for the next few days. Better to throw them away and buy new ones; no price could be too high . . .

He saw an opening between two buildings that led to an empty lot. He hurried to it, hid the shameful bundle in a corner with some other rubbish, and walked on. At least that was done.

Halfway to the hospital, he came to his senses. He had no idea where to obtain new linen. The hospital? No good – it was desperately short of everything. His uncle? The embassy? Likewise overwhelmed, with refugees. Surely, he would think of something – anything could be found if you could pay for it. But he was nearly penniless – had had no remittance for months. Now he had befouled his bed, he would not be able to bring Lawrence back to his room. And, somehow, he would have to replace the mattress, too. The impossibility of it made him want to cry.

Would Lawrence want to see him, anyway? The sight of his body this morning had repulsed him; the raw welts on his torso reminded him of illustrations of leprosy. If Lawrence knew the full extent of his squalidness, he would never want to see him again. He must put off seeing him for the time being – any excuse would do – until he had sorted out this mess.

He gave in to a moment's despairing wish: if only they could have met when he was young and unsullied; not yet a drunkard; not yet a failed surgeon, failed poet, failed man. Ten years ago, only, but it seemed impossibly far. The Ellis he had been then, the youth who had shared his ideals and hopes with B. – that had been him at his best. And yet, he could not avoid the thought that followed: even that had not been good enough.

43

The voice saying his name was an amused whisper. Lawrence opened his eyes; there was just enough light to make out the face next to him. He was flooded with well-being, aware, more than anything, of a perfect comradeship. From the lassitude in his limbs, he knew that they had both been through some enormous, undefined endeavour, something involving great difficulty and risk, but now it was over. There was no need to speak, or even touch; it was enough just to lie there.

The feeling persisted through his waking in his own room and was so real that it took him some moments to understand that he was alone in his bed. The disappointment was acute. There was someone in the room: a figure knelt by the fire, coaxing it into life. Lawrence closed his eyes and heard Fanny blow on the kindling. There were the familiar sounds as she stood up, walked to the door and closed it behind her. He didn't move, hoping he would slide imperceptibly back into the dream. Instead, he became more awake and noticed that his groin was wet and sticky. He hoped fervently that it hadn't happened when Fanny was in the room – that would have been too unfair when, even in the dream, he had not been aware of ecstasy, just an intimacy that seemed more complete than anything he had experienced in life.

Since the letter arrived, he'd dreamt of Yves more than once. It had turned up a week ago, part of the huge backlog of letters that trickled into Paris in fits and starts. This letter had clearly been written some time ago, although water damage rendered the date indecipherable. It was only a single page, but it was warmly affectionate. At this point, Lawrence hadn't seen Ellis for weeks, had heard nothing since the vague note saying he wasn't well. Two further notes from Lawrence had gone unanswered. Suddenly fearing that Ellis had fallen seriously ill, he went to the American hospital and asked after him. He was told that Mr Butterfield was busy in surgery. Did he want to leave a message? It wasn't important, he said.

Yves' letter felt like providence. Yves was missing him (well, had missed him then). Yves couldn't wait to see him again. The feelings of last summer and autumn flooded back. It wasn't so long ago, really – the winter and the siege had only *seemed* to go on forever. Lawrence wondered when he would return. The Lamys noticed his short temper, his distraction. At the end of February, he fell ill with a severe cold and felt nothing but relief. He could honourably succumb to a state where no decisions could be taken.

Madame Lamy nursed him herself. She was once again occupied with the business, where bookings were picking up with the return of Parisians from their country houses, and with preparations for Ernestine's wedding, but she climbed the stairs to his room several times a day, as well as sending Fanny with hot drinks and morsels to tempt the invalid. Lawrence was content to lie in bed and be cosseted while he listened to Louise discoursing on floral arrangements, guest lists and the choice of restaurant. She took it for granted that he would be there, including him quite as one of the family. He was so grateful for the undemanding affection that he was more than once brought to the brink of tears.

He formed the impression that she hadn't warmed to her future son-in-law. On the face of it, she was complimentary, but he detected a lack of real enthusiasm. He wondered – as she poured him a tisane and talked of the grand house at L'Étoile that Ranvier was buying for his bride – if she was a little disappointed in the way things had turned out for her daughter.

'The house was left over the whole winter with wet plaster on every wall – all shut up, of course, so the smell was terrible. You can imagine . . . but it will be beautiful when it's finished. How's your throat?'

Lawrence nodded and croaked.

'No need to talk. Wait, a letter came for you – I did wonder whether I should bring it up here today, since you're ill, but . . . it's not for me to decide . . .' She took out a cheap envelope and handed it to him. 'Well, I'd better be getting on. Lawrence . . . is everything all right? It's not bad news, is it?'

The letter was from Michel, informing him that the funeral of Séraphine's father would take place in two days' time.

On Thursday, still weak and feverish, Lawrence waved away Madame Lamy's objections, got out of bed and caught an omnibus to the eastern edge of the city. He hadn't seen Michel or Séraphine since Christmas Day. Since then, the relationship with Ellis had occupied his time and his thoughts to the exclusion of all else. He was ashamed to have neglected them. He hadn't even known Séraphine's father was ill.

He arrived early at the church, and thought to sit inconspicuously at the back, but Michel spotted him and came over to greet him. He still wore his Guard uniform. Despite the occasion, he looked delighted to see him.

'It's so good of you to come,' he said, shaking Lawrence by the hand. 'But, my dear fellow, I see you are ill . . . You needn't have come all this way. To be honest, we were hardly expecting you.'

'I'm not that ill,' Lawrence said. 'Just a cold – and I wanted to see you both. I'm very sorry about Monsieur Bignon. And I'm sorry it's been so long—' he broke off, coughing.

'Oh, heavens, but it hasn't been. What, it was only Christmas! I know a lot has happened since, but . . .'

Pneumonia had taken Monsieur Bignon, and had nearly stolen

Séraphine's sister too. The father had fallen ill a month ago. Many others had gone the same way. Paulette, the sister, was recovering, although she was still too ill to attend the funeral.

'Are you well, otherwise? We must talk afterwards – we're going to Monsieur Bignon's favourite wine shop to raise a glass. You will stay, won't you?' He put his hands on Lawrence's shoulders and smiled.

'Of course. How are Madame Bignon and Séraphine?'

'Oh, you know – very sad. However, they are bearing up. We must talk properly later. You've promised, now!'

Michel left him to greet the arriving mourners. Lawrence sank into a seat near the door, pulling his muffler tighter around his neck. Why were churches so cold?

He kept his eyes fixed on the front of the church, so that he wouldn't appear to be watching the door, but he couldn't help it, and, when he saw the unmistakable shape of Ellis in the doorway, he had the sensation that each organ in his body turned a somersault. He felt, rather than saw, Ellis notice him, and his hesitation before coming over. Ellis smiled at him, and Lawrence made himself smile in return. He stood up and they shook hands.

'Lawrence. Good to see you.' He only held his eyes for a moment before looking around. Lawrence thought he seemed nervous.

'How are you now?' Lawrence asked. 'Better?'

'Yes, not too bad. Just been so busy . . . And how are you—? But I see you're ill.'

'It's just a cold. Nothing serious.' He glanced towards Séraphine and her mother. 'I feel I've neglected them. I should have known . . .'

'I know. Me too. I've been . . .'

Lawrence waited, but nothing more was forthcoming. 'Are you staying for the wake?'

Ellis looked around the church. An elderly couple were sitting down a couple of seats along from Lawrence.

'I expect so. Well, then . . .'

Lawrence watched his indecision. Would Ellis sit next to him, as two friends might well sit together?

With a smile, but avoiding his eyes, Ellis took a seat on the other side of the aisle – not far away, but not too near. He could have given Lawrence a brief touch, a look of complicity, an apology, even. Ah, well.

A thick, almost tangible fog had descended over the cemetery by the time they reached the grave site. The hillside cemetery was a wilderness of mud and winter-soured grass, and the mourners struggled to keep their footing on the slope where the grave had been dug. The trees had all been felled, leaving stumps – or craters, where roots had been wrenched up. Perhaps, last summer, it would have looked different; now, it was a wretched resting place. Lawrence and Ellis walked with the other mourners from the church, slightly apart from the others, but in silence. Lawrence coughed into his handkerchief.

'Are you sure you should have come?' Ellis said, and the jesting note in his voice made Lawrence flush with irritation.

'It seemed important,' he said stiffly. He was annoyed to be seen at such a disadvantage: his nose was streaming and his eyelids, he knew, were pink.

Lawrence wasn't the only one who was ill. The priest's words were punctuated by sniffs, and by the coughing, sneezing and weeping from the mourners at another burial, further along the hillside. The fog shrouded them, granted each graveside a fleeting privacy. As it drifted and eddied, other black-clad figures appeared in a ghostly distance and were then snatched from view.

Michel stood beside Madame Bignon, physically holding her up when she seemed on the point of collapse. Séraphine stood on her other side, dry eyed, as her father's coffin was lowered into the muddy hole. Madame Bignon finally burst into sobs and was gathered into her daughter's arms. It started to rain in earnest. Lawrence watched muddy water dribble off the lid of the coffin and wondered how soon he could leave.

They squashed into the café's low-ceilinged, dark interior, and, in the melee of finding and committing himself to a seat, Lawrence ended up wedged into a bench between people he didn't know. Vapour rose off the mourners' wet coats and mixed with pipe smoke, and bottles of wine were plonked on to the table; Lawrence felt the change in the air as the mourners, niceties observed and platitudes spoken, prepared to let their hair down.

He survived the afternoon by drinking glass after glass of hot toddy and wine – whatever came his way – which soothed his fever, as well as dulling his sensitivity to the surroundings. Even so, he couldn't but be aware of Ellis sitting a few feet away at the end of the table, his voice rising in volume as the afternoon wore on. Lawrence became increasingly irritated. Ellis had decided to be the life of the party: now, talking some braggartly rubbish about his uncle; now, laughing uproariously; now, airing his opinions about something or other. Lawrence felt a wave of dislike; he was loud, boorish, obnoxious. Good riddance. On every side, the guests' faces were red and gaping with laughter. He hated them all. Yves would never behave like this.

He stayed because he couldn't summon the energy to fight his way out, with the explanations and farewells that would entail. It was late when the party broke up. A forest of empty bottles stood on the tables. The remaining guests staggered outside into the wet evening, chatting and lingering. He could not see Séraphine – he hadn't managed to speak to either her or Michel all afternoon.

Ellis was by the door, talking to a stranger. Lawrence tried not to watch. They would both be heading in roughly the same direction, could reasonably be expected to walk together. Not that he wanted to go home with him, but, if Ellis didn't try, if he didn't apologize – at the very least, say something – that would be that. He should just leave.

Michel came up and put a hand on his shoulder.

'Lawrence! There you are! I'm sorry we haven't had a chance to talk. It's been crazy today.' Like everyone else, he seemed happily drunk. 'I hope you were all right in there. How are you feeling, my poor fellow?'

'Fine. I feel better, now. It was a very nice wake.'

He heard Ellis's voice, droning on behind him. One way or another, the day would soon be over.

Michel said, 'It was a beautiful service, wasn't it? He was a quiet man, you know, but greatly liked.'

'Please tell Séraphine I'm sorry I didn't manage to talk to her. I hope she doesn't think I ignored her. I got rather stuck.'

'Oh, don't worry. Séraphine had to go back to her sister, but she was touched that you came. She made me promise to invite you to dine with us soon. When you're better, of course – yes?'

'I'd love to. I'm sure, after this week . . . Write and let me know the day.'

'I will. But . . .' Michel led him a few paces away from the café. He was composing his face into something serious and rather severe. 'There's something I must tell you. I don't suppose you've heard from Alfred?'

'Alfred?' Lawrence could not even think who this was.

'Alfred Quinet – the artist who shared Yves' studio.'

'No. I hardly know him.'

Michel nodded and his eyes dropped. 'I had a letter from him . . . It only arrived a couple of days ago. It'd been held up, you see, like the rest of the post. It's bad news, I'm afraid. Yves is dead.'

Lawrence's mind went blank. Michel was mistaken.

'What do you mean? No, I just had a letter from him – I just . . .'

'I know, the post has been all mixed up. I got one, too. It's . . . I'm sorry.'

Michel's lips went on moving. Already floating in an unmoored state, so cocooned from the world that he couldn't feel the rain he knew was falling on his face, Lawrence could barely make sense of his words. Something about November, something about Gambetta. He kept thinking, But his letter: I got his *letter* . . .

'What happened?'

Michel looked puzzled – Lawrence realized that he had been explaining this.

'He was killed in action. Back in November, during the Battle for Orléans. He was shot. It was instant. He wouldn't have suffered, they said. His father went to . . . to find him, to take him home. The funeral was at the beginning of December, at their home. His father wrote to Alfred.'

'Oh.'

'I still can't believe it. Dear Yves. He was the best fellow you could ever meet.'

Lawrence became aware that Ellis was standing behind Michel, and, from the look on his face, he saw that he knew. Ellis was watching him. His eyes were narrowed and he was frowning, but that could have been due to smoke from his cigar, or the rain. Lawrence looked back to Michel, at his kind, weary face. He was upset too, but, on a day like today, Yves could only be his second or third greatest sorrow.

Lawrence turned to look down the street. The horizon was soft and uncertain behind the veil of rain, and he felt too addled and slow to gather his wits, to know what was the right thing to say. He thought, simply: Yves, no . . . and felt the spin of the earth beneath him, threatening to hurl him off.

44

Louise had known no good would come of Lawrence's insistence on going to the funeral. She'd tried to talk him out of it, but of course he wasn't to be dissuaded. She said as much to Monsieur Butterfield when he brought Lawrence home, his face a terrible ashy colour, and Monsieur Butterfield told her that Lawrence had felt unwell at the wake. They had been drinking and their clothes were as wet as if they had walked all the way, rather than taking a cab. Both men were red-eyed. She was rather surprised by the intensity of their gloom, given that the deceased was a friend's father, not someone they'd known well. Lawrence mumbled an apology to her and an abrupt farewell to his friend, and went upstairs.

'It was very kind of you to bring him back, Monsieur Butterfield. You're a good friend. I hope we'll see you again soon, when he's better.'

Monsieur Butterfield muttered something unintelligible, turned to go, then turned back. 'Madame, I think . . . it wasn't the funeral. We have just found out that a friend of ours was killed in the fighting last winter. The news has only just come. Monsieur Harper and he were close friends. It's a terrible shock.'

'Oh, no! I'm so sorry to hear that. What was his name?'

'Yves Michaud. He was a painter. He died fighting with Gambetta.'

Louise crossed herself. 'When did it happen?'

'In November. At the defeat of Orléans.'

'That's terribly sad. My deepest condolences, monsieur.'

'Thank you. I hope I didn't speak out of turn. I thought perhaps you ought to know.'

Louise went up to Lawrence's room, and found him lying on his bed, fully clothed. She clicked her tongue. There was no fire in the grate and the room was clammy with the smell of wet clothes.

'No, no, no, Lawrence! I'll send Fanny to make up the fire. You must not lie there in those wet things. I mean it. Take them off! Now. Come on.'

Lawrence obediently sat up and began unbuttoning his waistcoat.

Louise tugged on the rope for Fanny. 'I'll get Cook to make up a hot compress, and a tisane. Or perhaps you should have a bath? What about it?'

'No, I'll be fine.'

'Come on, everything – that too.' Louise stood over him as he peeled off his long underwear and rolled into bed. His exposed body was thin and vulnerable. He was so young and so beautiful, it was very hard not to put out her hand and touch him, but she knew she mustn't. It broke her heart that she couldn't comfort him, as a mother would embrace her son when he was ill or sad. He looked as though he needed someone to do so. She pulled the blankets up to his chin and laid her hand on his forehead. He trusted her; for that, she was grateful. 'That's better. You're cold as ice.'

'I'll warm up in a minute.' His eyes met hers and she was struck by the unhappiness she saw in them. She dared to brush the tendrils of damp hair off his forehead.

'Monsieur Butterfield said you just found out you have lost a friend.'

His eyes slid away and his forehead buckled in distress.

'I'm so sorry, my dear. I'm so sorry. Oh dear . . .'

He was trying to say thank you, and not cry. She couldn't bear it. She laid a hand on his shoulder, through the blankets.

'There, there. It's all right. Shh, shh.'

He felt breakable. Young people were skin and bone. You forgot how fragile they felt, once your own child had grown up and you couldn't cuddle them anymore.

'There you are, Fanny. Can you stoke up the fire – make it nice and hot. Monsieur Harper was caught in the rain, on top of his chill. I'll go and talk to Sabine about some tisane. I'll bring up more blankets.'

Lawrence muttered his thanks and turned to the wall. As the girl set about the fire, Louise withdrew.

She went downstairs, deep in thought. Her feelings had shaken her. So what if she had seen his body? She would feel no shame for stealing such a treasure, would preserve the memory of it in amber. Anyway, really, she saw him more like a son, and wanting to put her arms around him was a maternal impulse. She loved him and wanted to protect him from pain. It was just that she was a little confused, because sometimes people got confused about the different kinds of love.

45

Before he started work, Swan came up to say he wanted a word in private. Ellis followed him upstairs to the room that served as his office. He sat with his hands in his lap, quite calm. He knew what was coming and felt nothing in particular.

'Well, Butterfield, I want to thank you for everything you've done – all the more, as I know your doubts about doing it. I want you to know that you've been a great help, and we appreciate it. But I guess you won't be too upset to hear that we no longer need you, now the fighting's over . . .'

'No, of course not, sir.'

'No reflection on you at all,' Swan went on. 'You've done a fine job. I spoke to your uncle and told him how grateful we are. But we don't need so many staff now, thank the Lord.'

'No. Quite.'

'I expect you'll be glad to get back to your poetry, and so on.' His folksy Southern drawl seemed to broaden by the second.

Ellis agreed and smiled, and Swan smiled. They shook hands. It was all very cordial.

He went to the door of the operating theatre – ballroom, as was – and looked for Soeur Débarras. She was standing at a table with another surgeon, Dennis Meehan, who was bending over a patient, his cuffs red with blood. He wanted to thank her. But he couldn't interrupt them.

He would have to wait or come back another day. No one looked up or noticed him go.

Ellis began to walk in the direction of Montmartre. He was relieved, he told himself. Free. Mainly, what he felt was numb. He had nothing to be ashamed of. He'd hated every minute of it, yet he had, as Swan said, made out all right.

He didn't fool himself that what he had done was so wonderful; some hospitals had turned to amateur surgeons to make up the shortfall in medical staff, and they had acquitted themselves well. There was an Irish journalist who was famous for his coolness with a scalpel. It was all perfectly absurd . . .

There it was again: that feeling of unreality he was experiencing often these days; an impermeable panel that shut him off from his own life, which had, when he was with Lawrence, briefly seemed to dissolve.

On waking this morning, he'd sworn he would not drink today. But, now he was out of a job, what else was he going to do? He could see about finding somewhere else to live; he'd often thought about changing his lodging, but had not had time to do anything about it. He hated walking into that building, knowing that the concierge might pop out at any moment. Nothing more had been said about his uncle's cat; Madame Gigoux no longer pretended to have spotted her on the street, and Ellis had given up his show of concern. It felt as though she had made a tacit admission of guilt, but, at the same time, he had lost the moral authority to accuse her. Since the incident of the bed linen, the hateful woman had gained the upper hand.

He could buy the papers and sit in a wine shop, read the advertisements. He could try to write something – although he knew that this would not happen. If he didn't drink, it would be all too easy to brood on the disaster that had been Monsieur Bignon's funeral, the news about Yves, on all the ways he had fumbled his chance to make amends with Lawrence.

He had meant to write to him before the funeral, but was embarrassed to tell the truth, and bad at prevaricating. He'd hoped that somehow, when they saw each other, explanations would be unnecessary. But he saw Lawrence's face, and saw that he was angry, and ill. He hoped for an opportune moment to apologize, but then came the terrible blow of Yves' death. Michel had told Ellis earlier, and his first thought was to ask if Lawrence knew. He urged Michel to tell him as soon as possible, but Michel was swept up with other guests. The last thing he'd wanted was to witness the telling – that made it all the worse.

Why had he chosen that precise moment to approach? Because, being drunk, he'd actually forgotten about Yves. He'd ambled over, full of wine and hope, and heard Michel's words; he caught Lawrence's eyes and read in them a terrible anguish. Then he committed the worst sin of all – he hadn't looked away. He couldn't stop looking at Lawrence's dear face, thinking, I have to know: if he is devastated, if he is heartbroken, I'll know what I suspected all along – that, no matter what he said, I was never as good. Lawrence had turned away to hide his face, and Ellis saw him stagger and collapse.

It wasn't too late. He just needed a new start – a new place to live, a new job (well, his old job, again). He would be able to cut down his drinking because he would no longer need to blot out the things he had seen. He would write to Lawrence now and explain all the things that he had not been able to say at the funeral. His heart ached with genuine pain for Yves, who was good and gentle, unfailingly generous and kind. Yves would never have got himself into the sort of scrapes that Ellis repeatedly found himself in. But, also, he was dead. However much he was loved – and they had all loved him – he was gone.

He turned the corner of the Rue de Castiglione and spotted a familiar, fox-like face. It was the critic, Gustave Daudel. At the sight of Ellis, the habitual, supercilious expression dissolved into a grin of delight.

'My dear friend!' Gustave pumped his hand, and then, overcome with an emotion that surprised Ellis, kissed him on both cheeks. 'What a happy encounter!'

'I didn't know you were in Paris.'

'I've just got back. Thank God! All those months in the country – I thought I would go stark staring mad. But you have had worse than boredom to contend with. You must tell me everything. You look thinner and more poetic – unlike me, I know. I have seen no one and know nothing. Where are you going now? Can I invite you?'

'Nowhere in particular. As a matter of fact, I've been laid off.'

Bemused, but flattered to be treated as though he was the person Gustave most wanted to see in the world, Ellis allowed himself to be steered to a nearby bar, where Gustave ordered champagne.

He indulged in the seedy pleasure of describing the siege: the cold, the shelling, the squalor of the hospital, the funeral of Séraphine's father. Gustave proclaimed himself in awe of Ellis's work as a surgeon, which both gratified and embarrassed Ellis. Staying with his parents-in-law near Bordeaux, untouched by the war, Gustave seemed to have been living in a different country. He had not shivered or felt hunger pangs, or been kept awake by bombs. He had heard from Yves, last autumn, and from Alfred Quinet, who saw out the war on the Brittany coast. He had learnt of Yves' death at the end of last year. To him, it was old news.

'His father went to the site of the battle, to look for him. It took days, but he didn't give up. It was snowing, freezing . . .' Gustave shook his head. 'Eventually, he found him. He had that comfort, at least, of taking him home.'

Ellis swallowed his champagne and allowed his glass to be replenished. He could visualize only too clearly what Yves' father might have found. They raised their glasses in a toast to their friend.

Gustave went on, 'What I can't understand is why he joined up in the first place – I would have thought him the very last person who would throw himself into fighting. Although –' Gustave's voice assumed a sly, confidential tone – 'I wonder – strictly between ourselves – if he wanted to prove that he was, you know, as much a man as any of us. That even one of his predilections . . . you follow me?'

Ellis felt frozen. 'Whatever the reason, he was very brave.'

'Yes. I just wish that he were less brave, and still here. But what of the Canadian boy – Monsieur Harper? You said he was at the Bignon funeral. Is he devastated – or is he one of those little trollops who long since found someone else?'

Ellis heard himself speak as if from an icy distance. 'I don't, er . . . Yes, he was upset. Of course. We all are.'

How could Gustave think any different? He had left Paris in August, before anything happened. The siege had changed them; there was an abyss between those who had lived through it and those who had not. Ellis thought, I have lived through two wars; he has lived through none. It's not his fault.

Gustave beckoned the waiter over, ordered more champagne and some oysters. He turned back to Ellis with a smile.

'Forgive me. I've had time to grow used to the idea, but for you it is new and painful. We'll drink to absent friends, and we must also think of the future, eh? What are you going to do now? I'm sure your experiences have, at the very least, furnished you with some good material for poetry.'

Ellis shrugged, and Gustave began to talk of art. The unreality was stronger, the glass walls around him thicker. There was no way he was going to stay sober now.

46

Right up until the last minute, Anne wasn't going to go. She wanted to, very much, because Fanny had asked her – but she also didn't want to, at least as much. Awful possibilities presented themselves: Fanny would not be there, and she would look foolish. Far worse was the possibility that Fanny *would* be there, but that she would have forgotten about inviting Anne, and would be embarrassed to see her. Or (perhaps even that wasn't the worst thing), Fanny would not know her at all.

On the Saturday afternoon, she served tea to Monsieur Papin in the drawing room. It was peaceful; being in a room with him was almost as good as being by herself. She was surprised, but not alarmed, when he bade her sit down.

'So, Anne,' he began, stirring sugar into his chocolate. 'It won't be long, now, before I leave. Have you thought any more about what you will do?'

Anne had been dreading this. She managed to put it out of her mind for long stretches, and, as she so rarely laid eyes on Victor Calmette, she managed to put the awful fact of his marriage proposal out of her mind also. Unable either to assent or deny, she said nothing.

'Are you finding it difficult to make up your mind? Perhaps I can help.'

Anne stared at the feet of a little fruitwood side table. The beautiful furniture would go with him. Could she countenance the loss of the lion feet, and the mahogany piano, and all the other wonderful things that were migrating to the country? Was she weighing the loss of them against the loss of Marguerite? Yes, because that was easier than weighing a life with Papin against a life with Victor Calmette.

'If you could do anything at all, Anne, what would you most want to do?'

She didn't hesitate. 'Stay on here, like this.'

'You mean, keep working in this house?'

She nodded. 'For you.'

'Ah. But, imagine this: if anything were possible – anything, no matter how silly it might sound – what is your heart's desire? Surely it's not to keep house for a foolish old man.'

Anne had no idea. How could you truly see things that weren't there? All she could picture was Marguerite.

'Maybe . . . work in a zoo.'

'You mean as a keeper? Or a veterinarian?'

'Oh, no, no – I don't know. Of course, that wouldn't be possible.'

'Well, nothing is possible – until someone does it.'

Anne sighed. There were things that were actually possible – in the sense that she was able to walk across Paris – and then there were things that were theoretically, but not really, possible. She'd have thought that, being so wise, Monsieur Papin would know that.

'This menagerie is a hidebound place. An old institution. But there may be zoos that are not so old, nor so bound by tradition.'

Anne didn't know what he was getting at.

'I think you would make an excellent veterinarian, given the right training. You know how to pay attention, you have passion without sentiment, and you never forget anything.'

Anne smiled at the carpet. Such nonsense, but it was sweet to hear.

'I wish things were different, but it is time for me to retire. I can't stay here forever, nor should I. And I fear there will be unrest in Paris before long. That is not something I care to see. Do you know to what I am referring?'

Anne shook her head. She had a good idea, but it was always as well to keep quiet and let men tell you things.

'The authorities made a mistake. They gave rifles to half a million men when we were at war. Now, those men have no jobs and are angry at the way things have turned out. I think there will be rioting. I doubt there would be real danger here, but it may be ugly. Does that frighten you?'

'I'd want to stay with the animals. They can't defend themselves.'

'I thought you would say that. Well, then, it seems that you have decided.'

Anne was mortified. Had he tricked her into refusing his offer of a job?

'I don't . . . I'm sorry, Monsieur Papin. I would always be happy to work for you.'

'I know. You don't need to apologize. You never need to apologize to me.'

'But I haven't decided. I don't know! I—'

'I wonder whether your decision has been more difficult, because I understand that, er, Monsieur Calmette has made you a certain offer. It is none of my business, of course, but I gather you have not yet given him an answer.'

Anne stared harder at the floor. She shook her head.

'Please, tell me if I am wrong, but perhaps the offer is not to your taste . . . yet you do not like to refuse, in case there were to be hurt feelings. Am I right?'

Anne nodded. 'He has been very kind. I don't want . . .' Strangely, she felt a tear run down her cheek. Strange, because she was not sad; she was, on the contrary, happy that he understood her. 'I'm sorry.'

'No, no. You don't want to lose that friendship. Monsieur Calmette is an understanding man. I think he would be willing to have you stay on here as the housekeeper, and he would say no more about the other thing.'

Anne put both hands to her face. She was happy, but she also found it unbearable.

'How would that be, if you could stay on here, as the housekeeper, like now? Would you like that?'

She nodded and whispered, 'Yes.'

'I think you could tell him in a letter; it might be easier to say what you mean than in conversation.'

'Yes. You think that will be all right?'

'I do.'

She made herself lift her eyes to his face. Made her eyes seek out his faded blue ones in their dear, wrinkled nests. She even willed him to look at her, which, at length, he did.

After that, she found that she wanted to go to Fanny's meeting. She was too excited and restless to stay in the house. If she didn't get out and move, she thought she might fly away, or burst.

The interior of the church was lit by oil lamps and seemed full of people. Anne scurried to one side of the nave, where she could peer from the shadows, hoping to catch a glimpse of Fanny. The noise of all these people talking made a rumbling, echoing din that crashed around her ears; she was assaulted by shouts and laughter, and the smells of pipe smoke and unwashed bodies. Her eyes skittered from one patch of light to another, seeking a familiar face, but Fanny was nowhere to be seen. In a panic, she turned to leave, just as someone pressed something cold into her hand. It was a glass of wine, and she found herself holding it, fixing her eyes on the feet of the person who had given it to her. They wore polished black boots. Black trousers. A gentleman. They were saying something in tones of great surprise.

'My goodness . . . surely – Anne! Mademoiselle Petitjean – it is, isn't it?'

Anne could not bring herself to look up. But there was something familiar about the voice. It sparked memories.

'It's Hippolyte Mazade. Do you remember me?' He lowered his voice discreetly. 'I can't believe it. Anne! My goodness!'

His voice was full of wonder. It made her look up, till she could apprehend his face. Yes, it was him, her Hippolyte, whom she had not seen for – oh – years. He wasn't her Hippolyte, though. He'd said he would come back for her, but he hadn't.

Hippolyte was talking, asking her something, but someone else was trying to talk to him at the same time, and he laughed. He seemed quite overcome. Anne stood there, not knowing what to say or do. Then Fanny was at her side, exclaiming with pleasure.

'You came! I'm so delighted. You must come and sit with me. Raymond is here too, but he's with his friends. You know Citoyen Mazade? How amazing! It was fate that I invited you!'

'Citoyenne Petitjean and I have not seen each other for a long time. But what a happy meeting this is.' Hippolyte seemed truly delighted to see her. But how odd that he even recognized her, from among the hundreds and hundreds of women in the hospital, and all the patients he must have seen since. The thought that he was pleased to see her shocked her a little. Flattered her.

The meeting began. It was an informal gathering, where both sexes stood up to participate. The audience was mostly men, but there was a good number of women too. Many had taken glasses of wine that were laid out on a side table, and most of the men smoked. The smells of a bar were stronger than the faint whiff of incense. Anne held the glass Hippolyte had given her, but couldn't quite bring herself to drink from it. They were in a church, after all.

The audience listened to each speaker and called out agreement or comments. They addressed each other as 'Citoyen' or 'Citoyenne'. Apart from Hippolyte – introduced as 'the well-known doctor', which made Anne warm with pride – the most memorable speaker was the last. This was a middle-aged woman, with a striking, frog-like face.

She spoke with a fluency and passion that held the crowd spellbound. She criticized the government in the strongest terms, and spoke of how things were unfair on ordinary, working people. The *citoyens* were going to change things by taking action. The action was not specified. They were using these meetings to work out just how things should be different. It would be hard; the government and the bourgeoisie wouldn't like it, but the rewards would be great. Change was inevitable – at which point, the audience erupted with clapping and cheers.

This was exactly what Monsieur Papin had been talking about: these were the dangerous people, revolutionaries, with wild, turbulent ideas. Many of the men wore Guard uniforms and there were rifles propped casually against walls and chairs, although they didn't seem that belligerent. They listened to the women with as much attention as they gave to the men. No doubt Monsieur Papin would be horrified to know she was sitting here, listening to such things. But, as much as she liked and respected him, she was certain that he was wrong. She had known, all her life, that things were unfair, that life for most people was hard. Every moment of her life had made that clear, but she had never before heard anyone propose what might be done about it.

Fanny made Anne stay on after the meeting. Anne submitted, although she was exhausted; she wasn't sure how much more she could take. The whole thing was overwhelming – the stirring words, the faces, and Hippolyte being there, and his being pleased to see her . . . Her head churned. Fanny introduced Anne to her husband as 'Citoyenne Petitjean'. She felt Raymond – Citoyen Klein – rake her with fierce, dark eyes, but she kept her eyes down and said little, and he soon turned away. He scared her a bit, not because of anything he said, but because he had a dark, discontented feeling about him. She wondered what it was like to be married to him. Certainly, he was handsome.

And it was fascinating to see Fanny here, among friends: a popular figure, known and liked by many.

'It sounds so funny, this *Citoyenne*,' Anne whispered, when they were, briefly, alone.

Fanny laughed. 'I thought so too, at first. But, think – why should women be divided according to whether they are married or not? Men aren't.' She saw Anne's face and laughed again. 'I told you there are new ideas around! Citoyenne Michel – that was the last speaker – she's amazing. She isn't married and wouldn't want to be. Some of the women say marriage is a trap set by the Church. That's not what I think, of course –' she laughed – 'but a girl shouldn't have to marry just to get somewhere to live, or something to eat, should she?'

'No,' said Anne, and the thought made the blood crash in her veins. 'What does she do, then, Mada— um, Citoyenne Michel?'

'She's a teacher. And a writer. Of course, she comes from a good family. They say that she's a friend of Victor Hugo.'

Hippolyte Mazade came towards them. He had changed in the last two years – he had grown a beard and he wore glasses, which made him look older and more like a doctor. But he was still softly spoken, with eyes that were, to Anne, less hurtful than most people's eyes.

'Citoyennes.' He bowed. 'Thank you for coming. Did you enjoy the meeting?'

They said they had.

'Citoyenne Petitjean and I met when I was a medical student, and she worked as a nurse's assistant.'

He said it so simply and naturally that Anne could have hugged him. Fanny said, how nice for them to meet again.

Hippolyte hesitated. 'I hope we can expect to see you at more meetings?'

Anne glanced briefly at Fanny, who smiled encouragement. 'Well, perhaps. If I can.'

'Now that we have met again, it would be a shame—'

Fanny excused herself to find her husband and darted away with a brief touch on Anne's arm, as if to say, *I'll be back.*

'I owe you an apology, Anne. I've thought of you often. I'm sorry that I never—'

'Oh, no. I didn't expect—'

'Still, I meant to come and find you. I'm very happy to see you like this. It must be fate, us meeting again.'

Anne caught that sense again, as when he used to compliment her. Could it be that he still liked her in the same way?

Then another of the speakers was by his side, muttering intently in his ear. Anne caught the words 'central committee', and 'critical', and, if she wasn't mistaken, 'bastards'. Hippolyte was a man of consequence here. The man was insisting he go with him to talk to the others.

'I'm sorry, I must go. We're here every Saturday evening. *Au revoir* – I hope.'

Fanny found her, a few moments later.

'I have to go,' Anne said. Her head was on the verge of exploding. 'Did you find your husband?'

'Not yet. Wasn't it interesting, don't you think? And you know Citoyen Mazade – I can't believe it! And, I'm sorry, but the way he was looking at you . . . Oh, come on, if I've ever seen a man smitten, it was him. Was there something between you, before? No, you don't need to answer; I know what I saw . . .'

Anne shook her head, cheeks aflame. She kept her eyes on the floor as Fanny talked non-stop. Fanny was exalted, bubbling with energy; her eyes shone, she laughed with pure happiness.

At last, Anne made her goodbyes to Fanny and Raymond and began to walk home. Thoughts swirled in her head. It was the most extraordinary evening she had ever spent. She'd drunk only half a glass of wine, but she felt as though she had been drinking Monsieur Papin's best champagne, or as though she'd woken up after sleeping her whole life, and, despite what Fanny said, it wasn't due to Hippolyte Mazade.

She felt ashamed about all the things she had never questioned. She walked at top speed, filled with urgency and purpose. Something had opened in her mind – a window whose existence she had never imagined – and it gave her a glimpse of something wonderful.

47

On Saturday morning, Ellis was woken by a tremendous din. There was a clangour of bells, rung without rhythm or pattern, and, underneath the bells, a rumbling from the street below. He got out of bed and peered from his window. The Rue Lamarck was filled with people; as far as he could see, there was a dense crowd, and it was on the move. The rumble was of thousands of boots on cobbles, the sound of sternly beaten drums and the mutter of singing and shouting. An atmosphere rose off the crowd – tense, excited, angry.

The crowd was making its way up the hill, to the Tour Solferino, where, a few weeks ago, National Guard troops had dragged two hundred cannon, parking them on the terraces around the tower in a show of defiance to the surrendering government. Ellis was on the point of going back to bed, but then he caught the word, 'Betrayed!' Curiosity got the better of him, and he pulled on his clothes.

In the street, he allowed himself to be swept along by the crowd. It slowed to a halt near the top of the Butte Montmartre. Ellis could neither see nor hear what was happening ahead, and the crowd was so dense he could barely move. Next to him were men in Guard uniforms, abattoir workers, a pair of laundresses, a teenage boy with fevered eyes. Listening to their snatches of talk, he gathered there was a regular army regiment at the top of the hill, and that, perhaps, some people had been shot. Citizens. There were ragged chants as people shouted against the prime minister and the head of the army. 'Down with Thiers! Down with Vinoy!'

A cold rain began to fall and a ripple of laughter spread through the crowd around him. There was cheering. The atmosphere was, more than anything, jubilant. He felt famished and decided it was time he found something to eat.

The letter from yesterday was still in his pocket. After reading it through once, he had shoved it there, unsure what he felt about it. When he had found a café and ordered rolls and coffee, he brought it out.

His mother had written in roundabout terms of what she called her 'new-found happiness'. The terms were so roundabout that, on first reading, it wasn't until the final page that he realized, with a sickening jolt, that she intended to marry again. Or, as she put it, 'to join in the nuptial endeavour' with a gentleman called Mr Reeves. She hoped that this news would not come as too much of a shock, but she had not wanted to write and tell him until the siege was over. Her first thoughts, she assured him, were always for him, and his happiness. However, Mr Reeves was keen to hold the wedding in July, in just four months' time. She desperately wanted Ellis to be there, and hoped and trusted he would be able to arrange his affairs accordingly. She wanted him to give her away.

The letter was the reason why, last night, after a period of exemplary moderation, he had ended up drinking too much.

It was not something to which Ellis had given much thought – the possibility that his mother had an emotional life independent of him. Stupid, of course. She was in her early fifties, slim, without a grey hair in sight, and had been a widow for nearly a decade. She deserved to be happy. He told himself he was glad. But, for the last ten years, she had constantly reaffirmed the central, inviolable place he held in her heart – had used that fact to squeeze him in a vice that had become intolerable. This news took a pressure off him that he had long railed against. At the same time, he was jealous.

The really irritating part (amazing, the number of ways that someone he loved could annoy him) was that, in one sentence, she seemed to be asking for his permission to marry, but clearly, in the next, assumed it. *I wouldn't dream of doing anything that might upset you*, she wrote, in reference to the memory of his father. Then she suggested the date he should arrive for the wedding: *There are so many things on which I want to consult you.* And, finally: *I couldn't bear it if you weren't there to give me away* – as though he couldn't possibly have commitments of his own. There was, of course, no reason why he shouldn't go. She even – cunningly, insultingly – offered to pay for his passage.

She described Mr Reeves as a bachelor of middle age, but did not specify his occupation. What if the man was a fortune hunter? His mother had a modest, but useful income. What terrible flaw had prevented anyone from marrying him before now? Was it up to Ellis to protect her?

During the siege, cut off from outside communication, it had been his habit to think of his mother more fondly, less judgementally, than usual. It was as though those who lived outside the walls of Paris were suspended in whatever attitude they had last presented. But, just as profound things had happened to him, so things elsewhere went on happening. His mother had fallen in love. Yves had died.

Why did the news make him feel so desolate? How should he reply? *Dear Mother. Congratulations. By coincidence, I too have fallen in love. But I'm afraid it's not a good time for me to come home, as, at present, I don't know where I am, or what he thinks of me . . .*

He was haunted by the memory of Lawrence's face after the funeral – the starkness of his shock, the silence of the cab ride. Until that day, Lawrence had seemed to him someone who moved through life with enviable ease and resilience. Perhaps he hadn't credited him with much depth. But the silent tears in the cab, his intense anguish, and the realization that he could do nothing to assuage it – all that shook him into a clearer understanding of his feelings. He had written to Lawrence at length, stressing his illness and his apologies. He had been honest. He didn't know if that had been the right thing.

He resented the way that his mother's wedding – any wedding – unthinkingly claimed precedence over all else. He could never ask her to validate the choice of his heart. There could never be any acknowledgement, let alone celebration. Of course, that wasn't her fault.

As he thought this over, he saw Lawrence's secretive, careless smile. He had said, during their short period of happiness, as they lay in each other's arms, 'I would never marry. If it weren't for this –' he trailed a finger down Ellis's flank – 'I'd find some other reason. I don't want to be like everyone else.' His face had such a beautiful arrogance as he said it. Ellis half admired, half feared that bravado. He was so young. Easy to make such statements at the beginning of your life. Ten years ago, B. had said very much the same thing.

Ephraim's residence had been emptied of the last of its refugees, and, though the hall and corridors had a knocked-about look, it was peaceful – pleasant to sit back in a chair and listen to nothing but the tick of the mantel clock and the popping of the fire. Ellis's uncle was not at home, but the maid let him sit and wait in the library. She even brought him a bottle of wine and some sandwiches. He chose a book from the shelves and soon became absorbed. When he heard the sound of his uncle's arrival in the hall, he was struggling to make out the print in the growing darkness. He stood up as Ephraim came in.

'Ellis, this is a nice surprise. Well, perhaps not such a surprise. I take it you've heard from your mother?'

'Yes. They said I could wait. I hope I'm not disturbing you too much.'

'Not at all. It's good to see you. I would have been here earlier, but my lunch went on longer than expected. You must stay and have supper, now that you're here. Have you eaten?'

'The girl brought me sandwiches.'

'Good. So, you've heard from Sophia.'

'I got her letter yesterday. Did you know anything about this impending marriage?'

'I doubt I know more than you. I have never heard her mention the name before.'

'Don't you think it rather sudden?'

'Perhaps that's only how it appears to us, so far away. I am happy for her, of course.'

'Of course. She deserves it.'

The maid came in with a tray. Ephraim had asked for a bottle of champagne to toast the good news.

They lifted their glasses and drank to his mother's engagement.

Ephraim said, 'I am relieved. I've often thought my sister was not cut out to live alone. At one point, I hoped she might come over and live here, with me – but I think she felt it would be intruding too much upon your life.'

Ellis was momentarily speechless. He had never imagined his mother holding back on his account. He searched for something to say. 'So, will you go to the wedding? July, she said. That seems rather soon.' It was the middle of March.

'We'll see. It may be difficult for me to leave. But you must go, Ellis. She would be devastated if you didn't.'

'I'm not sure. I have several things going on. Why might it be difficult for you? Surely you can take a holiday, now? When was the last time you went home?'

Ephraim frowned. 'The situation here changes daily. Only today, while I was at the chateau, we heard some nasty rumours, though that is nothing new.'

'What sort of rumours?'

'I would have to corroborate them before passing on such a thing.'

'There was a bit of a stir in Montmartre this morning: crowds in the street, grumbling about the government – you know the sort of thing – but it seemed quite good natured.'

'Well, as I say, you must go. I believe she wants you to give her away.'

Ellis nodded. He gazed into his empty glass.

'She loves you very much, you know. You are everything to her.'

Ellis smiled, trying to accept this assertion with grace, rather than alarm. Before he could reply, there was a knock at the door, and Warburton, the secretary, came in.

'Telegram,' he said, nodding at Ellis as he handed the envelope to Ephraim, who opened it.

It was a long message. Ephraim read it and the ensuing silence changed, darkened. At length, he folded it.

'James, will you call for the carriage?'

The secretary rang the bell by the fireplace.

'I'm sorry, Ellis, I have to go out.'

'What is it?'

'It seems the likelihood of my going anywhere has just receded a little further.' He looked at his nephew, his face weary. 'This afternoon, in Montmartre, two generals were murdered. The National Guard has taken the Hôtel de Ville. The government has fled.'

'But then—' said Ellis, at the same time as Mr Warburton said, 'But the army—?' His face was milk white.

'From what I can gather, it seems the army – a good part of it, at least – has sided with the rebels.'

'The government has fled – what does that mean?'

Warburton looked at Ellis with a mixture of terror and contempt. 'It means a revolution! It means the Reds have taken over!'

Ephraim stood up and turned to Ellis. 'I have to go out. You must stay the night, of course, at least until we find out what's going on.'

'I'll be fine. Let me come with you. You shouldn't go alone.'

'Stay!' It was not so much a command as a plea. 'For God's sake, Ellis, please. James will come with me.'

Ellis acquiesced. After all, what had he to go home to? His thoughts had flown to Lawrence – where he was, what he might be doing. But a man who was ill in bed could hardly be mixed up in a revolution. If a letter awaited him at home, it would still be there tomorrow.

48

While Lawrence was ill, he was haunted by an incident from his child-hood. It must have been spring, as he could recall the delight with which he ran around outside after a long winter's imprisonment. The thaw had come and everything was wet and bright. Colours seemed wonderfully vivid after the grey-white months. He came to a big silver birch, mesmerized by its shaggy trunk, and became absorbed in peeling off the old, loose bark, revealing new skin beneath. He held his breath as he removed longer and longer strips. It made him shiver, as though he were hurting the tree, but he couldn't stop until he had pulled off every last scrap. He collected the long curls of birch paper from the forest floor and had the enchanting idea of making them into magic hair. He was adorned with birch tresses when he became aware that someone was watching him. He looked around to see his father, on his face an expression he never wanted to see again. Even at that age, he had known it was only a matter of time before he was found out.

Sunday 19th March dawned clear and sunny – a welcome change after the long spell of damp weather. Lawrence got dressed for the first time in days. Yesterday, his fever had dropped, but it left him feeling weak and desolate; he'd spent a good part of the afternoon crying into his pillow. He grieved for Yves, of course, but the initial shock had abated. It felt more as though he was grieving for himself and his friends – how naive they had been, thinking they had all the time in the world.

Yves would never have the chance to paint those paintings, or make up his mind about himself. Lawrence's sadness spread to encompass the failures and disappointments that went on every day. He wept for the way his mother's letters were dull recitals of seasons and waypoints in their neighbours' lives, in which she was no more interested than he. She hardly mentioned his father, except to sign off her letters, *with love from us both.* That was a bromide, if not a downright lie.

The curious thing was that the news of Yves' death changed little. Lawrence's memories of him were the same. He had thought of him often, not knowing he was dead. Now that he knew, what difference did it make? He had long since extinguished hope and expectation from his thoughts. Or thought he had. He made himself reread the letters that Yves had sent him: three sheets of paper, barely ten minutes' worth of words. He folded them all into one envelope – such a small sum of evidence – and pushed the envelope to the back of a drawer.

Yesterday he had received another letter. He saw Ellis's handwriting and opened the envelope with feelings so mixed he could not name them all, then found his heart quickening as he read. It was the frankest letter anyone had ever written him. In it, Ellis explained that his silence was due to exhaustion after Buzenval and an attack of hives that had made him feel very low. The physical affliction was distressing enough, but worse was the black mood; when it came over him like that he hated himself and felt he wasn't fit to be seen, especially by the one he cared about more than any other. He knew he had tested Lawrence's patience to breaking point, and at the funeral had been horribly clumsy. He hoped, against hope, that Lawrence could find it in his heart to forgive him.

Madame Lamy smiled when he joined them at breakfast.

'How nice to see you downstairs. You look much better – you have colour again. He looks much better, doesn't he, Serge?'

She turned and signed to her husband, who nodded amiably, but returned immediately to an intense perusal of his paper. Lawrence realized that the atmosphere was strange. Louise's smile had a forced quality. Ernestine was also reading a serious newspaper – something Lawrence couldn't remember seeing before.

'Has something happened?' he asked, as he drew up his chair.

There was a pause. Madame Lamy looked at her husband, opened her mouth to speak, and burst into tears. Lawrence was shocked; even at the height of the shelling, he had never seen her cry. Monsieur Lamy put a hand on her arm.

Ernestine dropped her paper and turned her gaze on him, in the grip of unusually strong emotion. 'There has been a coup d'état.' Her voice was strangled.

Louise uttered a sob. 'I'm sorry. Stupid of me. It's just—'

'What sort of coup?'

'Have a look. I can't read any more.' Ernestine pushed Le Figaro across the breakfast table and stood up abruptly. The legs of her chair snagged on the rug, and it fell over with a crash. She turned to her parents and signed swiftly without speaking, then turned and left.

'Titine! Wait!' Her mother got up and went after her.

Le Figaro voiced dire mutterings about anarchy and the risen ghosts of the Terror, but, to Lawrence, the news seemed to add up to little more than another change of government, only a few weeks after the last election. After breakfast, although still weak and easily tired, he walked the short distance to the Hôtel de Ville, curious to find out more.

The bright morning matched his lifting mood: the Seine sparkled and the streets were full of people with smiles on their faces. The National Guardsmen he saw were accompanied by cantinières – women in uniform, with casks of brandy slung around their shoulders, who called out and laughed with passers-by. The atmosphere was exultant and Lawrence found himself smiling at them. He touched Ellis's letter in his breast pocket. Some changes were for the better – why shouldn't this be one of them?

A red flag was flying over the Hôtel de Ville, and the square in front of it was a sea of uniformed guardsmen. They lounged in the sun, loaves of bread impaled on their bayonets. Some had flowers in their caps. It felt like a holiday.

Amid the huge, good-natured crowd, Lawrence caught sight of an unmistakable, bright head, and made his way towards Séraphine, whose hair flamed in the sun.

'Mademoiselle Bignon!'

'Monsieur Harper! Or, rather, I should call you Citoyen Harper!' She laughed merrily. Her face was alight with joy.

'I wish you would call me Lawrence,' he said.

'Very well. Lawrence – and Séraphine, then – yes? As this is a new beginning.'

'Is it?'

'Yes. A wonderful one. I walked all the way from Ménilmontant to see this.' She waved a hand towards the Hôtel de Ville. 'Michel is here somewhere, with his battalion. I'm so happy. This is the best thing that could have happened!' She couldn't stop smiling.

'My employers were terribly worried, this morning. They're nervous of what it means.'

'They are bourgeois. It's understandable. Governments have been on their side forever, against working people. Maybe they don't know what to expect, but it will be fair. This is the first time I've been happy in months, after Papa and everything. My brother is coming home, did you know? And Paulette is getting stronger every day.'

'I'm so pleased. And your brother – it must be such a relief.'

'Yes. For months, I had dreams that he was dead. And now . . .' She looked at Lawrence and impulsively seized his hand. 'Oh, I'm stupid. I'm so sorry. I know you were a good friend of Yves Michaud. It's horrible. I miss him too. Such a waste. There has been too much death. Too much . . . all of it.' She smiled and released his hand. 'But something good is coming out of the whole mess, at last.'

49

The last time he hit her, Raymond had been utterly contrite, as sweet as Fanny had ever known him. He got down on his knees and cried, begging her forgiveness. When she was with him, she believed his protestations that he would change. Then she went to work and saw the shock on Madame Lamy's face, the pity in her eyes. It was so humiliating, having to lie, knowing that she was not believed.

Raymond's battalion, the 101st, was one of those sent to fight at Buzenval. She had told herself this: that he might die in battle. Perhaps God would punish him for what he did to her. The thought made her weep with horror, but there was something . . . almost something exciting about it. Imagining his death meant imagining herself without him. Then he came back.

He wouldn't talk about what he had seen, but he was very quiet. He went with the remains of the battalion when it marched on the Hôtel de Ville. Fanny was at work and heard nothing about it until she got home. Her neighbour came to tell her that the 101st was involved, that there had been a gun battle and people had been killed. Fanny nodded and was very calm. She didn't want him to die, not really.

She walked through a thin, penetrating rain to the Hôtel de Ville, to find the square in front of it awash with yellow mud, scattered with debris. A few rag pickers scavenged in silence. She spoke to one woman, trying to find out what had happened, where the guards had gone. Children had been killed, the rag picker said. A woman was shot in the head. Most of the bodies had been taken away; the last of them was now being loaded on to a cart. It was that of a well-dressed middle-aged man. Surely an onlooker, from the look of him; it was hard to believe that he was a Red, but he had been shot through the chest nonetheless and his shirtfront was scarlet with blood. Fanny turned around and walked home. War was one thing: soldiers went off to fight an enemy with guns; they were trying to kill each other, even if the odds were desperately unequal. But today was different: in the heart of the city, French troops had fired on unarmed Frenchmen and women. Had killed them.

To her relief, Raymond was there when she got home, red-eyed with weeping; he thought she had left him. He came to her, and she embraced him.

Since then, something had changed in their marriage. All his anger had turned elsewhere, against those who had done such a thing. As she comforted him that night, Fanny was infused with a new strength, as though some of his power and dominance had shifted into her. Raymond said that, while he was under fire, he had prayed: if he was spared, he would never hurt her again.

Fanny heard about the coup from Raymond late on Saturday night, when he came in, somewhat the worse for wear, but wildly excited and happy. It was a miracle – the revolution had finally happened; the government had fallen – and all without a drop of bloodshed. Apart from the two generals who had been shot, but, apparently, it was their own troops who had shot them; the Central Committee of the Guard weren't to blame. Now he, Raymond, would be paid again – they were sure to restart the Guard stipend, he said – and so she would be able to stop working as a maid. Excited as she was, Fanny just kissed him goodbye in the morning and promised to come to the Hôtel de Ville when her work was finished.

The sky had cleared of rainclouds and the eastern horizon was growing pale behind her. At this early hour, the streets were quiet; not even the church bells had woken. Her route took her alongside the wall that bordered Père Lachaise, past the corner where the Mussulman graveyard lay apart from the populated southern section. Recent breaches in the wall had yet to be repaired – made by people raiding the cemetery for firewood – and it was through one of these gaps that a movement caught her eye. She looked around; it was dark at the base of the wall, but the street lights were working again and, if someone had been there, she would have seen them. She walked on, but again had the feeling that something was moving just outside her field of vision. She turned around again, to assure herself that no one was following her. Nothing. She smiled at her silliness – she wasn't a girl who was prone to fancies.

Then, through the tear in the wall, darkness oozed. Fanny was rooted to the spot. The creature was the darkest thing, black as a hole, and it moved like liquid, without sound. It flowed down the wall and along its base, towards her, before darting across the road and into the deeper shadows of an alley. She had an impression of large size and tremendous, coiled power, of eyes that glowed a ghastly white as they turned towards her. Then, just as quickly, it was gone. At least, she couldn't see it anymore, although she couldn't have said exactly where it went, or even if it had been there at all.

She was frozen with terror. Her heart hammered fiercely, and her breaths came short and shallow. She turned and hurried down the road, her footsteps loud on the cobbles. She did not slow down until she had left the cemetery far behind, but the morning was clouded by unease, as though the thing, the apparition – what else could she call it? – was an evil portent.

At work, she tried to forget about it, but all day she was subdued. She couldn't really talk to anyone in the house; Madame Lamy claimed that her nerves were shredded by the political news, and Sabine was full of dire warnings. Mademoiselle Lamy dashed off after breakfast, looking daggers. Madame Lamy even wept a little at breakfast, and then sighed gustily as Fanny cleared the table.

'I don't know. I really don't. What is to become of us all?'

Fanny understood this was not a question she was expected to answer; nonetheless, she ventured a response.

'Nothing bad will come of it, madame. It will be a good thing.'

'Will it? Is that what your husband says?'

'Yes, but many people are saying it. I say it. It is a government of the people, for the people.'

Madame Lamy looked doubtful. 'I suppose we'll have to put up with it, whatever it is. Thank you, Fanny. I know you're a good girl, so it gives me some comfort to hear you say that. But what will happen now, with the wedding and everything, I don't know.'

'People will still marry, madame!'

'But what if they shut down the churches?'

'They won't shut down the churches!' Fanny laughed, although she was less certain on this point. 'Can you imagine the French letting anyone do that?' She smiled at her. 'I'm sure, when we know more, there will be no cause for worry.'

She put the coffee pot on the tray and paused. She had an almost overpowering urge to mention the thing she thought she had seen that morning, which had cast a shadow over this wonderful day. She wanted someone cheerful and sensible like Madame Lamy to laugh it off with her, to agree that shadows before dawn played frightful tricks. But madame was not cheerful today. She looked at the clock and clicked her tongue.

'I must fly, or we will be late for Mass.'

Fanny picked up the tray and went downstairs. She had not prayed much over the last few weeks. Raymond did not attend Mass, and even she had stopped her regular Sunday attendance, caught up in the heady atmosphere of the clubs, where churches were simply places to gather and talk of change. But her first thought, when the shadow flowed towards her, had been a prayer for her protection. She'd trembled like an aspen. She'd opened her mouth to scream, but nothing came out. The thing she'd seen was not of this world, so nothing in this world would have helped her.

50

It took days and much wasted paper, but Anne at last wrote her letter to Victor. She wrote that she wanted to stay on as housekeeper. She was honoured by his kindness in making her a proposal, but she did not wish to be married. She was sorry. She was not made for marriage. That seemed the most honest way of putting it. She thought about why she was so certain, especially in the light of Fanny's teasing about Hippolyte Mazade. She forced herself to think, what if someone else had proposed to her – someone like Hippolyte? It would be different, of course – she had liked Hippolyte to an unusual degree – but, in the end, it would be the same: enforced proximity, enforced intimacy, presumably motherhood . . . She balanced the idea in her mind. She could not imagine it. If she were married, she would not belong to herself.

When the letter was finished, she went to the menagerie to deliver it. She haunted the zoo for some time before she spotted Victor leaving the director's office. He smiled when he saw her.

'Good morning, Anne. How are you?'

'Well, thank you.' She looked down. As soon as she took the envelope out of her pocket, he would know. 'And you?'

'Yes. We've found a jaguar. It should arrive in the next few weeks. That will be something to celebrate, won't it?'

She nodded. Perhaps he had forgotten all about the proposal. It had been weeks ago.

'Were you looking for me?'

She took the envelope and held it out. He took it, his head dropped and he sighed. So, he had not forgotten.

'Is that your answer?'

Anne had never felt so wretched on behalf of another person.

'I see.' He was trying to smile, she could tell. Now it was he who could not look at her. 'Well . . .' He nodded several times. 'I must be getting on.'

He walked away, down the path that led to the elephant enclosure, although there were no elephants there.

The Sisters at the school had told her she was too wilful, and it was true. She felt sick with fear. Victor would be angry at her ingratitude. She thought of running away, but, as before, couldn't think of anywhere to go, so she continued to go about her duties. And, despite the recent upheavals, Paris under its new, revolutionary government also continued much as before. There were municipal elections in which the rebels were returned with a handsome majority. Predictions of chaos and violence proved baseless. The Commune settled to the business of running the city with few outward ripples – the rubbish was collected as before, street lights were lit, omnibuses ran. As Anne did the shopping, the streets were, if anything, quieter than before. Some shopkeepers addressed her as 'Citoyenne', some did not. As when the war had broken out last year, she had the sense of vast, nebulous changes going on somewhere over her head, like the weather, but the pattern of her life did not change. She wondered about the vision she had glimpsed at Fanny's meeting, of a new life for people like her. So far, it did not feel any different from the old. Still, the vision did not dim.

The next day's post brought Victor's reply. She opened the envelope with shaking hands, her throat tight with fear, but it was good news. Victor informed her that she was welcome to stay on as housekeeper. He hoped the same terms as before would be acceptable. He made no reference to his proposal or her refusal. She understood his wish to sweep it under the carpet. Soon, the whole incident in the dining room came to seem like a dream.

Anne was kept busy overseeing the packing up of Monsieur Papin's furniture and belongings. The house grew empty and dull. The colours had gone. Noises echoed off the bare walls. Patches on the walls were the ghosts of mirrors and paintings. Even the smell changed. A number of things remained, including the furniture in Anne's room, and new furniture arrived, but it wasn't as nice.

On the day Monsieur Papin was due to leave, Anne awoke with a desolate feeling. It was the last time she would take Monsieur Papin his hot water, the last day she would serve him breakfast. In the kitchen, she watched Lucie for clues as to how she should behave. She didn't know what was normal for a housekeeper to feel when her employer left for good. Was it appropriate for her to be sad, or should she appear unmoved? Monsieur Papin ate his breakfast while reading *Le Figaro*, as usual, but, as she brought in a fresh pot of coffee, he folded the paper and set it by the side of his plate.

'Well, Anne –' he dabbed his mouth with his napkin – 'many changes, eh? I must say, I'm looking forward to my retirement. I feel my years.'

Anne stood with her hands folded in front of her.

'I hope you will continue to be happy here. Monsieur Calmette is a good man.'

Anne bobbed her head. 'I know.'

'But if, for any reason, you find that you want a change, or if ever you need help, then you can always count on my friendship. I hope you will remember that.'

Anne nodded again. She felt a heat at the back of her eyes, and recognized that she was sad. She had never thought of him as a friend, because she worked for him – and yet, that was how she felt. He was no longer her employer, he was someone she would miss.

'Monsieur, I'm grateful for all your kindness.' She wanted to say something more personal, but couldn't think what.

He smiled. 'Well. I have to see Director Lapeyre, then the last of my trunks will be collected this afternoon. So, we had better say goodbye now. I have something for you.' He took an envelope from his breast pocket and handed it to her – one of his thick, creamy envelopes.

She curtsied, but didn't think she should open it yet. 'Thank you, monsieur.'

There was an awkward silence. Was that it?

'I wish you the best of luck, Anne.'

'Thank you. Goodbye, monsieur.' She curtsied again.

There was no reason for her to wait around, so she returned to the kitchen. She went out to run her errands, and, when she came back, he had gone.

51

Ellis waited in the café where they had agreed to meet, unable to swallow for the tightness in his throat. Then Lawrence walked in and, as soon as Ellis saw his face, he knew it was going to be all right. Lawrence sat down and brushed his hand against Ellis's thigh under the table. They smiled at each other and couldn't stop, and, shortly after, got up and left.

In Ellis's room, they did not undress when the door was locked, but embraced in the middle of the room, too close even to kiss, rocking a little, keeping their balance in an awkward shuffling dance, and all the things he had marshalled to say – the arguments on behalf of, well, on behalf of himself – seemed unnecessary. All except one. He pushed Lawrence far enough away that he could look in his eyes.

'I know I'm not Yves—' he said.

Lawrence made a noise that was between a laugh and a snort of exasperation. 'I don't want you to be Yves! I never wanted you to be Yves.'

'But—'

'I'm sad about him, of course. But I missed *you*.'

'Really?'

'I thought, when I didn't hear from you, that maybe you'd met someone else.'

Ellis shook his head. 'God, no. I just wasn't well. I got into a state. What with the hospital, the exhaustion – I had terrible hives. I didn't want you to see me like that. It's disgusting.'

'You make me sound like some shrinking maiden. You can trust me more than that.'

Ellis pulled up his shirt, exposing fading red marks on his stomach. 'Look. They're almost gone, but it was ten times worse, all over me.'

Lawrence pulled the shirt up further. 'Ellis, I wouldn't have minded.' He bent and pressed his lips to the red marks. 'Does it hurt?'

'Not now. But sometimes I get into such a mess I can't bear it. I can't stand myself. So how could anyone else stand me?'

'It's not your fault.'

'It was partly my fault. It wasn't just the hives – I was drinking again. I disappoint myself.'

'You don't disappoint me.'

They kissed for a while, then began to undress. Lawrence helped take his shirt off altogether. He stroked the sides of his ribs, his arms. And he looked at him in that unnerving, assessing way he had, softly tracing the red marks on his skin. He came to the pink scar on his arm.

'How did you get this?'

'Oh, God . . . Not my finest moment. In fact, it was during the fight that lawyer mentioned. I *think* the woman attacked me with a broken bottle. I don't remember.'

'Do you know what it looks like?'

'No, what?'

'The letter *L.*' Lawrence bent his head and kissed the scar.

It seemed too good to be true, that he was being exonerated like this. Lawrence said, 'Shall I tell you something about Yves?'

Ellis felt his heart sink. 'All right.'

'Last summer, I wanted to love him. I thought he wanted it too, but he wouldn't let himself. Whenever I got too close, he would sort of – recede. I can't help thinking that's why he joined up. He was running away from me.'

'It wasn't your fault.'

'No, I know. I *know* that. But, maybe if I hadn't . . . he'd still be alive.'

'You can't think that. It would have happened another way. It wasn't to do with you. I never felt I knew him that well. He was always so calm and equable on the surface. I suppose I assumed he was calm all the way through. But no one is, are they?'

'No. The reason I'm saying this is because . . . you shouldn't think he was better than you. In some ways, he was a coward. And you're not a coward.'

'Me?' Ellis laughed. 'I'm the biggest coward going. I'm scared all the time.'

'But you don't run away.' Lawrence stepped closer and touched his face. 'That's not why I love you, because you don't love someone for a reason. I just can't help it.'

Ellis experienced such a flowering of joy, he felt light-headed. It was worth being alive for all these years, after all.

'I can't help it either.'

Then they were kissing, and, at the same time, Ellis was laughing. He wanted to yell his happiness out of the window. Tell the whole city. Instead, they stumbled to the bed. When they were naked, Lawrence knelt over him and sucked him until he could hardly bear it. He released him only to whisper in his ear, 'I want you to fuck me.'

Ellis ignited with a mix of excitement and panic. This was the threshold he had always resisted crossing. The illegal thing, the undeniable – the thing that was punishable by vague but terrible fates. It was . . .

Lawrence saw his hesitation. 'Would you rather—?'

'No, I don't . . . I mean, I've never done that . . . Scared again, you see.' He tried to laugh. 'I've always been, er, law abiding, in that respect.'

'Really?' Lawrence raised an eyebrow. 'Well, it's not against the law here. Unless you don't want to—'

'No. I do. I do want to.'

But he closed his eyes as Lawrence spat on his hand and manoeuvred himself until he could insert the tip of Ellis's cock into his ass. Ellis gasped and opened his eyes again. The intense yet refined pressure was extraordinary, but not as extraordinary as the expression on Lawrence's face: eyes wide, mouth rounded, his eyes alight and locked on a distant point, as if he had been granted some indescribable vision.

At the beginning of April, things were calm. The streets were quiet and orderly. There was hardly any crime. Theatres reopened and the sun shone. Ellis, whose pose it was to hold himself aloof from political discussion, had to admit that the Commune seemed to be no bad thing. They heard the odd disturbing rumour that so-and-so had been spirited away in the night, although they always reappeared shortly afterwards. They saw the posters that blossomed on walls overnight, listing the names of citizens 'appointed to receive denunciations of those suspected of being in complicity with the government at Versailles.'

He was too intoxicated by this new-found happiness to pay much attention. He suggested that Lawrence ask for some time off, and they spent three whole, idle days together. If he'd had qualms that prolonged proximity would dim their passion, he was happily surprised. They walked in the spring sunshine and drank in local bars, but most of their time was spent in his room, trying to make sure his neighbours did not hear anything untoward.

At Easter, Ellis took Lawrence to lunch with his uncle. On the omnibus on the way there, he was amused to see that Lawrence was nervous.

'You'll be a relief after a peasant like Alfred Quinet – you've seen his table manners. Oh, and Gustave – he was very suspicious of him, with reason, I've always thought. You're a Canadian, and a Presbyterian. He'll love you.'

Lawrence smiled enigmatically. Almost as charming as his apprehension was the way he smoothly resumed the cool, judgemental manner he had worn when they first met. By the time they walked into the residence together, the disguise was complete.

Every day, now, Ephraim Quine took a carriage to Versailles to meet with members of the official government. Twenty miles there and back – it was wearing him out. His face looked greyer and more tired than at any point during the siege. Ellis shook his hand and clasped his arm briefly, and introduced his friend as a Canadian photographer. There were a handful of other guests, but no one Ellis knew, except Warburton. As he had expected, his uncle took favourably to Lawrence. He asked intelligent questions about photography and spoke of sending acquaintances to the studio for portraits. He was good at setting people at ease.

After lunch, buoyed by their success and several glasses of Montrachet, Ellis took Lawrence outside to show him the old orchard and the gardens where the livestock had been kept – now empty and scruffy with neglect.

'It was so beautiful, last summer – hard to imagine, isn't it? There were masses of roses here. They tore them up to make room for the hens.'

'It's still beautiful. Like being in the country. So, where did the goats live?'

They wandered into the orchard. The trees were starting to come into leaf and blossom; a haze of colour softened the black branches.

'These are the first undamaged trees I've seen this year. How on earth did they survive?'

'I suppose it's just too far away from the poor districts. And the refugees were guarding the animals, too, of course. They patrolled with revolvers.'

Ellis looked around them. They had walked deep enough into the orchard that the house was invisible. He pressed Lawrence back against a gnarled trunk and kissed him. After a moment's hesitation, Lawrence responded, before gently pushing him away, his hands on his face.

'I had to make sure you were still you,' murmured Ellis. 'In there, you were so proper . . .'

Lawrence grinned. 'I'm still me.'

They were kissing when a low roar cut through the soft air of the orchard, shocking them apart. Sharp, yet heavy. Dreadfully familiar. They froze where they stood, looking at each other. The crash echoed off distant hills and died away. It was somewhere to the west, towards Versailles.

Lawrence said, 'Again?'

Ellis said, 'It's starting already.'

Lawrence looked into his eyes. 'What does that mean?'

'Those are government cannon. You didn't think they were going to sit quietly in Versailles forever?'

'But they say the army refuses to march on Paris.'

Ellis shrugged. The orchard had felt full of peace and the promise of renewal. The artillery began its thunder again, and didn't stop.

Editorial in *La Justice*, 10 April 1871:

The government is now in possession of proof that the agitating forces behind the revolution in Paris are foreign agents. Key among them are men who have been exiled from their native countries for revolutionary activities: Anarchists, Socialists and members of the Working Men's International, who have already been the instigators of strikes in this country. These men are abetted by the class of women who frequent the Red clubs, who spurn the sacred duties of motherhood, hearth and home: here you will find infanticides, prostitutes and other criminals, a former inhabitant of the Harem at Constantinople, and one notorious Fury who prowls the barricades in order to cut off the heads of the dead and perhaps of the living . . .

Front page of *Liberté*, 17 April 1871:

Our valiant Guard battalions were pushed back from Fort Valérien after heroic fighting, but they were only sixty against continuous heavy artillery fire and two thousand government troops under Marshal Vinoy. Those manning the guns until the last minute included two boys, one thirteen years old, the other fifteen, who had been at their posts for ten days straight. Those who could, escaped, swimming across the Seine after a bridge was destroyed, but those taken prisoner by the Versaillais were summarily executed, without trial, and without mercy . . . Government shells fell on a school in Neuilly, killing five young girls as they set off for an outing . . . The funerals of all those brave souls martyred in the defence of Paris will take place tomorrow, at the Hôtel de Ville.

From the Versaillais paper *Le Soir*, 25 April 1871:

The savage residents of Belleville have taken over your homes, broken into your wine cellars and lain in your beds! Once the Commune has fallen, and honest people have reclaimed their property, it will be necessary to have it fumigated!

52

When Victor Calmette first moved into the veterinarian's house, Anne considered shoving the armchair up against her bedroom door at night. She felt guilty even thinking it. He had never done anything untoward, but her past haunted her. She told herself it was foolish – told herself, even, that taking such a precaution, by acknowledging it, might make the thing she feared more likely to happen.

She served his meals in the dining room, just as she had with Monsieur Papin. The old veterinarian's silences had been restful, but a silence with Victor seethed with unspoken things. He tried to break it with remarks about her favourite animals, to which she responded politely. But, as the days passed without incident, her unease lessened. They fell into the habit of conversation when she was in the room – always instigated by him, venturing remarks, asking her opinion. He encouraged Anne to visit the cats, saying Marguerite had missed her. He urged her to resume the practice of calling him Victor instead of Monsieur Calmette. So far, she had managed not to call him anything at all. A week passed, then another. She was clearing the remains of the dinner – he had been unusually silent – when he interrupted her.

'Anne, wait a minute. Please – put that down.'

She did as she was bid.

He attempted a laugh. 'Won't you sit down – just for a minute?'

She perched on the edge of a chair, at the other end of the table.

He didn't usually drink to excess, but the second bottle of wine was nearly empty. She stared at the carmine rings he had made on the tablecloth.

'I was thinking, the other day, it must be a year ago – more or less – that we first met, that day at the bear pit. You remember?'

'Yes.'

'I told you about when Marguerite was a cub, and I nursed her back to health. And then we became friends, did we not? On your days off, you would come to the zoo and find me, and we would talk.'

It wasn't quite like that, she thought. I came to see Marguerite, and you were there. But she nodded.

'Then you came and worked here, for Monsieur Papin, and ... I suppose what I'm trying to say is that I miss our friendship. Those talks. And now that we are both here – in the same house, seeing each other every day – I hope we can be friends again. I want you to forget about ... you know, any awkwardness in the past. Just because you're the housekeeper, it needn't mean that we can't ... I suppose what I'm trying to say is, sometimes I feel, almost, that you are afraid of me, and that distresses me.'

He was twisting the stem of the wine glass in his fingers. He looked quite wretched. She waited, but he appeared to have finished.

'I'm not afraid of you. Of course. We can be friends.'

'Good. You do like me, don't you, Anne?'

'Yes. I like you.'

He let out a deep sigh. 'That makes me very happy.'

She felt his eyes on her face. She tried to look up and meet his eyes, and smile. Managed it. It wasn't so bad.

That night, she started awake at a noise. She knew what was happening: someone was turning the handle of her door. Of course. Deep down, she had always known this was coming. In a way, there was even some relief that it had arrived, and she wouldn't have to go on any longer with the fear hovering in the back of her mind, the nagging memory of when she was fifteen.

She listened to the door opening, swishing its bottom edge over the carpet. There was a pause, before he came in and closed the door. Then he seemed to just stand for an age, breathing in the darkness.

Anne kept her eyes shut and her breathing regular, although her heart was slamming against her ribs like a mad thing. Perhaps he would come to his senses and go away. Perhaps she was dreaming; perhaps— A floorboard creaked. He was coming towards the bed. If she screamed, would Lucie run from the other end of the house? She doubted she would hear. Closer, until he was right by the bed, and she could smell the wine on his breath. She was catapulted back to the house where she had lived with her mother, the room, the thick smell of alcohol . . . and her allowing it to happen, because Maman had told her that she must.

'Anne?' It was a soft whisper.

Before she knew what she was doing, she had reared up and lashed out with her arm. The arm encountered something soft but resisting. He grunted.

'Anne . . . Anne! Shh. It's only me. It's all right—' He leant forward, his hands pinning down the blankets, and she felt his breath on her face.

Terrified, she wrenched herself free with a cry and slithered out of the bed, along the wall towards the window. She knew where things were in the dark and nipped behind the armchair. He was up again. He was between her and the door.

'Anne, please don't be frightened—'

'Go away!' she hissed, through clenched teeth.

She couldn't see his face, could only perceive him as a pale, night-gowned shape, as she must be to him. She, on one side of the armchair; he, on the other. She heard her own breaths coming as high whimpers and was angry to sound so weak. She was not weak.

'Anne, we're the same, you and me. We're alike; don't you see – I could make you so happy.'

She knew, with a sparkle of fear, that he was very drunk – even more than he had been at dinner. He had gone on drinking to give himself courage to do this. Why would that be a surprise to her?

'Just go! Please.'

'I want you so much. Dear Anne . . . If only you'll let me—'

He came towards her and cursed as he stumbled against the chair. As he fell, he grabbed hold of her nightgown. She reached out in desperation and her hand met something – the handle of the clock on the mantelpiece – heavy, cold, topped with the stallion with its spiky mane – which she swung in his direction. It collided, with a horrible, dull sound.

Victor gave a grunt, let go of her arm and collapsed with a thud. Anne backed away. He seemed to be sitting half on the chair, half on the floor. He groaned. She held the clock in front of her, like a shield.

'I'm sorry! I'm sorry. I didn't mean . . . Monsieur Calmette?'

There was no answer. What did she expect him to say?

'Monsieur – are you all right? Victor?'

The breathing went on. Rough. Thick, somehow. What was she waiting for? For it to stop? That was not what she wanted. With trembling hands, she found and lit the candle that stood by her bed. By its light, she peered at his face. His eyes fluttered open, and he seemed to regard her without judgement. A thin line of blood welled from his cheek and trickled down his face and neck. A rivulet ran under the collar of his nightshirt and made a stain on his shoulder. There wasn't so much blood, but it kept trickling. The breaths kept coming, hoarse but regular. What had she done?

53

Anne walked the streets, waiting for sunrise. If she kept walking, they wouldn't know where to find her. In her pocket was the envelope Monsieur Papin had given her. It contained more money than she had ever seen. And she had made herself invisible. She was not helpless. This restless wandering made her think of Nero, slinking through darkened streets. The street lamps might have come on again, but she took heart from his vanishing. If a creature like that – so strange and out of place – could disappear so completely, then so, surely, could she.

When the shops began to open, she stationed herself in a shadowy doorway from where she could see the bakery in the Rue des Ciseaux. She kept her head down, face shaded by her hat, and watched. On her way in, Fanny passed quite close to her, but noticed nothing. Anne waited until she came out again, then fell into step behind her. She had only a few paces to go; she had to get on with it. But how? Before she had decided, Fanny sensed a following presence and whirled around. When she saw Anne, words stuck in her throat.

For once, Anne *had* to keep her eyes on Fanny's and let herself be penetrated. She had to communicate her desperation, her need. And her friend, bless her, didn't say a word. She gaped for a moment, then lifted her chin and smiled.

The household had not yet risen. Fanny made her wait in the back corridor while she took the bread to the kitchen. After a few minutes, she returned and indicated that Anne should follow her up the stairs. She led her up to the fourth floor and hurried her into an unused bedroom. She closed the door behind them and put her finger to her lips.

'We'll have to be quiet. Monsieur Harper's room is just over the landing. He's the lodger. But no one ever comes in here, apart from me, so you'll be safe.'

Anne sat on the bed, suddenly exhausted beyond measure. Fanny sat beside her and picked up her hand.

'Anne, what's happened? Why are you dressed like that?'

Anne looked down at the entwined hands. It felt odd to be touched, but she had no energy to protest.

'I . . .' Her thoughts were scrambled, and she couldn't remember what Fanny knew and didn't know. So much had happened in the last few weeks. 'I thought it was going to be all right,' she began, and managed to tell Fanny the whole story, up to Monsieur Calmette stealing into her room during the night. Only a few hours ago, but it seemed like a lifetime.

Fanny listened with a frown. 'Oh, Anne. I'm so sorry. Did he hurt you?'

Anne shook her head. 'He grabbed me . . .' Black light shimmered at the edge of her vision.

'It's all right, Anne. You're safe here.'

'I didn't want to hurt him. I just wanted him to stop.'

She really thought she was going to pass out. It hadn't happened for so long, but she could be thrown back there in one instant of—

She heard her breaths coming in tight, constricted gasps, but she didn't pass out. She found that she could focus on Fanny's face, and Fanny's hands, which were holding hers.

'You didn't do anything wrong, Anne. It's not your fault.'

'But I hit him. With the clock.' Anne mimed swiping out at him. 'It had a horse on it. And he . . . I don't know. I don't know if he's . . . His face was bleeding. But he opened his eyes, for a moment.'

'He did? And then what?'

'Then he closed them again. He was groaning. What if I've . . . ? What if he's . . . ?'

She waited for Fanny to run for the police.

'If he was breathing, and he opened his eyes, it sounds like he's all right. Perfectly all right, probably. I wouldn't worry too much about *him*. What about you? Where are your own clothes and things? Did you leave them there?'

'I can't go back. I'll be arrested. He was *bleeding*. I have money. I'll go – somewhere.'

After shutting the door on that awful breathing, she'd gone to Victor's dressing room and pulled an old suit she had never seen from the back of his wardrobe, thinking that, if it was there, it wouldn't be missed. The shirt and jacket fitted well enough, although the trousers were a little loose at the waist. She had to secure them with a belt, but, at first glance, no one would notice. With her hair stuffed under an old hat, there was nothing about her to arouse immediate suspicion.

'I don't want to make things difficult for you. I just need somewhere to stop for a while, until I work out what to do. I couldn't think of anyone else . . .'

Fanny pressed her hands again and smiled. 'You did the right thing, coming here. I'm going to help you. Don't worry. Now, are you hungry?'

Anne thought, then nodded.

'I have to go and do the rooms, or they'll wonder what's happened. You can stay here. If you're quiet, no one will come in. I have to serve breakfast, but after that I'll bring you something. It'll be all right.'

Suddenly, Fanny leant over and kissed Anne on the cheek. Anne was too surprised to move.

Fanny got up and went to the door, then turned and whispered, 'By the way, you make a very handsome man!'

Grinning, she slipped out.

Anne lay on the bed, trying not to make the mattress creak. Her body felt like a sack of stones, but she was too nervous to close her eyes. What if someone walked in? Who was Monsieur Harper? Was he the foreigner from the zoo, the one who had come to her rescue in the bread queue? She crept to the door, found there was no key, and went to lie down on the floor behind the bed, so that – from the doorway, at least – she would be out of sight. She took a pillow from the bed and curled herself around it, holding it tight.

When she woke again, it was to find that someone – Fanny, presumably – had laid a blanket over her. In front of her, on the floor, was a plate of bread and cheese, and a jug of milk. That she had been oblivious to the visit gave her a turn. How long had she slept? It was an overcast day; she had no way of telling the time. She hardly dared look out of the window, in case someone on the street glanced up and saw her face.

When she had eaten, she used the chamber pot and lay down again. Maybe the police weren't looking for her. She hadn't stolen anything except the suit. And she had abandoned everything of hers, other than the envelope in her pocket, which she touched every few minutes. She had left nothing that was of value to her. Except, perhaps, the book Victor had given her for Christmas – aeons ago, it seemed. She loved that book, had read and reread the chapter on Haiti, poring over the exquisite colour plates, dreaming. She had never told him that she loved it; it was too personal, too intimate; it would have made her . . . beholden. But she had been beholden anyway.

If he was all right, maybe he would be too embarrassed to report her. On the other hand, if the worst had happened, by now Lucie would have called the police. It had been his fault. Why couldn't he have left her alone? She hadn't hit him that hard – or hadn't meant to. But the thought of that heavy marble clock made her stomach hurt.

She wormed herself further out of sight, under the bed, palpated the envelope over her heart and made herself tune in to the boom of the far-off artillery. This new bombardment had been going on for days, but it was fainter and less threatening than it had been during the siege. They said it was the government cannon attacking the western forts, but they also said that French soldiers refused to march on Paris, so there was nothing much to worry about. The distant growling brought back the cold winter nights – in the first room she had ever called her own, where, for a while, she had felt safe.

54

Lawrence stood beside Ellis at the *rond-point* on the Champs Élysées. A crowd had gathered, as though they had to see it with their own eyes before they could believe such a thing was happening. It beggared belief. As they watched, a shell screamed out of the sky, landed further up the boulevard and exploded in a cloud of smoke and dirt, engulfing the arch and the square around it. There were cries of awe and dismay from the crowd. After a minute, the shape of the arch reappeared through the haze, and children raced forward, drawing murmurs of alarm and cheers of encouragement.

'What the hell are they doing? Are they crazy?'

Ellis and Lawrence had to squint to make out what was happening. The late afternoon sun lit up the dust, making it hard to see, but, before another shell could fall, the boys came running back, some staggering under the weight of heavy objects. When they reached the crowd, the children began to hawk their trophies. Most prized were fragments blasted from the bas reliefs of the arch itself; anything recognizably human – an amputated marble hand, a stone ear – drew keen bidding.

Since beginning this second siege, the government guns had razed the villages of Courbevoie and Neuilly, to the west. Then they pounded the western suburbs, and now they were shelling the Arc de Triomphe, L'Etoile, the Champs Élysées. Their reach was creeping ever nearer the heart of Paris, and there seemed nothing the combined forces of the Commune could do about it. According to Ellis's uncle, it could only be a matter of time before the Commune would have to come to terms. Although Paris was not completely cut off, the Prussian army was still camped a few miles to the east, waiting and watching. The onslaught had made refugees of the wealthy inhabitants of Auteuil and Passy, who were outraged at being attacked by the government they supported. The refugees included Ephraim Quine, who had abandoned his official residence in favour of an apartment above the consulate.

Ellis had just been to see his uncle. He told Lawrence he had agreed to go back to work in the American hospital. He said this flatly, without looking at him.

'When do you start?' Lawrence asked, in a lull between explosions. He wished he could talk him out of it, but knew he would not; however reluctant Ellis was to return to hospital work, his failure to do so would probably be worse.

'As soon as possible. They're overwhelmed.'

Another high-pitched whine grew louder, silencing them, followed by a crash they felt through the soles of their boots. This time, the arch immediately vanished and the cloud of dust boiled down the avenue towards them, growing with frantic speed. The onlookers scattered with nervous cries, covering their heads. The explosion was half a mile away, but it was impossible not to flinch. Lawrence had reached for Ellis's arm and grasped his sleeve as they were jostled by the crowd. They ran. Hot dust surrounded them, making them cough. Then the outline of the arch reappeared through the murk. Fine particles hung in the air, settling on the heads and clothes of onlookers. The *maison particulier* which had housed the American hospital was in the next block – now, it too was engulfed in the grey haze. For the last week, it had been empty – beds and staff removed to a safer location.

'Are you all right?'

Lawrence nodded, coughing to clear the dust from his mouth. Ellis's hair had turned grey, his eyes red in a dust-whitened face. Lawrence's own eyes stung.

'Seen enough?'

Ellis nodded. They began to walk away from the destruction.

'I wish you would go and sit it out elsewhere. My uncle says the trains will stop before long, then it'll be almost impossible to leave.'

He had said this before, but Lawrence didn't take it seriously. The government's attacks were more destructive than the Prussian bombardment; the hastily reconvened hospitals were filling up again, only this time with the results of French bullets and French shell splinters. But the army wouldn't invade Paris itself. It wouldn't attack its compatriots. Sooner or later, the Commune and the government in Versailles would reach some, probably mutually unsatisfactory, compromise. He wasn't worried for himself.

'I'll be all right. Who will bother with us? Anyway, you're staying.'

'That's different. I can't decently refuse.' He poked at the ground with his cane.

'Ellis, promise me something.'

Ellis snorted. They both tensed as the sound of another shell landed behind them.

'No, listen. Promise that you'll tell me . . . if things get too difficult, like before. Don't hide it from me.'

Ellis was silent. Lawrence had gleaned a little more about his illness, how ashamed it made him.

'I can't bear it if I don't hear from you. I don't care how disgusting and hideous you are.'

Ellis laughed, as he'd intended. 'All right. I promise I'll write with all the gruesome details.'

Lawrence brushed his hand softly down Ellis's sleeve; it was as much as he dared. He would have done more, but it made Ellis jumpy.

'Good. Anyway, I have my new job.'

Lawrence had accepted a commission to take photographs at the Hôtel de Ville. Ellis worried it would put him on the side of the Communards. Lawrence shrugged this off; he would be a journalist. His sympathies might lie, more or less, with the Communards, but, as a foreigner, he kept his views to himself. Since Thiers' government had begun to bomb the city, the Commune's support was growing among the formerly hostile bourgeoisie. Even Madame Lamy was appalled by the indiscriminate ruthlessness of the government onslaught. The Communards might be anticlericals, not to mention communists (Fanny had told her she was wrong about that, in his hearing), but, in practice, she had to admit, they didn't seem too bad.

They turned up a street, heading to Ellis's lodgings as the day faded, and Lawrence began to walk quicker. He couldn't wait till they were alone. Each time they met, the time passed so quickly. He almost resented the urgency of his desire, for the time it took up. He wanted it, of course, but he wanted time, too, to talk, and there never seemed to be enough.

Ellis had told him that his mother was going to remarry and was begging him to go back to America for the wedding. When Lawrence asked him if he intended to go, Ellis shrugged and said he didn't know. Then he changed the subject and hadn't referred to it since. It was like a hole yawning in the road ahead. Lawrence was torn: as keenly as he wished the fighting to be over, a part of him hoped it would continue – long enough, at least, to prevent any plans being made until it was too late.

Now that they had found this understanding, he felt it incumbent upon him to protect their delicate equilibrium. Tonight, he knew, they wouldn't talk about work, or the hospital; they wouldn't discuss the future. They would make love, then go out to eat. They would go to bed and fuck some more. They would fall asleep in each other's arms. It was more than he'd ever dreamt of.

On his first day at the Hôtel de Ville, Lawrence waited in the entrance hall while someone went to look for the man who had engaged him. The job had been arranged with the Lamys, but Serge, suffering from arthritis, was not fit enough to undertake it. Lawrence supposed it would involve taking portraits of the Committee members, and he was excited. It was a chance to have his work widely seen, perhaps even make his mark. He sat on a bench near the door, looking at the high ceilings, the sweeping staircase with gilded banister, and the vast paintings, which made a marked contrast to the rather scruffy, black-coated figures who hurried to and fro. The atmosphere was grave; often, he heard raised voices. He waited a long time, but the man didn't come back. His excitement dimmed. After more than an hour, and several attempts to find out what was happening, a bearded, bespectacled man came towards him. He, too, seemed to have little time to waste.

'You are Citoyen Harper, the photographer? I'm Citoyen Mazade, of the Committee for the Interior. Please, accept my apologies.'

They shook hands. Citoyen Mazade was one of the Commune's busy, black-coated men. He wasn't much older than Lawrence – indeed, most of them were young men – but he looked as though he hadn't slept for a week. His black beard was unkempt and there were dark shadows under his eyes, but he radiated energy.

'I'm sorry you've been kept waiting. Things are rather busy at the moment.' He waved his hand around them. 'If you will come with me . . . You have your equipment? Good. Jean-Luc!' Mazade gestured to a lantern-jawed youth hanging around by the front door and instructed him to push the mobile darkroom.

Lawrence followed them along a vaulted corridor and around corners, until they stopped in front of a pair of elaborate doors. A uniformed guard with a rifle kept watch outside. Mazade nodded to him and he stood aside. Lawrence had registered that the mix of odours in the entrance hall – damp wool, unwashed bodies and tobacco – blended with something else as they went deeper into the building, something which seemed to thicken outside these doors.

Mazade took Lawrence by the arm and lowered his voice. 'We

appreciate your coming to us, citoyen. This is vital work – a vital service to the Commune. I appreciate that it is not easy. I must say, I feel it's an advantage that you're not French.'

Lawrence nodded, puzzled. Mazade opened the door and led Lawrence inside.

At first glance, Lawrence was unsure what he was looking at. They were in a large salon, as richly painted and gilded as the rest of the building, but the high windows were shuttered and the interior was bathed in shadow. The stench was overpowering. All the furniture seemed to be shrouded in dust sheets – then he saw that it wasn't furniture. And they weren't dust sheets. On tables, on benches and on the floor – everywhere he looked – men's bodies were covered in makeshift shrouds. It was a morgue.

He turned to Mazade, thinking he must have made some mistake, but the man had closed the doors behind them and was indicating that the youth put his equipment in a corner.

'You must set up as you see best. Perhaps using light from the window . . . You may open the shutters, over here – this side gives on to an internal court; no one will see in.'

Then he registered Lawrence's expression.

'Didn't they tell you what the work was to be?'

'No. What is this place?'

Mazade looked impatient. He sighed. 'These are the brave men who have died fighting for us, but they have yet to be claimed, or even identified. Sometimes there is no one with them who knows them. So, they bring them here.'

He lifted the shroud – a rough piece of canvas – over the nearest mound. The face was too shadowed to discern much other than a dark beard and moustache. A piece of paper was pinned to the front of the dishevelled jacket.

'Each one is marked with a number and the place where he died. That must be in the photograph, of course. We need photographs for their families, you understand, before it's too late. Are you all right, citoyen?'

Lawrence nodded, although he found it hard to breathe. He was sucking in the air through his teeth, but he could taste it – the cloying, sweet smell of the dead. 'Yes. Quite all right.'

'I'm sorry for shocking you, like this. I thought someone had explained the nature of the work.'

'It doesn't matter.'

His eyes grew accustomed to the dimness. At some point, they had run out of shrouds, for a dozen bodies lay on the floor near the window in their uniforms, filthy and bloodstained. His eyes were drawn to one face, which was slightly turned towards them from his spot on the floor, mouth and eyes open, as if he had been frozen in mid-cry.

Mazade was talking rapidly: '. . . Jean-Luc will help you with anything heavy. And Citoyen Lhermitte, here . . .'

Lawrence hadn't even noticed the fourth person in the room; he was dressed in rusty black and bending over one of the corpses. Something about his posture and his stealthy, silent movements made Lawrence shudder.

'He is the layer-out,' Mazade continued. 'He will prepare them for you. Clean them up. Make sure they're as . . . recognizable as possible.'

The man barely looked around from where he was bent over a table. With slow, caressing movements, he was cleaning a face that, even in the gloom, had a greenish tinge.

'You will do it, won't you?' A hint of desperation had crept into Mazade's voice.

Lawrence nodded. His throat worked and he worried that, if he tried to speak, he might vomit.

'Come outside for a moment.'

Mazade led him back out into the corridor. He seemed a kind man, not without pity, but Lawrence could tell he was impatient to get on with his next task.

'I'm a doctor, so it doesn't shock me, but if you're not used to it . . .
It's important that we do this – for the families, you understand? We
keep them as long as we can, in case someone comes looking for them,
but, for many, their families are in the provinces.' He shrugged. 'After
a few days, we have to bury them. Without this record, they would
never know.'

'Yes, of course. But . . . The light in there – it's too dark.'

Mazade was nodding quickly. 'Jean-Luc will fetch lamps. Just tell
him what you need. Oh, and . . .' From his pocket he took a small pot
of pungently scented balm. 'Just do this.' He moistened his finger and
dabbed it beneath his nostrils. 'You can keep that. Also, you'll find
you get used to it.'

'Right. Um, the letter didn't say how long you would want me for.'

'Well, citoyen –' Mazade let out a sharp laugh – 'as long as it takes.
We will fight until the last man is drained of blood. Make no mistake
of that.'

Left alone in the corridor, Lawrence anointed his upper lip with
the balm. It made his nose prickle and his eyes water, but at least he
didn't gag. Inside, Jean-Luc looked at him expectantly. Neither he nor
the layer-out seemed unnerved by the presence of the dead.

55

Victor frowned at the sight facing him. His cheek was still swollen around the wound, but the bruising was turning from purple to green and yellow. Worst of all, beneath the swelling, there seemed to be a bump or ridge in his cheekbone. He poked at it with a fingertip. He feared he would bear it, a painful reminder, for the rest of his life.

He had woken to find himself on the floor of Anne's room, sprawled on his back, his neck awkwardly bent up against the armchair, one arm numb beneath him. He was cold and confused and his head hurt like the devil. What had happened to get him here? Then it came back to him in a rush and he groaned aloud. He had frightened Anne, and she had responded as . . . well, as he might have predicted. He should have known what would happen, but he had thought – no, he had not thought, that was the trouble. He had drunk too much, and she had seemed, over the last few days, to be warming to him.

He groaned again as he tried to get up. His face throbbed, and his cheek exploded in pain when he touched it. He got slowly on to hands and knees, crawled a short way, then sat down. He thought he was going to vomit. Eventually, he managed to stand up. From the silence around him, he was sure that Anne was gone. She would not come back – of that he was certain. No second chances from her. What an idiot he had been: insensitive, clumsy, stupid. He staggered back to his own room, where he washed off the blood as best he could.

He had a few hours to come up with a story. What reason could he give to Lucie the cook when she found out – as she shortly would? That he had surprised Anne in an act of theft? That she had gone mad and attacked him in a fit of hysteria? Perhaps that was more likely, given her past, but could he make out that it had happened anywhere but in her bedroom? He racked his brains as the sky lightened, and then there was a knock at his door. Lucie, of course, simmering with annoyance at the disappearance of her underling. Then she saw Victor's face, and screamed.

Haltingly, Victor told her that he had heard noises in the night, and had gone to investigate, only to find Anne having some sort of hysterical fit. When he tried to prevent her from harming herself, she had attacked him and run off.

Lucie gasped and crossed herself, looking aghast. 'She's always been so quiet and modest.'

'Yes. But she has a history, you know.'

Only last night, at dinner, Anne had smiled at him, laughed with him – so what was he supposed to think? They were both lonely and they had so much in common.

Victor whimpered a little and touched his head. Lucie wasn't stupid; what if she put two and two together?

Lucie tutted. 'But one never knows. Once a madwoman . . . We must report it to the police, monsieur. She might hurt more people! Maybe she already has! And I'll send for a doctor, of course, to look at that. Oh dear, to think . . .' She crossed herself again.

Victor agreed to see the doctor, but declared that he didn't believe she was a danger to others, that she hadn't meant to hurt him. There was no need to involve the police. Let Lucie make of that what she would.

When Lucie had gone back to the kitchen, Victor got out of bed and went back to Anne's room. It was only the second time he had been there. The bed was unmade, the bedclothes swept aside and rumpled on the floor. Her clothes were hanging in the wardrobe and draped on the commode. She didn't appear to have taken anything with her. There on the shelf was the book on the Antilles. Perhaps she had never cared for it. There was a stain on the carpet: his blood. A wave of nausea came over him and made him sit down on the bed. He wondered about the weapon Anne had used. A water jug? A candlestick? He looked around, and his gaze came to rest on the Second Empire mantel clock – a hideous lump of a thing, topped with a rearing horse. There were rusty stains on the horse's spiky mane. He went to the mantelpiece, picked it up and his skin crawled with fear. It weighed a ton. Lucie was right: Anne might have killed him.

Victor took to his bed for the rest of the week, sent word to the zoo that he had a fever, and listened to the distant explosions to the west. He worried about Marguerite and the others, but Robitaille sent regular updates, and Robitaille's wife baked him a cake.

Lucie was talked out of going to the police, but she revelled in her new-found power. She became his conduit to the outside world. She reported that she had found a replacement – a young, meek girl, who wouldn't give them any trouble. As he had feared, once she saw that the attack had taken place in Anne's bedroom, she drew her own conclusions. A look of sly satisfaction stole across her face and had been there ever since.

56

Michel's battalion had been detailed to defend one of the Commune's western forts against the government forces, but, before he left, he asked Lawrence to look out for Séraphine in his absence. Lawrence was flattered, and then concerned. Did Michel guess he had nothing to fear from Lawrence as a romantic rival? Did that mean he *knew*? Or did he simply trust them both? There was also the laughable idea that Séraphine could not look after herself, but he gave him his word. Michel laughed and embraced Lawrence, kissing him on both cheeks without a trace of self-consciousness.

'There's a good fellow! I know I'll be all right, but it puts my mind at rest.'

Séraphine rolled her eyes, but she, too, seemed pleased. Lawrence had the warm feeling of being needed. They were his best friends, he told them impulsively, meaning it, and they raised a toast to each other, and to Michel's luck.

None of them spoke of the thing that hung like a dark cloud over the Bignon household. Benoît, Séraphine's brother, had been held prisoner by the Prussians for months. Under the terms of the armistice, he was released, but, as a serving soldier, was sent to fight on the government side. Séraphine did not know exactly where he was posted, and it was possible (although very unlikely, they all assured each other) that Benoît and Michel would come into conflict.

Since Lawrence began work at the Hôtel de Ville, he had told no one except Ellis what he was doing. Now that Michel was 'out there', there was a dread at the back of his mind, of coming across his friend's face among the dead. Or the face of anyone he recognized. That apart, the work was not as distressing as he had anticipated. Like the others who worked in the morgue, he grew blasé, and, once he had seen each man's face, and knew it was a stranger, he could get on with the business of arranging and lighting the bodies as if they were elements of a still life.

It was an odd and intimate thing they did. Lawrence came to respect Citoyen Lhermitte, the layer-out who that first day had struck him as ghoulish. He was swift and methodical as he wiped dried blood and dirt from the men's faces and sponged and tidied their clothing, re-pinning their identifying paper so that it was straight. He talked to each one in a sing-song voice as he did so.

Lhermitte and Jean-Luc would carry the prepared body over to the window, where a table waited under the eye of the camera and the light fell kindly. Lawrence had thought they would need more help, but almost every man was scrawny, his flesh winnowed by hardship. The state of their clothing was pitiful: some had only half a uniform; some had no shoes. Some were painfully young. Every day, a few of the bodies had to be removed; in the dead of night, a cart came to collect those that had been there the longest. He didn't know where they were taken. Each morning, there were fresh corpses to record. In most cases, this photograph would be the only likeness these men ever had.

Séraphine threw herself behind the cause of the Commune with intense fervour, and she invited Lawrence (it was his duty to Michel, she told him) to accompany her to her local political club. It was a fine evening when he walked to Ménilmontant to meet her, and they sat in the smoky church nave and listened to speeches. The clubs had become popular during the siege, and after the surrender they mushroomed, springing up in every district. For Lawrence, this was his first such meeting. Séraphine was knowledgeable and opinionated about the workings of the Commune; she knew the names and reputations of those involved. Since starting at the Hôtel de Ville, Lawrence had gathered that there was a serious rift in the ruling Committee. The moderates and the Jacobins were at loggerheads. He asked her what she thought of Citoyen Mazade, still the only member of the Commune Lawrence had spoken to.

'Mazade? He's the doctor, isn't he? The Creole. He's one of Varlin's group, a moderate. He's a good man.'

'He didn't seem very moderate,' Lawrence said, and told her about the 'last man drained of blood'.

'But a Jacobin would have said, "We will fight until Paris is razed to the ground and the last child is drained of blood!"'

Lawrence knew he was being teased. 'And which are you, mademoiselle? I mean – I beg your pardon – citoyenne?'

'I wanted to go with Michel's battalion,' she said, more seriously, 'but I was afraid to leave Maman and Paulette on their own.'

'Really? What would you do? Would you fire a rifle?'

Everyone knew that there were women joining the fighting – women like Citoyenne Michel, the Red Virgin, who fired a rifle alongside the men. Other women served as *cantinières*, handing out food and drink to the fighters in the field, or worked as medical aides and nurses.

'What? You don't think I would shoot a government rat?'

Séraphine fixed Lawrence with such a fierce glare that he laughed. 'No, I believe you would.'

Tonight's audience was a noisy crowd: mostly artisans, a smattering of men who looked like journalists or students, and a good many women. The font had been drained and filled with tobacco, to which everyone helped themselves, and a statue of the Virgin had a Guard's *képi* on her head. Lawrence was interested in what was said, but did not find the speakers impressive. The style tended towards the florid, but was short on facts. It is hard to disagree that freedom is good and injustice bad. Séraphine leant over and whispered that the best speakers didn't come to the clubs anymore – like Citoyen Mazade, they were members of the Commune and too busy running things. But the audience was appreciative, and when one of the speakers trumpeted the mystical importance of Paris as 'the sun of the civilized world' – which alone would ensure their triumph over the Versaillais – they went crazy, shouting and stamping their approval.

Out of all the bluff and bluster aired that evening, one thing lodged in his mind. The Commune had decreed that all women living with a man killed or wounded defending the Commune would be paid a pension, whether married or not. There was an excited stir in the audience at this announcement, and prolonged applause. Lawrence joined in with enthusiasm. When he glanced at Séraphine, her eyes shone with tears.

The atmosphere began to affect him. These were ordinary people, used to being ignored or denigrated. The lives they led were hard and narrow, but tonight their faces glowed with joy. Their eyes were lifted up, not to heaven, but to a better version of their lives on earth. It made him know in his gut what he had previously appreciated in the abstract: the possibility that the project of social reform could affect him on a visceral level. If the Commune was breaking the grip that Church and tradition held over relations between men and women, what else might be broken? There were philosophers Lawrence had heard of, like Fourier, who attacked marriage and preached true equality and freedom of love – between men and woman, but also women and women, men and men. He and Ellis had talked about it, but he did not dare speak of such things to Séraphine and Michel. No one at the club went that far. A woman stood up and denounced the power of the priests, to great applause, but no one suggested that women should take an equal part in governing, or even be able to vote for those who did.

When the meeting broke up, Lawrence walked Séraphine home. After the heightened excitement of the meeting, she was quiet.

'Thank you for inviting me, citoyenne. It was very interesting.'

'You don't have to pretend.'

'I'm not pretending.'

'Perhaps we'll make a revolutionary of you yet.' Séraphine smiled, then turned away, and he noticed she was crying.

'Séraphine, oh . . .' He was at a loss. 'What is it? You haven't heard—?'

She shook her head angrily. 'No, no. Well, I know nothing. But I can't help thinking, what if it's this minute, or this one, that—?'

'I know.' He didn't know. It was not as though Ellis was being shot at.

Séraphine wiped her eyes on her sleeve. 'I want to join him, Lawrence. It's the least I can do.'

'Do you think Michel would want you to?'

She looked down. 'It angers me that he risks his life while I do nothing. Sometimes I think I care more about this struggle than he does. He's angry about Paris and the surrender, but I think of the changes that this government could make – that Thiers and his like will never make. And then, if I was out there, we would be risking everything together. Wouldn't that be a fine thing?'

Later that night, Lawrence sat at the table in his room, trying to write down his thoughts about the evening. A thud outside his door made him jump. Surely it was too late for the family to be wandering about, and he always heard the stairs creak when they came past. He got up and peered out on to the landing. He saw nothing, but he heard something else – it sounded like a moan, and it came from the room opposite.

He went back and picked up the poker, just in case. He crept on to the landing, flattened himself against the wall and put his hand on the door handle of the spare room. He flung open the door and stood back, poker raised. Nothing happened. The room was dark apart from the glow from the uncurtained window, but he thought he smelt something – a snuffed candle?

'Hello?'

As his eyes adjusted, he saw that the room was empty. Relieved, he nonetheless fetched his lamp, to assure himself that it had been his imagination, or the wind, but, when he walked in again, he nearly dropped it. Standing behind the bed was a figure, holding up both hands in supplication.

'Please, please, don't call them.' The voice was hoarse with fear.

Despite his shock, Lawrence recognized her – it was the girl from the zoo, from the bread queue, who, for some reason, was wearing a man's shirt and trousers. She looked terrified.

'You won't remember, but we met outside the bakery one night. You told me about the animals being sold for meat . . .'

Lawrence stared, at a loss to see a connection between butchered animals and the girl's presence in the guest room. He took a step back. 'Yes, I remember. No one told me that someone was staying the night, mademoiselle. I'm sorry to have disturbed you.'

'They don't know. Please, you mustn't tell them.'

'You mean . . . ? What do you mean?'

'I . . .' She closed her eyes. 'Someone attacked me – I needed somewhere to hide.'

'But – here? How did you get in? Ah – you know Fanny?'

The girl's eyes were huge in the lamplight. The way she flinched told him he was right.

'It wasn't her fault. I can't get her into trouble. Please.'

She backed away from him until the wall stopped her, then she slid down into a crouch. She looked pathetic, and yet there was something impressive about her. She might plead with him, but she wasn't giving anything away.

'Will you tell me what happened? Perhaps I can help. Wait a minute . . . You're bleeding.'

He gestured to her face with the lamp, making the shadows leap. She touched her forehead and looked at her fingers. A trickle of blood had run out of her hair.

'Oh. I hit my head. On . . .' She indicated a rumpled blanket on the floor under the bed. 'I must have started up.'

'You're sleeping on the floor?'

'So no one can see me.'

'Let me get you a cloth for that, and . . . do you want something to eat, or drink?'

He cast around; there was no sign of food, although a jug stood on the floor next to the bed.

'Fanny brought me things, but . . .' She looked up briefly and nodded.

He noticed how her eyes slid away if he looked at her. He remembered she had been the same in the queue, when the guardsman had been so rude. Remote, as if she wasn't quite of this world.

When he came back with a tray, she was sitting exactly as he had left her. He laid the food on the ground and then, since sitting in a chair looking down on her seemed wrong, he lowered himself to the floor a few feet away. He had brought two glasses and filled them with wine.

'Please, you have nothing to fear from me. I'm not going to come closer, I promise.'

At length, she accepted the glass he held out and drank from it. She tore into a hunk of bread, and he let her eat in silence. After a minute or two, she whispered, 'Thank you, monsieur.'

'My name is Lawrence Harper.'

'I know.'

'Oh. What's your name? What brought you here?'

She told him in a few sentences.

'And you think he's looking for you?'

She shook her head. 'I don't know. Yesterday, Fanny went to the house to ask after him. But there was no answer, so I don't know whether he's all right or not.'

'What? Why—?'

'I hit him with a clock. He was breathing, but I don't know how bad it was.'

He took a gulp of wine. 'I see.'

'You know him.'

'I don't think—'

'The veterinarian. He was at the zoo when you took the pictures of the animals. Monsieur Calmette.'

'Oh. *He's* your employer?' Lawrence remembered an inoffensive-looking man with a copious moustache. 'Yes, I met him. But I haven't seen him since—'

'So you could go and ask for him. Find out if he's . . . Because then . . . then I'd know.'

Lawrence drank while she finished eating. She accepted another glass of wine. She ate half the bread and covered the rest with a napkin.

'Is your head all right now? Does it hurt?'

Her hand went reflexively to her forehead. It had stopped bleeding. 'No, it doesn't hurt.'

'Well, then – I'll leave you.' He picked up the bottle and glasses.

'Thank you for helping me.'

He nodded. Suddenly, the girl gasped. Her eyes were enormous, fixed on something over his shoulder.

Lawrence turned to see Louise Lamy standing in the doorway, a look of utter consternation on her face.

He scrambled to his feet. 'Madame Lamy! I'm sorry . . . This is entirely my fault. I . . . I . . .'

Louise shook her head and held up a hand, as if to fend off anything he might say. She withdrew, shutting the door behind her.

57

Fanny had barely exchanged a handful of words with Monsieur Harper since the morning she found him in bed with his friend, although the image of it came to her mind, unbidden, with bothersome regularity. So, today, when she took in his hot water and he sat up and hissed her name, she started in surprise. Then he told her what had happened last night with Anne and Madame Lamy. He said that he had taken the blame for Anne's being here.

'Oh. But why?' Fanny felt a stab of annoyance. Anne was *her* friend.

'I thought it was probably best, don't you think? Madame Lamy is . . . well . . .'

Yes. In love with you, thought Fanny. If only she knew what I know.

In a way, it was a relief. Keeping Anne's presence a secret was exhausting, and, for the past days and nights, Fanny had worn herself out with the fear of discovery. That first evening, she went to the veterinarian's house and rang at the door, but there was no answer. She saw no black crepe or outward signs of mourning, but the silence told her nothing. She reported to Anne the next day, and Anne looked alarmed, and then Fanny was alarmed too. What if he was dead, and Anne was a murderess? What if the police came? Anne had lived in an asylum; perhaps she was capable of things Fanny could not imagine.

She went downstairs to fetch the breakfast things. Anne and Monsieur Harper had clearly found a moment of sympathy. Perhaps she had drawn the wrong conclusions all along. Did he, she found herself wondering, think Anne was pretty?

Preoccupied, she stood idly in the kitchen. Sabine looked at her crossly.

'Fanny! The bell!' she shouted. 'They've been ringing. Are you deaf?'

In the dining room, she was astonished to see Anne at the breakfast table with the family and Monsieur Harper. The atmosphere was tense; Mademoiselle Lamy was looking daggers.

'Fanny,' said Madame Lamy with a tight smile, 'we have a guest for breakfast. Could you set another place and bring more bread and coffee?'

Mademoiselle Ernestine got up without a word and went out.

In her confusion, Fanny curtsied, even though she hardly ever did that, mumbled a reply and returned to the kitchen.

When she had a quiet moment, Fanny went up to see Anne, who had been lying on the bed, but started up when Fanny knocked at the spare-room door.

'So, what happened? What did she say?'

'She was all right. I think she was angry, at first, but then . . . You didn't tell me she was Creole.'

Fanny stared in astonishment. 'Madame Lamy?'

'Yes. Her grandfather came from Martinique.'

'Oh. I didn't know. She's letting you stay, then?'

'For the time being. She said she would discuss it with her husband.'

'Oh, well, it'll be all right. He's a dear.'

'I have to go. The daughter – I think she hates that I'm here.'

'Oh, Mademoiselle Lamy . . .' Fanny couldn't disagree. 'Where could you go? Do you have any family?'

Anne shook her head. 'No. My only friends are at the Salpêtrière. The police will look for me there, if anywhere.'

'Well, you can come home with me.'

'But your husband? Won't he—?'

'His battalion has gone to fight the Versaillais. He left this morning. I wish you would; I hate being there on my own.'

'Oh. Well – if you're sure. Thank you. I can help.' Anne came to her. She lifted her eyes to Fanny's and smiled tentatively. She reached out and took both her hands. 'You're too kind. I don't know why you're so nice to me.'

Fanny smiled into her eyes. 'Because you're my friend, silly!'

Anne pressed her hands.

Fanny kissed her on the cheek. 'For a moment there, I was afraid you liked Monsieur Harper more than me.'

Anne looked amazed. 'Why would you think that?'

It was what was so unusual about Anne – as though she carried an immunity to the general affliction of being a woman. Well, not entirely, since her employer had tried to force himself on her – nothing unusual in that – but it had occurred to Anne that she could fight back. In fact, the really extraordinary thing, Fanny reflected, and knew it for a certainty, was that it would never have occurred to her not to.

For the rest of the day, she thought about Anne, and her reactions to things, and how different they were from her own. She found herself dwelling on the time she had been courted by her husband. At first, she had felt in control; handsome Raymond had wooed her, implored her, made her feel that she was a rare treasure, and he her helpless, willing slave. Then, she had let on about her modelling, and he acted as though she had stolen something that belonged to him. To appease him, she had decided to give him her virginity, and it had won her a proposal. She thought him wonderful because he hadn't cleared off after deflowering her.

That was the history of their courtship – her foolishness and her sacrifice; his devotion and forgiveness. But, thinking back, she hadn't exactly chosen to present him with her virtue. Raymond had more or less demanded it. He was furious that other men had seen her naked, when that should have been his privilege, and, if she really loved him in a way she had never loved anyone else, she was obliged to prove it.

58

In the afternoon, Fanny brought her a pair of scissors, a mirror, a few other things. When she left, Anne picked up the scissors and cut her hair as close as she dared. When she had done as well as she could – patting the back of her head and combing the hair between her fingers – she stared at her reflection, fascinated. With her cloud of hair gone, her head looked oddly small and naked. It made her skin look darker, her eyes larger. She was newly aware of the cords in her neck. She placed a bowler hat – an old one of Monsieur Lamy's – on her shorn scalp and tilted it at an angle, regarding the effect. Who knew this person? It was exciting. Who would she be now? She forced herself to meet the eyes in the mirror, with a little shiver, for it was her and, at the same time, it wasn't.

Fanny waited for her until after dark. Anne had not been outside since her flight from Papin's house. She had nothing to take but the envelope, pinned inside the pocket of her jacket. She and Fanny walked side by side, and no one paid them much attention. At first, Anne was frightened she would be caught, but Fanny was confident that no one would know her, and, once they had crossed the river, she began to relax. On a quiet stretch of street, Fanny slipped her hand in the crook of Anne's elbow, as if they were sweethearts.

'Why are you laughing?' Fanny asked.

'I'm not.'

'You are! Making faces, then.'

'It's walking in these. It's so peculiar.' She plucked at a trouser leg. 'You have this thing in between your legs – it rubs.'

Fanny gave a yelp of laughter. 'Don't do that.'

She batted Anne's hand away. 'Go on ahead . . . Swing your arms more.'

Anne walked ahead, self-conscious. Once she swung her arms, she began to take longer strides. Fanny followed.

'Keep your head up. And look around – remember, you're not afraid of anything. You don't have to be modest. No, you're doing it again.'

Anne sighed. 'There's so much to remember. How do you know all this? Have you been an actress?'

'I use my eyes. And I've modelled, remember.'

Anne tried to keep her head up, her eyes on the middle distance. She had walked her whole life looking at the ground. It was alarming to keep her head up; she felt vulnerable to any casually swung glance from a stranger. But it was dark, and no one looked at her closely. It was funny to think that people didn't bother to look into your face – they just saw the overall picture. She began to enjoy the freedom conferred on her by these trappings – it was a power of invisibility.

That night, Anne woke from a deep sleep to hear Fanny crying quietly beside her.

'Fanny? What is it? You know, I can go somewhere else. I'll go tomorrow.'

'No, Anne! I'm so glad you're here. I just worry about Raymond. Every day, men are being killed – and how would I even know if something happened to him? I try not to think about it, but I can't stop.'

Anne didn't know what to say to make her feel better. 'Where is he?'

'They're defending Fort Issy. The 101st battalion. They call themselves the Lost Children.'

The Lost Children seemed an odd name for a fighting force. 'I'm sure someone would tell you if anything happened. They have messengers, don't they?'

Fanny nodded. 'I'm sorry, I woke you.' She rolled towards her in the dark.

Anne could feel her warm breath on her face. Smelt her slightly sour smell. 'I could be a messenger.'

Spring was generous, as if to make up for the horrors of the winter. Throughout April, the weather had been beautiful. Leaves sprouted from the ruined stumps of trees. Flowers burst from cracks in the pavement. For the first time in months, Anne was aware of birdsong: the sweet chirrup of sparrows, the whistle and clack of starlings. It was wonderful to hear, even though, underneath the birdsong, there was the bass grumble of artillery. But, as she walked towards the river in her new suit of armour (that was how it felt), she thought how normal it all seemed. Fishermen sat on the banks of the Seine. Cabs rattled past. Her eye was caught by one particularly fine horse – neck arched, high stepping, its coat seeming cut from burnished metal. A pied dog scampered across the road, some stolen prize in its mouth, tail a-whir. Her heart lifted.

No one bothered to look twice at a young man in an old suit. She tried to remember Fanny's lessons. She swung her arms, strode out, covered ground. She didn't know how far it was to Fort Issy, only that it lay on the far side of the city, on the road to Versailles. By midmorning, she was in an unfamiliar suburb and the growling of artillery was louder. This part of the Left Bank lay outside the old city walls; it was semi-rural, semi-industrial; the air had an acrid tang from the factories, mixed with the smells of damp soil and grass. Anne passed craters where bombs had fallen during the winter, heaps of rubble and ruins already colonized by coarse, rangy weeds. But there were also patches of ground where the trees grew green and whole, and a stream ran for a while alongside her path. Her eye was caught by a jewel flash of blue as a bird darted low over the water. Imagine living in the country and seeing such things every day . . .

There, ahead, lay the long rib of the city wall, and a gate patrolled by men with rifles. Approaching it, she caught up with a woman struggling under the weight of the basket on her back. The woman swore as one of its straps broke.

She wore a red sash and brass-buttoned jacket, which meant she was a *cantinière*. She let the basket fall to the ground, and stood, massaging her neck.

Anne took a breath and deepened her voice. 'Can I help you, citoyenne?'

'I don't know. It's gone at the buckle. Are you going through?' the woman asked.

Anne nodded. 'I'm going to the 101st battalion. At Issy.'

'That's where I'm going.' She looked pointedly at the basket, then at Anne. 'Would you help me carry it, citoyen?'

Anne agreed, and they stood while the woman got her breath back. She introduced herself as Suzanne Carbonel.

Anne reached for the outstretched hand, feeling slightly dizzy. 'Noury. Antoine Noury.'

Antoine, she'd reckoned, sounded sufficiently like her own name that she would respond to it. And Noury was the surname of her friend Marie-Jo.

'You're not with the Guard?'

Anne had wondered what she would say to this. Out here, civilian clothes were rare. With a sick feeling in her throat, she said, 'I'm a journalist.'

'Goodness. But you're so young!'

'I'm twenty-two,' said Anne, annoyed. But, of course, her smooth cheeks marked her out as a youth.

Suzanne chuckled. 'A mere child. What paper do you write for, my lad?'

'Whoever pays, citoyenne. *La Cri du Peuple, La Lanterne* . . .' She named two Communard papers that had been lying around in Fanny's kitchen. Sweat broke out under her armpits and trickled down her sides.

'Ah, well,' Suzanne looked down at her basket, more important to her than newspapers and those who wasted their time on them. 'I'd better get on.'

After that, it was easy; they picked up the basket and were waved through the gate. Many people came and went without hindrance, on foot and on horseback – men and women, carts ferrying supplies. They were passed in the opposite direction by an ambulance full of wounded.

Underneath it all, and growing in volume, was the thunder of artillery. Anne began to distinguish different layers in the noise: a deeper booming that was the government artillery, and the sharper, closer Communard guns. The air was heavy with dust, which made talking difficult. They trudged silently through the village of Issy, then passed farmhouses and a yellow chateau, the square towers of which rose above the trees. Then they saw the fortress itself, on a hill, belching smoke and thunder.

Before that, they reached a straggling encampment, the supply base for the fort. The atmosphere was calm, even leisurely. A bearded guard called out to Suzanne, and she replied cheerfully. Then he looked at Anne, who kept her face still, her eyes just beyond his face. Her heart pounded. She told herself she wasn't afraid of him, or of anything.

'And you, citoyen – who are you and what do you want?'

'Antoine Noury. I'm looking for Sergeant Klein, of the 101st. I've a message for him.'

The man grunted. 'Message? What message?'

'From his wife.'

The guard rolled his eyes and muttered something under his breath.

'He's up there, with the rest of them. You can't go up. You'll have to wait until evening, if you want to see him.'

*

It was curious seeing the fighters close to, like this – unshaven and filthy, their uniforms smeared with dirt and dust, sometimes blood. Some were only half in uniform, the regulation striped trousers paired with a smock, or a brass-buttoned jacket over workmen's overalls. All looked exhausted. Fort Issy was critical to the defence of Paris, Fanny had said. If the Communards lost it to the Versaillais, it would all be over. Men lay in the mud and dozed with their heads on their packs, relieved themselves in the open. There was a reek of sulphur and human filth. Anne had never been in a place where men so out-numbered women. She reminded herself it did not matter.

What should she do? Wait, to try to see Raymond, or slip away with the news that, this morning, at least, Fanny's husband was alive? She made her way to the corner of the camp that seemed the least busy and looked for a place to rest where she would not be noticed. There were a few women, mostly identified by their sashes as *cantinières*, but she also saw a middle-aged woman dressed in a man's uniform, trousers and all, though in no attempt at deception: long hair streamed down her back. She stood talking to a couple of guardsmen, all of them smoking cigarettes and leaning on rifles. Fascinated, Anne tried not to stare.

The spot she had chosen to wait was near a large tent with a red cross stitched on the side. After a while, a nurse emerged from the tent, quite close to her, before emptying a bucket of bloody water beneath the bushes. Anne had the feeling she was in the wrong place. The nurse's red hair straggled from beneath her cap and one cheek was smeared with blood.

'You don't want to sit there, citoyen,' she said. 'It's where all this rubbish goes.'

'Oh, I'm sorry.' Anne stood up. She kept her face down, hoping the nurse wouldn't look at her.

'What are you doing here?'

'I'm waiting for someone. I have a message.'

'Waiting . . . here?' She made it sound like a ridiculous thing to do.

A half-choked, agonizing scream came from the tent. As though plucked by the sound, the nurse jerked up and took a deep breath.

'I don't suppose you could lend us a hand for an hour? We're desperate.'

A fractious male voice shouted, 'Citoyenne Bignon! Where are you? Hurry, for God's sake!'

'Well, actually . . .' Anne said.

The redhead gave her a look of weary disbelief and turned back, and Anne, after a moment's hesitation, followed.

59

The queues outside food shops were growing again; prices were spi-
ralling in a grim echo of autumn. There was a numbing familiarity
to all this, as to the noise of shells exploding, the closure of railway
stations, the embargo on leaving the city. But this time there was no
solidarity among citizens. Doctors were tolerated by all, but, if asked,
Ellis said that he was impartial. It seemed to him that the government
attacks were indiscriminate and cruel, while the Commune, split into
warring factions, was ineffective.

Accusations of atrocities were hurled by both sides. The government in Versailles claimed that the Communards were criminals, not
combatants, and treated prisoners worse than criminals. The Commune's favourite general had been captured unarmed and murdered;
his mutilated corpse was taken to Versailles on a dung cart and put
on display, where women poked at his brains with umbrellas. Shortly
after, the Commune's chief of police arrested the Archbishop of Paris
and several priests and flung them in jail. Newspapers on both sides
were incandescent with rage. That Lawrence was working for the
Commune frightened Ellis to death. When Ellis discovered what his
job entailed, he was appalled. The thought of his darling surrounded
by decomposing corpses was horrible. And, at the same time, rather
magnificent. Lawrence was bemused by his reaction.

'It's not so different from what you're doing,' he said, 'only less
difficult.'

Ellis couldn't say why it so distressed him: he didn't want this treasure tainted by the horrors with which he was so familiar; he didn't want his lover to be haunted by the ghosts that haunted him. He told himself his worry was misplaced; Lawrence was blessed with a resilience he had never been able to find.

'At first, I thought I wouldn't be able to do it. Now, I just think, I'll do the best I can for them. I mean, it's the least I can do, for their families, isn't it?' He shrugged.

'You're an angel.' Ellis took Lawrence's hand, the fingers stained black with silver nitrate.

Lawrence grimaced as Ellis kissed them. 'They're awful. Don't . . . I have to do so much printing, it never comes off.' He took his hand away, then pulled Ellis's face towards him and kissed him.

Ellis found Ephraim Quine in his new lodgings above the consulate. Even though it was Sunday, his uncle had just returned from a diplomatic mission to the Mazas Prison, where Archbishop Darboy was held, the main hostage in negotiations between the Commune and Thiers' government in Versailles. For their part, the government had imprisoned a veteran revolutionary, Auguste Blanqui. Although elderly, Blanqui wielded enormous influence. The Commune had offered to release all their hostages in exchange for him, but the offer was refused.

'The Communards thought that Thiers would do anything to free the Archbishop. They don't realize he's as ruthless and entrenched as they, if not more so.'

Ellis heard the despair in his voice.

'You'll be able to do something for him. They'll listen to you.'

Ephraim shook his head. 'I'm just a neutral who is allowed in with newspapers. The poor man is not in good health, and getting weaker. I can't see what will cause either side to move. The pig-headedness of it all would make you weep.' It was almost a cry.

Ellis persuaded him to leave his desk and sit by the fire. The window overlooking the Rue Royale was a lovely, twilight blue, but the artillery still beat its drums in the distance.

'I go back to Versailles tomorrow, so . . .' His eyes closed. His eyelids were papery, shiny with weariness.

'Speaking as a doctor, I should order you to rest.'

Ephraim smiled at him. 'Yes, I know. Unfortunately, it is one of those times. I do rest.'

'I wish I could do more to help.'

'You're doing your bit. How is the hospital, now? Don't think I don't know –' he leant forward and touched Ellis on the arm – 'what it cost you to go back.'

Ellis shifted. 'Oh, you know. It's fine.'

On his first day back at work, he'd became aware of an aristocratic English drawl coming from one of his new colleagues. So many Americans had left Paris after the first siege that the staff was now international, and the newcomer was an Anglo-Irish surgeon, Patrick Logue. Logue was a tall, thin man, about his own age, nattily dressed, with a fresh complexion. His flamboyant manners gave him a certain notoriety, and Ellis was wary, as he was always wary of men who were too . . . obvious. He knew this was ridiculous; his colleagues were perfectly accepting of Logue, who gave the impression of not caring a fig what other people thought of him. They discovered that they had literary interests in common, and, when Logue invited him to a salon concert, the prospect of hearing some good music was too tempting to resist.

The hosts had hired a string trio. Ellis closed his eyes and let the music wash over him. The voices of the cello and violin in particular were exquisite. It was a nagging frustration that he was so moved by music, but had no talent for it. He wished Lawrence were here.

The last piece in the programme was a Corelli sonata. It had a melancholy sweetness, the cello and viola exchanging notes back and forth, like voices murmuring sadly. Ellis closed his eyes until he wasn't listening to the music, but feeling it like something on his skin. When he opened his eyes, he found they were wet. He brought himself back into the room with difficulty. Collecting his coat, he was not surprised to find Patrick Logue by his side.

'Where are you headed, Butterfield?'

'I have lodgings in Montmartre.'

'Would you mind if I walked a little way with you? I feel the need to stretch my legs.'

They stepped out of the building and turned northwards. They had to pick their way around holes in the roadway, where the paving cobbles had been prised up to form a nearby barricade. These obstacles were increasingly familiar. But it was a soft spring evening and the guns, for once, were silent – you could almost believe that life was normal.

Ellis lit a cigar. He thought he knew what was coming. 'Thank you for this evening. I haven't heard anything that good in months.'

'Do you play?' Logue asked.

'Only the piano, a little, and badly.'

They walked on for a moment in silence, their canes tapping a rhythm on the pavement. Then Logue said, 'I saw how moved you were by the Corelli. It's one of my favourites, too.'

'Yes, it was beautiful. And beautifully played.'

'The violinist, that young Italian – he was charming, wasn't he?'

Ellis hesitated a fraction before agreeing.

'Did you know, Corelli was an invert?'

'Oh? I didn't.'

'I suppose people don't mention it because they think it might affect people's taste for his music. It doesn't affect yours?'

Ellis laughed. 'No. Of course not.'

'I wonder, since you are *au fait* with the area – perhaps you could suggest a place for a nightcap? And, if I haven't imposed too much already, perhaps I could persuade you to join me?'

Ellis glanced at Logue. His face wore a bright but vague expression. An expression he himself had probably worn on occasion. 'Well, I . . .'

Instantly, the man's face closed, as if this was what he had expected. 'No – I'd be delighted.'

There was a bar he knew, not far away. He knew it because he had been there with Lawrence, half reluctant and half excited at the frisson of going to such a place as a couple, where that was what they were assumed to be. He had been nervous; such bars did, periodically, get raided by the police. This was a discreet place, but the glances that crossed and recrossed the room made the air crackle with possibility. Being there with Lawrence was bittersweet – the eyes of every man in the bar followed him, then they turned to examine Ellis, assessing him, measuring themselves against him. He wasn't used to being assigned an erotic value, being deemed worthy – or not – of such a prize.

'Shall we go soon?' he'd muttered before long, conscious of one man in particular – a grizzled individual, with a handsome, aquiline face, who gazed at Lawrence with a morbid intensity.

'Because of him?' Lawrence laughed softly, and let his hand rest on Ellis's neck. 'He can see that we're together.'

Lawrence appeared alight, vividly thrilling and aware, in a way that Ellis adored – but he wanted that spark to come from him, not from the desire of strangers. He tried to turn it into a joke.

'What if he's a policeman?'

'Darling, he's not a policeman. Or, if he is, that's not why he's here.'

Lawrence basked in the atmosphere, but Ellis became quiet, so, when they had finished their drinks, they left, Ellis feeling eyes burning into his back.

Outside, Lawrence took him by the arm. 'Don't you find it a relief? Not having to hide?'

Ellis shrugged. Even at night, he was nervous of being seen. 'I don't know. That man wished I was dead.'

'Well, I don't.' He leant towards him. 'They were looking at you, too.'

That evening had been unnerving. But, once they rounded the last turn of the staircase in Ellis's building, Lawrence had seized him and kissed him with such abandon – excited, he knew, by the attention – that he couldn't regret it.

Tonight, in the bar, no one looked at Logue that way. In response to the Irishman's questions, Ellis said, 'I've been here once – with my friend.'

'Oh.' Logue smiled. 'A close friend?'

'Yes.'

Logue sat back in his seat, recomposing himself. 'How long have you and your friend known each other?'

'Nearly . . . yes, a year.'

It had been a warm May evening when they met at Yves' studio. It made him smile to think of it, because they hadn't taken to each other – at least, Lawrence admitted he hadn't liked Ellis. Ellis couldn't remember what he'd thought; he'd been too drunk. He thought, I have changed in that year.

Logue smiled again – very sweetly, this time – and looked into his glass. He said quietly, 'How lucky you are.'

'Yes. I am.'

After this, Logue subtly turned his attention to the other customers in the place. His cheeks were pink, and his demeanour seemed to tighten with longing. At last, sensing that a youth – not unappealing – was glancing towards them, Ellis took the opportunity to plead tiredness.

'I think I might stay and have one more, old chap – that is, if you don't mind?'

Ellis assured him he didn't, thanked him again for the evening, and left. But, outside, he noticed the youth following him. Halfway down the street, Ellis turned and said, very firmly, 'Monsieur, I have nothing for you. But, if you were to return, I think the other gentleman . . .'

The youth gazed at him lasciviously; then, with a shrug and a smile, he turned back. Ellis didn't wait to see where he went. Maybe Logue would be too humiliated and hurt. But then, maybe not.

60

Louise had been shaken to discover Lawrence Harper with a girl. Though her reaction – she admitted it was down to jealousy – had been unfounded, she was uneasy at the thought of sheltering a fugitive. The whole affair of Anne Petitjean upset her – and that she was dressed in men's clothing made her seem furtive and guilty. Then there was her manner: intense yet evasive; the stillness that suggested not calm, but opposing forces held in great tension; the way she wouldn't look her in the eye.

'If she's done nothing wrong, then she has no reason to be afraid,' she signed to Serge, when the girl had gone back upstairs after breakfast. She offered to intercede with the girl's employer, who, she was sure, would take her back – these things happened every day, after all – but no one agreed with her. It turned out that Fanny and the girl were friends. She implored Louise's forgiveness, and begged that she not report it to the police. Serge and Lawrence were both stalwart in the girl's defence, so Louise had given in. Ernestine simply refused to have anything to do with it. She wagered they wouldn't have been so gallant had Anne not been a girl, and a rather striking one.

After lunch, Lawrence came to tell her that Anne would be leaving that day – the whole thing apparently arranged without consulting her, in her own house!

That night, Louise was in a bad mood; the incident had thrown her off balance. Although it was a relief, for once in her life, not to be responsible, it made her feel old and irrelevant, she told Serge.

Don't be ridiculous, he signed; she was wonderful, and he loved her. He just didn't agree with her on this occasion. The girl deserved a chance.

'I know. I was wrong,' she signed. 'I love you.'

'I'm lucky you put up with me,' he replied.

Now, things were happening so fast that the problem of an errant servant no longer seemed important. Louise and Ernestine stood side by side at the dining-room window, watching men with mattocks prise up the cobblestones in the street outside their house. Women and children carried them to the corner, where a barricade was rising. In the morning, they had sweated in the sun; now, rain plastered their hair to their heads, but they toiled on. Last night, persons unknown had overturned an omnibus and pressed it into service to plug the small street off to the right. Further barricades loomed at intervals down the boulevard. Vehicles could no longer pass. Daily, it was becoming more difficult to get around, even on foot. This morning, Fanny reported that the Pont d'Austerlitz was closed.

This newest barricade was massive: a thick stone wall pierced by a narrow, angled slit. On one side of the street, it met the wall in front of the chocolatier, Lefevre; on the other, it butted up against the café, obscuring its list of beers. Some of their neighbours had already cleared out. Last week, the majolica dealer packed up his goods, shuttered the shop and left for the country. Ernestine argued that they should do the same, but neither Louise nor Serge wanted to leave. Studio Lamy was theirs and all they had was here; who other than them would protect it, if the worst came to the worst?

Twenty-three years ago, in the summer of 1848, Louise had felt the same dread as rioting spread through the centre of Paris and the army took to the streets to shoot down the insurgents. Then, Louise and Serge lived with little Ernestine in a tiny apartment near the Madeleine. Louise stayed indoors for days, anxiously hovering over her daughter. Serge continued to go to work – it had not been long since they had set up in business on their own and their finances depended on it – but Louise was too scared to leave the child with a nurse. In the end, their neighbourhood had escaped the rioting and shooting, but, this time, it didn't look as though they would be so lucky. The army was coming, crying out for revenge, and the Communards had sworn to fight to the death.

'Well, there's no point standing here doing nothing,' Louise said, for the fourth time. 'Titine, you'll worry yourself to shreds. Come, there is plenty to be getting on with.'

Ernestine sighed. 'I wish you and Papa would come with me. It will only be for a few days – a week at most.'

Monsieur Ranvier had offered to get them all out of Paris until the fighting was over. He had rented a house to the east of Paris, and Ernestine was going – she had packed her things, and was waiting for him to send a carriage, although the prospect of a carriage getting anywhere near their door was dwindling by the minute. Louise and Serge were reluctant to leave. They had metal shutters for the shopfront, but would that be enough? If people were kidnapping omnibuses and overturning them in the street, what was to stop them tearing shutters from windows? Twenty-three years ago, the insurgents had thrown tables, beds and wardrobes out of windows to shore up their rubble barricades – small calvaries, where many of them subsequently died.

'I don't know why you're being so stubborn.'

'We've gone over this, Titine. We'll be perfectly safe. They say there's nothing to worry about.'

'But you don't *need* to stay. Charles wishes you would come. And so do I.'

Louise touched her daughter's hand. She was warmed by this admission. But their life savings, and all the money they had inherited from their families, had gone into buying the building and equipping it with the best of everything. Louise hadn't told Ernestine, what with plans for the wedding and all, but money was rather tight. And they had recently taken delivery of a quantity of darkroom chemicals, most of which were highly flammable, even explosive. Serge believed it was his duty to keep them, and all around them, from harm.

'Right. I'm going to the butcher's,' Louise finally announced.

'But it's raining, Maman,' Ernestine protested.

'I'm going to go shopping, while I still can.'

'Citoyenne,' said the guard in charge of the barricade, touching his hat in a civil manner. He had been there since yesterday, when construction started. He was a middle-aged man with a heavy moustache, well spoken and not unpleasant. 'Do you need to pass?'

'I'm going to the butcher's on Rue Soufflot.'

'Well, bring me back a sausage. I've been here since five o'clock this morning.' He added a smile and a grimace, to show that he was joking.

'Tell me, mon— er, citoyen, is it possible for a horse and cart to get through, anywhere, perhaps to the east?'

He shrugged. 'I don't know. I doubt it.'

She passed through the slit in the wall, restating her mission at each barricade. The streets around the Panthéon had been turned into a fortress, and the massive barricade on Rue Soufflot was a marvel of engineering, a complex of interlocking walls and smooth, sloping faces. Something about it put her in mind of the pyramids; despite herself, she admired it. But cannon stood in the embrasures – great black beasts, with long, evil snouts. The rain made them gleam. She shivered.

She managed to get through to the butcher's, which was, thank goodness, still open. She bought meat and sausages, cured meats, things that would last – who knew when she would be able to get out again? She nodded sympathetically as the butcher complained of the difficulty of getting deliveries through the blocked streets. He said he had never missed a day in fifteen years of trading, but he was going to shut up shop in a couple of hours, because it wasn't worth losing your life over, was it?

61

All that afternoon, it poured with rain, and, even inside the tent, the ground underfoot turned to glue. Shells fell incessantly, pounding their eardrums, but, from inside the tent, you could not tell how near they were, nor was there time to worry about it. Since following the nurse inside and helping restrain a delirious man who was trying to tear off his bandages, Anne hadn't stopped. She had sized up the problem, sat on his cot and used the blanket to hold him down, as she had done to hysterical women countless times in the Salpêtrière.

'Do you have any chloral?' she asked the redhead.

'Er, no,' the girl replied, uncertain. 'We have ether – would that do?'

Once the man had been bound to his cot and stupefied with ether, the redhead looked at her with boundless relief.

'You know what you're doing!' she said. 'Are you a doctor?'

'No. I've worked as a hospital orderly, that's all.'

'Well, thanks be to God for sending you. You're the answer to our prayers.'

After that, she couldn't leave, as a constant stream of wounded were carried down from the hill and into the tent, or laid on the ground outside to wait. Fort d'Issy was under furious attack. One man, whose gun had blown up in his face, blinding him, said the fortress was in ruins. They could not hold out much longer.

Anne had not a moment to wonder whether she was afraid. In a rare lull, the doctor in charge signalled for Anne to join him outside. She wondered if she had been discovered, but he merely offered her a cigarette.

'I can't tell you how thankful we are to have your help, Citoyen— I don't even know your name.'

Anne gave him her new name, and they shook hands.

'It's been like this for days . . . We can't keep this up.' He shook his head, then yelled for coffee and bread.

A *cantinière* fetched cups of black coffee and some food. Anne was desperately thirsty, and gulped down the coffee, scalding her throat. She sucked gingerly on the cigarette in between bites of bread and sausage. The smoke was hot to her lips, and cool in her throat. She held the cigarette as the doctor held his. Fanny would have been proud.

The doctor talked non-stop. He seemed to accept Antoine Noury without question; perhaps he was too exhausted to question anything. Another cart was making its way down the winding road from the fort: more wounded on their way.

'Citoyenne Bignon and I haven't slept for three days,' he said, tossing the end of his cigarette into the mud. 'You'll stay, won't you. I can't tell you what a difference you're making.'

So Anne stayed. By nightfall, she was moving automatically, so tired she had forgotten who she was meant to be. No one cared, anyway. Then someone lifted the tent flap and shouted that the fort was being evacuated. That explained the change in the noises from outside – the grinding of cart axles and tramping feet. The doctor muttered, 'God, about time,' without looking up from where he was sewing a cheek back together. But the redhead cried, 'The cowards! They can't leave!'

The guard shrugged. 'There's no bastion left. The government are right below the glacis. It's hopeless. Finished.'

Guardsmen brought carts and horses to take those who could not walk. One came in and spoke to the redhead, and they embraced, briefly but urgently.

Anne heard no more gunfire. She wondered if it meant the war was over. She did not ask, as she thought men would know such things without asking. Once the wounded were loaded up, the doctor gathered his instruments, bloody as they were, throwing them into a bag.

'No time to waste,' said the doctor. 'You'd better get back to Paris – that's all that's left. No, wait!'

Anne froze in place. This was it. It had been too good to last.

'Give me your address, citoyen. We're in desperate need of orderlies.'

Anne thought rapidly. This work was something she could do. She gave him Fanny's address, said she was living with her sister. She shook hands with the doctor and the nurse – both were effusive in their thanks. The doctor said he would be in touch. It had all been surprisingly easy. No one had looked at her twice. She knew that, as the former patient Anne Petitjean, she would not have done any of these things. But that was now a skin that she could shed and take on a new one.

She watched the stream of men leaving the fort and went up to a man with a slightly smarter uniform than most, to ask him if he had news of Sergeant Klein.

The man threw out his arms as if to say the question was absurd. 'There's no one left up there, at any rate.' He gestured towards the hill, the shape of the broken fort barely visible against the night sky. 'They've all gone.'

'Thank you,' said Anne. But he had already wandered off, moving with a dazed, stumbling gait.

She watched the exhausted men for a while. Raymond might have left before her. She joined the ragged march away from the fort, and realized she felt faint with hunger. In the village, she found a baker that had stayed open, catering to the thick stream of the defeated. Anne bought a loaf of bread and walked on towards the city. Other figures were strung out along the road, but they walked in silence, heads low, feet dragging, emanating an odour of shame, bewilderment and failure. Anne turned up a side lane to get away from them. It was too sad.

She followed the lane past a farmhouse, climbed a gentle slope and turned to look back the way she had come. She saw red and orange light coming from behind some trees and wondered what it meant. Then she realized, with a shock, that it was the chateau she had passed earlier in the day; a shell must have sailed right over the encampment and fallen on its square-roofed towers, setting the beautiful old building on fire. This morning, the chateau had struck her as the essence of permanence: solid, proud, safe. Now, she could hear the crackle and roar of flames gnawing at the stones. She could see the smoke rising and sparks flying into the night sky.

There was no sign that anyone was attempting to put out the blaze. In the village, they must have seen the flames, even if the chateau was empty – impossible to save, or not worth saving? She could smell the burning, and the smell made her heart pound in her throat with a ferocious power that was part fear and part excitement.

It was like the smell that had presaged her seizures, but this was not her madness. And, though she felt fear, it wasn't the same kind of fear; it was comprehensible, one she could walk away from, if she chose. Yet she stayed, because this new skin allowed it, her hand resting on the trunk of a tree, watching a burning that was real – both awful and lovely.

Letter written by Louis Rossel, Commune's Minister for War, 10 May 1871:

I am incapable of continuing to bear responsibility for a command where everyone discusses but no one obeys. The Commune has argued and prevaricated while the enemy took Fort Issy. I could have repulsed it had I the least military force at my disposal, but the petty wrangling of the Committee prevented the deployment of artillery and paralysed our troops. I therefore resign . . .

From the diary of Communard Hippolyte Mazade, 15 May 1871:

. . . the Committee tried to arrest the only competent tactician we have. So Rossel has resigned – and there are those who accuse him of treason! Without a coordinated strategy for the city's defence, the outlook is bleak. The Commune must put aside its differences or it will not survive.

Headline from *Le Cri du Peuple*, 16 May 1871:

This morning, at the Hôtel de Ville, twenty-two elected officials of the Commune announced their resignation. They wrote an address to the majority, violently criticizing its methods, its attitude towards the minority, and the decisions of the Committee. At the gates of Paris, the situation is critical. The fort of Vanves was evacuated yesterday evening. The villages of Issy and Vanves were also lost. The circle closes on the city, caught between Prussian troops and the soldiers of Versailles.

Proclamation issued by Prime Minister Adolphe Thiers, 17 May 1871:

I hereby warn that the moment has come when, to shorten your sufferings, the Versaillais army must attack Paris itself. Honest citizens will have nothing to fear from our soldiers; they must simply stay indoors, and follow instructions when required.

Poster for a concert in the Tuileries:

The Commune of Paris presents:
A GRAND OPEN-AIR CONCERT
in the TUILERIES GARDENS
Sunday, 21st May, at 19.00
1500 MUSICIANS!
Mozart – Meyerbeer – Rossini
REFRESHMENTS!!
Entrance: 20 sous
All proceeds to go to
the Wounded of the Commune.

62

To Fanny's surprise, Madame Lamy decided to join her at the concert on Sunday evening. Only the day before, she had said she was too frightened to leave the house, before apologizing – Fanny had been walking to and from work, as usual. Sunday was a lovely day, and madame was more like her usual self. So, they walked through the barricades, over the river, to the Tuileries Gardens.

They found an atmosphere of an extraordinary gaiety. Fresh flowers garlanded the gates and statues. Uniformed guardsmen and *cantinières* mingled with families dressed in their Sunday best. Children ran around, shrieking with delight. There was a Punch and Judy show, and refreshment stalls sold all sorts of dainties. Madame Lamy bought them *sirop de vanille* and brioches, and they sat on the warm grass, listening to the distant strains of the orchestra. The crowd made so much noise that, at times, they could barely hear the music, but neither of them minded – the chatter and laughter were infectious, and it drowned the distant thunder of guns.

Fanny got home late, and found Anne already there. A few days ago, she had started work as an orderly in one of the private hospitals. The doctor she had helped at Issy recommended her – or, rather, recommended Antoine Noury. Anne liked being useful. When she was lifting patients, or stripping beds, or carrying bandages, no one questioned her. Fanny understood. If she hadn't had her work, she would have gone mad with worry.

'The concert was wonderful. Such beautiful music – and there were flowers everywhere! It was a shame you didn't come. But I've brought these.' She unwrapped bread and sausage, and began to slice them up.

Anne smiled. 'I've been with people all day. I just want to be alone.'

'But I don't count as people, do I?' Fanny cut off a chunk of sausage and put it in her mouth. 'I'm glad I have *Antoine* to protect me!' She grinned at Anne.

Anne ducked her head, but she too smiled.

The bells began to toll shortly after midnight. The first to sound was the bell of Saint-Jean-Baptiste de Belleville. Almost immediately, it was joined by the tenor of Notre-Dame-de-la-Croix de Ménilmontant, ringing the tocsin, the sound of alarm. The message spread from church to church, district to district, multiplying as it went. It sounded without stopping, and underneath swelled the deep rolling of drums.

Anne and Fanny started awake at the same moment. Notre-Dame-de-la-Croix was just on the corner, and the deafening clangour made the air in the room shake.

'My God!' Fanny sat up and scrabbled to light the candle. 'Shit. Oh, God. It's happening!'

Anne looked at her, her eyes wide with fear. 'What is?'

'It's the signal. They've got in.'

The bells meant that Versaillais troops had finally breached the walls of the city. They – the Communards, everyone – had been preparing for this, knew it was coming, but still, it was shocking. Fanny began to dress in a distracted fashion.

'What are you going to do?' Anne asked. She pulled shirt and trousers towards her. She wasn't sure why, except that, in grave emergency, she wanted to be dressed, preferably in men's clothing.

Fanny didn't look at her. 'I have to find Raymond.'

After the fall of Issy, Raymond Klein's battalion, the 101st, or what was left of it, limped back behind the city walls. *Les Enfants Perdus* had defended the fort with desperate courage and sustained heavy losses under the Versaillais' overwhelmingly superior fire power. Raymond – miraculously unharmed – was proud of the way they had acquitted themselves. They put the other battalions to shame, he said. Then, the 101st was redeployed to defend barricades in the west. Two nights ago, he had come home, eaten ravenously, listened without interest while Fanny explained Anne's presence and attire, and had gone to bed. He barely spoke to Anne, which suited her. She spent the night on blankets under the kitchen table, trying not to listen to the painful-sounding noises from the bedroom. In the morning, he left before she woke up.

Fanny was anxiously pinning up her hair. 'I have to do something. I can't just go to work as though nothing's happening, can I?'

She went to the window and peered down. Anne joined her. Below, some figures were standing under a street lamp, talking. They didn't appear in a hurry to go anywhere.

Anne thought of Papin's warning: the 'ugliness' – whatever he had meant by that. Back then, she'd assumed that, whatever happened, she would be safe in the veterinarian's house.

'What would Raymond want you to do?'

'I don't know. Anne, I think you should put on one of my dresses. If you go out like that, you'll be conscripted.'

Anne shook her head firmly. 'I'm going to the hospital. It'll be safe there. Probably the safest place.' She pulled on her red-cross armband to prove it.

There was another factor. She didn't say so to Fanny, but the prospect of putting on women's clothing depressed her. After her first day at the private hospital, she felt valued for what she could do. She began to think that maybe she could go on like this, live like this. It made all manner of things possible.

Fanny's eyes brimmed with tears. Anne took a deep breath, caught and held her gaze.

'Don't worry. Raymond is lucky. He hasn't had so much as a scratch, has he? Not from all the fighting.'

Fanny pressed her hand and sniffed. 'I know, but . . .'

'In any case, you can't do anything till morning. There's no point. We'll know more then.'

Fanny nodded and pulled herself together. Anne was right, she said. She was so glad she was here with her; she would have gone crazy if she was alone. In the end, they lay down again, keeping their clothes on, just in case. Anne allowed Fanny to put her arm around her, as it seemed to comfort her. They counted the unquiet hours till daylight.

In the morning, Anne walked to her hospital in the centre of town. It was one of the private hospitals that had sprung up in response to the new flood of casualties, and it was housed in a former hotel on the Rue Rambuteau, just a few streets from the butcher's shop on Rue de Rivoli.

The hospital was run by foreigners, but they spoke reasonable French, so Anne didn't find it too difficult to fit in. In fact, she was glad they weren't French; it gave Antoine Noury another layer of obfuscation. In the end, a hospital was a hospital. What surprised her was their attention to hygiene. It was a far cry from the Salpêtrière. Monsieur Noury and the other orderlies were kept busy running to change beds, lift patients and ferry the wounded from ward to surgery. She watched as they used a weak solution of carbolic acid to keep everything clean. She wiped down tables and washed instruments between surgeries. They even used it on the patients' wounds. At the end of the second day, she overheard a surgeon say to one of the nurses, 'Tell Monsieur Noury to get it. He doesn't make mistakes.'

She kept herself to herself, ate alone, but they were so busy, she felt safe, almost invisible. She was a pair of nimble hands and strong arms. She remembered instructions to the letter. If anyone noticed anything odd about her, they didn't say anything.

During a break for bread and coffee, she squatted against a wall, feeding morsels of bread to a dog that came nosing round. The smell of blood attracted strays from all over the neighbourhood. She eavesdropped as a surgeon talked with the ambulance men who had brought in a cart of wounded Communards, and heard that government troops had taken the western suburbs, but encountered resistance near the Place de la Concorde, and had been forced to retreat to L'Étoile. More Communard battalions were being moved up to reinforce the defence.

In response to the surgeon's questions, the ambulance men reported that the barricades which guarded the centre were holding. They were stoutly built and well stocked, defended by cannon. The Versaillais might have been welcomed by their friends in the bourgeois west, but now, by God, they had their work cut out.

Fanny arrived at the Studio Lamy late and out of breath, due to the crowds on the streets and having to make her way around or through the barricades. Troops of guards and artillery were flooding from east to west. She heard distant gunfire – the usual rumble of artillery, but also, when the wind caught it, the lighter stuttering of rifles. More barricades were being hastily built on the main roads. She only managed to cross the river at the Pont de Constantine with much pleading. Everywhere, people pitched in to help – women, children, the elderly – all bringing paving blocks, iron gratings, sandbags, bricks, rubble, even furniture, to add to the barricades. She gathered that the Versaillais had breached the defences at Point du Jour, on the right bank, but, when she asked which battalions were fighting, no one could tell her.

At the Lamys, a grim calm prevailed. Madame Lamy was surprised but glad to see Fanny. She voiced her relief, again, that Ernestine had left – in the end, her fiancé had had to hire footmen to carry her trunks through the barricades to the nearest point his carriage could reach, over two kilometres away.

'Why didn't you go too, madame?' Fanny asked.

'Because someone needs to look after this place. Otherwise, all our furniture will end up on one of those barricades.' She jerked her head to the window. 'We will be quite safe behind these shutters. Of course, you and Sabine are welcome to stay, Fanny dear. Sabine can make up a bed downstairs. You will be safe here also.'

'Thank you, madame, but . . .' Fanny didn't know what to say.

Madame looked at her. 'Monsieur Klein – is he . . . safe?' She knew that he was a Communard, and a fighter.

Fanny shook her head. 'I don't know, madame. I don't know where he is.'

She bit back tears. Madame was no friend to the Commune and hadn't thought very highly of Raymond in any case. But she was looking at her with sympathy.

'I'm sorry, my dear; this must be difficult for you.'

Fanny felt the tears fall, then blotted them on her sleeve. 'Thank you, madame. But I'm fine.'

She was torn – she felt a duty to Madame Lamy, who had always been so kind, but she also knew she couldn't stay in this house while . . . God knew what was going on, out there.

Over breakfast, Madame Lamy was shocked to hear that Monsieur Harper still intended to go to the Hôtel de Ville, where he'd worked for the last fortnight. Fanny paused, listening.

'The army is coming, Lawrence – I wish you wouldn't go. It would be best not to be associated with the . . .' She glanced, a little late, at Fanny. 'I think you should go upstairs and help Serge with the inventory. We'll say you have been here all along.'

Monsieur Harper shook his head and smiled. 'I'll be careful. I'll leave if I have to. But I'm a foreign photographer, not a partisan. Anyway, you don't need to worry. Look what Monsieur Butterfield sent me.'

He took from his pocket a crumpled red-cross armband, worn by medical staff to ensure they could go about their business unhindered. Madame Lamy crossed herself.

'He is a thoughtful friend. But promise me you'll be careful. Don't get caught there.'

As he was heading for the door, Fanny made up her mind and ran after him.

The square in front of the Hôtel de Ville thronged with people, all of them, like Fanny, suppliants desperate for help or information. Lawrence told her to wait outside and fought his way through the crowd to enter the building, shrugging aside those who seized him by the arm, begging for intervention.

Inside was just as chaotic. He searched in vain for an official. It was difficult; he knew so few of the delegates by sight. At length, he saw a familiar dark head vanishing down a corridor and ran after it.

'Citoyen Mazade! It's Citoyen Harper. A moment, please.'

Mazade slowed without looking around. 'I have no time to— Ah, Citoyen Harper, I'm afraid I can't stop.'

'Just one thing – the 101st battalion. Do you know where it is?'

Mazade stopped in surprise. 'Doing their duty to defend our city, I imagine. Unofficially, I have no idea. Why?'

'A friend – her husband is with them and she hasn't heard from him.'

'Someone at the War Commission might know – but, to be honest, I doubt it; things are moving too fast for them to keep up.' He paused and lowered his voice. 'Some of the guards have gone home – they're refusing to fight away from their own districts. I'm sorry, you'll have to excuse me—'

'Of course. But – what should I do?'

Mazade stared at him through the thick lenses. The shadows under his eyes were more pronounced than ever, and he looked thinner. His clothes stank of tobacco and sweat. Lawrence wondered when he had last slept. Mazade smiled grimly.

'Do your job as long as you can, citoyen. But, if things get worse . . . We cannot guarantee your safety, you understand.' Mazade came closer and held out his hand. 'If I don't see you again – thank you for all you've done for the families. It's important work.'

Lawrence took the man's hand and they shook – it felt oddly final. He had the urge to wish him luck, but held his tongue in case it would seem insulting to suggest that he – or the Commune – would need it.

Too late, Lawrence thought that he should have asked about Michel's battalion too. The 95th . . . or was it the 59th? But Mazade wouldn't have known. He set off down another corridor, searching for the War Commission. Someone, he thought, must know something. They were, after all, in charge.

63

This morning, heading to his office in the Hôtel Lagny, Victor found the front door blocked by horses and wagons. A blond man in uniform was giving orders in a foreign accent, while dozens of guardsmen were ferrying crates down the stairs and into the cellars. Victor walked into the entrance hall, where he found Lapeyre hissing at his secretary. Lapeyre was gesticulating, his face white with rage.

'You shouldn't have opened the door for them, you fool. You had no right to do so.'

The secretary held his ground. 'The general said he would arrest me if I didn't give him the key.'

'What's happening, director?' asked Victor.

Lapeyre glared at him. 'That foreign upstart out there is requisitioning my headquarters.'

'But why?'

'Because the *Commune* –' he spat the word – 'wants to turn this place into an arsenal. Gunpowder and ammunition for the defence of the entire Left Bank, and it has to be here!'

Victor felt the blood drain out of his head. 'But they can't do that!' he said. 'What about the animals?'

Lapeyre strode past him as if he hadn't spoken. Victor looked at the secretary, who shrugged and raised his hands in a gesture of helplessness.

'But we can't just . . . We can't . . .'

He hurried out to where Lapeyre was shouting at the general, who held up his hand as a lieutenant spoke urgently into his ear.

'You have no right to take over my headquarters! All of these buildings are under my control as director of the menagerie, and I am an official of the French government.'

The general, who looked no more than thirty, nodded to the lieutenant and turned to Lapeyre. He had a neat beard and high cheekbones: a Pole, and a soldier. His face was haggard, but patient.

'And I am General Dombrowski, in charge of the defence of the Left Bank, and my orders come from the Committee of Public Safety, which is the legal government of Paris. This is war. Such measures are inevitable.'

He ended the argument by striding away, judging that Lapeyre would not lower himself by scurrying after him. The soldier brushed against Victor's shoulder as he went past.

All morning, wagon after wagon was unloaded and crates of munitions were swallowed up by the tunnels beneath the zoo. A Guard detail was set up around the park's perimeter, but Victor and other zoo employees were allowed to stay. After lunch, Lapeyre left, taking his secretary and several boxes of files with him. He entrusted the care of the animals to Victor. Victor wasn't going to leave. He had nowhere else to go.

He tried to comfort himself with the thought that the cats' pavilion was at the far end of the zoo, away from the soldiers and their explosives. Robitaille had been giving them extra food in an attempt to distract and soothe them, but they sensed something was amiss. Marguerite paced her cage, staring out over his head, tail twitching from side to side. The new lioness had only recently arrived and had yet to settle; she snarled and spat at anyone who came near. And there was the lynx, a very young and beautiful creature, which huddled, petrified, at the back of its shelter and refused to move. Tancred the lion was more lethargic than ever. He looked thin and dusty – the worn-out king of a dwindling kingdom.

'The director has gone. We're on our own,' Victor told Robitaille.

Robitaille nodded, unsurprised.

Victor's mouth was dry with fear. He pictured himself standing in front of Marguerite's cage as the mob advanced, brandishing weapons.

'I will stay, monsieur. It will be all right.' Robitaille was matter of fact, as if this were all part of the day's work. He showed little reaction to the presence of troops or the possibility of gun battles in the park.

Victor suspected Robitaille of Communard sympathies, but he didn't know for sure; it was not something they talked about.

Last week, they had closed the zoo. The government in Versailles had issued a proclamation that it would soon launch a full-scale military attack to reclaim the rebel city. It was in all the papers. The threat of retaliation had now been hanging over them for weeks, and Victor wished they would get on with it. It was inevitable. The idea of the rabble who had taken over the Commune actually being able to form a government was doubtful in the extreme. Saying they were going to build a better world for working people was all well and good, but he didn't believe it. When had it ever been better for working people?

Victor had done his best to ignore the news, to focus on ensuring the animals didn't suffer more than they had to, but now the whole thing was shoved right under his nose. He'd watched the barricades going up, the cannon being dragged into place. What would happen if troops began fighting amid the flowerbeds? The animals would go mad. It would be torture for them. He wished Papin were here. He would have known what to say to the little Polish general. He wished Anne were here. She would have . . . what?

He remembered talking to her, before Christmas, about the slaughter of the animals, and her look of contempt. Her look? She had excoriated him without even looking at him.

He gripped the bars of the lynx's cage in his anguish. The cat was a panting ball of fur, its head invisible, tightly curled with fear and misery. But what could he do?

Victor had spent his whole life – his whole life! – saying, *But what could I do?*

He remembered Anne's stony reply: 'Refuse.'

64

At the American hospital, they could only take the worst of the wounded. Those that did not need urgent surgery were bandaged up and sent to other private hospitals nearby. The most severely injured lay in the corridors, groaning, crying out, or – worse – silent. Nurses and even orderlies were triaging men as they lay on the floor – bringing water, cleaning them, staunching their wounds with rags. Medical staff were near impossible to find; they practically dragged people off the street to help and still they did not have enough.

At the table next to Ellis, in the former breakfast room, Logue kept up a desultory flow of remarks unrelated to the resection he was working on. He talked about his club in London, about memorable meals he had eaten – anything but what was going on around them. Ellis was grateful for the thread of triviality, as the warm westerly wind brought the sound of gunfire to the open windows.

The unconscious body on his table was female. Women had joined the fighting in the western forts and, now that the army was pushing into the city itself, more women were involved. This patient was in her forties, he guessed, and wore the blood-soaked uniform of a *cantinière*. She had been brought from the Trocadéro, where a shell fragment had torn into her side. In all his time working in the hospital in Washington, he had never treated a woman for battle wounds.

Ellis passed his sleeve over his damp forehead. He had no Soeur Débarras by his side. He had asked for her when he came back to work, but this time the nurses were from a different convent. He missed her calm confidence. The nurse assisting him now was young and inexperienced, and deferred to him at every step. She gave the impression of thinking him possessed of infallible knowledge and skill, so he found it difficult to talk to her. He finished sewing up the ragged tear in the woman's flank. The shell fragment had missed the major arteries, but had nicked the liver. She might live.

At lunchtime, the surgeons went to a neighbourhood café. Another cartload of wounded had just been delivered. The ambulance men said that the Versaillais were shooting anyone who surrendered. Ellis knew not to believe everything he heard, but, while he ate, he scribbled a note to Lawrence, begging him not to go back to the Hôtel de Ville.

Logue and another surgeon, an Englishman called Reid, were talking about a patient who had died that morning. The man had a bullet lodged in his shoulder, which was removed without complication, but shortly after surgery he stopped breathing. Reid, who had operated, was morose.

'He was in an advanced state of alcoholism,' said Logue. 'With such debility, death is not to be wondered at. Half my patients are drunk when they come in.'

'You can't blame them. They're afraid,' said Ellis.

Fear wasn't the only reason. The injured Communard had been suffering from full-blown delirium tremens before the operation. They gave him bromide of potassium, the usual treatment for such cases, and he calmed down, but he never woke from the anaesthesia. Ellis pictured Lawrence, briefly, as he would have touched a talisman.

Reid went back to the hotel. Logue and Ellis called for more coffee. None of them expected to go home that night.

'How are you? All right?' asked Logue quietly.

'Yes. I'm fine. And you? The noise doesn't bother you?'

'No. Strange that it doesn't.' He lowered his voice further. 'I meant to ask, how is your friend? Is he safe?'

Ellis glanced at the envelope beside him. 'Yes. I hope so. He's working as a journalist – at the Hôtel de Ville. Not the best place.'

'But he's a foreigner? The French army won't dare attack foreigners. They can threaten vengeance on Communards all they like, but he'll be all right.' He patted Ellis on the shoulder.

As they walked into the hotel, Logue smoothed a hand over his hair and drew himself up, pulling back his shoulders. He'd confided to Ellis the reason: Logue, an eternal romantic, was smitten by one of the new members of staff – an orderly. The young man was a Creole, quick and efficient, with a handsome, boyish face and a teasingly remote manner. Ellis thought Logue was unlikely to find favour there, but you never knew. War made stranger things happen.

Fanny followed the women west, towards the fighting. The Red Virgin, Citoyenne Michel, was at the head of the group, wearing a filthy Guard uniform, a red sash around her waist, holding a rifle as if it were part of her. Her words had swept them from Chateau d'Eau to Clichy – words full of passion and anger. She had two lieutenants in the impromptu brigade: one was a young, well-dressed Russian, with a fierce, beautiful face, and the other was a woman Fanny knew. This was an aspiring actress and model called Céline Cerf, and their paths had crossed at Studio Lamy. They had posed together, on occasion, and Fanny remembered her as a terrible flirt, but good fun. Now, she wore a red liberty cap, and her uniform was much the smartest of the three – Fanny wondered if it had been specially tailored, it was so dashing – but she handled her rifle with just as much aplomb.

'You should come with us,' she'd said, after they had greeted each other.

'But I wouldn't know what to do,' Fanny said, still reeling from the surprise of seeing her in such different circumstances.

Céline grinned. 'Nor did I, last week; nor did any of us. It's easy, once you've practised a bit.'

Fanny took a deep breath. What were her choices? To sit at home, eating her heart out with worry, or cowering in Madame Lamy's kitchen, feeling like a traitor to all she believed. Neither would help Raymond.

There were at least three dozen women in the group, all full of a righteous fervour that spilled over into high spirits and singing. On their march, Fanny learnt some names, and a smattering of reasons for their choosing to fight: Léodile's son had been mortally wounded at Issy and she swore revenge on the soldiers who killed him; Elisabeth was a seventeen-year-old laundress, who believed passionately in the Commune's programme of social reform; Jeanne, a grandmother, was sick of being treated like a dog. Fanny was elated to walk beside them.

They stopped for a lesson in rifle shooting, firing at a wall covered with advertisements. Fanny expected the heft of the rifle she was given, but she was stunned by the recoil, which bruised her shoulder, and by the deafening noise, and the heat of it. But twice she managed to hit her target, and she grinned across at Céline after hitting her poster for the second time. She was taking charge of her future in a way that counted, perhaps for the first time in her life. She had no qualms imagining a human being in her sights, instead of a poster for nerve pills.

As they marched westward, the noise of warfare grew louder: the rumble of cannon, overlaid by the intermittent crackle of rifle fire. If she felt her courage waver, Citoyenne Michel would turn around from the head of the column just at that moment, it seemed, and shout words of encouragement that were better than brandy. The excitement was so powerful that Fanny's worry over Raymond retreated until she barely felt it. If the others felt no fear, why should she?

Poster issued by Commune's Committee of Public Safety, afternoon of 22 May 1871:

Citizens of Paris,

We have suffered the siege, the bombardments, the famine, the plots and the betrayals.

Are we going to allow our efforts to be destroyed by an army of reactionaries?

It is up to the people to defend our revolution.

We fought to obtain it, we will die to defend it.

To the barricades!

65

Overnight, the gunfire stopped. Perhaps, Victor thought, it was already over. But, even before dawn lightened the sky, heralding another beautiful day, the cannon started up again, louder than before. Victor threw on his clothes and hurried to the menagerie. In the depleted enclosures, there was a palpable sense of terror. He went straight to the feline pavilion, where the cats were snarling, roaring and trembling. The lynx was pressed into the deepest corner of its cage, but he could see the rapid pounding of its heart through the fur. Tancred was pacing, uttering low, angry warnings. The lioness was on her hind legs, hissing with fury, trying to escape from her enclosure. He hurried to the last cage and what he saw there scared him the most: Marguerite stared through the bars and swayed from side to side – something he had never seen before. Her eyes were fixed and glassy. He felt as if he, too, were on the verge of madness.

Robitaille arrived, his normally impassive face twisted with emotion.

'Monsieur, they're coming to evacuate us.'

'What do you mean, evacuate us? Who is?'

'I've just seen the sergeant at the munitions dump. He says we have to clear out. I told him, of course, we couldn't, because of the animals, and he said, then . . . he said we must shoot them. Or they will.'

Victor felt strangely calm. 'Why do they want us evacuated? What do they think will happen here?'

'He wouldn't say. But I think things are going badly.'

Robitaille meant going badly for the Commune. To Victor, this was good news. On the other hand, drunken soldiers with guns – any soldiers – were not to be trusted around his animals. He told Robitaille to bring him a couple of men and a hand cart. The head keeper came back an hour later, with two disreputable-looking elderly men. One was clearly drunk, the other bleary eyed and frail looking, but Robitaille assured him that they were the best he could find.

Victor had calculated the doses according to weight. They began with the lynx, loading his comatose body on to a cart and wheeling him to the veterinarian's house. Lush spring foliage shielded them from the guards in the park, had any of them been looking. Victor had already sent the servants away, telling them it was for their own safety. They laid the lynx on the floor of the study. Drew the curtains. A bucket of water. A bucket of meat. They repeated the trip until all the cats were shut up in separate rooms: the lioness in the dining room; Tancred in the library. Marguerite was the last, taking the longest to lose consciousness. She was so heavy that, even with four of them, they could hardly drag her. If she hadn't lost so much weight during the siege, they would not have managed it, but at last she was laid out on the floor of the drawing room where Monsieur Papin used to take his tea – where they had sat with Anne, all those months ago, eating *puits d'amour*. The shutters were closed and the curtains drawn; the animals had food and water. He hoped and believed that, over the next day or two, the Versaillais army would reclaim Paris and the cats wouldn't have made too much of a mess. Anyway, what was some mess compared to the life of his Marguerite?

He paid the old men and swore them to secrecy with threats. They assured him they wouldn't breathe a word and went off to drink their wages. Victor felt some of the long-held tension seep out of his body.

'The others will have to take their chances. Kako won't make a noise – hopefully they'll just ignore him – and I don't suppose anyone will bother with the reptile house.'

He turned to see Robitaille fumbling awkwardly with his cap.

'What is it, Robitaille?'

'Monsieur Calmette, I have done my duty, have I not?'

'Always, Robitaille.'

'And God knows when I was last paid. No, it's not that. I'm sorry, but I have to go now – you understand?'

Victor looked at Robitaille, with whom he had worked for the last eleven years. He had seen him almost every day, but he knew next to nothing about him. But he did understand. Robitaille was too old for conscription to a battalion, so, if he meant to fight, it was because his heart told him to.

'Do you think that's wise, Robitaille?'

'Sometimes one has no choice.' He seemed unable to go on.

God, thought Victor, has his son been killed, or something terrible like that? He hadn't seen the son since he was a boy – he must now be, what, in his twenties?

'Of course you have a choice.'

'I have to go,' Robitaille repeated.

'Well, yes . . . all right, then. I will see you soon,' he said firmly, and held out his hand.

Robitaille looked grave as he took it. 'I hope so, monsieur.'

Fanny spent the night behind the big barricade. The shooting died down with nightfall, and they took turns to rest and keep watch. She had curled up on the pavement in her shawl, thinking, I will never, ever sleep like this, and had woken up when the sky was milky with dawn. Some women had gone off to find food, and came back with bread and cheese, which they shared between them. She wondered briefly whether Raymond was also waking up like this, behind a barricade somewhere.

She had fired her rifle yesterday, aiming at distant red-trousered figures just visible several hundred metres down the boulevard. She did not know what happened to her bullets; there was too much smoke and dust, and she found it extremely difficult to keep her eyes open when squeezing the trigger. It was not that the thought of killing a Versaillais soldier bothered her. They had tried to kill Raymond and had shot and killed so many others. Yesterday, they put an old woman, whose son they had killed, up against a wall and shot her in cold blood. Citoyenne Michel had told them this, her eyes blazing.

'And yet she did not falter, citoyennes. She cursed them with her dying breath.'

After the meal, Céline Cerf came to crouch beside her. Somehow, her hair still looked shiny, her dark curls full of life. She was excited; her eyes and teeth gleamed. Fanny grinned back at her.

'They've probably brought up more artillery. Today, we'll see some fun!'

War showed you who people really were. Céline had told her that she was doing this because of her mother, who had been evicted from her lodgings after the siege, whereupon she caught a chill that turned into pneumonia. It was all over in a week. Her death was the fault of the government, whose laws were in favour of the landlords and their class. They did not care about people like her.

'They call us communists. Fools! If being a communist is to ask for respect, to ask for a decent chance in this world, then, fine, I am a communist.'

Céline laughed and Fanny nodded in agreement. The first golden streaks of day lightened the sky behind them. Even the sun was on their side.

From the last edition of *Le Bonnet Rouge*, Tuesday, 23 May, 1871:

Parisians, we have suffered the siege, the bombardments, the famine, the plots and the betrayals, are we going to allow our efforts to be destroyed by an army of reactionaries? We have had enough of generals with gold braid and ornaments. Make way for the people, the bare-armed fighters! The hour of revolutionary warfare has struck!

66

By lunchtime on Tuesday, the Hôtel de Ville was filling up with wounded. They came in limping, supported on shoulders, piled in carts, carried on sacks. They were left on the floor of the entrance hall, or laid, end to end, down the corridors. There were no doctors to treat them. The Versaillais army had simply swept around the main barricades in the centre to take Montmartre from the north, and the Tricolore was flying from the Solferino Tower. Another army of Versaillais was working its way up the Left Bank. Even in the Hôtel de Ville, few pretended that the ramshackle defenders, grossly outnumbered and faced with overwhelming firepower, could resist much longer.

That morning, Jean-Luc had not turned up at the mortuary. Lawrence and Lhermitte left the dead to their own devices to do what they could for the living, which was almost nothing. They brought them water, dribbled from large jugs straight into their mouths, cleaned off the worst of the blood, took down names and addresses. They ran out of paper and scribbled names on the wall above where they lay – walls already spattered with blood. Lhermitte was as matter of fact with the wounded as he had been with the dead, as though this was just another waystation on the journey they would all take, sooner or later. Lawrence found himself wiping away tears; men called to him, crying out, and wailing in pain, or terror, or because they were desperate to send a message before it was too late. He smiled and reassured them. His face ached from the effort; his voice sounded false and hearty. Was this how Ellis felt every day?

Then – he had no idea what time it was – a young, frock-coated Communard was beside him. A man he had never seen before.

'Are you Citoyen Harper? I've been looking for you. We need you and your camera.'

'Really? Can't it wait? I'm trying to—'

'No. Now. If you please.'

Lawrence followed the man up the gilded staircase and through parts of the building he had never seen before. He was led down a hushed corridor, where his feet sank into thick carpet, and then was surprised to be ushered into an ornate bedroom. On the bed, on a bedspread of blue satin, lay the body of a man in uniform.

'You have to make his portrait. It's important.'

Lawrence stared. The dead man was quite young, with fair hair slicked over a high forehead, wide cheekbones and a neatly trimmed beard. Despite his youth, he wore medals, and there were gold flashes on his shoulders.

'Who is he?' said Lawrence, keeping his voice low.

'Why, it's General Dombrowski.' The Communard's voice cracked with tears.

Lawrence felt a surge of unease. He knew the name – everyone did. General Dombrowski was the Commune's commander in chief, their military genius. The Versaillais had offered him half a million francs to give up Paris, but he had refused. Some thought he'd taken the bribe, and that was how the army had entered the city. Now, he was dead, like any common soldier, gunned down at a barricade.

'His last words were, "Do they still think I'm a traitor?"' The youth took out a handkerchief and blew his nose.

After he'd printed the plate of the dead general, he handed it to the Communard, who took it with both hands, as if it were a holy relic. They walked downstairs together, and Lawrence said, 'Citoyen, what is happening? Is the city going to fall?'

The young man shook his head, but the look in his eyes was pure terror. Then he gave a gasping laugh and clapped him on the shoulder. 'Long live the Commune!' he cried, and disappeared around a corner.

The government onslaught erupted suddenly with daybreak and was relentless – a barrage of artillery aimed directly at their barricade, pounding into the massive wall of cobblestones and sandbags. Fanny could not see, or hear, or breathe. The barricade swallowed shot after shot after shot. It held, but they were deafened and deluged with dust and sand. Choking, she scrambled up to the notch in the barricade and peered through, but could make out nothing. To her left, she saw something move: an arm waving feebly among the cobbles. She put her hand on a sandbag, which moved in a strange way, and she recoiled, realizing it was someone's back, grey and warm, but still, utterly still. Baring her teeth, Fanny put her rifle muzzle through the breach and fired into the heart of the cloud.

For some time – hours? minutes? – Fanny fired and reloaded and fired into the murk. Sometimes she saw flickers of movement, flashes of red clothing. Sometimes they stopped moving. Céline, who was at the notch to her right, aimed carefully, and she heard her whoop: she had got one! But Fanny never saw anyone fall. She fired a couple more times, then ran out of bullets.

She slithered down the side of the barricade to find more ammunition, staggering towards a grey figure whose dust-smeared face was unrecognizable. She pointed to her gun, explaining. The figure shouted at her, but, though Fanny saw her lips moving, she couldn't hear any words. It was the Russian, her beauty blotted out by a thick layer of dust. Another shell landed just in front of the barricade, making them both throw themselves to the ground. When Fanny finally uncoiled and looked around, there was no sign of the Russian.

Where would she find bullets? She staggered back to the barricade, recognized the smart boots emerging from the embrasure above her and reached up to tap Céline on the ankle. She would tell her that she had to go and find ammunition, so she didn't think she was deserting her post. Céline didn't respond, so Fanny climbed up to her, shouting her name. They were all made deaf, but she had shouted at her for a good minute before she realized that Céline would never hear anything again. There was a hole above her right eye. Her eyes were still narrowly open, as though she were sighting along her rifle, but the irises were already filmed with dust. The only thing that moved was a curl on her forehead. Fanny stared. Then she wrested Céline's rifle out of her hands and unbuckled her munitions belt. It took her an age to drag it from under the limp, heavy body. Then she was aware of voices, and someone tugging at her skirt.

'Citoyenne! We have to fall back. Come on!'

Fanny looked around – it was Elisabeth, the laundress. Her round, childlike face was smeared with blood.

'She's dead!' she yelled. 'Céline—'

'Come *on*! For God's sake – before this clears and they start again!'

Fanny slid down the barricade without another glance at the body and followed the girl. They ran after the others, bent double, keeping close to the wall of blind shopfronts, given temporary amnesty by dust.

When Lawrence emerged from the Hôtel de Ville into the square, he was struck by the sky. It was a sick colour, the sunlight turned to ochreous haze, and a pall of smoke obscured the view to the west. He smelt burning. Up ahead, smoke cast a veil over the Rue de Rivoli, but more smoke rose to his left, across the river. Automatically, he checked the line of sight towards the Studio Lamy, beyond the towers of Notre Dame. No smoke there, at least. Did that mean it was safe?

He had to take a tortuous route to get to the Rue Rambuteau, avoiding the barricades. When a National Guardsman grabbed him by the arm, he pointed to his red-cross armband and said, 'American hospital,' very firmly, and was allowed on his way.

He hoped Ellis would be there, but, even if he wasn't, he meant to ask for help. Perhaps they could spare some nurses for the wounded at the Hôtel de Ville? But, the hospital seemed as chaotic as the city hall. A nun in a winged headdress asked his business. He said he was looking for Monsieur Butterfield. He explained the situation at city hall, and the nun shrugged helplessly.

'Monsieur, we have not enough nurses for our wounded here. Not enough doctors, not enough orderlies, not enough anything.'

She turned to a slim figure bending over a body in the corridor. 'Monsieur Noury! This gentleman is looking for Monsieur Butterfield. Is he back from lunch?'

At first, Lawrence thought he was hallucinating, but the smooth, still face and downcast eyes were unmistakably those of Anne Petitjean. Also, she was wearing an old suit of his. Anne's eyes flickered towards him with a flare of alarm, but she said, 'Please, monsieur, if you wait outside, I will come and find you in a moment,' and he nodded and turned back to the street. It was no more shocking than any other event of the last few days.

In a couple of minutes, Anne appeared by his side. She walked up to him, frowning, and looked right and left before speaking.

'Are you going to give me away?'

'No, of course not, An— er, tell me your name.'

'I am Antoine Noury.'

'Very well, Monsieur Noury. You have nothing to fear from me, I promise. But . . . how do you come to be here?'

She shrugged. 'I worked in a hospital before. I can work in one again.'

'Of course. And – Monsieur Butterfield? Does he know?'

'No! Why would he?'

'No, I just . . .' Just assumed that Ellis would know whatever was in his own mind. But Ellis had never seen Anne, only heard the story about a poor, feminine fugitive. 'No reason. Don't worry – I'll say nothing to anyone. I'm glad you're safe.' *Safe* was probably the wrong word.

'Monsieur Butterfield is still at lunch. The surgeons go to the Café des Archives, down there, on the corner. You won't miss it.' She pointed eastwards.

'Thank you, Monsieur Noury.' Lawrence's hand went to his hat before he could stop himself, so he turned it into an unnecessary adjustment.

Incredible that, only a few blocks away, men were killing each other and shops on the Rue de la Paix were burning like Roman candles, but cafés were still serving chops and tarte tatin. Lawrence smelt roasting meat, onions and garlic as he walked in, and remembered he hadn't eaten for hours.

He saw Ellis's blond head at a table with two other men and felt his stomach clench. He made his way over. Ellis's eyes narrowed when he saw him, but he smiled and introduced Lawrence in English, and asked if he had eaten. The other doctors stood up, saying they had to get back, but one, an etiolated Englishman, urged Ellis to stay.

'You got my note?' Ellis asked, as Lawrence picked up an end of bread and began eating.

He nodded. 'I don't think the Hôtel de Ville will last much longer. I was told – unofficially – to get out. But the halls are full of wounded, with no one to see to them.'

Ellis bent towards him and pressed his thigh against his under the table. 'The army are attacking down the Rue de Rivoli now.'

'I saw the smoke. You might have to evacuate.'

'We should be all right. We're protected. Geneva Convention and all that. And they won't want to antagonize the Americans.'

He looked up as the waiter brought a plate heaped with chops and sautéed potatoes. Lawrence fell on it. Ellis watched him.

'Listen – you can't go back to the Hôtel de Ville now.'

'But all those wounded. It's awful. And I'm worried about the Lamys. There's an enormous barricade right outside the house.'

'They're bourgeois. They'll be fine. All they have to do is sit tight. All of western Paris is rejoicing, now they've been liberated.'

'It can't last much longer, can it?' Lawrence lowered his voice. 'I just photographed General Dombrowski's corpse, so who's in charge now?'

Ellis frowned at the news. Even he knew the gravity of it. Then he shrugged. 'I'm just glad you're here now. I was worried about you.'

Lawrence swallowed a mouthful of potatoes and felt warmth flood through him. 'And I you. Can't you go home tonight? You have to sleep somewhere.'

'I don't think so. It's safest indoors. You must stay off the streets. In fact, why don't you help us at the hospital? We're desperate. We're reduced to taking down the names of the dying, so at least we can tell their families.'

'Do you mean it? Won't they think it odd?'

Ellis almost laughed. 'They would see it as a great favour. We're practically pulling people off the streets as it is.'

Lawrence scribbled a note to the Lamys to tell them where he would be. He felt a twinge of guilt, as though he was abandoning them, but Ellis was right. They would be safe in their home and, in any case, his presence would not help them.

Fanny was furious with herself. She had discovered for the first time that her eyesight was poor – too poor for her to shoot a rifle with any effect. She had never seen a body fall as a result of her effort. When her neighbour at the barricade said, 'By the lamppost. Big beard. He's mine . . .' she couldn't see anything. She said as much to the Russian, weeping with frustration, but the Russian told her to keep firing at chest height. Level the weapon to just above the ground, into the thickest smoke, fire, slide down, reload; creep up, check, level, fire, slide, reload.

Citoyenne Michel was amazing, almost superhuman – one minute on the barricade, shooting, then running to and fro, succouring the wounded, encouraging the faint hearted, her voice hoarse with shouting orders. She managed to magic up bread, ham and wine from somewhere to keep them going. But, even so, after a few more hours, Fanny didn't think she could go on much longer. Every part of her body ached, she had hurt her hand climbing a barricade, and there was a pain in her left knee whenever she bent it. A couple of hours ago, she had watched as the young laundress, Elisabeth, was hit by a shell fragment which tore away half her neck. They'd dragged her into a doorway and tried to staunch the blood, but her panicked eyes dimmed and she died. Fanny rejoined her post.

Place Blanche fell to the enemy at lunchtime. Those who were too badly wounded to walk had to be left, and some of them, out of ammunition, despairing, exhausted, turned their rifles upside down and waited for the Versaillais to take them prisoner.

But Fanny heard that the Lost Children were on the Left Bank, defending the Panthéon. Amid all the blood and horror, one thing seemed clear: if she was going to die, she would do it beside her husband. There were fires burning all along the Right Bank, but that was the way she had to go. She followed the others along the Boulevard des Martyrs. She simply turned down a side street, hobbling on her sore knee. She pulled her shawl over her head and held the rifle close to her skirts, her munitions belt looped over her shoulder. No one tried to stop her.

Anne was worried when she saw Monsieur Harper come back to the hospital, but he didn't so much as look at her. He walked in with the big, fair doctor, whose name was Butterfield, and it seemed that he had come to help the medical staff. Later, she saw him in the wards, speaking to wounded men and writing down their details. Then she was too busy to worry about where he was or what he was doing. She felt a rush of gratitude towards him. He had helped her in the bread queue, and at the Studio Lamy, and now it seemed he was helping her again. Why? She could see no benefit to him in it. Perhaps, she thought, he was simply kind.

At some later point, she was finishing cleaning up in the theatre, when a hand landed on her shoulder, and she jumped. She was so tired, she hadn't heard the footsteps. It was Monsieur Logue, the Irish surgeon, and she relaxed slightly. He had spoken to her before and was always polite and friendly.

'I didn't mean to startle you, Monsieur Noury! I was concerned; you haven't stopped work all day! You really need to go and get some food, and rest. I insist on it.'

Anne nodded and straightened up slowly. Her body was stiff with exhaustion.

'You look done in. Have you eaten at all today?'

'Um. I don't—'

'That's what I thought. I haven't eaten either. You can't work if you don't eat. Come, I'm inviting you.'

They went to the Café des Archives, where the dinner was far better than the sort of thing Anne was accustomed to, and she ate hungrily. She contrived to sit beside Monsieur Logue, rather than opposite him, so he couldn't stare at her face too much. Really, she thought, rather pleased with herself, she was getting quite good at this. She kept her eyes on her plate and answered the surgeon's questions with monosyllables. She had heard somewhere that Irish people were talkative, and he certainly was, and very interested in her background. Before she could stop herself, she had told him about her father.

'From Haiti? Goodness. Have you ever been there, yourself?'

'No.' Extraordinary question. She almost smiled at it. 'Both my parents are dead.'

'I'm sorry, Monsieur Noury. You must certainly try to visit the Antilles. I myself stopped off in Jamaica when I was coming back from America. It's a very beautiful country. The colours are extraordinary. Almost like one imagines the Garden of Eden.'

Anne muttered something non-committal. She determined to keep close to the truth, but not say too much. Monsieur Logue seemed to sense that his conversational overtures had run aground. He filled up their wine glasses again. She hadn't noticed finishing the last one. Now, he was asking her where she lived.

'Er, in Ménilmontant.'

'And what do you do when you are not working, Monsieur Noury? I expect you have a sweetheart?'

Anne sensed dangerous ground. 'A sweetheart? Um, no.'

'Ah? Well. Nor I. Nor I.'

Monsieur Logue ordered them the English pudding, telling her that the café was famous for it. If she'd been wearing stays, she wouldn't even have attempted it. No reason not to, now.

They had nearly finished the pudding when Monsieur Butterfield and Monsieur Harper came in. Monsieur Butterfield said that she was needed on the wards, and she scrambled up guiltily, wiping her mouth.

'Of course, monsieur. I'm coming. I'm sorry—'

'No, don't worry – whenever you're finished.'

'I'll walk back with Monsieur Noury,' said Monsieur Harper.

Monsieur Logue looked up, and a strange, pained expression flickered across his face, before vanishing behind a bland smile.

Walking along the Rue Rambuteau, Anne noticed there was grey powder on her coat. She brushed at it, which just smeared it into the cloth. Ash was raining softly from the orange sky.

Monsieur Harper glanced at her. 'They've set fire to the Records Office.'
'Oh? Who has?'

'Actually, I'm not sure, but it's on fire. Listen, there's something you should know. Um, Monsieur Logue, well – Monsieur Butterfield says he is *interested* in you.'

'Does he suspect? He did ask a lot of questions. I thought he was being friendly.'

'No, not at all, not like that. It's ...' Here, he lowered his voice, although distant cannon fire made this unnecessary. 'He is a man who prefers men to women, if you see what I mean.'

'Oh! But ...' Anne was astonished, then confused, then – 'Oh,' she repeated.

'We thought it best to warn you, in case he ... well ...'

Anne was taken aback; she'd assumed that Antoine Noury would shield her from all that.

'Monsieur Butterfield will drop some hints that he should leave you alone. He'll say that we know each other slightly and that ... that you are not that way.'

'Oh. So, does Monsieur Butterfield know?'

'I ... yes. But, rest assured, he will never tell a soul.'

Anne wondered, not for the first time, what it was men talked about when they were together. She had no idea. They turned into the court-yard in front of the hospital.

'Thank you, monsieur ... but, I don't understand.'

'What do you mean?'

Anne was lost, and it seemed important to get her bearings.

'Why are you being kind to me? What do you want?' She glanced at him just long enough to see him look unhappy, or perhaps cross. 'I mean,' she went on, 'you keep helping me, and I don't understand why. People don't help, usually.'

By 'people', she meant men. But it felt funny to say that to him. She could tell that Monsieur Harper was looking at her face.

'All I want is to be your friend. Perhaps because I think you know what it is to feel different. As do I.' He shrugged then, and walked into the hospital.

Anne waited before following him. She felt shame – she had clearly been in the wrong to ask him that. People were so confusing. What had he meant, about being different? Then something came to her: perhaps Messieurs Harper and Butterfield were like Marie-Jo and Lisa at the Salpêtrière. Like Monsieur Logue, come to that, which was why they had known . . . But now she was afraid she had made him angry.

When her shift finally came to an end and the nuns on the ward told her to get some sleep, she went outside. She had made up her mind she would walk back to Fanny's, but, once outside, she simply stood, feeling the exhausted weight of her limbs. It was night, but a sullen red glow lit the sky to the west. She went to the end of the street, from where she could see leaping orange light silhouetting a barricade on the Rue de Rivoli. Fires to the west, fires to the south. Fires on Île de la Cité, and other fires, over on the Left Bank. The Rue Royale in flames, the Rue Saint-Florentin . . . all those streets, with their beautiful shops: the grocer's where she'd bought oysters and fruit for Monsieur Papin. And the butcher's which had sold the bodies of the zoo animals – it, too, was up in flames. *Deservedly so*, said a wild, devilish voice in her head. *Burn it all down.*

Anne hunkered down in a doorway and watched the fires. Somehow, she knew she was safe here. An enormous roar made her flinch, but, wedged into the deep doorway, she couldn't fall. Above the rooftops sprouted a gigantic flower of flame, and thunder reverberated through the ground and in her bones. Was that the Louvre? The Tuileries Palace? She thought of Hippolyte Mazade, the Hippolyte of the Salpêtrière, when she and he had argued about the evidence of her own eyes and how she would know that her fear of fire was unfounded. Look to the evidence. Well, Monsieur Mazade, here is all the evidence you could ever need.

She was too tired to move, too tired even to be afraid; she drifted into a half-waking dream of Sister Bonaventura and her winged horses, and the fiery chariot of hell. Deep down, she felt a grim satisfaction, almost a triumph – perhaps, all along, it was not hysteria that had afflicted her, but foresight.

67

Towards mid-afternoon, Fanny found her husband. The 101st battalion was dug in at the western end of Boulevard Saint-Germain. A corps of Versaillais was attacking from the south-west, but the fortification manned by the Lost Children was a vast construction of sloping walls and hidden passages. Raymond was first astonished and then delighted to see her; he teased her about her rifle and munitions belt, and said they did not need more fighters. She would be more help to them as a *cantinière*. Fanny was relieved to give up her rifle to someone who could use it more effectively.

Raymond examined her weapon. 'Shit, it's a new one! Better than mine. Go up there and ask for Mireille – she runs the canteen. You may not be good at this, my dear, but I am – you'll see.'

He kissed her, positively cheerful as he went back to his place on the barricade. His confidence was contagious. When Fanny introduced herself to the women, one of the other *cantinières* said that Sergeant Klein was the best shot in the battalion, and looked at Fanny with an admiration tinged with envy.

A few hours later, the sky was dark and enormous fires lit up the Right Bank. Government cannon had pounded the barricade for hours and it was finally disintegrating. The Communards had only two pieces of artillery, and they had run out of ammunition. Fanny's relief on finding people who believed they would win had vanished. She had not spoken to Raymond since arriving. The position seemed to be going the way of the barricades in the north this morning: a desperate defence against insurmountable odds.

Then, one of the fighters – a boy no more than fourteen years old – came running up, calling, 'Is Citoyenne Klein here? Citoyenne Klein, that's you? Your husband . . .'

She ran.

Raymond was only wounded, shot through the shoulder, but he had lost a lot of blood. The boy, whose name was Fred, said there was a church that was taking in wounded further along the boulevard, and offered to help Fanny take him there. She bound Raymond's shoulder with pieces torn from her petticoat, and they supported him between them. He didn't complain of the pain, he was just bitter at leaving his post. Fanny sent up a secret prayer of thanks. She did not say it could only be a matter of time before they were overrun.

They found the church, but it was locked. Fred was dismayed, thinking he had made a mistake. Fanny looked around them.

'We'll just have to go on a bit further. It's not much further to the Lamys' studio. Come on, my love.'

They struggled on, avoiding the main road with its succession of barricades. The side streets were only lightly blockaded. At last, they reached the narrow alley and Fanny was hammering on the green door behind Studio Lamy. Raymond was getting heavier every moment. His face looked bad. Fanny cursed – what if the Lamys had left town?

'Madame! Sabine! It's Fanny!' she shouted in a cracked voice, over and over.

At length, there was a noise from inside, and Sabine's white face appeared in the crack of the door. She didn't want to let them in, but Fanny insisted she fetch Madame Lamy. Fanny prayed. She hadn't been to confession – even to Mass – for too long. She swore she would make up for it, if only, please God— Then madame opened the door, and, when she saw Fanny, and the boy, and Raymond fainting, soaked in blood, she ushered them inside.

Monsieur Lamy came and Fanny told the couple of their plight. Both of them looked worried, but Monsieur Lamy took her hand and pressed it, and Fanny burst into tears.

Between them, they managed – her, Fred and madame, since monsieur's arthritis was too bad – to get Raymond up the five flights of stairs. It took forever, but they agreed that the attic was the safest hiding place. The studio was so cluttered with equipment and set dressing that they could camouflage half a dozen people. Madame made up a bed for Raymond on the divan that Fanny had spent many cold hours draped over. Soldiers probably wouldn't suspect a prosperous, bourgeois business like theirs, but it was best to be on the safe side, so the bed was camouflaged by the Chinese screen and by stacked backdrops and drapery. No one giving the studio a cursory glance would think it was anything other than that.

Madame brought up bread, soup and brandy. Fanny thanked her profusely. She was so good; she could never repay her.

'Don't thank me. What are friends for?'

'And Sabine?' Fanny was worried about the cook.

'Don't worry about Sabine. I've put the fear of God into her. She might grumble, but she's got a good heart. No one saw you come into the alley?'

'No. I'm sure no one saw.' Fanny looked at Fred for confirmation.

He shook his head. 'I was looking behind us all the way. There was no one.' His voice wavered awkwardly between the child and the man, and that, added to his shyness, meant he hardly spoke.

Madame smiled at him. 'It was very good of you to help Fanny and her husband.'

Fred nodded, blushing, his cheeks bulging with bread. Filthy blond hair, stiff with dust, stood up in a halo around his face. Fred had no ideological fervour, didn't even seem to understand what he was fighting for; he had simply followed his father and brother. He told Fanny they were from Belleville, that they had been fighting together, but had become separated. He didn't know where they were.

'I'm sure they're all right,' said Fanny, putting her hand on his.

Fred nodded, his eyes on the floor.

'And your mother? Is she at home in Belleville?'

He shook his head. 'Maman passed away three years ago.'

'I'm sorry. Listen, we'll stick together, okay? You're with us, now.'

Fred looked at her, round eyes shining with tears, and nodded. When he could eat no more, he gave Fanny an awkward hug. Feeling his skinny shoulders, she was touched. She couldn't help noticing that he badly needed a bath – but then, so did she. Fanny made him a nest out of the costumes she had worn in the past, and he curled up on it, exclaiming with wonder at the fineness and glamour of the materials, then fell, mid-sentence, into a deep sleep.

Fanny fed Raymond soup and brandy, which revived him a little. They had one oil lamp, shielded so that no light would show in the skylights. It was like being in a tent of red-striped fabric, beyond which Fred snored.

With his good hand, Raymond took hers and squeezed it. 'Thank you, my little one. No, that's enough, now. I'll be all right, tomorrow . . . Have to get back . . .'

Fanny kissed his hand. 'I love you, my darling.'

Raymond looked at her. 'I love you, too. I don't deserve you. Promise you won't ever leave me.'

'Don't be silly,' she said, and kept his hand in hers until she was sure he was asleep.

From the window of Lawrence's room, Louise watched the fires spread until they made a curtain of flame that pulsed in the sky and made the Seine glitter with crimson jewels. She knew each burning landmark as well as she knew her own hands. There the Grand Palais was on fire, and there the Palais de Justice; the Tuileries, where the Emperor had lived, and the Palais Royale. The Prefecture of Police, the Records Office, the Conseil d'Etat and the Ministry of Finance; the Champs Élysées, and the grand streets of the 8th and the 1st arrondissements, with their fashion houses and jewellers, the grand hotels and the elegant churches. Everywhere the beau monde gathered and promenaded and spent their money was on fire. It felt as though the city's heart – or, if that was not its heart, then its beautiful, famous face – was being consumed before her eyes.

She went to bed when she couldn't bear to watch any longer. Then she got up because, when she closed her eyes, she imagined flames bounding towards them, overwhelming them. Serge reassured her – the fires were serious, but the Seine and the islands separated them. He promised he would keep an eye on the front of the house, in case of trouble there. So they took turns, having got Sabine to fill as many buckets and pans with water as she could find, and place them near the windows.

The street lights were out, which made it hard to tell what was going on. On this side of the great barricade, they saw occasional pinpricks of light as the guards lit their pipes and wandered about. Sometimes, they heard voices. Louise would occasionally climb the stairs to look out of Lawrence's window, to check on the Right Bank. The fires were still burning, but were no nearer, and the wind was in their favour.

'Surely this must be over soon,' Louise signed again. 'I hope we've got enough meat in; I only planned for three, and I doubt anyone will be open . . . I expect we'll cope. That poor boy – he's just a child. You know, Serge, in a way, I'm glad Fanny is here, even like this. I was so worried for her, thinking what she must be going through, worrying about *him*.'

Serge signed his agreement. Like her, he was deeply fond of Fanny. He had been a little in love with her when she first began working for them – but that was life, and an increased tendresse on his part led to some of his best work. But Fanny was special to both of them. She had an extraordinary affinity with the camera, and was such a sweet girl besides, always modest, sensible and cheerful. The sort of daughter anyone would want.

'I think I'm going to lie down for a bit,' Louise signed. 'Is that all right with you? I'll be up at six anyway, and then you can rest . . . Yes, you will, dear. Otherwise your hips will let you know about it.'

She touched her hand to her husband's cheek and went up to bed.

68

Sleep was hard to come by. The mutter and roar of the fires fought with the tocsin, rung from every church in the east of the city. It went on all night, sometimes falling still, then taking up again, now joined by the desperate rolling of drums. Lawrence was given a cot in one of the upstairs bedrooms shared with some other aides, but he slipped out to find Ellis, who, as a surgeon, was allocated a private room. It was cramped and smelt of carbolic, but they could be alone.

'I think I understand, a little, what it's been like for you,' he murmured, as they lay in the single bed.

Ellis, already falling asleep, merely grunted.

He listened to the tocsin. It was a desperate sound, struggling to keep time, faltering, not giving up.

'When this is over, let's go away . . .'

He remembered that Ellis was supposed to be going to America for his mother's wedding. He hadn't mentioned it again.

'We could go to Greece. Visit Thebes.'

'Mmm.'

Ellis rolled on to his side, and Lawrence shaped his body against his, pressing nose and lips against the skin in the centre of his back, inhaling its waxy warmth. He told himself that, even if Ellis went back, it didn't have to mean the end of them. But what was there to keep men like them together? There was no covenant, for them; no approbation. He kissed the patch of skin, over and over. I claim you, he thought. I claim you. This is my covenant.

Ellis groped for Lawrence's arm and pulled it around him.

Lawrence knew that he was strong enough to swim against the current. He felt strong enough for both of them, but he knew there was no such thing.

On Wednesday, the sun didn't rise. The sky was as dark as an eclipse; smoke blanketed the city with a thick pall, as far as the eye could see. It had been hot and dry for weeks, and now a wind got up and the fires spread. The warmth was the suffocating heat of things burning. Everything smelt of petrol – the air, the bed linen, their clothes, their hair. Even the water tasted of it.

The hospital was some blocks away from the burning streets, but, before they closed the windows, gusts of wind blew in flurries of charred fragments – the tax records of Paris from the burning Ministry of Finance and the Cour des Comptes, it was said. They seized on the joke: one good thing, at last!

A newly arrived orderly reported that the Hôtel de Ville was ablaze. The Commune had fired it and withdrawn to a town hall in the eastern districts. That was it, surely: an admission of defeat. Lawrence felt sick – had all the wounded been evacuated? – but he was kept so busy carrying patients from ward to surgery and back that he forgot about it. On his way back from lunch, he made his way to a junction from where he could see the Hôtel de Ville. It had been the centre of the Commune; now, he glimpsed its chimneys only through roiling smoke, silhouetted by flames. Where he stood was north of the block that contained the Boucherie Ranvier; that whole stretch of Rue de Rivoli was ablaze. Presumably, Ranvier himself was with Ernestine in the country, but his business was being devoured. Lawrence couldn't avoid a sneaking satisfaction: some recompense for the butchered beauties – for Pépin the gentle giraffe and Cleopatra the camel, the joyful elephants and all the others. Surely Ranvier would be impoverished by this loss. Would Ernestine still marry him?

Something jabbed him in the kidneys and he turned with an exclamation of annoyance. He saw an ash-smeared uniform, a heavy moustache, a rifle with stained bayonet.

'Careful with that thing, citoyen,' Lawrence said – then, too late, realized his mistake.

'What did you say?' The Versaillais peered at him. Two more government soldiers were close behind.

'Look, I'm on my way to the American hospital.' Lawrence gestured with his left arm at the red-cross armband. 'I work there. I'm Canadian, a British subject. So, if you'll excuse me—'

'Papers,' said the first soldier – an officer, going by the gold on his shoulders.

Lawrence felt in his pocket for the hospital letter; thank God, it was there. He held it out and the man studied it. Lawrence held out his hand to take it back, and the man stared, looked him up and down. His face was slack and he smelt of brandy.

'Sergeant, the hospital is gravely understaffed and it is vital—'

At some signal, the other two advanced and seized him by the arms.

'Bring him!' The officer turned and began to walk. The others kept a tight hold and began to drag Lawrence between them.

'What are you doing? I am no Communard. I'm a Canadian citizen. I work for the American hospital, and therefore I am protected by the Geneva Convention—'

One of the soldiers holding him wrenched his arm in its socket, turning his palm upwards.

'What's that, then? You've been firing a rifle, *citoyen.*'

Lawrence looked in horror at his black-stained palm and fingers.

'I'm a photographer! That's staining from silver nitrate! It isn't powder stains! All photographers have stained hands, for God's sake!'

'Thought you worked in a hospital. Now you're a photographer. Which is it?'

'I'm both . . . It's true! Just take me to the hospital on Rue Rambuteau. Hotel Florentin. Take me there. Ask them!' Lawrence cried, and pulled back against the vice-like hands.

It was a mistake. The officer turned and pressed the point of his bayonet into Lawrence's stomach. Just far enough to hurt. He didn't breathe.

'Another word from you and I'll leave your corpse in the gutter.'

Lawrence allowed himself to be led. His mind raced: When we get to their superior, he will understand. There will be someone of intelligence, somewhere – someone sober. Then they turned a corner and his heart missed a beat. A group of men were huddled together, heads bowed and faces blank. Many wore bloodstained Guard uniforms. One man – his head swathed in a makeshift bandage – could only stand with the support of his neighbours. Prisoners.

That was when panic set in. He began to shout: the wounded men were entitled to medical care; the man with the head wound should be in hospital; they were bound by the Geneva Convention to ensure that—

The officer turned to Lawrence, and the hatred in his eyes made him quail.

'No, *citoyen*, the Geneva Convention protects combatants wounded in a justified war. You are not combatants; you are common criminals.'

Lawrence barely knew what he was saying: This was all a mistake; he was Canadian. He wasn't a Communard but a photographer; they couldn't do this to him. The embassy would find out and there would be trouble . . . He was innocent!

He yelled for help, in French and then in English. Something hit him on the side of the head – so hard, he staggered and nearly fell. When he righted himself, his eyes met those of one of his fellow prisoners: a small, spare man, at least twice his age, in the blue smock of a worker.

Skin and clothes alike were smeared with ash. Bloodshot eyes bored into his. Lawrence's protests died away. He felt ashamed.

The group was jerked into movement, stumbling in a line. After they had shuffled along for a few minutes, there was shouting and they were halted. Two soldiers came out of a doorway, pushing a man with his arms behind his back. He wore the red belt of the Commune. The officer went over and spoke to the soldiers. Their captive lifted his chin and spat in the officer's face. Lawrence felt his bowels turn to water.

The man smiled, took a deep breath and managed to shout, 'Long Live the—'

The shots were deafening. In the ensuing silence, the man sagged forward, crumpling into a heap, with his head on the officer's foot. The officer made an exclamation of disgust, then kicked the body away.

'Move this rubbish out of the way.'

The two soldiers who had fired the shots looked at each other with a long-suffering air, then bent and picked up a foot apiece. They dragged the dead man to one side of the street, his head bouncing off the cobbles with a sound Lawrence would never forget.

69

Ernestine's fiancé had found them safe shelter in a village thirty kilo-metres east of Paris, in the area still occupied by the Prussian army. Monsieur Ranvier – Charles – had rented a *maison de maître*, where Ernestine had her own rooms, while Charles, his elderly mother and his young son stayed in a separate wing. Given the circumstances, it was quite respectable.

Since the war with Prussia was now over, they could be friends with their new neighbours, and last night they had been handsomely entertained by Kapitan Dreiberg, who was billeted at the local manor house. The kapitan had informed them that the pall of smoke hanging over Paris came from buildings along the Right Bank, from the Tuileries to the Hôtel de Ville. The communists, knowing they were going to lose, had set fire to them out of spite.

Charles's face drained of colour. His shop was directly in the path of the burning. When he admitted as much, the kapitan, a merry, mous-tachioed man, who was very gallant with Ernestine, looked crestfallen.

'What about the Left Bank? Do you know if there is any damage there?' Ernestine asked, trying to swallow the tightness in her throat. Her parents were so stubborn. Why couldn't they have accepted Charles's offer to bring them here?

'As far as I know, mademoiselle, there is no conflagration there. So – ah, your parents – I understand your concern, but they have the wide and mighty Seine between them. It is buildings associated with the state – the government, the old empire and so on – that are a target for the mischief makers.'

Charles put his hand on hers and patted it, and smiled sympathetically, which did not make her feel better.

He controlled his rage until they were in the carriage on their way back.

'My God, these people are animals! Savages! Atheists! I hope they get what's coming to them. The Emperor was far too lenient with dissent and look where it has led! These vermin must be destroyed once and for all!'

He slammed his fist into the palm of his other hand. His lips shone with spittle. Ernestine looked at him. This was more passion than she had ever seen him show about anything. Charles saw her look and collected himself.

'I'm sorry to be such a fire breather. You are shocked, of course, but then, you are a tender-hearted woman –'

Ernestine smiled. Sometimes, she thought he had absolutely no idea who she was.

'– you would show even these miscreants mercy, I am sure.'

'No, I would not. I would show no mercy to those who shoot French soldiers and who set fire to palaces. But my parents' maid, for example: I know she is a sympathizer, but she is a good, modest girl and a churchgoer. They are not all atheists and communists.'

'Well, I'm sure your little maid is not taking potshots at soldiers. I am talking of those who do such things – who set fire to the businesses of honest, hard-working—' His voice rose an octave: 'I finished those refurbishments only a year ago! Do you know how much it cost me? I will never get that back!'

Ernestine was not unsympathetic. She shared his anger over the destruction of his business. It offended her soul to think of communists and anarchists setting fire to nice buildings – it was all jealousy and spite, wanting to tear things down because they themselves had nothing, so everyone should have nothing, but—

'Ernestine, tomorrow, I thought we might take the carriage over to Saint Maur; Dreiberg said there are some very fine views around there. Mother would like it. She loves the spring flowers.'

Ernestine sighed. 'I can't think about it, right now. My parents—'

'Of course, it is a worry. If only they had come with us. Let's see how you feel in the morning.'

He looked towards her and took her hand in his.

In the morning, Ernestine claimed a headache and stayed behind when the others went for their drive. The windows of the sitting room faced west, so she could see the grey pall that hung over the city, now spread into a vast cloud that blocked out the sunlight. With deep misgiving in her heart, she wrote a letter to her parents and rang for the maid. Was there still a post? Could she send the carriage for her parents? Charles's carriage had been unable to reach their home before the fighting started ... Would they agree to leave, anyway? If only she could see what was happening at home, perhaps she would worry less.

She was angry at Charles for insisting that she leave Paris. She was angry with herself; she could have refused. She was angry at her parents' stubbornness, but she knew that they, too, loved the business that they had built up, and wanted to protect it from harm. She was angry at many things, not least her fiancé showed less concern for her parents than for his glorified pie shop. Last night, as they sat in silence in the carriage, she'd had to quell the urge to pick up his hand and bite it.

70

Blue smoke swathed the Rue des Ciseaux in drifting veils, making it hard to see anything, and there was a peculiar sound in the air: a spitting and buzzing. The blue smoke came from the cannon and rifles; it eddied through the warm air and mingled with black smoke from the burning buildings. Through it all, a black snow was falling – soft flakes danced through the air and rained gently on to the pavement. Everything was covered in a soft grey layer of ash.

The plane trees that shaded the house in summer were losing their leaves. Swarms of green confetti fluttered to the ground and mingled with the ash. After the first hour, Louise realized that the spitting sound was bullets cutting through the air, stripping the leaves from the branches. Horrified, she signed to Serge, who could not hear it – he must not go outside; the air was full of death. He signed back – he had realized it before her. No one was going outside.

The Lamys kept their vigil by the dining-room window as the battle came nearer, peering through the drawn curtains. Dead bodies lay where they fell. Even in the June days of '48, neither of them had seen anything like this. At least the poor horse that had been caught in the crossfire now lay still.

The Communards had retreated, barricade by barricade, and were now defending the one nearest them, between the chocolate shop and the café. They fought tenaciously, heroically, hopelessly. It seemed insane to Louise that they were willing to die for this – for what exactly? A few metres of street? A principle? For the Commune? They were going to lose in the end, so why wouldn't they save themselves while they still could?

The fugitives in the attic made no sound. This morning, when she had taken up food and water, she told them the soldiers were coming closer, so, at some point, she hoped, the wave of fighting would wash past and then it would be safe to leave. Last night, she'd been struck by something almost frightening about Fanny – she looked so bedraggled, yet she was so resolute.

Back in March – it seemed far more than two months ago – she and Fanny had talked about the Commune, and what it stood for, and Louise conceded that better lives for working people was a laudable goal, and, yes, the government had been wrong to expect people to pay their rents and debts after four months of hunger. But then the Commune had flung the poor old Archbishop in jail, and, by unspoken agreement, they never discussed it again.

A part of her wished she had not opened the door last night, and she didn't want to go up to the attic now. Perhaps, if she didn't, they would magically disappear. If only Fanny had not been with her boorish pig of a husband. But he was injured and needed help. You had to help people in trouble, that was what Christianity was all about. No one could blame her for that, surely?

She must have drifted off in her chair, because, when she started awake, her chin was wet with saliva. She heard Serge's limping footsteps on the stairs – he was going down to the shop – and then it came again: a deep pounding that made the very walls of the house shake. Dust trickled in a light shower from the ceiling. Louise wiped her face and heaved herself to her feet.

In the shop, there were clouds of dust, inside as well as out. A shocking hole had appeared in the wall behind their counter. Dust-covered figures wielded sledge hammers and a ram: they were tunnelling into the shop from the bakery next door. They shouted to them to stand back. Louise clutched Serge's arm as they retreated, shielding their faces from the dust.

When the soldiers had climbed through, they explained themselves, quite politely. They wanted to use one of their upstairs windows to attack the big barricade from behind. The officer in charge spoke with confidence that the Lamys, a couple of good *honnêtes gens*, were happy for this to happen. Serge pointed to his mouth and made the usual sign that he couldn't speak, but gestured that, naturally, they could follow him upstairs, and welcome.

'But messieurs . . .' said Louise faintly, her eyes flicking to her husband's. He looked calm. Her own face felt stiff with horror. These men were going to shoot the defenders from their house – shoot them in the back. But, if they refused, they would search the house, find the fugitives and take them prisoner – take Serge and her prisoner as well . . . All this crossed her mind in an instant. 'Yes, of course.'

'Who else lives here, madame?'

'Just me and my husband, and our cook, Sabine. Our daughter has left town, thank the Lord.'

'And this is your business?'

'Of course. We've been here for years.'

They trooped upstairs, the soldiers' boots sounding heavily on the floorboards. Louise hoped that Fanny could hear and that they would stay absolutely still and hidden. She felt sick. Serge showed the Versaillais into the drawing room, but the soldiers wanted to go higher, to get a better angle.

She led them, talking loudly, up to their bedroom. They were still two floors away from the attic. The soldiers went to the window, peered out and pronounced themselves satisfied.

'Thank you, madame, for doing your patriotic duty,' said the officer, as she withdrew, shutting the door after her. She was trembling. She believed the soldiers were in the right, but to aid and abet them in this ... Where did you wait while men shot other men from your bedroom? She went upstairs to Lawrence's room. She closed the door, to put another door between her and the sound of rifle fire. Dear Lawrence. At least he was safe at the American hospital – that was a mercy. A loud crack from below made her blood freeze. A fusillade of answering shots. Then a soft noise from the landing. Serge must have come away from there too.

She got up and opened the door, and her heart seemed to fall out of her body. The figure disappearing down the stairs had a bloodstained bandage around its shoulder: Raymond Klein, in shirt sleeves and stockinged feet, a revolver in his hand. Fanny was rushing down the stairs behind him, her eyes enormous with fear. His face was set in a grimace and he ignored Fanny's hissed entreaties. Louise was on the stairs behind Fanny when Raymond reached their bedroom door, flung it open and fired into the room. Yelling. He fired again. There was a rattle of bullets, and he fell backwards on to the landing. Fanny let out a terrible wail and threw herself on his body.

Two Versaillais exploded out of the door and bounded up the stairs towards Louise.

'Who else is here? Bitch – how many?'

He hit her in the face before she could finish the words, 'No one.'

She collapsed heavily on to a stair. Soldiers pushed past her and leapt up towards the attic.

'Serge!' she wailed. 'My husband didn't know they were here. I let them in! It was all me!'

'Shut up!' the soldier shouted into her face, so she smelt his stinking mouth. Then he had gone and, at the same time, she saw Fanny groping under Raymond's body, and realized with dreadful clarity what she intended. She launched herself on to the girl and they both fell heavily to the floor.

'Don't, don't, don't,' Louise was crying, her weight pinning Fanny down. She felt Fanny's hand loosen on the revolver. Other hands gripped her shoulders, dragged her away. She was screaming her husband's name.

At some point on Wednesday afternoon, the Commune's defence of the Left Bank was given up as hopeless. The handful of defenders who remained on the barricades fired their last rounds on the Rue Soufflot before retreating to the east. They abandoned Saint Germain, the University Quarter and Montagne Saint Genevieve, spiking the guns as they left, leaving the wounded they could not carry. Many surrendered, hoping for mercy. The last to leave the Latin Quarter was a group called *Les Pupilles de la Commune*, the oldest of whom was fifteen.

Hippolyte Mazade was involved in regrouping the dwindling numbers on the Boulevard de L'Hôpital, a short distance from his former place of work, the Salpêtrière. He probably didn't give much thought to his memories from that time, being too busy plotting their withdrawal eastward and northward, barricade by barricade, towards the river.

By then, even the most intransigent Jacobin knew what was coming: a war of bloody attrition, until they were holed up in the working-class strongholds of Belleville and Ménilmontant, fighting for their lives. At midday, they'd abandoned the Jardin de Luxembourg, which quickly became an execution ground for captured insurgents. They backed away through the narrow streets of La Glacière, across the stinking Bièvre, into districts where the *beau gens* had never cared to set foot.

Towards evening, they abandoned the Jardin des Plantes. Victor Calmette was the only man left in the zoo. They had forgotten about him. He couldn't see what was happening outside the walls, but the gunfire never stopped. As it drew nearer, he could distinguish between the more measured, almost leisurely crackle of rifles, and the sudden, staccato bursts of the *mitrailleuse*.

Last night, he had gone back to the house. He dared not open the doors to check on the animals, but odd noises from downstairs – thuds, a loud crash as something shattered – kept him awake. The next day, he passed unchallenged into his office in the Hotel Lagny and lurked there, dealing with paperwork. He felt he had to stay in the zoo until – what? Just before six o'clock, two guards came through the hotel.

'Out, out!' they shouted. 'Get out! They're going to blow this place up. Unless you want to go up with it.'

Victor retreated to his house. He thought it would be safe there, although that word had lost all meaning. He was in his bedroom when a deep roar made the house tremble. There was not one explosion, but a long subterranean thunder. He couldn't see the Hotel Lagny from his window, but he imagined it collapsing, going up in flames. It occurred to him – rather late – to think, What if the tunnels full of explosives stretch right underneath this house? He was peering out the window into his garden when there was another crash from below, and a lissome, tawny shape sprang out into the bushes. It was the lioness, forcing her way through the dining-room window. Just a flash of pale brown against dark foliage, so quickly did she disappear. His heart leapt with joy and fear.

He didn't know how long he'd stayed there; long enough that he felt sure the thunder was over, and the house wasn't falling down. He opened his bedroom door, listening for more escape bids from downstairs. His bedroom was on the opposite side from the rooms where the other cats were imprisoned, so he didn't know what had happened. He debated whether to go down and open the doors, but, playing that out in his mind, he could only foresee one, murderous ending – possibly for him, certainly for the animals. The lioness had gone – not his choice, but hers. Perhaps she would be seen and shot by one of the thousands of men with rifles. Perhaps she would be granted a miracle. If the others – if Marguerite – went, so be it. Soon, now, surely, the Versaillais army would be here, and order would be restored. Things would go back to normal. Robitaille would come back – please, God, let him come back.

It was late afternoon before Ellis realized he hadn't seen Lawrence since that morning. He told himself not to be concerned – there was enough to worry about with the backlog of wounded and the still-raging fires; and there were many reasons why Lawrence might have left. After a house in the next block was hit by a shell, the staff were ordered not to go upstairs, but Ellis combed the building, asked people, searched anyway. No one had seen him for hours. The attic room where they had spent the night was empty, the bed still showing the impress of their bodies. Last night, when Lawrence suggested that they go away together, Ellis had thought of asking him to come to America, but that promised to be a complicated conversation and he didn't bring it up because, when this was all over, there would be time enough.

The rattle of gunfire was so unceasing that, while he was working, he hardly registered it. Now, it hammered into his brain, and he couldn't stop imagining horrors: Lawrence, caught up, somehow, in the fighting, his body torn and bloodied . . . He would be fine. He just . . . Why had he not left word?

Downstairs, he found his uncle and Mr Warburton talking with Swan. Now that the western suburbs were in the hands of the Versaillais, the ambassador had moved back to his official residence. He had called in to ensure that the hospital's neutrality was being respected.

'I'm sorry to say that there have been reports of Communard prisoners being abused,' Ephraim said. 'On the way here, we saw groups of prisoners being harassed and taunted by people from the neighbourhoods. There was no mercy, not even from the ladies.'

'We've had no trouble here,' said Swan. 'We have the red-cross flags, and a sign that we are the American hospital. I don't think they would dare.'

Ephraim and Swan were discussing the possibility of moving the hospital back to the west, but Ellis became increasingly agitated. As soon as his uncle mentioned that they should leave, Ellis jumped up and asked for a private word. He told him that he was worried about a friend; perhaps his uncle remembered the Canadian photographer? Ellis wondered, could Ephraim bring any influence to bear, in the event of . . . ? Ephraim reassured him that a foreigner, a non-combatant, was most unlikely to be molested. Ellis tried to smile and agree.

'I'm sure there's a simple explanation,' said his uncle, as he and Mr Warburton were leaving.

Ellis walked his uncle to the courtyard to say goodbye, then turned back. He saw an orderly in the corridor and shouted to him. It was Antoine Noury.

'Monsieur Noury, when did you last see Monsieur Harper?'

The young man gave him a flickering glance and shook his head. 'At lunchtime, I think. Or even before. We've been so busy—'

'He didn't say anything? Did he leave a message, about where he was going?'

'I'm sorry, monsieur, I don't know – although, I did ask him about Fanny – that's my friend, the Lamys' maid – and he said he would try to find out about her when he went there again. But I don't know if he did. I mean, it would not be easy to cross the river now.'

Fanny wanted to kill Madame Lamy. All she wanted – all she had left – was to shoot one of Raymond's murderers before they killed her. Anything else, she didn't care. But madame had landed on her, her weight crushing her arm to the floor, and she had lost her grip on the revolver. They struggled, Fanny too winded to speak or shout, then the weight was lifted off her, and she was hauled to her feet. The gun was gone. Her hands were roughly tied behind her back. She waited for grief to overwhelm her, to take away her consciousness, but it was not so merciful. She could still see Raymond's stockinged feet from the corner of her eye.

There was the sound of pounding footsteps overhead, then slower footsteps as they dragged the boy downstairs. Fanny glanced up to see Fred's frightened face, his eyes huge, his hair sticking up. She had told him to hide under the pile of costumes, but it hadn't helped. She didn't care if she lived, didn't care about herself at all, but she felt a stab of rage and pity on his behalf. She made herself nod at him, said, in a low voice that didn't sound like hers, 'It's all right, Fred. I won't leave you. Will we, madame? We're not going to leave you.'

Madame calmed down when they brought Monsieur Lamy downstairs to the shop. Sabine, too, had been dragged up from the kitchen, terrified into silence. Madame spoke to the soldiers, saying that her husband and her cook had no knowledge of the fugitives. It was she who had let them in and hidden them in the attic. Fanny could see that her words, and her accent, were sowing some doubt in the soldiers' minds. She spoke too, but only to confirm madame's account: madame had not had much choice, since Fanny's husband, Raymond Klein – she felt a fierce pride at voicing his name – was seriously wounded. Madame was a kind soul, but she was no friend to the Commune.

'Shut up,' said the officer.

Eventually, they were taken outside. The big barricade was in the process of being dismantled. The officer made them wait in the street as the soldiers went back inside. They carried out the bodies of their comrades, the two men Raymond had shot, and laid them on the other side of the street. Then the soldiers went back inside. Monsieur and Madame Lamy exchanged looks, but no one dared ask what they were doing. The soldiers reappeared after a few minutes and muttered to their officer. He smiled and looked up at the roof. Fanny and the others looked up too, and, after a minute, they saw wisps of smoke rising. Madame gave a sob. Fanny stared; her chest seemed to be full of something cold and hard and heavy. They were going to leave her husband's body in the house as it burned. By her side, Fred was crying. Fanny didn't cry. She didn't beg. She wouldn't give them the satisfaction.

The soldiers lit their pipes, apparently waiting for something. Madame Lamy had her hand under her husband's arm, as if she was helping him to stay upright. Fanny held Fred's hand, which was sticky and hot.

A blinding white flash erupted from the roof of the studio. Smoke poured upwards and the studio began to burn with strange coloured flames.

The officer removed the pipe from his mouth. 'No friend to the Commune, you say?' he said in a musing sort of voice and smiled.

There were no street lights, but the night was lit by the glow of the fires. Ellis made a wide loop eastward, to the Place Royale, and then down through Saint Antoine to avoid the furnace that had been the Hôtel de Ville. He crossed the river at the tail of the Île Saint Louis, pausing to look back across the water at the crimson glow in the sky. The Seine gleamed like a river of blood.

At the Halles aux Vins, Ellis turned west and found the end of the Boulevard Saint Germain without difficulty, but, from then on, it was hard to be sure of anything. The streets were littered with the remains of broken barricades, shops were shuttered, doors nailed up, signs defaced or missing. He picked his way through the heaps of rubble and the holes where cobbles had been prised up. He passed the muti-lated corpse of a horse, the stink of it reaching him even through the stench of burning. When he thought he had come far enough, he looked around for a familiar landmark. He knew there was a tree outside the house – but was it that one? All the shopfronts were hidden behind sheets of metal. But the next tree along – scarred by bullets, denuded of leaves – stood in front of a burned-out shell. The houses there had been fired, the roofs collapsed. He knew that the Communards were setting fire to some houses in order to stop the Versaillais ambushing them. Or perhaps they'd been hit by shells. He retraced his steps and banged on some shutters – but there was no reply.

He walked back and forth for some minutes, refusing to accept the evidence of his own eyes, but, in the end, he couldn't avoid it. There was the café on the corner. There was the chocolate shop. There was the sign for the bakery next door.

The building that had housed the Studio Lamy was now a smoking ruin.

The prisoners were forced to walk at gunpoint, and, after less than a hundred metres, Serge was moving with difficulty, his breath hissing through his teeth. His arthritis had been bad these past weeks, and Louise knew he was in pain. She held his arm and murmured in his ear: it could not be far; they would find someone to listen to them. Behind them, Fanny and Fred walked hand in hand. Louise had hardly dared look Fanny in the eye, after they left the Rue des Ciseaux. Her white blouse was one great, dark stain from where she had lain across her husband as the life left him. She looked like a creature from myth – her hair loose, her face smeared with blood. After that first terrible cry on the landing, she had not uttered so much as a whimper. Her eyes were fixed on the middle distance. At least the boy was there, and Fanny had promised to look after him; otherwise, Louise dreaded to think.

After an age of struggling along, endlessly held up by piles of rubble, they were shepherded on to the Champs de Mars. Mutterings and groanings came from a mass of prisoners; the field was black with people.

Now, she could make out that, although most of the prisoners were working men and women, she and her husband were not the only bourgeois. She saw a middle-aged man in a smart black coat and top hat. He looked like a lawyer, or a doctor. And over there was a woman whose pale, gleaming dress was surely silk.

She had made Serge as comfortable as possible on the ground, when the crowd began to surge around them. A soldier came through, jabbing people with the butt of his rifle.

'Get up, get up. Move along. Move along, there! You're not staying.'

Louise called to him that her husband was ill and in pain. He couldn't walk any further. It wasn't reasonable to expect him to go on.

The soldier might not have heard her. She grasped at his sleeve, but he wouldn't look her in the face. Serge struggled to his feet, his hand on her arm indicating it was all right. It wasn't all right, but now they were moving again, and Fanny was on the other side of Serge, putting her arm around him to take his weight.

Despite her efforts, they couldn't manage. Serge tried with all his might, but his face was grey with pain, his breaths ragged groans. They were by the river, plodding on towards Versailles, when he stumbled, and they could no longer hold him up. Serge shook his head, his legs buckling beneath him. Louise looked around for help. He wasn't the only one. A very old woman – she couldn't understand why someone like that had been arrested – was sunk in a small huddle by the side of the crowd. No one helped her.

Serge signed her to leave him.

'No. No! Darling, I'm not leaving you.'

Louise knelt beside him. Fanny and Fred were trying to help him up, but they couldn't manage his weight. Serge was even making noises, shooing them away.

Then, from behind them, came a crack. A low moan – a general drawing in of breath from the prisoners. Louise didn't dare look around at the old woman, but she knew what was coming. She flung her arms around her husband and waited.

71

There are some things you cannot comprehend. Lawrence could not comprehend that he was going to die in the Jardin des Plantes, just a few yards from the menagerie. From where he sat, he could see the curlicues of the gloriette silhouetted against the sky. The fence behind him marked the enclosure where he had tried and failed to photograph the wolves, a year ago. He had walked along these neat paths countless times. Now, he was sitting by the same path, next to where a man had just dropped his trousers and voided a stream of evil-smelling liquid, waiting to be shot.

They had arrived, the previous evening, to find the park turned into a prison camp. There were hundreds of prisoners, sitting or lying on the grass. Government soldiers with rifles stood around the perimeter fence. Most of the prisoners were men. Many looked too old to have been in the Guard. Just as many were boys. There were several women too. It was a crowd of people that you could see every day in the streets of Belleville. Lawrence thought, not for the first time, of Michel and Séraphine. Where were they? Michel would be fighting, possibly Séraphine too. If he was afraid for himself, he should be much more afraid for them.

His attempts to talk to his fellow prisoners had been met with stares and monosyllabic answers. The most forthcoming was the man with the bloodshot eyes: Etienne was a printer, a passionate Communard, who had surrendered at his barricade when he ran out of ammunition. The others ignored Lawrence. They knew he was not like them, and, at first, he had taken hope from that. They resented him because they believed he would soon be taken away – rescued, somehow. But, as the hours passed, his hope faded. He heard Russian accents, Italian and something he couldn't identify. Being a foreigner was not the trump card he had hoped.

Come nightfall, the atmosphere changed. There was a crackle of rifle fire. A man had tried to escape and was shot as he attempted to climb the fence. Then a rumour spread through the park that the Archbishop, the Commune's main hostage, had been executed.

'How do you fancy your chances now, Canada?' Etienne said, with a bitter grin.

Lawrence felt tears threaten. Yesterday, he had cried when he knew he would not immediately be released, tears of furious self-pity washing over him. He didn't want to cry again. He tried not to think of Ellis. Mainly, he cried for himself. He didn't want to die like this. It was all so stupid.

They watched as a group of prisoners were rounded up and led out of sight around the side of the Natural History Museum. Then silence. Then came a long burst of rifle fire. Then silence again. Or, there were cries, screams, then more shots, stuttering on and on. Christ, how many shots did it take? Then silence.

In the small hours, storms came. Thunder drowned out the gunfire. The rain began to put out the fires, but it did nothing to dampen the fury of the Versaillais once the death of the Archbishop became known. Before that, there had been a modicum of restraint in the summary court martials; afterwards, there was none. Parisians were arrested in the street, or in their houses, for many reasons, or no reason. They were shot because they answered back, or because their clothes were dirty, or because they had working-class accents, or grey hair, or were wearing a watch, or had Communard-issued boots, or because someone didn't like their face. Some were spared when they begged for God's mercy. Others weren't. White-haired men were killed, and boys whose voices hadn't broken. Women of all ages. Herded like cattle, they were shot in the Lobau barracks, in the Parc Monceau, in the prisons, in the Montparnasse Cemetery, in the Tuileries, in the railway stations. In the Luxembourg gardens, blood dyed the ground red. It ran down the central gutters of the streets. It ran into the Seine, where witnesses saw ribbons of blood flow along both banks.

Prisoners who survived their initial arrest were force-marched to a field outside Versailles, there to await trial. Many, who were ill or had not eaten or slept for days, fell by the wayside, and were left to die, or they were shot out of hand, like Serge Lamy. Louise would have been shot too, if Fanny hadn't pulled her up by the hand, and Louise, to her lasting surprise, had allowed herself to be dragged away. The will to survive was so strong, she was ashamed.

There was no reason for Ellis to believe that Lawrence had been in the house when it went up in flames. He kept telling himself that. He returned to the hospital and scribbled a note to his uncle, begging for his help. Help with what, he didn't know. He didn't know where to start. There was no information, just rumour, and the rumours got uglier by the hour. Every member of staff had tales of the atrocities they had seen at first hand: a bystander shot for looking at an officer the wrong way; the student killed because his name was Marx; the chimney sweep gunned down for being covered in soot. At this last rumour, Ellis felt sick; Lawrence's hands were permanently stained with chemicals. If you knew what you were looking for, these stains looked nothing like the marks left by firing a rifle, but he had little faith that such distinctions meant anything now.

He didn't sleep. In the morning, there was still no news of Lawrence. He walked through the rain to the Café des Archives and ordered a bottle of brandy. The café was full of government soldiers celebrating their imminent victory. Steam rose from sodden uniforms, and the café owner boasted that he hadn't lost an hour's business throughout the past week. There was a weird normality to the waiters hurrying by with plates and bottles, and the crowded tables and laughter, as though a gigantic convulsion hadn't just torn the city apart. As though some of these same soldiers hadn't come into the hospital the evening before, dragged out two patients and killed them. The doctors and nurses protested vociferously. The officer in charge laughed at them for citing the Geneva Convention. The wounded men were members of the Commune, he said – traitors. This had happened while Ellis was contemplating the burned-out ruins of Studio Lamy, but Logue had told him about it, his eyes haunted, his voice clipped with shock.

Victor was kept awake by the rifle fire. It went on all night without stopping, and throughout the next morning. He peered at the park from windows blurred with rain. He caught glimpses of the grey figures trampling over the neat flowerbeds, churning the ground to a swamp, relieving themselves where they sat. He saw rifles and bayonets. He saw groups of prisoners being moved around, but he did not know what was happening. He didn't want to know.

Eventually, hunger drove him downstairs and he listened at the closed doors. Tancred paced in the library, coughing his throaty grumble. There was a thud from behind the study door – it sounded as though the lynx had knocked over a chair. He could hear nothing from the sitting room. Had Marguerite made her escape? He noiselessly opened the door and peered in. Marguerite was lying in front of the fireplace. She lifted her head and looked at him, her eyes shining. He was both glad and saddened that she was still here.

'Not long now, darling,' he murmured, closing the door.

He should find more food for them today, somehow. He went into the empty dining room, its furniture overturned, smashed, soiled, the broken window letting in rain. Xanthe, they'd called the lioness, for her golden coat. He found it hard to picture her alive anywhere in the city. He could only hope.

There was a violent pounding at the front door. He froze. The pounding came again, imperious and demanding. It had to be soldiers – the Versaillais who had taken over the park. They were on the same side; he wasn't afraid of them – but he closed the door of the dining room and held his breath. There was more pounding, and shouting for someone to open up. He bit his lip. Lower, conversational tones. Then the unmistakable sound of an axe on wood.

Two soldiers looked at him in astonishment as the door swung open on broken hinges. Victor tried to look stern, but a grimace – half smile and half snarl – tugged at his mouth.

'Messieurs, I couldn't come to the door earlier. I have no staff anymore. This house belongs to the Jardin des Plantes, and I am the chief veterinarian of the menagerie. This is my home. What do you want?'

A stout, heavily whiskered captain looked at him with suspicion. 'I am requisitioning this house on behalf of the army of Versailles.'

Victor drew himself up. 'I'm afraid that's not possible.'

The officer's eyes bulged. 'This is an order. We are not here at your convenience.'

'I regret, I cannot let you do that.'

'Arrest him.'

Two soldiers stepped towards Victor and grasped his arms.

The officer turned to his lieutenant. 'You – upstairs. Search for federals.'

'I give you my word, there are no fugitives here. You don't understand!'

He might not have existed. Two soldiers bounded up the stairs, and the men holding him marched him towards the broken door. The officer made for the drawing room.

'Stop! You can't go in there, monsieur! It's dangerous!'

The officer hefted his rifle and opened the door. Victor cursed himself for not locking it; he didn't even know where the key was.

'There are dangerous . . .'

For a long moment, nothing happened. Apparently seeing nothing untoward, the officer lowered his rifle, relaxing. Then there was a great, tearing hiss, and a torpedo of black and gold muscle exploded from the room and out of the front door before anyone could react. The officer was left sprawling on the ground, brushed aside by the tigress like a bothersome fly. The soldiers holding Victor let him go in their shock. The officer struggled to his feet, his mouth a round gape of astonishment, as Victor, without thinking, ran to open the doors of the study and the library. The lynx was invisible, probably cowering under some furniture, but Tancred bounded out of the library with a roar; he paused at the bottom of the stairs, seeming to swell in size as he glared at the hypnotized men, before he, too, followed Marguerite through the front door and disappeared.

Lawrence sat on the sodden grass, with his elbows resting on his knees. The storm had broken in the small hours, but there was nowhere for prisoners to shelter, nor any point in them doing so. They let the rain wash the soot and dust from their hair, opened parched mouths to its water. Lawrence was wet through, chilled to the bone after the oily, unnatural heat of the last days. Sitting in this position kept the rain from his face, although it trickled down his neck and under his collar. He watched drops of water gather on the lock of hair that hung in front of his eyes, tremble for a while, and then fall.

The fires on the Right Bank had been extinguished, and the pall of smoke was clearing. He imagined how Ellis would react to news of his death. He would be upset, of course, but for how long? He would meet someone else, eventually. He was too handsome and too kind, and, underneath the noisy persona, he was lovable. Lawrence hoped he had made Ellis believe that. It wasn't fair; they should have had longer . . . The tears came again, self-pity masked by rain.

Overnight, Etienne had softened towards him. The printer seemed calm in the face of death – he had always known it might come to this.

'You can see how much they hate us. They fear us, too, because we remind them that all their wealth rests on our backs, and we are many, while they are few. I don't expect mercy. It's too bad for you, though, Canada.'

Lawrence shrugged and wiped his face with the back of his hand.

There was a noise behind them: a convulsion in the crowd of waiting prisoners. Lawrence lifted his head. Shrieks and yells, and a swelling surge of movement, as though a stone had been thrown into a pond. The Versaillais' guns swivelled towards the commotion. People jumped to their feet and ran this way and that. Shots were fired. Lawrence scrambled to his feet as panic rippled through the park, but still he couldn't see the source of it.

He ran for the menagerie fence and hurtled over it. He didn't care if anyone saw – may as well be shot now as later. He landed, was alive, stumbled, carried on. Behind him, the prisoners ran in all directions. One moment, Etienne was beside him, then he wasn't. He didn't look back. He could hear others panting and crashing through foliage nearby, but he zigzagged through the zoo's familiar land-marks until he was alone in a dense thicket of trees. He came to a wall – he threw himself over it, catching and ripping some cloth. He fell to the ground on the other side, and found himself in thick, wet undergrowth. He tried to quiet his breathing. Only yards away, beyond the wall, through the trees, he heard yelling and shooting, but more distant now. A new growl of thunder came, close to, that sounded like a lion's roar.

He huddled lower into the sharp, scratchy foliage. Where now? They would be searching for fugitives, wouldn't they? But he was one among many ... He peered around his leafy hiding place. The menagerie wasn't far from the Studio Lamy – if he could just make it back there ... or – the veterinarian! Wasn't his house in the menagerie? Perhaps this was its garden. Maybe, if he was here, he would remember Lawrence, and if—

A rustle of leaves nearby made him shrink into himself, heart pounding, scalp crawling with fear. He made himself look, braced for the sight of a red jacket, the muzzle of a rifle. Instead, he caught a flash of cinnamon and black, and he thought his heart stopped.

An impossible pair of eyes stared into his. Jewel-like, massive, like great quartz lamps. A presence that was neither hostile nor benign, before which he was wholly inadequate. Lawrence closed his eyes and listened to its breathing. As he waited for its decision, he could hear the beating of its great heart.

72

The surgeon in charge of everything, Monsieur Swan, came looking for Antoine Noury. The hospital was going to pack up and move to a more suitable location. Not only was the hotel too small, with too many stairs, but the stench of burned matter had only worsened with the rain, and the floors were covered with an intractable paste of soot, blood and filth. Monsieur Swan was particular about cleanliness. Anne listened – did he want her to clean it up? She had tried. Then he surprised her: he said he had been impressed with his work – they'd all noticed how neat Monsieur Noury was, how quick. Reliable and intelligent. They valued him. They wanted him to go with them to Passy . . .

All of a sudden, Anne thought of Fanny. The hospital had kept her so busy, she had forgotten to worry about Fanny since . . . yesterday? The day before? She hadn't seen her since Monday morning, and now – she didn't know what day it was. God knew what had happened to her.

'Um, thank you, monsieur. I don't know . . .' She stared at the floor.

'Please give it some thought, monsieur. We would very much like you to come.'

'All right. I will.' Anne risked a glance in the direction of his face.

'Right— Oh, and I don't suppose you have seen Mr Butterfield? No? Hm. He seems to have vanished off the face of the earth.'

Anne reckoned she could walk to Fanny's and back in under three hours, if she didn't hang about – but, before she even reached the courtyard, she heard someone call her name. She cursed under her breath, then she saw who it was and couldn't help staring: Monsieur Harper, normally so dapper, was a bedraggled shadow of his former self. His hair clung to his skull, his clothes were soiled, and there was a long rent in one trouser leg. He was unshaven and his eyes were red rimmed.

'Monsieur Harper. Where did you go? Monsieur Butterfield has been looking for you.'

Perhaps her voice sounded a little sharp. His mouth fell open and he stared at her. Then she thought, How many days was it since he went out? But she couldn't remember, and added, 'Are you all right?'

He gave a short laugh, although she couldn't see what was funny.

'Yes, yes. I'm . . . Where is he? Monsieur Butterfield.'

Anne had an idea where he might be. They walked together to the Café des Archives, but, outside, as she made to leave him, he put his hand on her sleeve.

'Where are you going? You shouldn't be out on the streets – it's too dangerous.'

'I have to find Fanny. I'm going to the apartment. I can be back in—'

'No, you mustn't! That's in Ménilmontant, isn't it? That's where the fighting is now. If you go there, they'll arrest you, or shoot you.'

'But I have this.' She twitched the arm that bore the red cross.

'That won't save you! *I* was arrested, for God's sake – a Canadian. I was nearly shot! Do you know she's even there?'

Anne shook her head. But where else could she look?

'She went with me to the Hôtel de Ville on –' he thought – 'on Monday. She was trying to find her husband's regiment.'

'Did you ask at the Rue des Ciseaux?'

'No. I mean, no, she's not there. Believe me, anyone at all is suspected of being a Communard. They shoot people without cause. It's too risky. If you stay, I promise I'll help you find her. I promise.'

Anne nodded her agreement.

She hung back as Monsieur Harper made his way through the tables. Monsieur Butterfield was sitting at a corner table covered with bottles and glasses, hemmed in by a bunch of Versaillais soldiers, yet not with them. His head was bowed, and it was some time before he noticed the sound of his name and looked up. Anne saw his face go blank with shock. He stared at Monsieur Harper as though he couldn't believe he was real. Then his face crumpled and he covered it with his hand.

Anne looked away. It was none of her business.

From *Le Figaro*, 28 May 1871:

Never has such an opportunity presented itself for curing Paris of the moral gangrene that has been consuming it. The Parisians must submit to the laws of war, however terrible they may be. Today, clemency equals lunacy.

From *The Times of London*, 29 May 1871:

The laws of war! They are mild and Christian compared with the inhuman laws of revenge under which the Versaillais troops have been shooting, bayoneting, ripping up prisoners, women and children during the last six days.

73

At the end of a week's intense fighting, the last spasm of Communard resistance was quashed – a hundred and fifty fighters were lined up against the eastern wall of Père Lachaise Cemetery and shot. Their bodies were propped up and photographed before being thrown into a trench. But the sound of the execution squads went on for days. The grinding of wagon wheels was heard all night, ferrying corpses to the outlying forts.

For days, the air continued to smell of burning, but now it came from the funeral pyres beyond the city walls and in the quarries of Buttes Chaumont. The army dismantled the barricades and repaired the damage to the streets, without being too nice about it. It was said that they threw rotting corpses into the craters in the roads and relaid the paving stones on top.

But this was Paris. Come July, it was quite the thing to make a tour of the ruins. A visit to the Hôtel de Ville was a must; the heat of its burning had been so intense that the limestone walls were swirled with colours, glossy as some exotic marble. Photographers and artists did a brisk trade in pictures of ruins and dramatic scenes of the fighting. Foreign tourists strolled the deserted boulevards, gaping at ghost shops on the Rue Royale and the Rue de Rivoli. They posed in front of twisted fountains and shattered statues, in rubble and ash. It was as good as a visit to Pompeii.

No longer on their itineraries was a visit to the menagerie, which, reeling from its latest losses, had closed for the foreseeable future. The head veterinarian received plaudits for staying at his post throughout, but he had not been able to prevent some of the animals escaping amid the mayhem. People told lurid stories of the escaped lions and tigers, but their real fates were unknown. No bodies were produced, but then, what were a few animals among so many human dead?

Victor heard all sorts of rumours. The one he clung to as an article of faith was that a great creature, perhaps a tiger, had been seen swimming in the Seine near Marly-le-Roi, although this was widely dismissed as fanciful.

74

Ellis went back to Montmartre only once, to collect his belongings under the venomous eye of the concierge's wife. In March, she and her husband had been quick to side with the Commune; now, she proclaimed her unwavering support for the government. Ellis knew she would be only too happy to denounce him as a Communard, if only she could think of a reason. That he was a surgeon annoyed her intensely. He handed over his key with relief.

'Monsieur, there is the matter of your outstanding rent. You failed to give a month's notice.'

Ellis laughed in her face. 'Madame, I know you ate the American ambassador's cat. I owe you nothing.'

Her face twisted with spite. 'And I know what you got up to, up there – you and that boy-wife of yours.'

Ellis allowed the shock to wash over him, and shrugged. 'That, in this country, is not a crime.'

He was surprised how easily the words came out, and at how little he cared.

For the time being, he had moved in with his uncle at his Passy residence. It was convenient for the relocated American hospital and it was a relief to be away from the centre of Paris, with its daily reminders of the massacre.

He invited Lawrence to stay there. His uncle was easily convinced that the Canadian, having lost everything in the fire that destroyed the Studio Lamy, was as much in need of refuge as the German professor – who still showed no sign of moving out. Lawrence was very quiet in the aftermath of the fighting, shocked by the loss of his home and work, and not knowing what had happened to the Lamys. He moved into a room along the corridor from Ellis with nothing but the clothes he was wearing.

Lawrence devoted his time to finding out what had happened to his friends. Certainty was hard to come by. He talked to neighbours on the Rue des Ciseaux, and learnt that the Lamys and their maid had been seen outside, prisoners, as the studio began to burn. He went to the Bignons' apartment to ask after Séraphine and Michel. He found it inhabited by strangers, but a local woman thought they had survived the fighting and managed to flee, but she had no idea where they might have gone. The district where they had lived was eerily quiet – from Père Lachaise to Buttes Chaumont, it had become a town of old women. He left messages and wrote letters, witnessed the denunciations of Communard sympathizers, saw more arrests.

He travelled to Versailles to enquire at the camps, where thousands of prisoners were being held in squalor and confusion. Conditions were appalling and typhus was running riot. Ellis worried that Lawrence would get ill, that he was clinging to his quest. He was afraid of what would happen if he did not find them, or if he discovered the worst.

One evening in June, he returned from Versailles with news that he had located Madame Lamy and Fanny Klein in the women's camp at Satory. He hadn't spoken to them yet, but it was a start.

That night, after dinner, Lawrence and Ellis left Ephraim in his library and walked in the orchard. The trees that had survived the government's attacks had flowered profusely, and now bore constellations of hard green fruit. The last of the sun was warm, and the air under the trees was loud with insects, drunk on the day's nectar. Lawrence stumbled with exhaustion. Ellis slipped his hand under Lawrence's arm and Lawrence leant against him.

'I'm so glad you've found Madame Lamy and the girl. Quite a lot of people are being released without trial. I'll try to get my uncle to intercede on their behalf. I'm sure he can do something.'

'Would he do that?' Lawrence felt tears pricking his eyes. He was generally so tired that he felt numb, but numbness was preferable to the alternative. 'He hardly knows me.'

'He knows you're important to me.'

Lawrence looked at Ellis. At night, he would slip into Ellis's room, but he thought they'd been scrupulous in maintaining the appearance of sleeping apart.

'What have you told him?'

'Nothing. The other day, he said, "I like your Mr Harper." But he said it in such a way that it made me wonder if he knows.'

Lawrence let this sink in for a moment. 'I owe you both too much already; I don't know how I'm going to—'

'You owe me nothing. I have some news, too. I'm not going back for the wedding.'

Lawrence was startled. The wedding of Ellis's mother was little more than a month away, but Lawrence had pushed it to the back of his mind: one more uncertainty among so many.

'Are you sure? Won't she be terribly upset if you don't go?'

Ellis shrugged. 'I've written to her. I've told her there is too much to do here. We don't even know if our friends are alive—' He broke off. 'But, most of all, I don't want to leave you.'

'Me?' Lawrence felt the warmth rush to his face.

'I want her to be happy, but how can her wedding be so important – yet not *us*? You are my love. When I thought I'd lost you, I didn't know what I would do.'

Lawrence looked around, but the summer leaves protected them. He took Ellis by both hands. 'You haven't lost me. You're not going to. I won't allow it.'

He said it as lightly as he could, but Ellis looked serious.

'So that's settled. I'll stay. But I think we should find somewhere else to live. Together.'

Lawrence felt dizzy. 'Really? Are you sure you want to do that?'

'Yes, I am. I want—' He stopped and cleared his throat. He sounded rather cross. 'I mean, I know I can be difficult, and say if you'd rather not, but I want us to live together. I want to cherish you, and love you, for as long as I live – or as long as you'll let me.'

Lawrence didn't know if he was laughing or crying. It was everything he wanted, in the midst of what no one would ever want.

'God, say something, Lawrence. Do you want that too?'

He hadn't realized he had not yet replied. 'Of course I do. My love. I do.'

They embraced. This time, neither of them looked around. Lawrence pressed his face into the flannel of Ellis's collar and breathed in his scent. Perhaps it was selfish, but he could only think that, as it had been given them to survive, now they had to live.

It was time. Anne was nervous, but resolute. If it didn't work, it wouldn't matter too much, because, as she had discovered, having money gave you power. It forgave you your mistakes. She would have to come back, anyway, to visit Fanny in prison. Monsieur Harper had promised to write to her when he found out about the trial. She could always go back to the American hospital to work, but now she had other ideas.

A whistle shrilled in her ear, making her jump. Here was the train – she had never seen one so close, let alone travelled in one. A vast, ugly thing that hissed steam like a shell falling in the River Bièvre, and the porters were shouting for people to climb on board. There was a deafening racket, all the sounds bouncing around inside the great glass chamber that was the station. She was nervous, decidedly, but people got on trains every day and survived, so why not her? She gripped her bag and climbed up the metal steps, glad to be in trousers. She walked along the second-class carriage until she found an empty compartment, and sat down, looking out of the window. She hoped no one would sit opposite and stare at her – but there were plenty of seats, so she could probably move, if that happened. A middle-aged woman arrived in her compartment with several pieces of luggage, puffing with effort, and Anne, grown crafty in the ways of her new skin, stood up and offered to help. Bags stowed, the woman thanked her and sat down, not quite opposite. Anne sat down again and pulled out the newspaper that was to be her shield for the journey.

The carriage juddered, metal clashed on metal, the wheels shrieked, the steam engine hissed. It was altogether a noisy affair. Anne felt her heart pound, but the train began to crawl out of the station. Her companion sighed and settled herself down to nap.

Anne briefly touched the top of her trousers, as she did a hundred times a day: the secret compartment which held part of her fortune. She had divided it up for safety, because losing it was one mistake she would not make.

Her own travelling bag, newly bought – a great heavy thing of Brussels carpeting – was stowed above her head. The clothing it contained was both male and female. She hadn't decided which she would wear when she went to see Monsieur Papin. Probably it would be best to wear a dress, the first time, although she was a little tempted to surprise him. She had a feeling he might appreciate it.

Anne looked out of the window, where Paris was sliding silently past. It was a long journey to the south; there would be plenty of time to make up her mind.

ACKNOWLEDGEMENTS

A huge thank you to my wonderful beta readers, who tell me when it's boring, but always in the kindest possible way: Orla Carney, Bridget Penney, Laurie Lynd, Clare Mockridge, Cécile Dumont, Paul Holman and Laura Lonrigg. And an extra special thanks to Laurie Lynd and Paul Hughes, for making me feel that I could.

Thanks, as always, to my much-loved agent, Diana Tyler, and the rest of the team at MBA, especially Susan Smith.

Thanks to Jane Wood, my wonderful editor at Quercus, and to everyone else who put such a lot of time and care into making this book the best it could be.

And always, for being my first reader and so many other things besides, to Marco van Welzen, all love.